DEADLANDS DRUID

A DRUIDVERSE URBAN FANTASY NOVEL

M.D. MASSEY

CHAPTER ONE

HOW DO you capture a demonic elder vampire with nearly god-like powers?

Very carefully, or as Crowley might say, "very sloppily indeed."

Said shadow wizard—the alternate timeline version—flew overhead, trailing smoky black tentacles and wisps of the shadow magic shell that covered him constantly these days. Having given himself over completely to dark magic and necromancy, he was crazy powerful now, and also crazy scary, in a Nazgûl-meets-the-Dementors kind of way. To be honest, the guy looked like shit, but I'd never tell him that.

Crowley's eyes were no longer human, and instead had become two swirling pools of darkness. His pale, nearly translucent skin was streaked with gangrenous lines, and a smoky black mist swirled all over his body. Add to that the black hooded mage's robes he wore, and he was the epitome of an RPG necromancer come to life.

Despite how scary this version of the Crowster was, I was momentarily worried that he'd been injured. But gauging by Crowley's expression, he was none the worse for the wear, merely perturbed at being shrugged off so easily by our prey. That was unfortunate, because with my partner temporarily out of the fight, Le Boucher would be solely focused on me.

At that moment, my self-preservation instincts kicked in. I spun and conjured a thick stone wall from the ground beneath my feet, just in time to partially deflect a punch The Butcher had aimed at my chest. The wall I'd summoned cracked without shattering, but only because it'd been shored up with druid magic. Had it been made purely from mundane stone, I'd have been a goner.

Well, maybe not. But it might have put me out of commission.

Taking a single step back, I allowed my druid oak to portal me fifty feet behind my attacker, just as he struck the barrier asunder with another mighty punch. On realizing I'd disappeared, the two-thousand-year-old vampire snapped his head this way and that, moving with a speed that was both unnatural and disconcerting. To buy some time, I amped up my chameleon spell, wrapping foliage around me to hide my heat signature from his supernatural senses.

"Naughty, naughty, druid," he said in a tone that conveyed annoyance and admiration both. "Portal magic is the sole province of the high and mighty. You've leveled up."

I remained silent and still, watching him from my hiding place as I waited for Crowley to get his smoky ass in gear and put the whammy on this joker. As I observed Le Boucher—the evil alter-ego of the "good" vampire, Saint

Germain—I noted that he too had been upgraded since our previous encounter. If not in powers, then certainly in appearance.

In his other form, Saint Germain was a short, portly individual, given to wearing expensive clothes and primping to the point of dandyism. *That* Germain was a middle-aged man of average height, with wavy brown hair, a prominent, aquiline nose, and dark eyes that alternated between mischief and sadness from moment to moment. Despite having some "dad bod" muscle beneath his paunch, he was altogether unintimidating at first glance.

But this thing? This creature was a monster out of nightmare and legend.

When I'd last seen him, he'd been starving after being restrained inside a magicked silver coffin for an extended period. Skin had hung off his skeletal frame and his face had been gaunt and sallow, a side effect of the primary vampiric entity within him feeding off his ample flesh to sustain itself. Right before we parted ways, he gorged on a legendary member of the Fomorian race—my race, on my mother's side—and apparently, that had changed The Butcher greatly.

Since then, Le Boucher had put on muscle, making him look more like a Greek statue than a famine victim. Pale gray, almost translucent skin covered flesh that was hard as marble, and silken brown curls flowed past his shoulders in locks that would shame any shampoo spokeswoman. Yet his hands and feet were more raptor-like than I remembered. The vampire's fingers and toes were too long, and they ended in curved nails that were likely tough enough to shred kevlar and boiled leather.

Then, there was his face. It had filled out like his body,

and while mostly pale, his cheeks had a slight ruddy glow, one that could only mean he'd recently fed. Rather than becoming more monstrous, however, his features appeared almost like a work of art. His visage was perfectly symmetrical, porcelain smooth, and lacking in a single flaw, save for the rather long canines that stuck out over his lower lip when he closed his mouth.

But the oddest thing? The bat-like wings that were currently folded against his back. Each consisted of a chiropteran skeletal structure, covered in paper-thin skin tough enough to turn tranquilizer darts. When he extended them, the overall effect was that of an outcast angel, an entity only just removed from heavenly heights, fallen to Earth and yet no less magnificent for the ride down.

As far as we could tell, he was faster, stronger, and more resilient than he'd ever been. Of course, that made apprehending him a bitch for Crowley and me, but it also served my purposes quite handily. If I was going to storm the Dallas coven's headquarters in the Hellpocalypse timeline and take out Alan Garr, I needed to recruit the toughest damned vampire killer I could get.

And according to the Luther I knew in my primary timeline, none of the Vampyri troubleshooters were more feared than Le Boucher. That was why I'd snatched him from Underhill and brought him to this deserted island in the alt-timeline Keys. All I had to do was convince him to work for me—while avoiding being eaten by him, of course.

I'd only momentarily been lost in recalling the events that had led us here, but a fraction of a moment was long enough for Le Boucher to determine where I was. One second I was staring at him across the sand, the next, he was in my face, looking me in the eye despite the fact that I was well-hidden by magic and nature both.

"There you are," he said in his odd, sibilant voice. He grabbed me by my neck, those elongated fingers wrapping around and locking in as he tore me from the undergrowth. "Now, I shall feed."

———

Shit, shit, shit, shit, shit, shit, shit…

That was all I could think as I panicked and shoved my palm in Le Boucher's too-perfect face, blasting him with part of my "break glass in case of emergency" sunlight spell. I didn't hit him with all of it because I didn't want to kill him. Yet, it was enough to cause him to release me and blitz away across the beach, trailing wisps of smoke from his now half-ruined porcelain face.

As for me, I fell to my knees, gagging. The bastard had nearly crushed my windpipe, and while I was pretty damned durable in my half-Fomorian form, I wasn't invincible. The choice to remain in this form had been a tactical one, as I'd worried that being in my full-on Hyde-side mode would be too great a temptation for The Butcher. The last thing I needed was to give him more of the "god blood" that had made him even more dangerous than he'd been before.

A cold, wet nose nudged my arm, and Larry the Chupacabra shimmered into view at my side. "Yo, druid— you alright?"

"Ack… Larry, the fuck are you doing here?"

He shrugged, at least as much as his weird, semi-canine shoulders would allow. "I dunno. When you and Super-Snape over there 'wuz planning your mission, I overheard and thought it sounded interesting. So, I decided to come along and see this legendary leech for myself."

"You mean you've been tagging along since Austin?"

"Uh-huh," he said, panting with his unnaturally long tongue lolling out the side of his mouth. One of his googly eyes rolled sideways as he stared at me, only to roll back and focus on me again. "Got any water in that Bag of yours? This tropical heat's killin' me."

"Bad… ack… timing," I rasped as I struggled to my feet. "Check back when I'm not trying to avoid dying."

Just then, Crowley strode parallel to us, roughly ten feet to my right, walking on shadow limbs that jutted from his torso like dark, wispy tentacles. He appeared unharmed, despite having been tossed across the island only moments before. The dark mists that formed the wizard's eyes whirled and churned, a bad sign if ever I'd seen one. The last thing I needed was yet another out of control, demon-possessed entity trapped on this island with me.

"Crowley…" I warned as he locked eyes with Le Boucher across the sand.

"Come, wizard, and meet your end," the ancient vampire taunted. "I might not be willing to feed on your tainted blood, but I'll gladly spill it on these desolate shores."

"Crowley!" My voice was returning, and I put a little extra magic behind it to get his attention. "Are you with me?"

He kept his gaze fixed on Le Boucher. Unlike me,

Crowley lacked character flaws like overconfidence and hubris. Sure, he was arrogant, but it was deserved, every last bit of it.

"The demon has not won the battle over my soul yet," he said. His voice was like dried basilisk skin drawn over barbed wire, an altogether unnerving sound. "You'll know when it has, and on that day, do what you must to put me down."

"Why, you sound like my pathetic host," Le Boucher chided as he paced back and forth on the other side of the narrow isle. "He's constantly trying to find someone or something who can put him out of his misery. Sadly, he's failed to find anyone who's up to the task—your companion included. Perhaps your faith has been misplaced, sorcerer."

Crowley spat thick black phlegm that sizzled when it hit the wet sand beneath us. I glanced at Le Boucher before addressing Crowley. "You ready to do the thing?"

The shade-cursed wizard nodded once. "But you must restrain him, druid. Else this will not work."

I leaned sideways, barely dodging a heavy piece of coral that Le Boucher had meant for my skull. "Yeah, I'm working on that."

Larry shimmered into view again. "I got an idea. I'll distract him so you two can put the kibosh on Fabio over there."

"That would be ill-advised, rat," Crowley said.

"Yeah, I don't think that's such a good idea," I added, addressing the scraggly cryptid as he vanished from sight. "Larry. Larry?"

No answer. Shit.

"It appears your covert cryptozoological canid has gone to play the hero," Crowley observed drily. "I shall not miss his company."

"Ah, hell," I muttered. "Get ready—I'm going to go save Larry."

"He's hardly worth the effort," the wizard mused.

"Yeah, yeah," I said as I blurred away at near-vampire speed. "Some would say that about you, too."

"There's no need to be nasty," the former changeling prince answered, his voice trailing off as I ran at Le Boucher, hurtling fireballs and lightning all the while.

The vampire was hardly bothered by my barrage, as he easily dodged every attack as if the fast-flying fireballs and electrified thunderclaps were moving in slow motion. The fireballs hit the beach behind him, as did the lightning strikes, each exploding and tossing sand and seashells everywhere. That was fine because it was pretty much what I wanted—lots and lots of sand and debris in the air.

"*Gusta gaoithe*," I whispered, infusing the air with druid magic that caused it to pick up speed as it whirled around the vampire.

The wind snatched the sand and beach detritus, spinning it in a maelstrom that nearly obscured Le Boucher from sight—and I from him as well. I was certain that, had he been a mortal creature, the magical sandblasting would've stripped the skin and flesh from his bones. Yet, for a vampire his age, it was merely an inconvenience.

He zipped around in an attempt to shake it, but the spell and sandstorm stayed with him. I'd placed a tracker on the spell, adding a little twist of druidry to keep it centered on the target. Meanwhile, I kicked up more sand, calling on my earth connection to toss wheelbarrow loads of the stuff into the roiling cyclone of sand and shells.

Within seconds, the vampire was completely hidden in the whirlwind, which meant that he couldn't very well see or hear me, either. All I had to do to track him was to keep an eye on the storm.

Part one of the plan, complete. Part two, coming up.

―――――

"Larry, where'd you go?" I asked aloud. Hearing no answer, I only hoped he wouldn't do something utterly stupid and completely catastrophic.

Time to light this candle.

"*Maighnéadas*," I said, raising my right hand in the air.

Instantly, the wind stopped howling around the vampire. Simultaneously, all the debris that had been flying through the air was immediately attracted to Le Boucher, like iron filings to a magnet. This effectively encased the vampire in a couple of tons of sand, seashells, and other beach debris.

Then, I clenched my hand into a fist. "*Cruaigh*," I rasped, as my throat was still healing after the assault I'd suffered.

Instantly, the sand, water, and seashells turned into mush that hardened into a substance not unlike reinforced concrete, some two feet thick. I'd worked the spells out myself, basing them on foundational druidic principles that involved coaxing natural substances and energies to do my bidding. In this case, that meant turning sand and seashells into stone.

Sea sand doesn't have a very high compressive strength, so the trick was drawing out the salt and water all at once to make it as hard as possible. What was left was a seven-foot tall, four-foot wide, bulbous statue, roughly in the shape of a man, that was covered in a white, powdery layer of salt.

I knew it wouldn't hold Le Boucher for long, and I was right. Within seconds, low cracking noises informed me that the vampire's concrete encasement was already weakening.

Damn.

I'd spent days figuring out and prepping those spells, and weeks scouting out this location. No way was I going to let all that work go to waste, never mind allowing that monster to fly away and terrorize Southern Florida. In a bit of a panic, I called on all the living vegetation nearby—grasses, vines, and kelp—ordering it to grow at an enormous pace, wrapping layer upon layer of it around the makeshift prison.

"Crowley," I said as I wove long, wispy strands of glowing gold and green druid magic around the plant life to shore it up further. "Whatever you're going to do, do it now!"

The shadow wizard strolled past, lowering himself to the sand as his tentacles dissipated into black mist that floated away on the breeze. The smoky, hazy black film that covered his body slithered away from his skin to gather in his right palm, leaving pale gray flesh behind.

Not unlike Le Boucher's skin. Huh.

Crowley tossed the compressed ball of shadow matter at the ground near the base of the vampire's temporary restraints. The tarry material spread out and separated seemingly of its own accord, etching black lines and glyphs into the sand that surrounded the vampire—concrete, plant life, and all.

When the spell circle reached completion, I felt my connection to the plants inside the area dissipate. A hissing noise rose up from the kelp and seaweed, then it shriveled up and died, drying and crumbling away from the amorphous blob of makeshift cement.

"Crap, Crowley—I was using that to hold the thing together."

He grunted, maintaining eye contact with the concrete shell. "You do know this is necromancy, do you not? The spell is incompatible with druidic life magic, and since my casting is stronger, it cancelled yours out."

"I wouldn't say your spell was *stronger*," I protested to no one in particular. Crowley arched an eyebrow, even as he concentrated on completing his enchantment. "Yeah, yeah. Just get it done, alright?"

The spell he was casting would cause Saint Germain's hitchhiker—the powerful vampire spirit that dwelt within his body—to recede, allowing his spirit to step "into the light," so to speak. To the naked eye, Crowley did nothing but stare at the concrete shell that contained Le Boucher. But in my magesight, I saw lines of sickly yellow and black magic emanating from his hands, weaving dark energies into the necromantic circle to force the spirit deep into Saint Germain's subconscious.

More cracks appeared in the cement shell as Le Boucher struggled to break free. Black beads of sweat broke out on Crowley's brow like drops of blood, shimmering softly in the pale moonlight. His face was a mask of agony, both from the strain and because he'd temporarily separated himself from nearly all of the shadow magic that now sustained him.

"Are you almost done?" I asked in a low voice.

"Nearly—there," he croaked.

That was when I heard Larry's voice echoing across the sands from my left. "Geronimo!"

"Fucking hell, Larry," I cursed. "Stop!"

Warning the cryptid was no use. The weird, dog-like creature coalesced into view as he launched himself at the vampire, eyes closed. Knowing that idiot, he'd been running laps around the island to gain momentum or some stupid shit, missing everything that had happened over the last thirty seconds or so.

Well, piss.

Things seemed to move in slow motion as the chupacabra opened his eyes. Just as the stark realization that he'd fucked up dawned across his bizarre, semi-canine face, a large piece of concrete fell off the side of the improvised prison, and Le Boucher's arm shot out, snatching Larry by the throat.

Next, the whole upper part of the cement blob crumbled away. Le Boucher held the cryptid up in front of his face, so he could stare the creature in the eye.

"Rat beast," he said as an evil sneer split his fallen angel's features.

The only good news was that Le Boucher hadn't managed to break out of the trap yet. "Crowley, is it ready?"

"Almost," he replied, in a hoarse whisper.

That could mean anything, and Larry might be dead by the time the spell activated. Rather than risk the possibility of the chupacabra getting himself killed for no good reason, I decided to play my final trump card.

I thrust my arm out, pointing my index finger at the vampire.

"*Solas!*" I shouted.

A bright, white-hot beam of pure solar energy shot out of my finger. The light struck the vampire at the bottom of his wrist, then I flicked my finger upward. As for the spell, it only lasted a split-second, but that was enough; the heat and light reacted with the vyrus in the ancient vampire's porcelain-hard flesh, severing his hand at the wrist.

Larry fell at Le Boucher's feet as the vampire roared, holding his charred, amputated limb up in front of his face.

"Grab the rodent," Crowley hissed as he tottered back and forth on the verge of collapse.

I burst forward, grabbing Larry by the scruff by reaching over the necromantic circle, careful to avoid touching it for fear my innate druid magic might scuff the barrier. Yanking the cryptid back, I fell on my ass, clutching the creature to my chest… just as Crowley's spell triggered with a low, sickly *whoomp.*

A wave of pure darkness emanated from the circle—not a glow, but the opposite of light, a force that seemed to suck all surrounding illumination inward. The lines and glyphs in the circle blurred, expanding for a second, then contracting and becoming more defined. Le Boucher locked his gaze with mine, and a look of pure, seething hatred passed almost palpably between us.

All at once, Crowley collapsed, and the enraged vampire shriveled in on himself as the spell took effect.

———

Dark shadow magic swirled like smoke around The Butcher, obscuring the vampire from sight. I set Larry aside, careful to avoid harming him, but not as to show undue care. The last thing I needed was to encourage his infatuation with me.

"Gee, thanks boss," the cryptid said. "I'd have been a goner if you hadn't saved me."

"I'm not your boss, Larry, and I only saved you because I have no idea what your blood might do that thing. For all we know, The Butcher might gain your powers of invisibility by drinking your blood. Then we'd all be up shit creek."

I rolled to my feet, making a beeline for Crowley to check on his status. On kneeling beside his unconscious form, I noted how pale and lifeless he looked. Yet, he was still breathing, and he had a pulse, albeit a weak one. Resisting the urge to use magic to heal him—my druid magic could very well kill him, even with most of his shadow magic absent at the moment—I instead left him to heal on his own.

Then, I turned my attention to Le Boucher. The shadow mist was dissipating, gathering like morning dew on the remainder of the druidic concrete that still encased our target. Soon that dark substance ran in rivulets down the sides of the containment construct. From there it gathered into a pool in the sand, subsequently flowing of its own accord back to its master.

Hopefully he'll be fine once he's reabsorbed his magic. As fine as he can be in his current condition, at least.

The more Crowley gave in to his demonic side, the less human he became, and the greater it affected him when he exerted his shadow magic fully. He'd confided in me once that, at a certain point, he'd lose control and the demon would take over. In that case, I was either to kill him with druidic life magic or, failing that, banish him to The Void.

In spite of myself, I'd grown fond of the shadow wizard during the time I'd spent with this version of him, and I was not looking forward to that day. But, now was not the time to dwell on those matters, as I had an ancient vampire to deal with—by whatever means necessary. I reached in my Bag and drew Dyrnwyn from its sheath, observing that the blade lit up with considerable brilliance as it crossed from the pocket dimension into this one.

Whether that was due to Crowley's presence or Le Boucher's, it was difficult to tell. Likely, the sword reacted to both of them. It had been designed to ferret out and destroy evil, after all. Besides my sunlight spells, Dyrnwyn was the only other weapon I possessed that could give an ancient vampire pause.

Certainly, a decent fireball might harm one, but as the monster had proven, they were easy enough for older vamps to dodge. As for Dyrnwyn's white-hot blade, I was enough of a swordsman and close enough to a vampire in speed to make evading the blade a difficult task, even for one like The Butcher. I held the sword extended in front of me as I approached the half-shattered blob of concrete, my focus trained exclusively on the figure revealed within.

Le Boucher stood there no more; in his place, a familiar figure slumped over the side of the container. Saint Germain's naked form was pale and a bit less plump than the last time I'd seen him, evidencing more muscle and perhaps a bit more youth than before. His typically perfectly coiffed hair was plastered in wet strands that concealed his face as he stirred, moaning softly.

"Gads, I thought that monster would never leave," he rasped, glancing up at me through that mess of long brown locks. "I owe you a debt, good boy, and that is a fact."

I held the sword at the ready, the tip pointed at his heart, keeping my gaze fixed on him all the while. He levered himself upright, using the side of the concrete shell for support. The vampire was smaller in this form than he was moments before, and I realized he could probably slip out of the remnants of my trap if he chose.

"Is that you, Jacques, and only you? Or do I need to run you through just in case?"

"If it would relieve me of this mortal coil, I might allow it. Yes, it is me." Jacques Saint Germain tucked his hair behind his ears as he regarded me with keen interest. I noted his hand had grown back during his transformation, a fact I filed away for later reference. "Perhaps I should apologize for calling you 'boy.' I can see you've shed your youth since I last laid eyes on you."

"The loss of my master forced me to grow up quickly," I replied, still holding the sword trained on him. "I had to become my own master, after Finnegas passed."

"That is unfortunate, and I am deeply sorry for it," he said, meeting my gaze. "Hmm, yes—the burden you carry is clear for any with eyes to see. 'Heavy is the head that wears the crown,' eh? I'm sure your master wished he could have given you more time before passing that mantle on."

I shrugged, then I sheathed Dyrnwyn. If Le Boucher were still in control, he'd have attacked by now. As I tucked the sword away inside my Craneskin Bag, I grabbed a bundle from within and tossed it to Jacques. It was a cheap duffle that contained clothing, toiletries, and a towel.

"Sunrise'll be here in a few hours. You'd best get cleaned up. We have a lot to talk about."

I gestured at the remains of the concrete in which I'd entrapped LeBoucher, exerting my will ever so slightly to allow the sand and other matter to return to its natural state. Then I backed away, keeping Saint Germain in sight as I gathered driftwood to build a fire.

CHAPTER
TWO

AS I SKEWERED my dinner on a pair of switches I'd cut from the island's vegetation, Crowley stirred and groaned softly nearby. He'd be well in no time, and could see to his own recovery—and sustenance. Although the wizard and the vamp might not need to eat real food, personally, I was starving.

Larry lounged beside me as I went about the task. "You trust this guy, boss?"

"Nope. Don't get me wrong, I like Saint Germain—heck, I might even feel a bit sorry for him. But so long as he has that thing inside him, he can't be trusted."

"What thing?"

"As a vampire, he's a unique case. Millennia ago, a primary vampiric spirit tried to take over his body when he was on the brink of death. Yet, Saint Germain's will was so strong, he resisted being possessed fully. Since then, he's fought a constant battle with the spirit to maintain control of his body, and his sanity."

Larry glanced at the vampire, who stood in waist deep water, bathing. "Kinda looked like he lost that battle."

"That was partially my fault. Hopefully, Crowley's magic will keep the other entity at bay." I didn't say what was I thinking, that if Crowley's hitchhiker took over, we'd all be fucked. "If not, well—let's just say I have a contingency plan."

"Never fear, boss. I'll keep an eye on him."

"Um, thanks, Larry."

Minutes later, I had a fire blazing on the beach, and a couple of large driftwood logs arranged around it for seating. Crowley had joined us, sitting silently as he was prone to do, staring into the flames and contemplating who knew what misery. In his timeline, he'd lost the love of his life— my ex, Belladonna. That had driven him over the edge, and now he lived for one thing only—revenge.

Recently, I'd taken him with me to the primary timeline, also known as my world. Not because he'd asked, but because I knew he needed it. There, I concealed us both with magic as we spied on Belladonna. Since then, alt-timeline Crowley had become even more pensive, yet his attitude seemed to have improved somewhat. He wasn't exactly cheerful, but he wasn't quite as gloomy all the time, either.

I rotated the skewers of fish that I was cooking—a couple of porgy I'd caught earlier using druid magic. I'd also cracked a couple of coconuts open for Larry, and he was busily digging out the meat with his forked tongue and crooked teeth. Saint Germain joined us, now fully dressed in the off-the-rack trousers, t-shirt, and loafers I'd given him. The vampire took a seat on a driftwood log across the fire from me.

Jacques opened the conversation by gesturing at himself full-length. "Now that you've humiliated me with these department store raiments, perhaps you'd like to share your purpose for hatching this elaborate scheme."

I pulled the fish away from the fire, propping one skewer upright in the sand and sliding the other off the stick and onto a flat, weathered plank of driftwood. "You mean to say, why did I capture and not kill you?"

"If that were possible, yes. We had a deal, you know."

"I remember," I said, nodding. "But, I need your help."

Saint Germain crossed one knee over the other, leaning forward as he warmed his hands at the fire. He wasn't close enough to benefit from the heat, but at his age, affecting human gestures to blend in was second nature. "You needed my help back then, too, as I recall. I killed that great giant for you, saving your life in the process. I'd say I've held up my end of the bargain."

"You didn't do that. The Butcher did. Then, he vanished into Underhill before I could stop him."

The old leech waved offhandedly. "Yes, I was there, sitting in the passenger seat, where I've been ever since." He glanced at Crowley. "At least, until this one performed that grim work just now."

"It will last a few days, no more," the wizard said softly.

"Can you repeat it?" Saint Germain's voice was flat, his face expressionless.

"Not without considerable preparation and effort," Crowley replied, still staring at the fire. "But this one is more than capable of slaying you, of that you can be assured."

Saint Germain turned his attention to me, narrowing his

gaze. "How did you gain such power in that brief period of time?"

"I won't tell you until you agree to help me." Pausing, I pulled the skin off my fish, then I tore a strip of flaky, hot flesh from underneath, popping it in my mouth. It was bland, but fresh, and it tasted of the sea. After repeating the process twice more, I continued. "As I said, I need your assistance."

Jacques rolled his eyes. "Fine, I'll bite. Tell me what you require."

"We're going after Alan Garr," I said matter-of-factly.

Saint Germain sat up a bit straighter, clutching an imaginary string of pearls as he did so. "I'm sorry, you're what?"

"He said we're going to kill Alalngar," Crowley responded. "And then we will slay his coven."

Saint Germain blinked twice. "Should I assume you'll be taking on the entire Vampyri Council as well? Then why shouldn't I wish to come along?" His voice dripped with sarcasm as he continued. "I'll just need to square away my personal and business matters beforehand. After we fail, you see, we'll all end up in a dungeon deep under some Romanian castle for the next several centuries. I've seen those places, having delivered many a disgraced bloodkin to their fate over the millennia. Once ensconced there, we shall not escape, of that I can assure you both."

I shared a look with Crowley, and he shrugged almost imperceptibly. It took only a few moments of consideration before I spoke next. "Not here, but in another timeline. I'm going there to save it, and I have to kill that motherfucker to do it. After you help me, I'll end you as well."

Jacques Germain cocked his head slightly. "*Mon Dieu*, you're serious."

"As a heart attack. You in, or what?"

"It all makes sense now," Germain continued, almost oblivious to my question. "Yes, yes—chronourgy would explain the rapid advancement in skill, that aged look in your eye, and this strange, much deadlier version of Fuamnach's Hound that accompanies you. *Sacré bleu*, you actually could kill me. You might send me to an alternate time stream where the vyrus cannot survive, or to the cold airless depths of space, or even age me forward or backward in the blink of an eye."

In truth, I hadn't thought of those things, but I nodded as if I had. There was so much that Gwydion had not taught me. "If I couldn't live up to my end of our bargain before, obviously I can now. So, are you with me?"

The old vampire met my gaze, his mouth set in a stern line. "It will take planning, certainly, and we will need additional assistance. Pfah, but this is nothing with which you cannot contend. Of course, I'm with you, you fool. When do we start?"

———

If you faced an insurmountable task and had unlimited time to prepare, what would you do? For me, the answer to that question was simple—I'd raise a team of the best possible recruits I could find, and plan and prepare like hell until I had a scheme that couldn't fail. I considered exactly how I might do that on a long, solitary stroll through my Grove in the Hellpocalypse timeline, where I'd retreated to gather my thoughts before I embarked on the mission.

Considering that I had the luxury of choosing members of my cohort from across multiple timelines throughout known and unknown history, picking the right team would be crucial. Pulling off the job in Vegas had taught me as much. On that recent job, I had been assigned an impossible heist by none other than Loki himself. The task was to steal the Apple of Discord, right out from under Eris' nose, from within the Vault of the Greek Gods, which was guarded by Typhon, the grandaddy of all dragons.

Successfully completing the heist required the assembly of a crack team of specialists, each with their own specific, unique, particular set of skills. Then I had to come up with a plan that would succeed, even if it failed. And finally, I had to outsmart not one, but *two* trickster gods.

All this time, over an array of capers and quests, I'd been trying to do things all on my lonesome. That heist made me realize that I couldn't do everything on my own. Moreover, it showed me that I couldn't go through life trying to protect my friends from their own choices. Some people were going to try to help me whether I liked it or not, and I was better off being there to guide them as a leader than trying to shake them off, so they didn't get hurt.

With that lesson learned, I now faced an undertaking that was many times greater and more challenging. This mission would span two timelines, multiple worlds and dimensions, and potentially affect billions of people for generations to come.

And if I failed? The druid order would be wiped from history, forever. No pressure, right? So, like I said, I'd need help.

Those with a rudimentary understanding of time magic —chronomancy and chronourgy, to the initiated—might think the primary challenge I faced was recruiting my team without disrupting the timelines. That actually wasn't an issue. All I had to do was find dead-end timelines from which to pluck my recruits, or recruit them from their timelines right before their moment of death.

In an infinite quantum multiverse filled with endless alternate time streams, there were bound to be timelines somewhere that were on the brink of self-destruction. And, there were certain to be versions of the people I required who were destined to perish prematurely in those timelines. That's where I would select my candidates—all except for one of them because I had always intended to make that individual permanently dead. As he'd said, I owed it to him as part of the deal we had struck.

Saint Germain—a.k.a., *Le Boucher*—had been a handful before I helped him suck Tethra the Fomorian dry. There was a reason "The Butcher" had been the favored troubleshooter for the Vampyri Council for centuries, and it wasn't due to his sparkling personality. As vamps went, Saint Germain was a decent guy, but his alter-ego was a stone killer, the meanest bloodsucking son of a bitch that ever walked any earth.

And now? Forty pints of the god-like giant's blood had made the bipolar vampire downright invincible. Thankfully, I had the world's most diabolical, demon-possessed necromancer riding shotgun to help me wrangle him. Unfortunately, our plan could go awry the moment we allowed The Butcher to surface once more.

But, one problem at a time. As for disrupting the timelines, Saint Germain wasn't an issue. All I had to do was ice him once his part was complete, which was what he wanted, anyway. So long as he didn't go back to our timeline after his gig was finished, we were golden.

The question was, who else would I need to recruit to

make this thing work? The prerequisites were pretty simple; they had to be powerful, ruthless, and inclined to help me save both humanity and the future of druidry on two earths. The team couldn't be too large, either, because as I'd learned in Vegas, too many chefs would result in one of them defecting to someone else's kitchen.

In the end, I'd boiled it down to two more candidates besides myself—Crowley, and someone else who I wasn't prepared to face yet. Honestly, though, I didn't really like those choices. One of them was a powerful wizard teetering on the brink of demonic possession, and the other one?

Well, let's just say they presented a Pandora's Box of emotions that I was terrified to open, simply because I didn't know if I'd even *want* to shut it again. Heck, I wasn't even certain I could go through with recruiting them, as the pain might be too much to bear. I glanced skyward as I thought about the consequences, my mood much darker than the storms in the distance.

Unlike the Grove in my timeline, it was always raining here, somewhere. That was the result of the death of my counterpart in this timeline, a version of me who'd died in the initial nuclear onslaught shortly after the vamps triggered World War III and the undead apocalypse. That trauma had affected my "children" deeply, turning one of them melancholy and the other nearly mad.

I'd managed to tame the Oak and restore its sanity, healing both Oak and Grove through bonding with the duo and restoring my presence. But deep down, they each knew I wasn't *their* Colin, and that loss left a scar that no amount of love and care could erase. I just hoped it wouldn't negatively impact the execution of my plan in this timeline.

Maybe I ought to spend a couple of years studying arboreal psychology before I continue with the mission. Surely, there's a timeline somewhere that has sentient Oaks in a branch of its evolutionary tree.

Amused at the thought, I chuckled softly, just as a large shadow drifted overhead. It passed more swiftly than any cloud could, growing larger until the shadow's counterpart glided into view some three hundred yards distant. Smokedancer swooped down in a meadow ahead of me, one that sat directly in my path, alighting as soft and soundlessly as a barn owl.

How she could fly and land so silently was anyone's guess, but I assumed it was a function of her magic. That she'd chosen to land along my chosen route meant that she wished to speak with me. Being typically dragon-like, she had given me the option of deciding *not* to make the abruptly proposed appointment.

However, that would've been incredibly rude. Not only was it a bad idea to blow off a dragon, I also liked Smokedancer very much. She'd helped me out of a terrible bind that involved being drowned by a river goddess who blamed me for the death of her homicidal, psychopathic son. And the bitch of it was, I hadn't even killed him—my mom had done that.

But like I said, Smokedancer had bailed me out, so I'd not deny her my time, especially when I had so much of it. I continued along the same route at the same pace, moseying my way toward the massive, house-sized red dragon who lay in the meadow ahead grooming her scales.

———

"Hello, Smokedancer," I said as I approached.

Hello, druid.

As always, she replied telepathically. From the moment we'd first communicated, I found it odd and slightly disconcerting that she could speak words into my mind so effortlessly. Apparently, this was how her kind communicated, but I had found it entirely unsettling.

The dragoness had picked up on my discomfort and taken to only communicating with me face to face. Certainly, she could easily talk to me from great distances, and she had previously. Yet, she knew this was my preferred method of communication, and thus she now always approached me before reaching out telepathically.

I often wondered if all dragons were as thoughtful as she, and whether she'd be so kindly disposed toward me if I hadn't offered her and her brood sanctuary and protection. There was no way I'd ask that, for fear of insulting her. As far as I could tell, she could only read surface thoughts that I *intended* to transmit, and I hadn't yet let those thoughts slip in conversation.

"It's a nice day for a flight," I remarked, apropos of nothing. Smokedancer seemed to enjoy small talk, so I made every attempt to engage her in it whenever we met.

Indeed, it is. Your Grove always seems to know how to maximize updrafts and air currents, making flying within this realm a pleasure.

We spent the next few minutes chatting about the joys of flight, and exploring the possibility that I might someday use my control of air molecules and wind currents to fly, despite my lack of wings. I'd already managed magical flight in another timeline where my powers worked differently. Since she seemed to enjoy sharing her insights, I kept that information to myself. After a time, she skillfully guided the conversation toward her intended point of discussion.

My dragonlings are growing quickly, druid, she said, blinking lazily.

The dragon had gold irises flecked with every color of the rainbow, shimmering in iridescence due to the protective nictitating membrane that protected each orb. Not long after she came to live in the Grove, I learned not to stare at them too long. For one, it was easy to become hypnotized by them, even without Smokedancer exerting her will to do so.

Moreover, she'd informed me that it was considered bad form in dragon culture to hold eye contact for too long. Whether that was due to their powers of hypnotism, or because they saw it as a challenge, she didn't say. Regardless, I often had to resist staring her in the eye whenever we spoke.

"I'm pleased to hear that, and to know they're thriving." I paused, waiting to see if she'd follow up with a clear request, making my life that much easier. She didn't, so I continued. "Is everything well?"

She blinked again, lifting her chin off her giant, taloned forepaws. *The Grove is a lovely place, magical and rife with food, with ample skies to fly in, and plenty of places to soar and roost. However...*

Finally, it occurred to me what she was getting at here. "However, it's beginning to feel a bit cramped as your broodlings grow, yes?"

She inclined her head slightly. *The druid is observant as he is wise.*

I smiled good-naturedly. "My late mentor would disagree, but thank you, nonetheless. In this case, however, he'd be right. I should have seen this issue coming long ago."

You are no expert on dragon ecology and biology. You had no way of knowing.

In fact, several of the tomes Finnegas had left for me were a series of bestiaries written by multiple druids over many centuries. Unfortunately, they'd been penned in multiple languages, and I'd yet to take the time to learn each in kind. It was a shortcoming I intended to rectify, just as soon as I dealt with the Hellpocalypse issue.

"Ah, but I can study, and in that regard I've been neglectful. My apologies."

No apology is needed. We reside here by the grace of your hospitality —

I held up a hand in protest. "Pardon me for interrupting you, but I beg to differ. This place is as much your home now as it is mine. Yes, I am bonded to the Oak and Grove, and ultimately, they do answer to me. Yet, I am no lord of the fae, nor am I human royalty. As a druid, it's my duty to serve all living things, protecting them, nurturing them, and maintaining nature's balance." I flashed her a warm smile, one that was heartfelt. "Besides, it's been a joy to have the dragonlings here in the Grove. Their presence has brought me happiness beyond measure."

Smokedancer closed her eyes and bowed her head. When she opened them to look at me again, they were misty, and her telepathic voice was filled with emotion. *Would that I could have met your druid master, Colin McCool. He must have been a very great teacher to have chosen well and trained you to become the druid you are today.*

"I wish you could have met him. You two would've gotten along splendidly." I looked to the horizon, where three dragonlings flew and frolicked in the magical 'sunlight' the Grove provided. "I'll speak to the Grove about expanding her borders. She enjoys doing so anyway, and I'm certain if you convey to her what you need, she'll be more than happy to provide it."

My thanks, druid. She shook her wings slightly as if preparing to take flight, but then stopped to address me once more. *Mark my words—when I return to my homeland, all will know that Colin McCool is a friend to dragonkind.*

She snorted and blew smoke that covered me from head to toes, not hot enough to burn me, but pleasantly warm like a towel fresh out of the dryer. The smoke smelled like burning incense, something exotic that I couldn't identify. When it cleared, she backed away about fifty feet, then she inclined her head one last time. After I returned the gesture, she snapped her wings and flew off to join her brood.

"You've gotten lots better at making words sound pretty," Larry said as he dropped his invisibility, coalescing into view at my side. The Grove in my timeline barely tolerated the genetic chimera, but strangely this one didn't have a problem with him. "I mean, sheesh—you had that dragon eatin' outta' your hand."

I stretched, feigning nonchalance because this topic made me uncomfortable. I might've looked twenty-two, but inside I felt much older. "Ten years of traveling the Twisted Paths to prepare for the battle of your life will do that to you."

"Yeah, but it ain't the years," the chupacabra said as he scratched behind his ear with a hind-paw. "It's how you spend 'em. That dragon's what—a few centuries old? But she treats you like an equal. There's somethin' to be said for that."

"Meh. She deserves respect, and I show it to her. Besides, I like her. She's polite and considerate, yet there's no guile about her. She just says what she means."

"Hah!" Larry wheezed as he broke into laughter that reminded me of that cartoon dog, Muttley. "Oh, the irony."

"How so?"

"You just described yerself." He sniffed, wiping his nose on the back of his paw in a very human-like gesture. "Well, except for the cussing, of course."

"How do you know she doesn't cuss? She only speaks telepathically."

Larry cocked an ear as he looked up at me. "C'mon, druid. A lady that classy never cusses. Everyone knows that."

———

Crossing back and forth between Earth and the Grove was easy, but crossing between timelines was difficult, and it took a lot out of me. That was why, when I'd abducted Saint Germain and brought him to the Hellpocalypse timeline, I went to the Grove to recover.

Yet, before we embarked on this mission, I felt the need to make one more trip back to my primary timeline to see Fallyn. After all, you never knew what could happen when you pitted yourself against ancient, powerful creatures with god-like powers. I didn't like to catastrophize, but I also realized that each adventure might very well be my last. The hell if I was going to face down a vampire army without kissing my girl goodbye beforehand.

First, however, I needed to discuss our next steps with Crowley. To that end, I had the Oak transport me to the place where I'd left him and Saint Germain. They awaited me in the shadow wizard's sanctuary, deep underground beneath an area of Austin that hadn't been completely decimated when the bombs fell.

Crowley's hideout was located in a large tunnel that had been dug as proof of concept by some billionaire before the apocalypse. Apparently, the guy had been trying to get a contract with the city of Austin to dig highway tunnels across the metro to alleviate traffic congestion. It was a stupid idea, but the tunnel he left made for a hell of a good safe-house in an undead apocalypse.

It was twenty-four feet in diameter, lined with reinforced concrete, ventilated, and sealed at both ends with thick steel walls and doors that were more than adequate for keeping out the odd zombie or revenant. The tunnel had also been dug beneath the billionaire's electric auto manufacturing complex, out near the airport. The entire place was fenced in and locked down like a damned military base, although there'd been a small coven of vamps hiding out there when Crowley moved in.

He slew them, of course, and used their body parts as components for his necromantic wards. Nothing was getting in this place—nothing undead, anyway. And, billionaires being billionaires, the tunnel had access to all the comforts of pre-apocalypse society, including solar power and diesel generators, a filtered ventilation system, kitchen facilities, and ample lighting.

How the wizard had found the place was beyond me, but it worked. He used the tunnel itself to house his "experiments," creatures like the rolling, amorphous ball of undead he'd used to track me down on my previous foray to this timeline. There were others, of course; flesh golems, undead held in thrall, and the like. They patrolled the length of the tunnel, making certain any undesirables who might find a way to cross Crowley's wards would then make it no further.

As for the living quarters, those were housed in a series of administrative offices adjacent to the tunnel. They'd previously been used as control rooms and places to house the mechanicals, and now they served as Crowley's living quarters, laboratory, and library.

When I popped in from the Grove, the shadow wizard was hunched over his apothecary table, staring through the lenses of an ancient brass microscope. Registering my presence, he raised a finger to indicate I should wait until he was finished. After he was done examining the results of his latest experiment, he swiveled around to face me, crossing his arms over his chest.

"Have a productive rest?"

"Always. There's nothing like taking a nap inside a sentient pocket dimension that is absolutely, one hundred percent dedicated to keeping you safe from harm."

"One should be so lucky," he said without a hint of sarcasm or envy in his voice. "Now that you've recuperated, we need to speak about the mission."

I scratched the back of my head and looked around. "First, where's Saint Germain?"

Crowley pursed his lips. "Feeding, I'd imagine. He asked me if I had any blood on hand, and I told him to get his own. Then I pointed him in the direction of a tribe of cannibal slavers who've been ambushing refugees along 71 east of here. That was perhaps two hours ago."

"You turned him loose—by himself?" I asked, shaking my head.

Crowley scoffed, but there was no malice in it. "He'll be stuck in his current form for days yet, and you and I both know he's relatively harmless to decent humans in that state. Besides, I placed a tracker on him. There's no place he can go in this hellscape where I won't find him."

"Fair enough. If something happens to me, and Saint Germain's alter-ego resumes control, do you think you could stop him?"

The wizard waved my comment off. "Nothing will happen to you. Now, we need to discuss the final member of our team."

I shook my head slowly. "I know what you're about to say, and the answer is still no."

"Colin, we'll be facing an ancient race that rivals the fae in both longevity and guile. Moreover, it is clear that, in mutating the vyrus, they meddled in magicks the likes of which mankind has not seen since the days when the gods freely walked the Earth. We shall need the old druid's guidance if we are to succeed, much less survive."

Of course, he was referring to Finnegas. Crowley and I had mutually agreed that we needed someone powerful and skilled in ancient magic to help us counteract whatever dark sorcery the Vampyri had dabbled in to make the Vyrus spread so quickly. What we disagreed on was who that individual should be.

As for the plan, it was clear we needed to eliminate a large percentage of the undead population. That would give humankind a chance to repopulate the Earth, and hopefully to grow strong enough to fight back against the undead. It was a long-game strategy, and hardly a neat solution, but practically speaking, it was the only solution that made sense.

There were now over a billion undead terrorizing the planet, making it impractical to try to decimate their numbers via violence or magic. The alternative? To defeat the vyrus with a counter-pathogen of some sort. Ideally, such a pathogen would directly attack the infection, spreading through the undead population and reversing what the Vampyri had done.

By weakening the vyrus carried by the undead, most of them would rapidly decompose and perish, for good. If we were lucky, the weaker version of the vyrus might also be used to develop a vaccine, with which we could inoculate the population at large. It was a long shot, and reducing the numbers of undead was the primary goal, but Crowley and I both thought it to be possible.

Spreading this counter-pathogen wasn't an issue. In my travels through the Paths, I'd discovered an alternate Earth where technology ruled instead of magic. Due to my magic malfunctioning, I'd nearly been stuck in that timeline, but I'd managed to escape along with the technology we needed to complete our mission.

Now, all we needed was the counter-pathogen. The only problem was that neither one of us possessed the skill to create something like that, despite each of us having the best training possible in necromancy and druid magic. Oh, we'd tried. Many times, in fact. And we'd failed each and every time.

I insisted that we needed to find the source of the infection to successfully come up with a cure. Once we had Patient Zero, we stood a much better chance of altering the vyrus to counter itself. Crowley, on the other hand, believed we'd still need assistance to see our plan through.

But who could we trust to go to for help? We needed

someone with skill in magic well beyond our own—
someone whose ideals and goals aligned with ours. I'd
suggested recruiting my half-brother from this alternate
timeline, the Celtic god Lugh. The wizard had vetoed that
idea outright, reminding me that none among the fae or
Celtic gods could be trusted.

Thus, we'd have to recruit a human. That person needed
to be someone whose mystical skill and knowledge rivaled
that of the gods and ancient fae, as they had most certainly
loaned their talents to the Vampyri to alter the vyrus and
cause the undead apocalypse. The list of candidates was
short, and it included only Finnegas the Seer and The Dark
Druid.

Clearly, that meant my former mentor, Finnegas, was
our only hope. I just couldn't bring myself to snatch him or
a version of him from some dead-end timeline, knowing I'd
have to return him thereafter to die all over again when that
timeline ended. Or worse, to abduct him from my timeline
before he died, healing him solely to help us while creating
a timeline paradox that could screw things up back home.

Because Finnegas had died in my timeline, if I snatched
him from there and healed him, I couldn't return him there
again. That would risk altering my own timeline irrevoca-
bly, and the repercussions could be dire. And hell if I was
going to heal him and then kill him, even if that were
possible.

As much as I wanted the old man back, even for a short
period of time, I couldn't bear to lose him again. Knowing
him, he'd find a way to off himself, purely to save the
primary timeline. Just thinking about it made me heartsick
all over, which was why I kept avoiding the conversation.

While I ran through the history of our conflict over this

matter in my head, Crowley stared at me with his creepy, swirling black eyes. "The answer is still no, Crowley, no matter how many times you ask it."

"Because it is the only way forward, I will keep asking it of you. You know this as well as I. There are none with the skill and knowledge we need whom we can trust."

"I still say we should find this timeline's version of the Dark Druid and make him help us," I muttered.

The shadow wizard hissed. "Better to make a deal with the Devil himself. Much safer, certainly. No, it is impossible. Even if we could subdue him, he'd find a way to sabotage our efforts, simply out of spite."

"Then we're still at an impasse, Crowster. So, let's just focus on Garr instead. He'll lead us to Patient Zero, and once we have the cleanest sample possible, we'll know for sure whether we can fix this thing ourselves."

Crowley stroked his chin, frowning deeply as he considered my stubborn refusal to do as he asked. "Fine then. When Saint Germain returns, we shall formulate a plan to abduct Alalngar and force him to tell us where the origin of the mutated vyrus may be found."

"Great."

"But Colin—"

"I know. We're going to need Saint Germain to pull this off. Can you handle him?"

"Yes. But you must be ready to help me should he turn on us. If he sides with Garr…"

"Don't sweat it. I have something he wants way worse than he wants to help his own kind. Trust me, it's under control."

The shadow wizard wheezed a long, drawn-out sigh. "Now, I am more concerned than ever."

CHAPTER
THREE

ACCORDING to Crowley's tracker spell, Saint Germain was running a zigzag pattern around a small hidden settlement to the east. Meaning, he was busy killing cannibals, which I didn't have a problem with at all. Since it looked like he'd be occupied for a while, I decided to head to the primary timeline to see Fallyn before we went after Garr.

For me, time magic was many times more difficult to perform than druidry, and it came with its own unique challenges and complications. Not the least of which was that it had been outlawed by all the major pantheons eons ago. Only a few gods were allowed to have knowledge of how to perform it—those being deities whose very nature demanded it. Even then, outside of their specific duties, they weren't actually allowed to practice it.

The reasons for this were obvious to anyone with half a brain. Time magic was extremely powerful and very dangerous, and the more you messed with it, the more likely you were to screw up a timeline and cause a catastrophic event. Challenge number one in traveling the

Twisted Paths—the extra-dimensional pathways that connected the time streams—was avoiding being the cause of such an event.

That was actually relatively easy if you knew what you were doing and had control over the magic you cast. To avoid screwing up your own timeline, all you had to do was make certain that you exited and reentered it at the exact same point in time, to avoid causing a paradox. For me, this had become second nature, although it still required a great deal of mental and magical energy to make the transition between the two timelines.

Besides that, it was all about not getting caught. That meant you had to enter and exit the Paths via a location where you were unlikely to be detected. Time magic caused magical ripples that emanated from the spot where the magician entered and exited the time stream. If a god or goddess noticed it, that disturbance could be tracked.

The solution I came up with to that conundrum was simple—I always entered and exited my time stream in the middle of bum-fucked Egypt. Or, to be more exact, deep inside Dog Canyon, on the northernmost edge of Big Bend National Park in one of the most remote places in the state. It was so far west as to be beyond the borders of Maeve's demesne, and also far enough from the border to avoid notice from the most powerful local entity, the shapeshifting *bruja* known as La Onza.

As usual, I stepped into my own timeline inside a small cave hidden high up on a mountain ridge, the entrance to which I kept hidden with vegetation, boulders, and magic. After making the transition, I followed all my usual security protocols. This started with dropping into a druid trance and scanning the area to make sure I hadn't been observed.

While in my trance I checked to ensure the cave remained undisturbed, finishing that task by shoring up the wards and spells that protected the place.

When I opened my eyes, Larry was sitting in front of me, staring at me with his tongue hanging out the side of his mouth. "So boss, what's next?"

As usual, he couldn't resist following me through a portal or timeline jump. I couldn't figure out how he managed the latter, but I assumed it had something to do with the *kitsune* DNA the government used when they created the genetically chimeric cryptid. I'd given up on trying to prevent him from following me around, but in this case, what I was about to do was too dangerous to risk letting him screw it up.

"What's next is that we have to part ways. We're back in the primary timeline now, Larry, and that's where I need you to stay."

"Going back, eh?" One of his googly eyes rolled around of its own accord, spinning lazily until it focused on me again. "That place is a complete shithole. Why'd ya' ever wanna do that?"

"Because it's my fault it's such a shithole, and I believe it's my responsibility to fix it."

"I guess I get that." He glanced around the cave, panting with a goofy-ass grin on his face. "You sure you don't need my help?"

"Not this time, bud. This is something I have to do alone."

He licked his balls, then he scratched behind his ear with a hind paw. "Alright then. Call me if you need me."

"Larry, you don't have a phone."

"I certainly do. It's just that I can't use it 'cept once a

month, when I change into my human form." He sniffed the air and chuckled. "Ah, you brought me back to my old stomping grounds. That was really thoughtful of you, kimo sabe."

That was definitely not why I chose this location, but I wasn't going to tell him that. "Sure thing. And if you don't mind keeping this location a secret..."

"Mum's the word," he said as he trotted for the exit to the cavern. "In case you need me, my number's in your phone. Leave a voicemail if I don't pick up, which is nearly always."

I almost asked him how he managed to put his number in my phone, then I thought better of it. Some mysteries were better left unsolved. "Of course. See you around."

"Not if I see you first," he replied as he was exiting the cave. "Then I'll see you for a while before you see me. And when you see me, it'll be a long while after I saw you..."

He kept babbling nonsense as his voice trailed off into the distance. "That's not creepy at all, you know," I yelled after him.

Damn it. Now I have to find a new cave.

After Larry left, I contacted my druid Oak and had it teleport me to the Austin Pack's clubhouse. Cell coverage was shitty up in the Guadalupe Mountains, so I figured I'd take a stab at finding Fallyn at the most likely location, the headquarters for the 'thrope pack she led as their alpha.

The Austin Pack's clubhouse was a private roadhouse-style bar on the edge of town that served as a place where they could party, conduct Pack business, and let their hair down away from mundane society. Most 'thropes lived and worked beside humans, unbeknownst to the mundanes, of course. Werewolves being werewolves, they needed to cut loose occasionally without causing a major incident, and the clubhouse allowed them the privacy to do so.

Despite being a member—only in the loosest sense of the term, mind—my presence tended to make a lot of the Pack uncomfortable. Most 'thropes disliked magic and magic users in general, and they were even more suspicious of fae creatures. To them, I ticked both boxes, first because I'm a druid, and second because I'm part Fomorian.

Never mind that Fomorians and the Tuatha Dé Danann are traditionally mortal enemies; to the Pack, everything that's not a 'thrope or a vamp is fae. So, I teleported in where I always did, inside the rundown storage shed that sat behind the clubhouse. Fallyn's scent hung heavy over the dusty, cobwebbed interior of the small wooden building, which told me she'd been here recently.

Finally, some good news.

Rather than text her to let her know I was coming, I decided to show up unannounced and surprise her. I exited the shed, fully preoccupied with the prospect of spending some quality time with my girlfriend, already making plans for dinner and a nice, quiet evening in the Grove alone. No sooner had I taken three steps out the door, than something large, heavy, and hairy jumped on me from behind.

———

At first, I thought someone might be playing a trick on me —maybe one of the Pack members who were favorably inclined toward me, or Fallyn, even. After all, werewolves were known to be playful, and they could get a bit rough in their play with their pack-mates and family. Then I felt it clamp its jaws onto my shoulder, and that's when I knew this was no prank.

The fucked up thing was, I wasn't even in my half-shifted state. With Fallyn being fully in charge of the Pack, it had been a while since I felt threatened on Pack territory.

Besides, sometimes it felt good to drop my other form and remain human. Sure, it was great being semi-invulnerable, but having denser muscle mass and connective tissue also left me feeling sort of dull and disconnected from the world around me. Maybe it was all in my head, but I'd grown up human, and it simply felt natural to be in that state.

Just my luck that the first time I let my guard down for months, I get attacked.

Without super-strength and supernatural reflexes, the thing dragged me down to the ground on all fours in short order. Werewolves tended to fight just like their animal kingdom counterparts, going for the throat and cervical spine first, vital organs second, and, failing that, hamstringing their prey as a final option. The only reason why it had missed my neck was because I'd seen a shadow and flinched. If I hadn't, I'd be bleeding out already.

As it was, the werewolf was savaging my shoulder by shaking its head back and forth, and blood was streaming down my chest and back. He also had his clawed hands clamped on my shoulders, his talons digging into my flesh while he drove forward with his legs, keeping me pressed toward the ground. I could barely see it out of the corner of my eye—a large white-haired male in his shifted form, from the looks of it. His blue eyes had a wild look about them, typical of a 'thrope on the hunt.

I felt and heard my collarbone snap between his jaws

and knew that if I didn't get him off me immediately, I wouldn't make it long enough to shift, heal myself, or even fight back. With few other options, I did the only thing I could do—I unleashed a spell right in the were-wolf's face.

Propping myself up on one hand while bearing the werewolf's weight was difficult, especially with the trauma I'd suffered and shock setting in, but I managed. That allowed me to reach across with my left hand, which I placed over his eyes.

"*Tine*," I said, and flames instantly poured forth from my palm, cascading across the werewolf's face, catching his fur alight.

The werewolf roared and released me, backing away as he batted at his ruined face and eyes with both of his massive, clawed hands. The upper part of his face and head were now a blackened mess, but he'd heal from that in short order. As for me, I was starting to feel woozy due to blood loss. I needed to do something quickly before I bled out.

Fighting a full-grown, shifted male werewolf in my current state was a no-go, so I reached out to the Oak to request that it teleport me back to the Grove. All I got was static, a sort of "line dead" situation that experience had taught me could only be due to deific interference. That, of course, meant this was a set-up.

Well, fuck.

It was clear I'd have to fight if I wanted to avoid ending up in this rogue 'thrope's belly. I started shifting, even as I knelt and grabbed a handful of weeds and grass from the ground, slapping it on my wound. The merest effort of will infused the foliage with druid magic, transforming it from useless lawn debris into a combination clotting bandage and wound closure.

The grass weaved itself back and forth across my wound, turning itself into thin strands of fiber that were tipped with thorny needles that sutured the wounds closed. The fibers also wove together as they released phytochemicals that would cause vasoconstriction and clotting. It was a spell I'd learned from the old man's library recently, and one I was glad I'd taken the time to master.

The entire process of closing the wound with druid magic took under three seconds, a painful but necessary bit of spell-work. Shifting would take longer, however. Unfortunately, I didn't have time to wait for my bones to become denser and my muscles and connective tissue to reknit, following patterns set by the Fomorian part of my DNA.

Plus, even once the shift was complete, it'd take several minutes for my healing factor to replace the blood I'd lost. No doubt, Fallyn and the rest of the present Pack were already on their way out here to investigate after smelling the scent of my blood. But one look at White Fang told me I didn't have even that long before he'd be fully recovered.

He was already growing new pink skin, even as the blackened, burned skin around his eyes flaked and peeled away. No sooner had that happened than he opened his eyelids, revealing a brand-new set of bright blue peepers that stared at me with a hatred I'd rarely seen outside of a confrontation between two Karens.

That indicated a major problem. I'd never seen a werewolf regenerate nervous tissue like that—not that fast, at least. Maybe Samson could do it, if he was fully fed and having a good day. But besides him, I didn't know of any werewolves who could heal that quickly.

It was just my luck to get jumped by a super-alpha. What I'd done to piss him off was anyone's guess, but that was a moot point. Somebody had to stop the fucker, and as usual, it looked like I'd be saving my own ass today.

———

Magic it is, then.

Since fire had worked so well the first time, I tossed a fireball at the werewolf with my left hand. My right arm hung uselessly at my side, so I'd be finishing this fight as a lefty. Fan-fucking-tastic.

As I was summoning a fireball, I heard Fallyn shout from the direction of the clubhouse. "Blaise, stop!"

Things were far too tense to spare her the barest glance, but my peripheral vision told me that a whole mess of Pack members were hoofing it over here. Far be it from a bunch of 'thropes to miss a good fight.

That Fallyn had asked him to stop and not me wasn't lost on me, but I had to wonder what her motivations were. Did she fear more for him than me? Or was it the other way around?

I decided it was best to worry about that later. "Blaise" looked ready to pounce, so I tossed my fireball at him and started forming another.

Like I'd said, the 'thrope's eyes had healed fast, so he saw my spell coming. That was the thing about fireballs— they dealt big damage, but were a little slow on the delivery. I tossed another, then another, backpedaling even as the werewolf zig-zagged to dodge the incoming attacks.

"She's mine, freak!" he half-snarled, half-roared at me.

"We bonded as mates, and that's for life. Yield my right, or die."

"I don't even know who you're talking about!" I shouted as I sidestepped a lunging forehand swipe that barely missed my face. "It's not like I've dated many women, and I'm a one-woman guy, so…"

That was when it hit me. He wasn't talking about one of my exes; he was referring to Fallyn. The realization stunned me for a second, freezing my brain and causing me to miss a beat. A beat was all it took for the werewolf to backhand me across the face so hard it flipped me over backward. I rolled ass over end, landing on my hands and knees in the dirt.

By now, I was almost completely shifted into my half-Fomorian form, but that fucker could hit. Not only did the reality of the situation throw me for a loop, but that backhand had me seeing stars. The fact that he'd dropped me wasn't lost on the big white lycan, and he promptly skipped forward to follow up with a soccer kick to my ribs that lifted me off the ground. Despite having a reinforced Fomorian skeleton holding the blood sack that was me together, I was pretty sure I felt a couple of ribs crack.

He'd knocked the air out of me, alright, but thankfully he kicked me on my left side. If it had been my right, he would have pulverized my liver—game over in this form. I could take a lot and heal a lot in my half-shifted form, but if a major blood-filled organ exploded inside me, it'd put me down for sure.

I wasn't about to take another kick like that, but I was also the one on the ground. In a fight like this, that was no bueno. If I was thinking clearly, I'd have used druid magic to even the odds, maybe turn the ground to quicksand and back to hard earth again, or suck the air out of his lungs, or something equally sneaky and sinister. However, I was definitely not thinking clearly at all, being concussed and having my world rocked all at once.

That said, I was one hundred ten percent pissed, and that counted for something. Furthermore, I'd just spent a decade roaming the Twisted Paths. I'd visited multiple alternate timelines and worlds searching for what I needed to heal the Hellpocalypse, all while studying druid magic to master the skills taught to me by Finnegas and granted to me when I sang the *teinm laida*.

During that time, I'd gotten an extended education in dirty fighting that could not be learned from books or gained in the sterile environment of a dojo. Some of the worlds I traversed were so barbaric as to make the Hellpocalypse seem tame, while others were inhabited by humans with powers that rivaled those of the gods. Whether this prick had me on my back foot or not, I would not go down easy, and I definitely was not going to be punked by some Johnny-come-lately who wanted my girl.

Besides, I wanted answers. And for that, I needed to make him my bitch.

Through the fog of brain trauma and battle, I knew a second kick was coming. Beyond the fact that he had claws on his hands and feet, this guy was pissed at me—any fool could see that. Angry combatants were stupid combatants, and this asshole did nothing to prove that axiom a lie. When the kick came, I sucked in my gut, arching my back to absorb the impact while hooking my left arm behind and around his ankle.

Then, I rolled into him. Not in a gentle way, but in a "you blindsided me like a gutless cur, and now I'm going to make you pay for it" kind of way. I used all the Fomorian strength and speed I could muster, and as I rolled, I felt his tibia and fibula snap, even as I tore out all the ligaments in his knee.

He screamed, or roared, or whatever the fuck were-wolves do when they experience the kind of pain that they aren't accustomed to experiencing. Me? I kept rolling into him, knocking him on his ass, at which point I released his leg. It flopped uselessly to the ground, grinding audibly due to the damage I'd inflicted. Then I transitioned into the mount, straddling his chest with my knees, from which I proceeded to rain hell down on him by way of pummeling the shit out of his big, ugly snout.

I can punch pretty fucking fast when I'm in this form, so I landed about a half-dozen blows before he could shell up and protect his head. He had good instincts, but like most supernatural creatures, he sucked at fighting on the ground. Most supes never lost their footing because they were so strong and agile, so they never trained in fighting off their back, either.

People who don't know how to ground grapple usually try to push the person on top off when they find themselves on the bottom in a scramble. I anticipated this, and when Blaise did so, I took full advantage. In response, I pushed his left arm to the left side of my head, dropping in tight as I slid my left arm around and behind his neck. Then I dismounted to side control, with my hips and torso now nearly at a right angle to his.

My right arm wasn't one hundred percent, but it was in good enough shape to complete the pillow choke I'd set up. This was a good place for me to be, considering I was fighting an anthropomorphic high-speed blender. I had his left arm immobilized, and I was choking the shit out of him, cutting off the blood to his brain.

Sure, he could rake me with the claws on his right hand, but he had no leverage, so he'd likely only do superficial damage before I popped his head off like a grape. He couldn't kick me, either, which meant he was unable to cut me with the claws on his feet—a win for me as well. And I'd ended up right where I wanted to be, which was snuggled up close enough to whisper in his ear.

A hell of a crowd had gathered by this time, at least a few dozen Pack members who all stood around in a circle watching the events as they transpired. Of course, they wouldn't intervene, not in a fair fight between two Pack members. It was practically Pack law.

Fallyn was there as well, wearing a worried yet inscrutable expression. She stood tall, shoulders set and fists clenched, but whether that tension was due to concern over the outcome or the white werewolf's presence, I couldn't be certain.

I'd say a little of both.

Standing next to her was a face I recognized from my recent—in this timeline, at least—visit to Greece. The woman was tall, and she dressed like she'd just stepped out of the Patagonia and 5.11 end of the outlet mall—cargo pants, hiking boots, a thermal shirt under flannel, with a puffy vest to top off the look. She had dark hair, a raptor's gray eyes, and she wore a bemused expression.

I hadn't been certain before, but this cinched it. She was Artemis, I had no doubt. Fallyn's much older sister.

I could figure out the implications of this startling coincidence later. My first priority was finding out why the fuck this guy thought Fallyn was his mate. I whispered so softly that only he could hear, despite standing within a circle of supernatural creatures with superhuman hearing.

"Tell me the truth, or I'll rip your head clean off your shoulders, then I'll cauterize the wound. You're here to defend your right as life-mate to Fallyn Randolph, yes?"

He struggled and squirmed, but I held him tight. Finally, he croaked his reply. "Yes."

"You said you were bonded. When and where?"

"A year ago, in the Alps. Leto herself presided over the ceremony. The Huntress stands here as my witness."

Which would have been a few months before I showed up and Macha restored her memory.

"Fuck," I said aloud.

My heart shattered then, even as my anger multiplied tenfold. I squeezed, twisted, and rolled, snapping the were-wolf's neck. I did not, however, separate it from his shoulders and shove a fireball down his throat, although I wanted to, badly. He'd be out of commission until his body repaired the injury, which in his case might not be long.

I tossed his limp body away, then I stood. The Pack were silent, but I cared nothing whatsoever for them. Presently, I only had eyes for Fallyn, and she couldn't even meet my gaze.

"Why? Why didn't you tell me?"

My alpha looked up with tears in her eyes, which she wiped away, quickly. "It happened while I was mind-wiped. Think about it, Colin—at the time, I didn't even know we'd been together. After I got my memories back, I had Leto annul and sever the bond, and she made everyone swear never to speak of it again."

I shifted my gaze to her sister. "Obviously, someone didn't listen."

The goddess spoke then, in a smooth, refined contralto voice that retained just a hint of a Greek accent. "I am a goddess of Olympus, druid. Leto's edicts hold no sway over me."

"Know this, *goddess*," I said, emphasizing the last word. "You've made an enemy this day."

Artemis shook herself. "Ooh, and look—I am shivering with fear."

I decided I'd have to deal with her later. Turning my attention back to Fallyn, I addressed her directly, my voice flat. "And you—" Honestly, I didn't know what to say, so I said the only thing I could think of to say. "Goodbye."

Oak, get me out of here.

"Colin, wait—!"

And then I was gone, although her voice echoed inside my head for days after.

CHAPTER
FOUR

I SPENT the next six months on an alternate version of Earth where all intelligent life had been destroyed by an asteroid impact event. The place needed help getting back on its feet, and I needed more practice in using druid nature magic—a win-win. Of course, I also needed time to process what had happened.

Besides the bugs, birds, reptiles, and small mammals, I was all alone there, and that was how I wanted it. Helping the planet recover provided me with plenty of work to keep my mind off Fallyn, and having a relatively clean slate gave me a place to experiment with druid spell work on a massive scale. I was free to make mistakes, and when I did, I'd simply reverse what I did in that area and start all over again.

Reforestation was my pet project, and once I got the planet's lungs breathing right again, everything else was a piece of cake. That kept me busy for several months, and I spent the rest of my time there just letting myself heal.

Those six months passed by quickly for me. When I

returned to the primary timeline, no time at all had passed. Once I was back home, I waited another day, keeping my phone off while I debated calling her. But what was there to say?

It wasn't that she'd done anything wrong in bonding with Blaise—that was on Leto. But keeping that from me? Sure, I'd have been devastated, but it would've been better than finding out the way I had.

I didn't want to hold it against her, but I wasn't ready to forgive her, either. The day after I returned, I turned on my phone, finding a dozen texts and a full voicemail inbox. The message I sent her was short and to the point:

I'm not mad, just hurt. Give me time. I'll be gone for a while. We can talk when I get back.

Thing was, I lied. Coming back opened old wounds, and I discovered that I was still well and truly pissed. To avoid blowing up the relationship completely, I decided to pretend I wasn't angry while engaging in a little—well, let's call it *anger management.*

First, I checked in on my Grove and gave it some instructions to keep it safe while I was gone. Then I crossed through the Paths back to the Hellpocalypse timeline and Crowley's underground lair. With no preamble, I marched into his lab and announced my intentions.

"I'm ready to break some shit. Let's go fuck Garr up."

Crowley swiveled his chair to face me, taking me in with a long, empty stare. "You've been places. Do you wish to talk about it?"

I crossed my arms over my chest, arching an eyebrow. "Do you?" I said in a sardonic tone.

"No, but I thought it polite to ask."

"Then go fetch Saint Germain and let's get this show on the road."

Crowley gave a put upon sigh, recapping several bottles and jars on his table. "One moment," he said.

The wizard stood, placing two fingers on each of his temples as he closed his creepy, hollow eyes. Then a large, black circle appeared just below the ceiling at the center of the room. No, not black—empty, like the Void. Just looking at it gave me the willies.

I didn't have to stare at it long; moments later, Saint Germain fell through it. He landed lightly, but not catlike, as he had no need to absorb the force of gravity. Vampires were weird that way.

I noted he no longer wore the ill-fitting clothes I'd given him back on the beach. Instead, he was wearing designer jeans, tooled and stitched cowboy boots, a white Western shirt, and a brand-new Carhartt jacket. He wiped the corners of his mouth with a bloodstained white handkerchief, appearing not the least bit surprised he'd been recalled from his hunt in that manner.

"Looks like you had a nice meal," I said. "How was the service?"

"Dreadful," he deadpanned as he held each arm out in turn, examining his sleeves. "But I did manage to locate a new wardrobe while I was out. Not exactly my style, but a damn sight better than those rags you'd given me."

It was a sure guess where he'd found his new get-up. "Nothing like shopping at Tractor Supply. Hell, I'm surprised they had anything left."

He sneered. "Those barbarians had been using it as their headquarters since shortly after society's collapse. They'd trashed the showroom, but the warehouse was stocked full to the ceiling with boxes of useful items."

Pristine caches like that were hard to come by in the Hellpocalypse. I made a note to get the location and visit the place, so I could deliver the choice bits to Guerra, Anna, Mickey, and the kids. Those boys would need clothes soon, and again every six months or so for the next ten years.

Just one more item to add to my logistical nightmare of a to-do list.

Crowley opened his eyes and the shadow portal closed. "Prepare yourself, bloodkin—we go after Alalngar tonight."

"Just like that?" the ancient vampire asked. "You're going to march right into the coven's center of operations and take out one of the oldest vampires in existence—and then what? Ask the rest of the coven to tea?"

I frowned and looked at Crowley. "Do you mind filling him in? I need to get ready before we take off."

We'd been plotting this attack for a while, and the plan we had was solid. I intended to hit them during the day, creating a diversion to draw the majority of the vamps and Renfields away from Alalngar's quarters. Then we'd pop in and snag the fucker right out from under their noses.

Sure, he was tougher than hell, and he'd been more than a handful for me the last time we locked horns. But this time, I'd had a decade in the Paths to prepare, and I was not the same druid I was previously. I chuckled to myself as I thought of what we were about to do.

Fucking Vampyri are not going to know what hit them.

The plan was simple—we'd strike in the middle of the day when most of the younger vamps were out cold, and the older vamps were buttoned up tight in their luxury apartments. Crowley and I would portal in and do a little prep work to make certain our target stayed put and that the other vamps stayed out of our way.

Then, I'd send the Oak into the center of their little post-apocalyptic utopia to rain hell down on their heads. That'd get the ant-pile good and worked up, drawing off most of the Renfields so we could keep the human casualties to a minimum. The Oak would deal with the humans using non-lethal methods while Crowley and I absconded with their leader.

And if Garr got frisky? We had a back-up plan for that possibility as well. As for Saint Germain, he was there to watch our backs while we did our thing. Hopefully, we wouldn't need him.

I had the Oak portal the three of us to the same building in the garment district where I hid out on my last visit to post-apocalyptic Dallas. On our arrival, we stood facing each other in a utility closet, avoiding verbal communication until Saint Germain gave us the nod.

"The building is empty," he said, stroking his cleft chin. "Now, if you would be so kind, I'd like to hear this plan of yours one more time."

I scowled at him. "Don't you have a photographic memory or something?"

"Unfortunately, that's not one of my vampiric talents," he said as he examined and buffed his nails on the cotton duck jacket he wore.

"You have more than one?"

"Hmm, in a manner of speaking. While I lack the sort of

magical talents those like Garr possess, my physical abilities exceed theirs in every single way. I am faster, stronger, more agile, and more durable than any elder vampire of a similar age."

"And when your alter-ego emerges?" Crowley asked.

"Then, I have no equal, at least not at close quarters." He smirked as he glanced at us each in turn. "Yes, I know you may have need of him, as I also surmised that the necromancer has means of bringing him forth. Just be aware that, should you uncork that genie, you may not be able to put him back in his bottle."

Crowley sneered, as he didn't like it when his magical skill was questioned. "Duly noted." The wizard turned his attention to me, his expression shifting to neutral as he addressed me. "You're certain you know where Garr will be?"

"Within a point-zero-three percent margin of error, yes. I searched the Paths for the most likely outcomes, and he appears to be a creature of habit. We'll find him in his bedroom, feeding as he engages in—"

"I do not need to know the details," Crowley replied, cutting me off.

"Oh, you'll find out shortly," Saint Germain said. "The oldest of our kind get bored, seeking ever more demented means of entertaining themselves as the centuries roll on."

"And you?" Crowley asked. "What keeps you from going mad with ennui?"

Saint Germain didn't miss a beat in responding. "The hope of a quick and permanent death." He fixed me with a searching look. "Let's get on with this, druid. The sooner I help you complete your task, the sooner you can grant me what I seek."

I interlaced my fingers and cracked my knuckles by extending my arms palms outward. "Alright, hang on tight."

I sent a message to the Oak. *It's time.*

The images it sent back were a collection of scenes of death and mayhem, involving vampires impaled on tree limbs and the like. It was a lot more gruesome than I was comfortable with, but this Oak still had issues after losing the other me. Did it worry me? A little, but to be honest, I needed him to be a killer to do what had to be done.

Remember, don't kill any humans. Just knock them out.

He didn't answer, but instead strengthened our mental connection so I could use my druid sense to see what was going on around him. The Oak had appeared at the center of the busiest intersection in downtown Dallas where the vamps, Renfields, and their human cattle resided. Traffic was light—because fuel and electricity came at a premium in the apocalypse—but the few cars present halted immediately.

Then, the chaos began. Thick green vines broke through the tarmac and concrete sidewalks all around the Oak in a block-wide radius. As they grew, the vines began picking up empty cars and tossing them through storefronts, ripping fire hydrants out of the ground, tearing down power poles, and generally causing mass mayhem.

I noted that the Oak only threw cars where people weren't, which was good. Soon, however, I heard sirens in the distance, and police cars began speeding toward the intersection. The first few tried unsuccessfully to dodge the foot-thick thrashing vines, only to get flipped over and smashed up, sending the officers inside scrambling after they escaped their patrol vehicles.

Subsequently, someone on the Vampyri's human police force wisely decided to order their officers to cordon off the area affected by my Oak. They took up positions behind their cars, shooting rounds at my Oak and the vines in a vain attempt to harm him. Every so often, one of them would slap their neck or some other area of exposed flesh, then fall to the ground unconscious. Closer inspection would reveal a dart-like thorn stuck in their skin somewhere, shot at them by the vines that were currently tearing up their city.

Excellent. Keep it up until I tell you otherwise, or until they get smart and start throwing Molotovs.

I cut off the connection, hoping like hell the vamps hadn't recruited any hedge witches who could perform more than rudimentary magic spells. When they'd triggered the apocalypse, the vamps had assassinated all the more powerful magic users in one fell swoop, a move they'd been planning for decades. I had yet to find any who'd escaped, which sucked for us humans, as we had virtually no one on our side who could fight the undead using magic.

However, it also resulted in becoming a weak point in the Vampyri's defenses, as they now had no one with magic to counteract offensives like this one. I understood why they took out The Cold Iron Circle and people like my counterpart in this timeline, yet it was pretty shortsighted of them not to find a few turncoats to keep in reserve. But, that was something I could ponder another time. Now that I knew the Oak's attack was in full swing, I had to put the second part of our plan in motion.

I opened my eyes and nodded once. "We're good. The

entire human police force is occupied. Best that we move before the older vamps get wind of it."

Crowley smiled, something he rarely did. Needless to say, it was creepy as fuck considering that his eyes were two slowly rotating black pools, and his mouth was full of the same swirling dark mist. "Now, the real entertainment begins. Brace yourselves."

He waved a hand at the sealed concrete floor beneath our feet, and a circle of midnight nothingness appeared below us. We fell through, headed for the next phase of our mission—to capture the most dangerous vampire in Dallas.

———

We landed on the rooftop of the Ritz shrouded in my silence and chameleon spells, but it turned out they were unnecessary. Like I'd seen earlier as I flipped through possible alternative futures, all four of the snipers assigned here were gathered on the eastern edge, taking potshots at my Oak. I reached into my Craneskin Bag and pulled out a handful of grass seeds, which I tossed in their direction.

The wind picked up at my behest, blowing the seeds so they landed on the tar and gravel roof surface behind the snipers. When they hit the roof, each seed immediately took hold and sprouted, fueled and fed by druid magic and sunlight alone. The grass blades thickened unnaturally as they grew at an incredible pace, turning into yardstick thick blades that whipped around the four police officers. As the grass whipped about, it disarmed the snipers while simultaneously restraining them in layer after layer of fibrous green vegetation.

Crowley sighed and shook his head. "I'd have simply tossed them over the side."

"And alert everyone that we're up here? Besides, there are few enough humans left as it is. We'll need as many as we can to repopulate after this thing is over."

"So you say," he replied in a snide tone. "But do we really want to repopulate the Earth with the seed of traitors?"

I dismissed his comment with a backhanded wave. "Just do your thing before the elder vamps are alerted, alright?"

"Fine." Crowley closed his eyes as he placed his fingers on his temples, instantly fully engaged in casting the spells he'd prepared.

"You really think you can overthrow them, don't you?" Saint Germain asked.

"I stopped them in our timeline, didn't I?"

"Sheer luck, more than anything." He paused, tapping a finger on his chin. "Or was it? I wonder, was someone behind the scenes pulling your strings all the while? It would explain much about how you always seemed to end up in the right place at the right time."

I kept my mouth shut, refusing to spill any information about how Finnegas, Maeve, and my mother had schemed to breed the perfect god-killing druid, guiding me from birth to become what I was today. Saint Germain was closer to the truth than he knew, as Finnegas and Maeve both had played me like a violin from the time I was old enough to start killing fae. I no longer held it against the old man, but I wasn't going to reveal those secrets to the enemy, either... even if he was more or less on our side.

"Never trust them, not a single one," the old man had

said time and again. But I always wondered, how then had he trusted Maeve?

While I pondered that conundrum and Saint Germain dealt with his quandary, Crowley had finished unleashing his spells. Black lines of shadow magic traced runes across the roof of the building, making intricate patterns that seemed to converge at each corner of the roof. Black mist seeped from the wizard's eyelids as he muttered incantations, then sickly yellow light shot out from his now outstretched palms, infusing the runes with necromantic magic.

The shadow wizard spoke one last command in some long-lost dialect taught to him by his former fae masters, and the runes lit up with the same pale, wan glow as the magic that had suffused them moments prior. Spell complete, Crowley's shoulders sagged slightly, and I noted that his deathly pale skin looked even more pasty now that it lacked the protective shell of shadow magic.

"It is done," he whispered.

"Good, I was getting antsy." I walked over to the side of the building and dropped five pebbles off the side. When they hit, they rolled up to the nearest entrance, slipping under the door and heading inside the building. With that task complete, I strolled back over to the wizard and looked at him askance. "Are you sure you're going to be up to doing the next bit?" I asked.

He nodded silently. "You two may go on without me to engage Garr. I will be along shortly to help you subdue him. I only need to regain my strength."

Crowley's spell had taken him weeks to prepare, which was why he was able to cast it and recover that quickly. The runes led all the way across every surface of every rooftop in the hotel complex, creating a necromantic circle that did two things. For one, it trapped all the elder and master vampires inside the buildings. And more importantly, it held Alalngar captive inside his penthouse suite.

"Are you ready?" I asked Saint Germain.

He laid a hand over his face, running it down to his chin before addressing me. "I suppose." He turned his gaze on the now haggard-looking Crowley. "Don't tarry too long, wizard. The druid and I will only be able to hold off Alan Garr for so long."

Translation? Crowley had better be ready to turn The Butcher loose if we were going to survive long enough to see this crazy scheme through. But if all went to plan, it wouldn't come to that.

Crowley met his gaze, head bowed beneath a hooded brow. "Never fear, I will be ready to do what needs must."

"Then I suppose it's up to us for the moment," Saint Germain said. "Lead the way, druid."

And with that, I sent a command to my Oak. *Leave the vines in place and retreat to a safe location. Then, send us in.*

The Oak replied by sending me an image of it ripping through the rooftop and reaching inside to grab Alan Garr. It didn't understand that Crowley's magic runes needed to remain unbroken to work, nor did it realize that it would be helpless against the ancient vampire's powers.

No, I forbid it. Just send us in and be ready to pull us out if I give you the signal.

A blink of an eye later, Saint Germain and I were standing in Alan Garr's living room, and it was on like Donkey Kong.

———

From the moment we entered the apartment, Garr knew we were there, a fact I was fully aware of before portalling us inside. You don't get to be 6,000 years old or whatever he was without developing crazy sharp, supersensitive hearing. At any moment, he'd *bamf* his ass in and start whaling on us both.

As soon as we stepped through, I reached one hand into my Bag, pulling out three specially prepared seed pods that I tossed on the floor. Then I triggered a spell that essentially covered my skin in a super-tough layer of bark that was self-healing and self-replenishing. As the bark layer coated my skin, I spoke aloud while scanning the room ahead of Garr's appearance.

"Keep him busy," I said as Alalngar appeared across the room in a puff of black mist.

Garr was Luther's maker, and he shared Luther's unique talent of instant and almost unlimited teleportation. Except, the maker was much better at it than his spawn. Which was uncanny, considering that Luther was hell on wheels in battle.

I didn't fully understand their powers, only that it involved shadow magic, and it made them nearly impossible to fight. I'd managed to land a couple of punches last time I faced Alalngar, but as it turned out he'd let me do so, just to see what I was made of. After that, he'd teleported circles around me as he wiped the floor with my face. It was not my brightest moment.

"I'll do my best," Saint Germain said. "But as you can see, I'm at a bit of a disadvantage."

"That's why I'm here," I said, raising my voice as I continued. Of course, I could whisper and Garr would hear every word I said, but theatrics were almost a requirement when you were fighting evil overlords. "Nice place you got here, Garr. I almost feel like I'm on the set of *Nip Tuck*."

The place was done up in black, red, and mirrors, like a satanic interior designer did a few grams of coke and then went to town on the place. The penthouse screamed, "rich bachelor trying way too hard," which was funny to me because the owner was older than written history. I mean, honestly—at some point, you'd think a guy would outgrow that ostentatious bullshit.

Garr looked much as he had the last time I'd seen him, except this time his face and hands were covered in blood. And, just my luck, he was naked as a jaybird at a nude beach in July. Honestly, the last thing I wanted to see was the king of Vampire Chads with his junk on display.

The ancient bloodkin was short and lean, maybe five-foot-six on a good day, with olive skin and neatly coiffed black hair, ever so slightly gone salt and pepper at the temples. He had a hawk-like nose, high cheek bones, and a jawline chiseled from granite, and when he spoke his voice was elegant and mannered, with a soft Middle Eastern accent.

"The reference escapes me, but you shan't, not this time—even with this traitor on your side." Garr glanced at Saint Germain. "Still on your quest to attain the true death, I see—eh, Jacques? And you think this boy can give it to you?"

Saint Germain chuckled softly. "Let's find out, shall we?"

Then, my vampiric ally was across the room, standing with his arm extended in front of a Garr-sized hole in the wall of the gaudily appointed living room. I would've whistled if I could manage it with my lips covered in bark.

"Impressive," I remarked.

Saint Germain scanned the space, turning his head left and right as he glanced over his shoulder to either side. "I merely hope you know what you're doing."

"Wait for it," I said, as Garr appeared next to Saint Germain in a puff of smoke and shadow.

Soon, Alalngar was *bamfing* around Saint Germain, the two trading blows as the younger ancient vampire spun, pivoted, and turned to face his attacker, almost as quickly as the elder of the two teleported from place to place. It was instantly clear that Garr was getting the better of the engagement, but this was what I'd needed to hatch the next part of my plan.

Precognition through chronomancy was not an exacting art. At best, you were choosing between several probable outcomes, picking the one that seemed most likely. This was based on the number of times certain events occurred in future time stream bifurcations, how one intended to alter their actions to impact those probabilities, and instinct.

Yet chronomantic prognostication was still just an educated guess. Moreover, the further into the future you made predictions, the less chance there was that your prediction would come to pass. There were simply too many variables to accurately predict what would happen in the distant future, or even a few months hence.

Instead, the best use of chronomancy was looking into the immediate future, perhaps a few seconds or minutes ahead. A magician was much more likely to get their predictions right by sticking close to the present. Obviously, doing so could provide the chronomancer with an undeniably unfair advantage in negotiations and combat.

However, maintaining that edge required the caster to maintain their "one step ahead" advantage, especially in combat. Chronomancy on the fly called for a level of mental focus and clear-headedness that physical injury could easily upset. That was why I'd lost to Alan Garr the last time we faced each other—I underestimated him and lowered my guard, and he used that opportunity to turn the tables and beat me to a bloody pulp.

If Crowley hadn't shown up to save my hide, I'd be in a Vampyri dungeon, or dead. That sobering reality wasn't lost on me, and I'd spent considerable time and effort ensuring it wouldn't happen again.

Having easily beaten me in the past, Alan Garr fairly ignored me this time, choosing instead to focus his attention on eliminating the more obvious threat, Saint Germain. I had expected him to do so, which was why I needed Saint Germain in the first place. That left me free to spring the trap I'd laid, and I did so as soon as Garr was popping in and out of material reality.

"*Péac,*" I said, infusing the word with a small amount of will and magic.

Instantly, the seed pods grew to the size of footballs. Then they burst open, releasing clouds of green druid magic, enchanted pollen, and eldritch spores in the air. Once the gas and magic had dispersed throughout the apartment, I spoke the second word.

"*Solas.*"

Instantly, the gas began to glow, suffusing the penthouse with a soft white light.

Dodge that, bitch.

Although Crowley's magic was better suited to defeating the undead, he'd have to restrain Garr to use it. Unfortunately, their powers were too similar for the wizard's shadow magic to be of use against the ancient vampire. Which, of course, left me in the driver's seat regarding who'd be the one to take the vamp out.

Honestly, I preferred it that way, my penchant for vengeance being what it was. Before we'd hatched this plan, Crowley and I had discussed at length ways I might counter Garr's vampiric talent. Crowley, being the expert on shadow magic, suggested using light to disrupt his powers.

Unfortunately, I'd tried that before using my sunlight spell, only to have Garr wrap himself in an impenetrable cloak of shadow essence. Based on that knowledge, my partner in crime and I decided I'd have to prevent Garr from using shadow magic at all. After a lot of brainstorming, testing, and significant trial and error, I came up with a plant-based light trap that worked on reverse photosynthesis.

Instead of absorbing light, the pollen and spores released it via a chemical reaction. And while not as strong as sunlight, it did express light waves in the UV spectrum, so it was harmful to vampires. Not so much that it would kill vamps as old as Garr and Saint Germain, but enough to be a nuisance—and to prevent Garr from using his magical talents.

Even better, the light was inescapable, as it emanated from the gas particles and was therefore omnidirectional. As soon as I triggered that portion of the spell, Garr became solid and was stuck in that form. Even better, some of my pollen and mold spores were caught inside his body, like little light-producing pathogens, burning him from within.

Heck, his skin even glowed a little. Then it turned red in places, blistering as he fried from the inside. The ancient, deadly vampire reacted as I'd expected—with utter confusion and complete disbelief.

Spend a few millennia racking up win after win, and it gets awful hard to recognize defeat when it's staring you dead in the face.

"What—ack—did you—hrrr—do to me?" he half-snarled, half-coughed.

I sped up to him using all the Fomorian speed I could muster, and I punched him in the throat. "Weaponized karma, that's what, you snide, condescending fuck."

Garr crumpled to the floor, weakened as he was by the spell, not to mention that I'd hit him hard enough to crush his windpipe and dislocate a few cervical vertebrae. He'd heal, but not before we restrained him and took him to a secure location. I hovered over him, wanting badly to soccer kick him into a pulp, only to have my violent reverie interrupted by a lot of loud, insistent throat clearing nearby.

I looked for the source, finding Saint Germain hunched over and covering his eyes with his arms several feet away. "Druid, do you mind?"

"Uh, right." I ran to a bedroom, doing my best not to lose my lunch due to the gory scene that assaulted my eyesight on entering.

A woman of perhaps twenty-five years of age was strapped to a large, X-shaped cross that was bolted upright via steel brackets that were bolted to the floor. Garr had performed the 'blood eagle' torture method on her, disemboweling her while she was still alive, then peeling back her abdominal skin, muscles, and rib cage to reveal her internal organs underneath.

I shook my head in anger, sadness, and disgust, looking

away as I snagged a semi-clean sheet from the bed. That's when I heard the woman wheeze.

"Kill… me…," she pleaded.

"Oh, have mercy," I whispered.

I sped back into the living room, tossing the sheet over Saint Germain, even as I gave a mental command for the pollen and spore particles to disperse and fade out. All except for the ones inside Garr, that was.

"Be right back," I said, reaching into my Bag to snag sets of silver-plated, tungsten alloy shackles and leg irons. I tossed them on the floor with a pair of leather gloves I'd kept with them. "Restrain him and wait for Crowley."

"But of course, oh Great and Mighty Druid," Saint Germain muttered from beneath the sheet. I resisted an almost obligatory eye roll, speeding back into the bedroom as I spooled up my druid magic.

In the past, my major weakness had always been in using druid healing magic. After the old man's death, I vowed to correct that shortcoming. During the decade I spent wandering the Paths, I dedicated considerable time to learning and mastering the magical healing arts.

With all that time to practice, I'd become quite good at it, although I wasn't certain if I could save this woman. Even so, I had to try.

"This is going to hurt," I said in the kindest, most sympathetic tone I could manage. "A lot."

She blinked once, whether in acquiescence or because she was too weak to do otherwise, I had no idea. Then it occurred to me that she might have thought I intended to grant her request, and I shuddered. Knowing that time was not on her side, I began to work furiously to save her life, dropping into a druid trance and reaching out with my druid senses to repair the damage.

First, I released the pins and hooks that held her skin and rib cage back, melting them away by using my control over the elements. This also served to cauterize the puncture wounds, which wasn't ideal, but at least it was expedient. Then I used magic to cleanse her intestines, which lay in a twisted heap on the floor.

Air magic lifted her innards up, forcing them back into her abdominal cavity. I held continuous pressure as I coaxed her body to heal at a tremendous rate, knitting her muscles and connective tissue back together. This I did all while rearranging her organs so they fit back into their natural position. After another infusion of cleansing magic, I "sutured" her up, fusing her skin back together.

To finish, I grew fibrous bandages from the bark skin that covered me, using magic and will to weave them around her torso to hold everything together. Next, I suffused her bone marrow with more magic to encourage her body to produce additional red and white blood cells. I drew moisture from the air as well, pulling it into her body to replace lost blood volume.

A final bit of druid magic acted as a painkiller and soporific, both of which I could only give her now that her trauma had been dealt with properly. Lastly, I released the straps that held her wrists and ankles, allowing her to fall into my arms.

Damn, she's a lot younger than I thought.

Eighteen, maybe twenty at the outset. She possessed farm girl good looks, with a strong, square jaw and prominent cheekbones, a straight nose, and thin, uniform lips. Blonde, athletic, and tall, perhaps five-foot-eleven. Also malnourished, either due to food rationing or the mandatory Vampyri "blood donations" all Dallas residents were required to provide.

Probably a college athlete, a volleyball player or something. I wondered how she ended up being singled out to be Garr's plaything.

Crowley's raspy voice interrupted my ruminations. "Leave it to you to find a damsel to rescue. If you're quite finished saving yet another downtrodden soul, it's well past time to leave."

Without waiting for a reply, he turned on heel and headed back to the living room, where Saint Germain and a subdued Alalngar presumably waited. I hefted the woman's limp body higher in my arms to gain better purchase, then I headed after him, wondering what I was going to do with her after she recovered.

CHAPTER
FIVE

CROWLEY HAD a portal prepared and waiting for me, although he, Garr, and Saint Germain were nowhere to be found. I paused before entering, triggering the spells I'd infused in the pebbles I'd dropped earlier. They weren't rocks, but miniature magical incendiary grenades, something I'd cooked up with the Grove's assistance.

On triggering them, each exploded, showering a fifty-foot radius blast area with a combination of magically infused phosphorous, sulfur, and magnesium that ignited as soon as it landed on something flammable. The blasts blew out the windows on the first floor of the hotel, which I could hear all the way in the penthouse due to having Fomorian enhanced hearing.

Crowley's containment spell would last for twenty-four hours at least, keeping vamps in and human help out. Plenty long enough for the entire hotel to burn to the ground, vamps and all. It wouldn't kill the toughest of them, but it'd thin the ranks of the senior Vampyri and most of their human sycophants placed in positions of power.

Man, fuck those people.

I was about to enter the portal, then I realized I was carrying a naked woman. I grabbed a white fur throw from a nearby couch and wrapped her in it, then I entered Crowley's inter-dimensional tunnel of horrors. Moments later, I stepped through the portal and inside the water tower behind the church in Bryan-College Station.

When we were trying to decide where to question Garr, this place immediately came to mind. I'd once cleaned out a nest of vamps here, rescuing their human captives, who were now presumably all members of Samson's pack. The main benefit to using the location was that it was disposable—the water tower was simply an added bonus.

As it turned out, the water containment tank had long since been drained, and with no power to run the pumps, the contents had not been replenished. The tank was thick steel, with one way in, one way out—a perfect jail for a vampire. After Crowley covered the inside with necromantic symbols and runes designed to keep a vamp contained, it was ready for Garr's arrival.

Saint Germain lounged in a chair, watching a shackled Garr, who lay on the floor inside a necromantic containment circle in the center of the tank. Crowley sat on the floor nearby *meditating*, although it was probably more like "fighting an inner struggle with his demons," literally. I didn't trust Saint Germain enough to leave him with Garr if Crowley was preoccupied, so I laid the girl on a cot near the wall, then I waited for the wizard to exit his trance.

Before that happened, however, someone opened the hatch and climbed down the ladder. It turned out to be

Sledge and another 'thrope, one of the former humans from their group who survived the turn. The big, burly biker took one look at Garr and whistled.

"I'll be damned, you really captured the fucker. I didn't think you had it in you."

"Um, thanks?" I said, smirking. Sledge sniffed the air, finding the source of the scent of blood after a quick survey of the room. He looked at the girl and arched an eyebrow at me. "Just a stray I picked up. She'll need food, water, and a safe place to heal, mind and soul."

Sledge gave a curt nod. "Can do. She got a name?"

"Not one I've gathered yet. Garr was—it's not worth repeating. She'll be out for a while, but she's safe to move."

"Say no more." He looked at his companion, a stout Asian woman no older than I should've been. "Leah, you mind?"

"Yeah, I got it." The young 'thrope slung the girl over her shoulder with care, climbing the ladder and handling her burden with ease as she exited the tank.

Sledge watched her go, then he turned his gaze on me. "Samson's back. He wants to speak with you."

I didn't answer to Samson anymore, and I wasn't about to set a precedent that I'd skip rope whenever he said jump. "Tell him I'll find him after I'm done here."

"Should I give him an ETA?"

"Nope."

Sledge pursed his lips, then he stroked his beard once for effect. "Alright, druid. If you need anything, send someone to find me."

The Austin Pack's sergeant at arms left the tank, which was just as well, since he was in as much danger around Garr as the girl had been. Not that Sledge couldn't hold his own—it was simply that Garr was so far out of his league, he wouldn't last ten seconds against him. No, it was best that we question the ancient primary vampire alone.

As for why the Pack was so favorably disposed toward me, I'd been bringing them supplies and intel for a while now. In this timeline, it was six months after Crowley rescued me from Garr's dungeon. Since then, I'd helped the Pack get set up in a new base on the outskirts of Bryan-College Station, away from the more dangerous downtown area where they'd been situated before.

So, they owed me. But with Samson's return, that dynamic could change quickly. Which meant I needed to question Garr, get the intel we needed, kill him, and get out of Pack territory before Samson decided two alpha males were one too many to keep around.

I waved to catch Saint Germain's attention. "Don't worry, I'll get you out of here as soon as we get what we need from him."

"How soon until my other half returns?" the old vampire asked.

I saw no reason to lie to him. "Crowley thinks a few days at the outset."

Jacques looked around the tank, at all the symbols and runes etched into the walls. "Perhaps you should leave me here, then."

"You really want to die?" I asked.

"I have had two thousand years to ponder that question. Yes, druid, I do."

I met his gaze unflinchingly. "When the time comes, I'll see that you do. You have my word." I looked at Garr where he lay sprawled in the center of the circle. "Now, let's attend to our guest. But first, why don't we make him a bit more disposed to discussion?"

————

Saint Germain merely cocked his head in response. I gave a wan smile, then I walked to the edge of the necromantic circle in which Alan Garr lay. He was only faintly glowing, but in the dim light of the tank's interior, he may as well have been a neon sign.

"I take it that's your doing?" Saint Germain asked.

"It is. Check it out."

I exerted my will, cranking up the intensity of the light emanating from the particles that were now floating around inside Garr's thick, vampire blood. His skin began to emit more light, especially along his vascular system, and he released a soft, almost silent groan. Soon, his skin began to bubble and peel.

Alan Garr closed his eyes tightly, pursing his lips in an effort to avoid any verbal display of weakness. Yet I knew that to be a vulnerability of his kind—of all supernatural races, really. That is to say, they grew accustomed to being impervious to injury, which of course meant their resistance to pain diminished over time.

If you're going to dish it out, you'd better be able to take it. That's what the old man always said.

I snickered and turned down the heat before I fried Garr completely. The skin over most of his body was now a blistered, weeping mess, and he remained curled up in a ball in the center of the circle. During our fight, he had proven he could take some damage, but that was when he had the luxury of rapid healing.

Anyone can tolerate a great deal of pain for a short time if they know it will soon end. But enduring immense pain for an indeterminate amount of time? That's another matter.

"I can make this stop, Garr," I said as I slowly paced a route around the outside of the circle. "All I want is a little info, that's all."

"Do I look like a fool, mortal?" he rasped. "Once you have what you want, you'll kill me. I'm only of use to you while I keep the secrets of the Vampyri under wraps. So, do what you will; I will not falter."

"Aw, c'mon, Alan. You don't even know what I'm going to ask."

"It does not matter," he said in a much more human voice. His body was healing from the inside out, although that would change once his heme reserves ran out. "Do your worst."

"Tell me where Patient Zero is," I demanded.

"I have no idea what you're talking about."

In response, I stepped into a small square of sunlight that shone through the hatch above. Using druid magic—and borrowing some of the Oak's natural talents—I absorbed the light energy into my body, channeling it through myself and into my right arm and hand. Then, I extended my index finger and pointed it at Garr.

The tip of my finger glowed, like an alien in an old Spielberg movie. Suddenly, a bright, white-hot beam of pencil-thin light burst forth, shooting in a straight line at the vampire inside the circle. I moved my hand only slightly, dragging the beam of sunlight and magic across his right ankle, severing his foot as neatly as if I'd cut it with a surgical saw.

Garr's eyes widened, and he sat up in a motion that was almost too fast to see. The vampire held his calf in his hands as he stared at his now severed ankle. He grabbed the amputated limb, holding it in place in an attempt to get the two segments to fuse and heal.

"Ah-ah-ah," I said, wagging my glowing finger back and forth.

I snapped for effect, adding a little magic to throw sparks off my hand as I did so. Instantly, the severed foot burst into flames, burning as brightly as Dyrnwyn's blade as it turned both flesh and bone to ash instantly. The tank now smelled of burned hair and meat, and Garr's palms and fingers were blackened as well.

The ancient, evil vampire turned his gaze on me, staring at me with the purest hatred I'd ever seen a humanoid express. "Insolent mortal child! I will see you flayed for this. You have no idea of the pain and anguish you have just brought upon yourself. I—"

I aimed my finger again, shooting another beam that cut off his other foot, this time at mid-calf level. "Oops—sorry, I meant to aim lower."

With a snap of my fingers, that severed limb burst into flames as well. Garr's body was attempting to heal him, as pink flesh and skin began to form at the edges of the cauterized wounds. I stopped that process by exerting my will, instructing the pollen and spores in his blood to release light in those areas, keeping the wounds raw, fresh, and painful.

"I—" Garr began, sputtering and spitting flecks of thick, pink saliva. He was sweating as well, not water, but thick, black drops of blood. "I am eternal! I am the dark gift made manifest! I am—"

"The night?" I said, cutting him off. "Sorry, man, I think that slogan's taken. Twice over, in fact."

Without another word, I directed another beam of concentrated sunlight and magic to take off his left arm at the elbow. I snapped once more, and *poof*, his arm went up in a burst of flame and light. Now he could barely prop himself up, and the look in his eyes began to change.

Before, his brow was furrowed with grim determination and outrage. Now, his eyebrows were drawn together in a peak, and his lip quivered slightly. I pointed my finger at his other arm, allowing the tip to glow a bit brighter.

"Stop!" he screamed. "We can make a trade, I'm certain of it. What do you want? Wealth? Power? Women? I can give you all that and more."

I glanced over at Saint Germain, who stared at me with an expression that said he'd never truly seen me at all until this moment. "Sheesh, the clichés," I said as I rolled my eyes. "Always with the clichés. Tell me, Jacques, are you guys required to read the same books and study the same movies? Is that where you get your lines?"

Saint Germain remained silent for several seconds before responding. "I—ahem—*prefer* not to include myself among the ranks of his ilk." He inclined his head in Garr's direction. "Thus, I cannot answer your question, whether it was asked in jest or seriousness."

"Hmph." I sniffed, turning my attention back to the multiple amputee in the necromantic circle at the center of the tank. "Meh, I guess it doesn't matter. So, tell me, Garr— where is Patient Zero? Where's the undead creature or vampire who acted as the incubator for the vyrus you modified when you kicked this whole fucking nightmare off?"

I made my finger glow just a little brighter, and he actually let out a small whimper. "I can't tell you that. If I reveal his location, he'll kill me, just as surely as you will."

"Yeah, but at least I'll make it quick. Or not." I made a small, circular motion with my finger, pointing it more or less in the general direction of his groin.

"No, stop," he pleaded, falling on his back so he could hold out his one remaining arm in a futile shielding gesture. "You will find Ateas in his laboratory, deep in the Deadlands."

"I'm sorry, the What Lands?" I replied, cupping a hand to my ear.

"The Deadlands," Crowley, said, choosing that exact moment to join our conversation. "The last place that any of us should want to go."

––––––––

"You've changed," Saint Germain said as we stood by, waiting for Crowley to finish with Garr.

Well, he stood, while I leaned against the side of the tank. That interrogation had worn me out, if not physically or magically, then mentally. As much as I hated Alalngar, I did not enjoy torturing anyone or anything.

As for Alalngar, his story never changed, and he stuck with the same line, no matter how long I tortured him or how many ways I asked him. He said we needed to find this Ateas guy, deep inside this place where nothing living remained, somewhere in the Northwest part of the Houston metroplex.

I glanced at Saint Germain, then away again, feigning indifference. "Meh. A few vacations in the Bahamas, a plant-based diet, a little plastic surgery to tighten up all the sagging parts, and badabing, badaboom—a whole new me. It's remarkable what modern medicine and healthy eating can do for you these days."

He flashed me a bemused grin that didn't quite match the seriousness in his voice. "You act as if you're the same flippant, arrogant youth I met not long ago, but that hard, distant look in your eyes says different. If I didn't know any better, I'd say you'd aged a lifetime since I left you standing over Tethra's corpse in Mag Mell."

Wisely, I kept my mouth shut. There was nothing to say, and no reason to say it. He was right, of course, but I'd learned to hold my cards close since then—especially with my enemies. And, regardless of what he might claim, Jacques was not my friend.

It did no good to engage Saint Germain further on that topic, so I kept my mouth shut as I watched Crowley work. With Garr weakened as he was, it took no effort at all for the shadow wizard to use necromancy to force the ancient bloodkin to talk. However, I'd left Garr somewhat of a mess. As Crowley leaned over our captive, Jacques whispered so low as to escape even another vampire's sensitive hearing.

"You frighten me, druid," Saint Germain said. "Perhaps more than any god or elder being that I have met in two millennia of roaming this Earth. Well, not this one precisely, but you know what I mean."

"Why's that?" I said, keeping my gaze on Crowley and Garr.

"Because you wield so much power, yet you have little comprehension of it." He remained silent for a moment, stroking his chin. "No, it's not a lack of comprehension, it's underestimation. No wonder the gods fear you as well."

"Gods, Vampyri, Fae—they can all go to hell." I gestured at the wastelands that lay outside the walls of the water tower. "Just look what your kind did to this world. They'd have done it to ours as well, if I had let them."

"And the gods?" Saint Germain asked. "What of them?"

"Some want to return to their former glory—and that's something I can't have. Not to mention, they want me dead. I guess I'll have to deal with them, too, just as soon as I set things right here."

The vampire clucked his tongue. "I do not admire the gods, any more than I admire my own kind. Therefore, I wish you the best of luck."

I gave him the side-eye. "If I have to rely on luck, I did a shitty job of planning." I caught movement out of the corner of my eye, and pushed off the wall. "C'mon. Looks like Crowley's finished."

The shadow wizard exited his necromantic circle, kneeling to tap it with his hand after he stepped beyond its bounds. Something dark and indistinct passed between his flesh and the circle as he did so, a bit of magic to reinforce the wards. Garr was little more than a torso, neck, and head now, so he wasn't going anywhere. Still, it paid to be careful.

As Crowley stood, I nodded at the hatch, then I addressed Saint Germain. "Stay here and watch him, so he doesn't commit suicide somehow. We may need him yet."

Jacques said nothing, not even deigning to make a snide remark at my presumption of command. He merely turned and faced the circle, standing absolutely motionless, as only very old vamps could do.

It was dark out and the moon was bright, and I was eager to get some fresh air. The inside of the tank smelled like burned toenails and charred pork, which gave me additional reason to take to the ladder ahead of Crowley. Of course, he merely climbed around me using his damned tentacles, the show-off.

When we stood on the roof of the tower, I spoke. "So, what'd he say?"

"An almost precise repeat of the information you managed to extract from him. The one we seek is Ateas, a three-thousand-year-old Scythian vampire. Ateas is a long-time member of the Vampyri council, and he's apparently dabbled in death magic for many centuries."

"Sounds like a real charmer," I deadpanned. "That's our Patient Zero?"

Crowley grunted. "He not only fashioned the mutated vyrus—with some high fae sorcerer's help, no less—Ateas used his body as an incubator."

"Hmm, smart. That would make the resulting organism much more stable and resistant to exposure and toxins."

"Although there isn't much that will kill even the normal vyrus." He stared out across the city to the south, where the odd fire blazed, and the moans of the dead echoed in the otherwise still night. "Ateas will be a formidable foe."

"Oh, how so?"

"Ateas is an ancient vampyri, perhaps the equal of Saint Germain or Alalngar. And, he is a necromancer as well. As such, he's had many centuries of un-death during which to hone his command of the mystic arts."

I snapped my head around to address Crowley directly. "Wait a minute—this Ateas is a lich?"

Crowley shifted his gaze as he turned to face me. "I do not know this word. What is a 'lich?'"

"You know, an undead sorcerer—a wizard who gets so powerful they don't die. They use necromancy to keep on living as an undead creature, doing evil magic stuff for ages as they acquire even more knowledge and skill in the dark arts, ever and always increasing their capacity for wickedness."

"But he was already dead."

"Gah—" I exhaled heavily. "That's not the point. The point is that he's undead, he's really good at magic, and he's going to be hellified hard to kill."

The wizard frowned. "Is that not what I said?"

"I—yeah, I guess you did." I scratched my nose, regretting it because my finger smelled like burned vampire. "What do you know about the Deadlands?"

"Merely what Alalngar said. It is a place where nothing living remains, and at its heart there lies a building where this—what did you call him?"

"A lich."

"Where this lich, Ateas, resides. Alalngar claims that Ateas commands a vast undead army, and that he has creatures at his command the likes of which no one has seen in generations."

"Think you can beat him? At necromancy, I mean. Could you take control of his army?"

Crowley shook his head. "Doubtful. One that old will be powerful. It is possible that we may only breach Ateas' territory with an army of our own."

"Or by stealth." I glanced at the hatch. "You know what this means, right?"

"We must keep Saint Germain alive a while longer."

"Ayup. Can you control him?"

"I might be able to suppress his alter-ego for a few more days at most. I will need rest afterward, however. Perhaps you should use that time to inquire with your lycanthrope friends and see what they know of this 'Deadlands' place."

"If anyone will know, it'll be Samson. He's been networking with all the 'thropes in the State, bringing them under his control."

"Oh? And what did their alphas say?"

"There are no more alphas left, Crowley. Fucking vamps killed them all, just like they killed the wizards and witches. Except they couldn't kill Samson because he's too fucking stubborn." I spat, trying to get the taste of burned vamp out of my mouth. "What should we do with Garr?"

"He is useless now. Let Saint Germain drain him, then burn the husk, so it does not regenerate."

I scratched the stubble on my chin as I considered his suggestion. "Do you think that's wise? What if The Butcher gains Garr's talent?"

Crowley waved my question away. "He cannot. He will only gain a bit of raw power and vitality for a time. Consider that he will need it if he is to accompany us into a place with no living beings."

"You make a solid point." I toed a spot of dried bird shit near my right foot. "Do you want to do the honors, or should I?"

"I'll leave it to you. As for me, I will need to preserve my powers for the struggle to come. Tomorrow I will cast the spell on Saint Germain again, and then rest for the remainder of the day. But for now, my shade needs to feed, and you need some rest."

Without warning, he leapt off the side of the water

tower. I skidded to the edge to see where he landed, only to find a large, tattered black hang-glider looking thing sailing off into the night.

Huh, never seen him do that before. If he starts using a catch-phrase, I might have to kill the fucker prematurely to keep him from upstaging me.

CHAPTER
SIX

WHILE CROWLEY WAS off feeding his demon, I tracked down Samson. The Austin Pack—now the Traveling Pack, I supposed—had taken up residence in an abandoned Department of Public Safety building on the northern outskirts of town. The Texas DPS was our state highway patrol, so the building was set up like any law enforcement headquarters, ugly and built like Fort Knox.

It had already been defensible before the apocalypse, and the state had fortified it when the troubles began. That meant there were plenty of sandbags, concrete highway barricades, and plastic water-filled barriers available to make the place practically impenetrable to the average zed. The fenced-in motor pool around back was an added bonus, as was the razor wire and armored vehicles that had been left when the authorities abandoned the facility.

The building was just a few miles up the road from the church and water tower, and with little else to do, I decided to hoof it over to the Pack's location. Unfortunately, that gave me a little too much time to think about Fallyn—definitely a mistake. Despite my extended leave of absence, the thought of her noshing with that white-furred 'thrope made my stomach churn and my blood boil.

I needed a distraction, so I began killing the odd zombie. Was it cruel? Not really. As far as I knew, these deaders were tortured souls, deserving of the final release. Besides, I was simply doing my part to save humanity, making a small dent in the estimated one billion undead who now dominated the planet.

This I did in a variety of ways, making a game of it as I moseyed on down the highway. Some I killed with thrown knives, some with Dyrnwyn, some with my war club—which had seen scant use recently—and I even got in some practice with the Red Spear. It was fun, and it helped pass the time, but I soon grew bored with the task.

Eventually, I decided to challenge myself, slaying them with thrown stones, and seeing how small of a stone I could reliably use to lobotomize a shambler. Then I started practicing my hand-to-hand combat skills. Recalling the time I'd contracted the vyrus, and the weeks I'd spent ill as my Fomorian immune system dealt with the infection, I covered myself in a protective layer of bark before going to work.

I began by allowing them to attack me, reviewing all the skills I'd developed on my first visit to the Hellpocalypse. This mostly involved dodge and counter tactics. Blocking was too risky, as you might get bit, and messy, risking infection via droplets flying in your eyes, nose, and mouth. So, I'd learned to either stab them cleanly through the skull with a long knife or pick, or to step around and trip them, then stomp on their cervical spines when they were on the ground.

Every so often during my little jaunt, I came across a ghoul, one of the faster, stronger zombies. These posed a bit more of a challenge, but the tactics I'd developed worked much the same. Soon I fell into a rhythm, killing dozens of the undead within the span of a few minutes.

The cadence of practice lulled me into a sort of trance, and it wasn't until I saw the revenant watching me from the open doorway of a nearby 7-11 that I realized something was up. It was a male, maybe fifteen when he died, thin and rangy the way many teenage boys are at that age. He was Anglo, with brown hair down to his shoulders, milky white eyes with black pupils, and half the skin on the left side of his face missing due to trauma and rot. The kid wore the remnants of a baggy pair of mauve skate shorts and a black Thrasher t-shirt. I immediately felt sad at what had happened to him, and guilty that I'd have to put him down.

Revs were dangerous, almost as deadly as young vamps, but this one shouldn't have been out at this hour. They were nocturnal, and while the sun wasn't up yet, it was still much too close to sunrise for the average revenant's liking. Equally strange, they tended to be aggressive predators, attacking humans on sight from ambush once they marked their prey.

I thought that it might be a scarcity of prey that had forced it to expand its hunting hours. Yet, it had seen me before I noticed it, and it should have snuck up on me and attacked. That odd change in its behavior piqued my curiosity, so I decided to wait before killing it, to see what it would do. It watched me, turning its gangrenous, mutilated head this way and that, and I watched it back.

Instantly, it became deathly silent as all the surrounding zombies stopped moving. I swiveled my head around, scanning the area, only to find that every last deader in a radius of a quarter mile had frozen in place. Where moments before they'd been stumbling around, moaning and groaning, now each stood stock still, staring at me as if I were the main attraction at the circus freak show.

Just like the revenant. Fuck.

A harsh, raspy voice came from behind me, one with just a hint of a Slavic accent. "You intrigue me, druid."

I turned to face the speaker, finding the source to be a middle-aged black man who was missing an arm at the elbow. He was clothed in the tattered remains of a tailored gray business suit, his blood-stained lavender dress shirt half-untucked, although the matching paisley tie he wore was still cinched tight. The man stood just a little straighter than the rest of them, seemingly adopting a cross-armed pose despite his half-missing arm. The zombie rested his chin in his remaining hand, as if he were a college professor considering a novel question fielded by a gifted student.

I said nothing, choosing to draw out whoever controlled the dead. Certain elder vamps could do this, but I'd never seen it done on this scale. Crowley could do it as well, but I doubted he could handle this many undead at once; at least, not without a lot of prep time. Since he was the only necromancer I knew, I had no idea if another could match his skill. Something told me I was about to find out.

"Oh, come now, druid, this isn't the time to be playing coy. Your reputation marks you as anything but the silent type, and I have so many questions." The zombie blinked with his one remaining eye. "Chief among them being, how did you avoid the purge?"

So, it is a vamp. Could this be…?

No, it couldn't. How would he know who I am, or where to find me?

Shit—I'd failed to consider Garr. Ateas could've been watching us through Garr's eyes. It was a trick any two-bit master of the undead could perform.

Damn, I am so fucking stupid.

"Based on that look of realization, I'll assume you've guessed my identity. Don't be so hard on yourself. You had no idea that I could link with Alalngar. He was my maker, after all, although I surpassed him in power and knowledge long ago. Garr was always too intent on worldly pursuits and distractions to reach his true potential. I never suffered from such shortcomings."

So, a talker and a narcissist. Color me surprised.

The lich—because that's what he was, and no amount of confusion on Crowley's part would get me to refer to him otherwise—looked me up and down through the zombie's eye. He wore a curious expression, eyes wide, browed arched, head cocked, lips pursed. The zombie chuckled, making a wet, gurgling sound deep in his chest.

"Since you won't engage me in conversation, I'll leave you to consider that I'm aware of your plans, and I look forward to your arrival. Until then, druid."

The zombie's shoulders slumped slightly, his posture sagging as the lich's spirit vacated his body. *Creepy.* I was about to have the Oak portal me back to the water tower, when I realized that the lich might still be watching.

The hell if I was going to play that card in front of him. Garr had been unconscious when we took him from his penthouse, so it was a good bet that the lich didn't know I could portal at will. It looked like I'd be hoofing it to the water tower to let Crowley and Saint Germain know what I'd discovered, and to kill Garr.

Before I could start heading back, every deader in a quarter-mile radius came at me all at once.

———

I'm fast in my half-shifted form, almost as fast as a young vamp and the match of most werewolves. As for strength, I'm no slouch there, either. In this case, though, hesitation cost me. Before I could decide whether to bail, leap, or run, I got dogpiled by a dozen undead.

Twelve-ish undead couldn't drag me down, but soon it became two dozen or more; after that, it was impossible to tell. They were biting me all over, so I covered my head and face with one arm, leveraging myself off the ground with the other. If I hadn't been smart and covered my body in bark earlier, I would have been covered in bites instead.

As even more zombies piled on, it soon became hard to keep my torso off the ground. And with all that weight on me, if I went prone, I'd be stuck. Then, my only option would be to shift fully. The problem? I'd get eaten alive while I was making the change.

Shifting was always messy. It involved a complete structural recomposition of my body—muscle, bones, skin, and all. Meaning, chances were good I'd get infected again during the shift, and that was an inconvenience I couldn't afford at the moment.

The question was, how to get fifty to a hundred zombies off me? With one hand on the ground and the other near my face, releasing a fireball was *not* an option. While the pressure wave caused by the detonation would knock them off me, firing that spell at point-blank range in an enclosed space was never a good idea—something I knew from past experience.

Anyway, the fire would burn my bark skin off as well— no bueno. I needed an alternative, and fast.

Fuck it, let's try chain lightning.

Among the tomes, scrolls, and grimoires left to me by Finnegas, there was one book I'd spent considerable time with lately. It was a collection of druid battle magic spells, passed down and added to by many generations of druids. The book contained some of my favorite spells, including Cathbad's Maelstrom and Mogh's Scythe, along with dozens of other incantations for killing lots of people on a battlefield.

Modern humans had this misconception that druids were the peaceful, tree-hugging environmental activists of their day, but nothing could be further from the truth. Sure, we protected nature, but that was where the similarities ended. Back in my master's day, druids were badass magic-wielding battle wizards who went to war beside their kings and tribes. Read the Celtic myths and legends, and you'll soon find that whenever war broke out, a battle druid would be there to turn the tide or even the odds.

Fighting was in my blood, so I took to druid battle magic like a fish to water. Most of it involved using the elements in unique and inventive ways. This particular spell was designed to neutralize multiple human or demi-human combatants at once, and with a minimal expenditure of energy.

Obviously, such a spell would be a useful tool if you were the lone druid on a battlefield full of people trying to kill you. The catch was, I hadn't had a chance to test it under battlefield conditions. I mean, it's not like I could just find a dozen people to test it on.

"Hey, Susan, would you mind if I tased everyone in the office today? No? Well, fuck you, and by the way, your keto cookies are disgusting, and I hope you never bring them to the office Christmas party ever again."

I suppose I could've gone to a timeline where no one knew me to test it, and then beat feet out of there. But electrocuting a few dozen random, innocent people wasn't really something I could justify. Knowing my luck, I'd kill someone accidentally. So, I'd tested it on a few lone monsters, and that was that.

Time to find out if it works on more than one target.

Focusing my will, I gathered static electricity from the atmosphere, building up a charge inside my body. Once I'd stored enough juice, I drew on the Grove's magic to really amp it up—no pun intended. Then I grabbed the closest ankle in the dogpile and released the spell into that zombie.

Immediately, a current of 300,000 volts and ten milliamps ran through the zed, short-circuiting her nervous system before jumping to her nearest cohort. Electricity moves pretty damned fast, even against resistance, so the spell whammied the maximum effective number of targets in less than a second. All at once, a couple of dozen zeds did the funky chicken. They flopped and jerked spastically for a second, just before they all locked up and went rigid.

That would have been great if I'd cast the spell at a distance. It was meant to immobilize large numbers, so the caster could escape pursuit, or follow up with a deadlier area of attack spell when in battle. But in this instance, I was still at the bottom of that dogpile, even as the whole damned thing fell on top of me.

Instantly, I collapsed underneath them, crushed beneath the now literal dead weight of a few dozen zeds. None of them were trying to bite me anymore, which was a plus, but I was even more fucked than before I cast the spell.

Way to go, genius. This is what you get for skipping Physics to make out with Jesse.

Adding to the depth of the shit I'd stepped in, the wind got knocked out of my lungs when the pile collapsed. Sure, I could hold my breath for a while in this form, but eventually, I'd need to breathe. Going without oxygen while under stress was a great way to weaken a half-Fomorian, which meant I'd be at an even greater disadvantage when the spell effects wore off.

Mentally scrambling for a solution, I flipped through all the spells I knew. Fireballs were out, and so was lightning. I could freeze them, but then I'd be in the same predicament. Wind couldn't move all these bodies, not unless I called down an F2 tornado or better, and then I'd be caught up in the blender right along with them.

That left my sunlight spells—which were ineffective against zeds—Mogh's Scythe, and Cathbad's Maelstrom. Mogh's Scythe might work. The spell created a molecule-thin blade of super-compressed air, which the caster then projected at speed to decapitate and dismember the shit out of all and sundry. Cool, deadly, and effective. But again, not suited for casting at close range.

But what about Cathbad's Maelstrom? The maelstrom spell was a form of mass telekinesis, but on steroids and meth alike. When you cast it, the incantation levitated multiple objects from the environment, orbiting them around the caster at speed, fucking shit up as they struck whatever came near.

The spell was designed to be used with inanimate objects, but could it be used with zombies?

Color me intrigued.

I'd have chuckled if I could breathe, so instead I wisely decided to focus on casting the spell. Dropping into a druid trance was difficult while I was being crushed like a grape in Tuscany, but I managed. Once I'd entered the proper frame of mind, I began directing the spell to latch onto bodies.

At first, it felt a lot like trying to pick up a teddy bear in a claw machine. Every time I tried to grab a body, it slipped right out of my grasp.

Finally, I figured out that I needed to focus the spell on their skeletal mass, and not the pus bag part of their bodies. Once I got that sorted, dead bodies began to levitate off the top of the pile, presumably to spin in the surrounding air. I couldn't see this happening, of course, but I felt the tremendous weight atop me lessen.

Eventually, a ray of sunlight poked through the pile. I took that as my cue to push myself upright and stand, emerging from the hole in the pile like a xenomorph popping out of an android's chest—goo and all. Having finally achieved the ability to breathe again, I took a few deep breaths, and then I opened my eyes fully to see what I had wrought.

It was both glorious and nasty as hell. All around me, zombies sailed and spun through the air. Most flailed, kicked, and snapped their jaws at each other as they regained the ability to move. Some were torn apart by the centrifugal forces, and therefore unable to do the airborne monster mash.

Those zombies closest to me had received the brunt of

the spell's effects, so they were the last to regain motor control. As soon as they began to stir, I added them to the spinning, swirling mass of whole and dismembered zombies. Other undead were drawn to the moans and movement. When they got in range they were torn apart, as bodies struck bodies with wet, sickening thuds.

Needless to say, the smell was horrendous. I'd grown used to it during my first stay in this timeline, but with all the wind kicked up by the spell, it was many times worse than the usual ambient odor. Just as I was about to toss my cookies, I released the spell, sending over a hundred zombies—dismembered and otherwise—flying in all directions.

Corpses hit buildings, cars, telephone poles, and buses, smashing limbs, crushing skulls, and further dismantling each undead missile on impact. The wet, crunching thunder of a hundred plus bodies hitting solid objects all at once was deafening and a bit sickening, but it was over almost as soon as it started. The result was a field of dented metal, broken glass, and mutilated zeds in a block radius from where I stood.

I spun slowly in a circle, taking in the devastation I'd wrought. Nothing moved or made a peep. That is, save for the odd twitch of a limb, or the slick sucking sound of a crushed body part sliding down the side of a semi or the wall of a building.

Great googly moogly.

After making a complete circuit, I caught movement from the corner of my eye. Snapping my head around, I was met by the stark, dead gaze of the revenant. The thing stood much too tall to be operating independently, so I had to assume Ateas was in control.

When it began to clap slowly, I knew I'd assumed correctly. I knelt to grab a stone to toss at it, hoping to put it out of its misery. By the time I grabbed a chunk of concrete and stood, it was gone.

Well, shit. I guess I tipped my hand after all.

CHAPTER
SEVEN

MY RUN-IN with Ateas had shaken me, despite the fact that I handled myself well enough to escape the attack. Somehow, I got the feeling he'd been toying with me— sandbagging, as it were. I'd only barely survived the encounter, and if that were the case, we were all in deep shit.

For a moment, I was torn. Should I warn the Pack, or Crowley and Saint Germain? Since I wasn't even sure if the Pack was on the lich's radar, I made a snap decision and beat feet back to the water tower. Crowley had to be made aware that Ateas could listen in on us. As Crowley was the only other necromancer left who was powerful enough to challenge him, it was a sure bet that the lich would target him.

Oh, fuck. What if Ateas can bust Alalngar out of Crowley's circle?

I don't think I'd ever run so fast in any form as I did on my way back to the tower, and it was a good thing, too. When I got there, several revenants and a couple of nosferatu were crawling up the supports at all four cardinal points, and the lesser undead were massing underneath at the base—thousands, from the look of it.

Most were merely milling around the water tower's legs. However, I spotted two ghouls at the base of the northwest support, holding what looked to be firefighter rescue saws. As I watched they started the saws up, and then they began cutting. While they weren't very coordinated in their efforts, sparks flew everywhere, and at the rate they were going they might actually do some damage.

All of this activity was making one hell of a racket, so where was Crowley? He should have already been aware of the issue and actively doing something about it. Yet, all was quiet atop the tower. Was it possible the lich already killed them?

No, the pair wouldn't go down that easily. Yet something was keeping Crowley's alarm wards from going off, and I wanted to know what. I leapt atop a nearby building and hid myself with a camouflage spell, then I scanned the area using my mage sight.

There.

A sort of dark miasma hung over the top of the tower, a sickly yellow and charcoal fog that could only be an anti-magic field. Such a spell could prevent Crowley from receiving the signal that his alarm wards were sounding—but surely, he'd notice it if all magic ceased working inside the tank?

There had to be something more to it. On closer inspection, I realized it wasn't a field, but a bubble. And it surrounded the entire damned tower.

An anti-magic shield? Damn.

I'd never seen anyone wield that much control over that

particular spell. How could Ateas have that much precision from so far away? Could he be somewhere nearby, directing the undead and casting these spells?

A search of the area yielded little until I looked directly beneath me. There, I spotted a wisp of magic that trailed from the upper floor of the house to the anti-magic field surrounding the tower. Moving as silently as possible, I crept to the side of the roof, peeking over the edge.

Beneath me, the revenant I'd seen earlier stood in the window, controlling the anti-magic spell. Or rather, Ateas controlled the spell through the revenant. This was yet another unexpected development, as I'd never seen Crowley casting magic through a proxy. Just how powerful was this lich, anyway?

I didn't have time to ponder that question, as the revs and nos-types had nearly reached the top of the tower. If they were able to wedge the tower door open, Ateas could send wave after wave of greater undead after them, drowning them in bodies. Or worse, if they shut the door and sealed it, Crowley and Saint Germain would have no way to get out.

What if the sea of undead down there collapsed one of the tower's support columns?

Saint Germain might survive that, but not Crowley. He was powerful in this timeline, but not invincible.

Shit, Saint Germain! Was that who Ateas was really after? There was no telling, but one thing was painfully clear—I needed to neutralize the spell and get those two out of there.

And, I needed to kill Alalngar. If I left him "alive," Ateas could patch him up and send him after us. The hell if I wanted a pissed off, healed up, possibly supercharged six-thousand-year-old vampire on the loose and coming after me right now.

Gotta have a plan. Think, Colin!

Step one… counter the spell.

Step two… get to the tower.

Step three… evac and leave nothing but scorched earth behind me.

It was a good plan. The question was, how the fuck was I going to accomplish all three? With no time to think, I fell back on what I knew best. And that was, unmitigated violence in close combat, using primitive weaponry and small ordinance.

Dropping a hand inside my Bag, I made certain that two objects I needed could be easily accessed. My Craneskin Bag had a pocket dimension inside of it, one that was set up like a huge storage warehouse automated by a magical AI. It was easy to lose shit in there, so I always kept my most important and cherished items right next to the opening. That way, I could just reach in and grab them without thinking about it.

Secure in the knowledge that I was geared up, I backed up to the other edge of the roof, then I took off at a sprint toward the tower. When I'd nearly run out of rooftop, I leapt for the top of the tower some thirty yards away, flipping in midair as I did so. Simultaneously, I pulled my Glock 17 out of my Bag, and I drew a bead on the rev in the window of the house I'd just leapt from.

I squeezed the trigger three times in rapid succession. The first round hit the rev in the chest, the second in the throat, and the third, between the eyes. It dropped like a puppet with its strings cut, and the connection between it and the anti-magic spell dissipated.

Step one, complete.

Of course, I was moving as fast as my Fomorian-enhanced body would allow. But would it be fast enough? Pushing doubt aside, I passed the Glock to my left hand and pulled Dyrnwyn from my Bag with my right.

The sword's blade lit up the dark as it burst into hot white flames all along its length. Just as I finished pulling the blade from the Bag, I completed my somersault and the full arc of my jump. My feet hit the top of the tower just a few feet from the edge, and as I landed, I bent my knees to absorb the shock of impact. Then I was running and gunning toward the hatch, firing silver-tipped rounds just as fast as my reflexes allowed.

Two revs went down in the blink of an eye, and I beheaded a third that had almost reached the opening. A nosferatu leapt from the edge of the tower, steering itself with the use of its vestigial wings. It must've been many centuries old, as I'd only ever seen fully developed wings on a nos that was older than Saint Germain.

I shot at it, but it seemed to blur as it flew toward me, dodging the bullets. I'd never seen a nos move like that, not since the one Luther and I fought. To say it spooked me was an understatement, and I'm not ashamed to say I forgot about the sword in my hand, instead emptying the magazine in a futile attempt to wing the vamp.

Then, it was on me, digging its clawed, dirt-encrusted fingers deep into my shoulders on either side of my neck. Like most nos-types, this one was bald all over, with wrinkled gray skin and a face that was only vaguely human. Its nostrils were reminiscent of those of a bat, more like curved slits than a facial feature, and its nearly lipless, tooth-filled mouth gaped wide as it leaned in to latch onto my throat.

Instinctively, I repeatedly punched it in the eye with the hot barrel of the pistol. "Get off me, bitch!" I growled.

The nosferatu held fast, despite the fact that I'd pulped its right eye. Undaunted, I switched tactics and shoved the pistol into the vamp's mouth, turning it vertically to avoid having my hand sliced off by all those needle-thin, razor-sharp teeth. I used the pistol for leverage, forcing it down the vampire's throat as I pushed the damned thing's face away from mine.

Then I realized I was holding something in my other hand.

Duh, Colin—you're holding a fucking magic plasma sword.

I could kick myself in the ass later; presently, I needed to focus on surviving this encounter. Casting aside all thoughts of self-castigation, I slashed across the nosferatu's midsection.

To my surprise, I encountered a shocking amount of resistance as I finished what ended up being a drag cut, then a draw cut coming back the other direction. Something did give, however, and I was rewarded by the nos-type's pained shriek—muted, due to the pistol in its gullet—and the sensation of nosferatu guts gushing all over my boots.

Well, that's something, I guess.

The vamp's grip weakened immediately. Knowing an opportunity to turn the tables when I saw one, I released the pistol, leaving it wedged in the vamp's mouth. Then I whipped the blade around in front of me, severing the vampire's arms at the elbows.

Now freed from the thing's grip—sort of—a step back was all I needed to gain the space necessary to stab it through the heart. I don't care how old a vampire is, sticking a white-hot piece of metal and plasma through its pericardial sac is gonna fuck up its day. Soon the damned thing was shriveling upon itself, even as I was pulling the sword from its bony, hairless gray breast.

The entire exchange had taken no more than a couple of seconds, but split-seconds count when you're fighting the undead. As I withdrew the sword, I crouched and pivoted, brandishing the searing hot blade in front of me as I looked for more assailants. None were close enough to strike. Apparently, the others had left me to the old nosferatu while they jostled and fought to be the first to enter the tower tank.

Two revs were fighting a nos to get through the hatch, and that was their undoing. I slung a lightning bolt at the nos, blasting it over the side. Following that with the fireball nearly turned out to be a mistake. Saint Germain popped his head out of the hole, only to see the fireball flying at him. His eyes widened, and he ducked back inside, just as the spell hit the closest rev.

My spell detonated in a conflagration of flame and expanding hot gases that turned the two revenants into secondary flaming projectiles. They sailed off in opposite directions, over the side of the tank. A second later, Saint Germain poked his head out again, a bit less enthusiastically this time. He fixed me with a sour look.

"Are you quite done?" he asked.

"With saving your asses? Sure." Just then, a loud shrieking groan echoed from below, and the water tower lurched and tilted slightly. "Ah, shit. We gotta get out of here."

"Oh, really?" Saint Germain snarked back. "And here I thought I'd lay out a mat and wait for the morning sun."

I flashed a sideways frown, even as I crouched and

caught my balance due to the tower lurching once again. "There are at least a couple of thousand undead down there, and they're all working to bring this thing down. Where's Crowley?"

"Trying to finish off Alalngar." He scowled and crossed his arms, looking more annoyed at our plight than anything.

"I'll take care of Garr. Could you grab Crowley for me?"

"He won't like it, and I'm not in the habit of irritating surly necromancers," Jacques replied.

"Fucking hell—do I have to do everything myself?"

"Wrong? Yes," he muttered.

Rolling my eyes, I sped past him and did a baseball slide into the hatch. "Crowley," I yelled into the hole, hanging onto it with one hand as the entire tower jerked a couple of feet to the side. Within, the wizard was messing with his necromantic circle, drawing new symbols and reinforcing them with shadow magic. "We have to leave!"

"We cannot. I am not finished," he replied.

"I'll handle it. Now, let's go," I hollered back.

"That simply isn't an option," he replied. "Unfortunately, someone is trying to unravel my necromantic circle so they can portal Alalngar out of here. Over the last minute or so, I have only barely been able to stay a step or two ahead of his work. If I stop, the Scythian will escape. So, you see, I cannot leave."

"Damn it..." I said, combing my free hand through my hair as I ran through our options.

The problem? I had to do this without tipping Ateas off regarding the true limits of my magical capabilities. That meant no time magic, and no teleportation, either.

Inside, I noticed that Crowley's runes were spontaneously disappearing, even as the shadow wizard drew them again with his index finger and shadow magic. In all my time in The World Beneath, never had I seen the like. At least, not when the opposing magician worked from a distance, sight unseen.

"Fuck it." I looked at Saint Germain, who now stood at the hatch's edge above me. He barely moved at all, even though the tower jerked and shuddered, tilting at a near thirty-degree angle.

The vamp tapped his toe slowly, arms crossed over his chest. "Would you like me to intervene?"

"How quickly can you get him?"

"If he hasn't locked the tank back down with magic again, I'll be back in two seconds."

I almost challenged him on it, but thought better of it. "Give me a second."

It took a moment to spin up the spells I wanted, but once I had them ready, I nodded. "Go."

Saint Germain disappeared in a blur of motion as I did my best to track his movements. He came into focus as he slowed to grab Crowley without killing him, supporting the Crowster's neck and head to avoid severing the wizard's spine. Once he'd secured his target, Germain sped off again. Rather than using the ladder, he ran up the side of the tank, exiting it through the hatch with a *whoosh* of air.

When they were clear, I cut loose with the spells I'd prepped. Mogh's Scythe shot out like a bullet from my hand, bisecting Alalngar's neck at an awkward angle. I'd wanted to cut it off completely, but it hung there from a ropy strand of skin and muscle, which could be surprisingly tough on a vamp that old. Hopefully, the follow-up spell would do the trick.

Time slowed as my fireball shot forth at the armless, legless, and nearly headless figure in the center of the circle. He was still alive, that much was clear, as I saw his lips moving and eyes blinking. That was likely because Ateas was channeling himself through Alalngar to undo Crowley's magic, but somewhere inside there, Garr's evil spirit was still present as well.

Let's hope he burns. I sure don't want to have to deal with his ass after that lich fixes him.

The fireball expanded as it neared the target, obscuring him from sight. However, I could've sworn I saw Alalngar smile, just before he started fading out at the edges. Then the spell struck and exploded. I swung myself out of the hatch, rolling away from the opening as I grabbed a handhold near the opening.

Flames and smoke shot out of the hole, a momentary roaring inferno that drowned out the cacophony made by the undead at ground level. The tower jittered and shuddered in response, then it leaned slowly and precariously in the same direction as before, but this time it did not stop. Instead, it kept inching over, bit by bit. Clearly, we had but seconds to evacuate.

I looked up to get a visual on my companions and found each staring at me with barely concealed contempt. Both stood nearly at right angles to the tank's surface, Saint Germain using his weird vampire powers, and Crowley hanging on with his sticky, shadow magic tentacles.

Meanwhile, I hung off the hatch lid like a school kid who'd just slipped and caught the top monkey bar. Crowley sighed, shaking his head.

"Do you not control elemental magic?" he asked.

"Yes, but I don't fucking control gravity," I groused.

They shared a look, and Saint Germain clucked his tongue. "I believe—that is to say, what the wizard is trying to intimate, is that—"

"You could make your feet stick to the surface of the tower in half a dozen ways," Crowley said, his voice dripping with barely concealed contempt. "Your shoe soles are either synthetic rubber, which is petroleum-based, or natural rubber, which comes from trees. Friction is a function of—"

"Fine, I get it," I said, nearly shouting.

Shit like this was embarrassing. It wasn't my fault that my druid master died before he passed on what he knew. They each continued to stare at me, one with amused pity in his eyes, the other with disdain. Finally, I'd had enough. Besides, the tower was slowly picking up speed.

"Okay, smart asses," I said. "Let's see you do this."

———

I sent a request to my Oak and had him teleport us the fuck out of there. Of course, I had the Oak land me on my feet inside Crowley's lair. Just for shits and giggles, I had the tree drop Crowley and Saint Germain in a cow pond in a nearby pasture.

Call me petty, but those fuckers should've thanked me for saving their asses.

Moments later, Crowley and Saint Germain portalled into the tunnel, stepping through a black oval of nothingness that appeared about a minute after I arrived. Crowley was dripping brown muck, while Saint Germain was as dry as British humor. The wizard scowled as he entered his lair, while the vampire hid a wry grin behind his hand.

"That was poorly done," Crowley hissed.

"Yeah, well—next time I save your tail, show a little gratitude."

"Oh? Like I saved you from Garr's dungeons?"

"That was for your own—" I remembered why he'd become what he was, and thought better of what I was going to say. "You know what, you're right. My apologies, that was childish of me."

With a thought and a gesture, I pulled all the water, grime, and pathogens from his clothing, gathering it in a ball. I was about to incinerate it, then I reconsidered, wrapping it in an airtight layer of bark before tossing it in my Bag. As a druid, you never knew when organic material would come in handy.

Crowley stared at me, his expression indecipherable. After several seconds, he huffed and hung his head. "Apology accepted. I should not have cast aspersions on your abilities. It is not your fault that you did not receive a complete education in druidry."

"Um, thanks, I think?" I said, shocked at this sudden flash of affability on the part of the world's surliest wizard.

"Oh, how very touching," Saint Germain remarked. He leaned against the wall of the tunnel, arms crossed, as he observed our conversation.

"How'd you avoid getting wet?" I asked. "Because I'm pretty sure I dropped you over the same pond."

The shadow wizard sneered. "He twisted in midair and then ran across the surface of the water. I'd not have believed it if I hadn't seen it for myself."

"How is that even—?" I scratched the back of my head, baffled. "You know what? Never mind. The issue we have to face now is, what we do next?"

My shade-cursed partner in crime sat heavily on a stack of cinder blocks that were partially covered by a thick, paint-stained tarp. "Clearly, Ateas has abilities and knowledge far beyond my own. You need to retrieve the Seer. There is no other path we can take."

Saint Germain's frown marred his typically cherubic visage. "But, I thought he died?" As realization dawned across the vampire's face, he shook his head slowly. "If you intend to do what I think, it could have dire consequences. You know that, yes?"

I side-eyed Crowley before meeting the vampire's gaze. "I intend to do no such thing. For starters, we aren't even sure what happened to Finnegas in this timeline. For all we know, he could be roaming the planes somewhere looking for a cure for the plague."

Crowley cleared his throat. "If I may? Consider your activities thus far in this particular bifurcation of time. As usual, you've traversed the earthly and eldritch dimensions with all the tact of an aughiskey in a glassblower's shop. Were the old druid still alive, don't you think he'd have shown up already?"

I thrust my lower lip out, nodding to concede the point. "Fair enough. But I still don't think it's a good idea."

"Then do you know how to fight this thing?" Jacques asked. "Because I certainly cannot. I felt the pull of his influence almost as soon as he began unraveling the wizard's spells. My alter-ego might be able to resist that creature's magic, but I doubt I could, and I shudder to think what might have happened if he'd turned his attention fully on me."

"That's what we have Crowley for, Jacques. We'll just

portal in, Crowley can hold him in place for a few seconds, I'll get the sample, and boom! Done and done."

"Trust me when I say that it will not be that easy," the shadow wizard replied. "I can assure you, his demesne is warded against portal incursions. And as for trapping him in a necromantic circle?" Crowley tapped a single, black-nailed finger on the wood pile. "I barely held him off for the span of a few minutes, and that was while I was in a prepared lair fighting him at a distance. Should I face him in person, despite the considerable power I've amassed lately, I fear it would be no contest. I believe recent events have made it painfully clear that we'll need help if we're to fight Ateas."

As much as it pained me to admit it, they were both right. We couldn't fight Ateas alone. While Crowley and I were both dangerous as all hell, we lacked the sort of knowledge and skill that only centuries of mystical study and practice could bring.

Sure, I could retreat into the Paths for a few hundred years, but without someone to guide me it was a crap shoot whether the effort would result in enough skill to beat the lich. Besides, we couldn't defeat him like we would any other vampire, since I needed his corpse intact. Incineration by fire or sunlight was out of the question, and beheading or staking him would risk spontaneous desiccation that could ruin the tissue and blood samples we required.

Still, I couldn't bring myself to make that decision. It had taken me years of time spent in my Grove and in the Paths to get over the old man's death. Seeing him again, hearing his voice, and having him to lean on, only to have to let him go once more—I couldn't take losing him twice. It was a pain I simply didn't want to face.

"I—" My voice faltered, as well as my nerve. "I need some time to think. I'll return by tomorrow morning, and by then I'll have made a decision."

Crowley's expression softened slightly. "Go where you must. I still firmly contend that we will not succeed in our task without the Seer's assistance. Consider this as we await your return."

Saint Germain smiled at me, but his voice was hard as granite. "You owe me a death, boy, whether it be clean or messy. I intend to collect, one way or another. Keep that in mind as well."

Those final words echoed in my mind as I had the Oak teleport me to the Grove. I had a lot to think about, but I needed to be clearheaded to do so. That meant heading back to my own timeline for a little personal resolution, and for that, I'd need to prepare.

Man, I hate relationship drama. Now I know why Finnegas never settled down.

CHAPTER
EIGHT

AFTER MUCH PERSONAL DELIBERATION, I exited the Paths in my timeline right after I'd left. Although Gwydion had never stated it, my instincts told me that it wasn't a good idea to remove myself from my own time stream for extended periods. For proof, I only had to look at what happened when I was gone from this reality for six months; I'd returned to pure pandemonium, a situation it took a great deal of effort to fix.

I was sure there was some principle of quantum mechanics that explained why it happened. Frankly, I didn't know what it was, only that my gut said, 'Don't do that.' So I didn't, as a rule. Which sucked because I really wanted to jump back in after six months of making Fallyn sweat—even though that wasn't really my style.

No, direct confrontation and radical honesty were more my things, rather than playing games that involved concealing feelings and intentions, and hiding the truth from your loved ones. Even after staying in the Paths for all that time, the knowledge that she'd been with someone else still stung. How was I going to face her?

Yet, I had to do it because the distraction I was experiencing was causing me to make stupid mistakes. I should've seen the trap Ateas set coming from a mile away, and I should have suspected some sort of link between Alalngar and the lich. Garr was the ranking vampire in Texas, and old as fuck, so it only made sense he'd have a connection to Ateas.

Since I'd had my world turned upside down, I'd gone back to making rookie mistakes. I was back to playing checkers instead of chess. It may have cost us dearly, as I had no idea if I'd destroyed Alalngar before Ateas managed to portal him away. Just thinking of facing a patched up, fully recovered, and pissed off Garr made me shudder.

Best not to think about it. Cross one bridge at a time, Colin.

The problem was, the bridge directly in front of me was treacherous. It was narrow, rickety, and spanned dangerous waters. This was a chasm of emotions I would rather not feel, much less face.

Still gotta cross it.

After cleaning up in the Grove, I put on clean clothes and shifted in and out of my Fomorian form—a painful process, but one that fully renewed me—then I headed back to Earth. When I appeared in front of the shed behind the Pack's clubhouse, I found Fallyn sitting on the door stoop.

Had she been waiting for me? Obviously. Was that a good sign? Who fucking knew?

She'd been braiding strands of grass, plaiting them into lengths of not-quite-rope. The girl had been at it for a while, as she had several feet of the stuff sitting on the ground between her feet. The alpha glanced up at me, her normally hazel eyes flashing yellow for a moment, then back to their usual color and hue.

"I didn't know if you'd come back," she said in a near whisper.

"Well, neither did I." This felt awkward. Suddenly, I had a Ricky Bobby moment, not sure what to do with my hands. I stuck them in my pockets and shrugged. "So I spent some time figuring that out."

"You smell like distant places and indecision," she said, turning her gaze back to her hands. She worked furiously at pleating the strands she held, eyes downcast. Suddenly, the braid snapped. Fallyn snarled and tossed the pieces away. "It's not my fault. I did it, but it's not my fault."

Not knowing the lay of the land yet, I stood my ground, making no move to draw closer or retreat. "Listen—it's not that you mate-bonded with… what's his name again?"

"Bleys."

"B-l-a-i-s-e?"

"No, with an 'e-y'." She growled and threw her hands up in disgust. "What does that matter?"

"Nothing. It just figures that he spells his name like a character from Zoolander."

My alpha glared at me. "This isn't funny. And it's not something you can joke away."

I cleared my throat, because fuck that, I held the high ground here. "As I was saying, it's not that you bonded with *Bleys*, it's that you concealed it from me."

Fallyn shook her head, eyes closed. "What was I supposed to do, Colin? Macha gave me all my memories back in a rush. Not only did I almost instantly remember that I'd been madly, deeply, and truly in love with you for the longest time, I also had to remember every fucking thing that Diarmuid did to me.

And while he didn't physically assault me, the way he mind-raped me—no one should ever have to go through that."

"I'm sorry."

She leapt to her feet, arms locked straight with her fists held tightly at her sides. "Would you stop being so fucking understanding and just let me talk?" she screamed, spittle flying from her mouth.

The fact that she had the gall to yell at me had a chilling effect. I crossed my arms over my chest, taking a step back. "So, talk."

The girl closed her eyes tightly, fighting back tears. I wanted to rush forward and sweep her in my arms, to hold her and tell her it'd all be okay. But I'd grown older, colder, and more guarded. No more wearing my heart on my sleeve. Nope, not anymore. It was time to play it safe, to see how it all worked out before I committed myself again.

Before I get hurt, even worse.

Fallyn kept her eyes closed as she continued, her voice low and desperate. Maybe it made it easier for her, not seeing my reaction—I truly wasn't sure. "What was I supposed to do, while we were getting to know each other again under those circumstances? Just up and say, 'oh yeah, and while I was in the Alps, I married and fucked some guy I met at my mom's castle'?"

I winced reflexively, and while she couldn't see me, she could smell my pheromones and hear the way my heart rate and breathing changed. By the way her shoulders tensed, she must've realized it'd been a mistake to say it like that.

Fallyn had been raised in a biker gang, and she was often blunt to the point of self-sabotage. This was one of those times. Almost unconsciously, my weight shifted to my heels as I prepared to step back into the Paths.

"Wait!" Fallyn said, opening her tear-filled eyes as she reached for me across the short distance between us. It felt like a chasm now, for sure.

I did wait, silently, watching her while maintaining a poker face even Honos couldn't decipher.

"Are you going to make me beg?" she asked, her voice the barest whisper. "Because I will, even though every cell in my alpha blood is screaming against it."

"No," I said, in a plaintive tone of voice. "I don't think it would do any good."

"Colin," she said as she met my gaze, tears streaming down her face.

"Fallyn, stop. If anyone in the Pack sees you like this, it'll be as if you laid down and bared your throat to the worst of them."

"That's the last thing I'm worried about right now. Besides, I sent them all away. My sister included."

"Ah, Artemis. Maybe she's the one you should be angry with, eh?" She started to speak, but I twitched a finger to indicate I wasn't done. "Look, I don't think this is it for us. There's no way I can believe that, not after the shit we've weathered. But finding out about you and Snowball? That's not something I can easily forget."

"What does that mean?" she asked, wiping her eyes with the back of her hand.

"It means... it means I need to go break some shit, wreck some motherfuckers, and possibly end a dynasty that's lasted since before written history. Maybe after I let off a little steam, I'll be ready to discuss *us*. But seeing you here, now, where *Bleys* jumped me—it's still too fresh and raw to deal with."

"Okay," she replied as she took an awkward step toward me. "I can deal with that."

I wasn't ready for physical contact from her, because the thought of her with him... *ugh*. Just thinking about it again turned my stomach. So I did the only thing I could do. I beat feet the fuck out of there.

"Goodbye for now, Fallyn. Take care of yourself."

She lunged forward, which was yet another mistake; I was jumpy enough as it was. Before she could reach me, I stepped backward into the Paths. Maybe it was my imagination, but the soft sound of sobbing followed me across the time streams, all the way back to hell on Earth.

————

I didn't want to go to the alt-timeline Grove, because I was way too upset, and my mood would have an impact on it. That version of the Grove was sensitive and easily affected by my negative emotions, as it didn't fully understand the nuances of the human experience. If it sensed I was angry, it might take that as an indication that danger was present, and that could result in unintended consequences.

Likewise, I wasn't ready to face Crowley and Saint Germain just yet, either. They'd expect an answer from me, and while I was nearing a decision, I hadn't quite made up my mind. What I needed was a pick-me-up, something to heal my wounded soul.

For that purpose, I had just the thing in mind. First, I searched for the stash that Saint Germain had discovered. After I found the location, I had to pick my way through the bloody mess he'd made of the former occupants. I hated cannibals as much as anyone, but damn—he'd gone a bit overboard on those clowns.

Some of them are nothing but body parts. Did Saint Germain really do this?

A particularly ravaged but mostly intact body lay draped across a pallet of deer corn, his chest cavity torn open wide. Something was clearly missing from his internal anatomy, and I didn't think a natural predator had removed it after the fact. Powerful vampires left a spoor trail that kept both lesser undead and animals away from their haunts for weeks.

Even I could pick up Jacques' scent here, that weird odor ancient vamps had. It was what I imagined King Tut's tomb had smelled like when they first cracked it open. I could only describe it as a combination of chemical preservatives, dried flowers, dust, and desiccated flesh.

The scene was concerning, as I didn't know Saint Germain could display that kind of savagery. Sure, he was a vampire, and therefore was not to be measured by human standards of moral turpitude... but damn. This was brutal.

I decided to chalk it up to predatory hunger and justice, and continued to the back of the store. There I found pallets of clothing in the original packaging, most of them still untouched by rodents. Over the course of the next hour, I stuffed my Bag with jeans, boots, socks, gloves, hats, shirts, jackets, belts, thermals, and anything else I could find that the boys would need.

As an afterthought, I grabbed a bunch of toys I thought they'd like, along with a few dozen blister packs of pocket knives and multi-tools. Not only were the knives and multi-tools useful in an apocalypse, they were also just the sort of doodads pre-pubescent boys loved to mess with and abuse.

Finally, I snagged stuff for the adults. Fuel cans and tools for Guerra, fertilizer and feed for Mickey, camp axes and machetes for Anna, along with clothing and footwear that would fit them as well. After rummaging around, I found an almost full bottle of Wild Turkey, not the best stuff but a useful antiseptic in a pinch.

Satisfied I'd sufficiently cleaned the place out, I had the Oak take me to the compound I'd set up for them at the castle mansion in Austin. The place had once been owned by a highly eccentric tech millionaire with a penchant for all things fantasy and medieval. It was in a secluded neighborhood, tough to get to, and surrounded by topographical features that would funnel most smaller hordes away.

More importantly, the place had been built like Fort Knox. The house was well appointed, and the grounds were surrounded by a high stone and wrought iron fence that we'd capped off with razor wire and spikes. It didn't take much to fortify it completely, and it even came with towers and an observation deck that allowed for a three hundred sixty-degree view of the surrounding area. Combined with the vegetation I'd grown to conceal and block every road into the neighborhood, it was nearly the perfect location for the group to thrive.

Speaking of using druid magic, my abilities weren't general knowledge among the human members of the group, although Anna suspected… something. Guerra knew, of course, as we'd been acquainted through the Pack in our previous lives. That was to say, he had been acquainted with my now deceased counterpart in this timeline—but it was the same thing.

To avoid complications, I preferred to keep the knowledge to myself. For that reason, I teleported in a few miles distant, into a neighborhood where I knew I was bound to find an EV. After a short search, I located one sitting in the garage of an upscale home that was nearly a mansion. A little druid-genuity and some tinkering was all it took to revive the batteries, charge it up, and get it roadworthy again.

After transferring everything I'd brought in my Bag to the back seat, trunk, and hatch of the vehicle, I drove it to a hidden access path that led to the castle house. At my mental command, vegetation parted and earth receded to reveal a weed-strewn, cracked, and overgrown suburban street. As I passed, dirt flowed back again and the plant life closed ranks behind me, wiping the tire tracks away in the process and leaving no trace I'd been there.

Once I'd reached the neighborhood where the castle mansion was located, I stopped the vehicle. After rolling down all the windows, I took a few deep breaths and dropped into a druid trance, expanding my awareness and senses to ensure that nothing and no one had seen me enter the area. Satisfied I was alone, I drove a little farther and left the SUV on the side of the road a few blocks from the compound.

Guerra was on lookout, of course, and he came out to greet me, having heard the sound of the EV despite the relative silence of the electric motors. Although he was still missing the lower half of his left leg, he slipped quietly from the undergrowth beside the road, lowering a crossbow as he approached. The prosthetic he wore was more modern than the last, this one a curved carbon fiber and metal blade that had likely originally been designed for runners.

The Danny Trejo lookalike lifted his chin at me, reverse nodding by way of greeting. "Hey *cabron*, you gonna wake up all the dead in a two-mile radius driving that thing in here."

Realistically speaking, the EV was only loud to supernaturally sharp ears. A vamp might hear it if they were within a quarter mile, but zombies and ghouls were unlikely to be alerted by the noise unless they were right on top of it. In other words, the old wolf was busting my balls.

"Good to see you too, Guerra." I extended my right hand, waiting for him to move his weapon to the crook of his other arm.

The 'thrope's left arm ended in a razor-sharp billhook that was attached to a prosthetic cup and sleeve. The injuries were souvenirs from a run-in we'd had with a nasty master vampire by the name of Dauphine. She was another of Alalngar's offspring, and had proved to be a handful. I'd ended her, but not before she took her toll on the old werewolf and our group.

Guerra clasped hands with me, meeting my gaze as he shook his head. "You got a haunted look, *viejo. Que te está pasando*, eh?"

"Later," I replied with a rueful, guarded smile. "How're the kids?"

"Good man, growing like weeds. Little fuckers are starting to give me hell in the pit." The pit referred to the sparring circle, where Guerra and Anna were training them in hand-to-hand combat.

"And Mickey? Anna?"

He hissed. "Mickey's fine, sticks to gardening, cooking

meals, and making hooch, and that seems to keep him happy. As for Anna, she's gone a little *loca*."

"How so?"

"Eh, you'll see," he replied as he glanced away, scanning the empty homes nearby as a pretext for not meeting my gaze.

"She's still mourning Brian." A statement, not a question.

"We all miss him," Guerra said as his gaze swept the surrounding woods and empty homes. "*Pobrecito*, it's like that bitch cut the heart out of the group. Kid was a natural leader."

Anna's little brother had been one of the casualties of my brief war with Dauphine. She'd snapped his neck, right in front of me. And hell if I couldn't do anything about it at the time, because I'd lost my connection to my Oak and Grove when I crossed over here.

I held my tongue as I stared at the weeds growing through cracks in the road. Anna still blamed me for Brian's death, and I couldn't help but agree with her. If only I'd been smarter, faster, planned ahead, looked ahead, had my powers…

Guerra snapped his fingers in front of my face. "Hey. It wasn't your fault, druid. There was nothing you could've done."

I tsked. "Yeah, there was. I just didn't do it. Not because I didn't want to, but because I was full of myself and I made mistakes. Not enough experience and wisdom under my belt, you know?"

"Shit, you think you're the only one that ever made a mistake? I've been around a while, longer than a lot of 'thropes, and made my fair share. You know what I've learned?"

"I sense a cliché coming," I said with a wan smile.

"*Payaso*. I'm being serious here."

"Go on, I'm listening."

"I learned that you can't cheat death. Everybody's got their designated time. Even if you gain enough powers and magic and shit to cheat the reaper for a while, nothing good ever comes of it. Seen it too many times."

Immediately, Gwydion came to mind. Click—as he called himself these days—alternated between mild cognitive decline and outright fevered delirium. He'd confided in me that his mental health issues stemmed from his efforts to achieve immortality without losing his humanity. Instead, he'd lost his sanity.

There's always a price to pay—always.

"Can't argue with that. You done lecturing me, old wolf?"

"You done being a moody little bitch?"

"That's sexist. Why not say, 'a moody little bastard'?"

"See what I mean?"

I chuckled softly, but my tone was serious as I continued. "Any sign of Richard?"

Richard was a kid I thought I had rescued from Dauphine's little vampire cult. It turned out that the kid was her human familiar—her Renfield. He'd been the one who let her in on that fateful night when Dauphine killed Brian.

"*Nada*. Killed a few revs, and a nos, but I haven't seen any higher vamps since that bitch got the jump on me. If she turned him, he must've beat feet to Dallas. Or he ended up filling the belly of some deader."

"Let's hope that's the case."

"What? That she turned him and he ran? Or that he got his ticket punched out in the badlands?"

"Either would be preferable to having him lurking around," I said as I tongued a molar.

The kid was dangerous, and a loose end. Honestly, I'd rather not be the one to clip him, but if Dauphine had turned him, I wouldn't hesitate. All it would take would be for Richard to gain the confidence of one of the boys, and trick them into letting him into the compound while Guerra was out on patrol.

Once he got past my wards — game over.

"Stop worrying, *viejo*. I already told you, there's no vamps for miles and miles around. The kids are safe."

After chewing my lip for a moment, I nodded. "Yeah, okay."

He passed the crossbow back to his remaining hand. "C'mon, let's go eat. Mickey just harvested some potatoes, and he makes a mean *picadillo*."

"You got tortillas?"

"Made with lard and everything. Raided a little Mexican grocery that I found untouched. You bring any booze?"

"Do Mexicans like tacos?"

"Now who's saying fucked up shit?"

I chuckled. "Hey, man, I'm Irish. You think I don't like fried potatoes and bread?"

He sneered, but his heart wasn't in it. "Alright, white boy, I'll let it pass. We'd better hurry before those kids eat all the tortillas."

———

When Guerra and I got to the compound, the boys were already gathered at the gate waiting for us. Based on the chatter I picked up on our approach, Matthew had been slinking outside the perimeter, spying on Guerra. It seemed the boys had a system, and they took turns keeping an eye on the old 'thrope when he went out on patrol.

"I take it you knew about this," I whispered, so softly only a supe could hear.

"'Course. They're boys, for fuck's sakes," he whispered back. "No matter how much Anna tries to keep them locked down, it's a lost cause. 'Sides, they need the practice. I only chew their asses when they fuck up and make too much noise. Little bastards are getting damned sneaky."

I gave a curt nod, reflecting for the millionth time that a bunch of pre-pubescent boys shouldn't have to learn how to survive in an undead apocalypse. But, as the old man always said, wish in one hand, shit in the other, and see which fills up first. We were dealing with the harsh realities of survival, and there was no room for error, or for going soft.

Dauphine and Richard proved that out.

We were still a block away, and while the kids were pressed up against the wrought iron gate, none of them made a sound, despite how they jostled and jockeyed for position. Yet, even this seemed to be too much clamor for Matthew's liking. The lanky child had grown taller since I'd last seen the group, and as he directed the other boys to silence with a series of hand signals, I noticed his pants were too short and his shirt too tight.

Good thing I brought supplies. At least they're eating well.

"I see Matthew's taken Brian's place as de facto leader."

Guerra scowled slightly. "When Anna leaves them

alone. If she's not—" he paused, his gaze flicking in my direction and quickly away again. "Anyway, she hovers too much these days. Not good for them. They need room to roam."

"You mean they need to learn to take care of themselves."

He gave half a shrug. "Where I come from, we don't shelter our young. Weak wolves lead to weak packs."

"She'll get over it. Give her time."

"I can't stay here forever, druid. Eventually, Samson's gonna summon me, and that's a call I can't resist."

What Guerra didn't say was that there might be a chance that his alpha could restore his lost limbs. 'Thropes gained strength from being in the presence of their pack, and sometimes alphas could draw on that strength to do extraordinary things. Pack magic was odd, and something I didn't fully understand, but it didn't take a genius to know that Guerra wanted to be made whole again.

For all I knew, there might be something I could do in that regard, some missing bit of knowledge regarding druid healing magic that Finnegas never taught me. Certainly, I'd learned a lot from this timeline's Lugh, but even his knowledge was incomplete. The nature of druidry was that each generation innovated and added to the whole; thus, only a true master druid could pass on the entirety of their knowledge to the next generation.

And I'm just a pale imitation, compared to the old man.

Guerra nudged me, bringing my attention back to the present. "Hey, put a smile on, or at least look like the world hasn't gone to hell in a hand-basket. The kids are watching."

For a grizzled old wolf, he sure was a softy at heart. I

pulled my shoulders back and lifted my head up, smiling as we approached the gate. Taking my time, I made eye contact with each boy in turn—Matthew, his best friend Christopher, Thomas, Danny, Cort, Dallas, Ly, D'Wayne, Bobby, Samuel, Kamal, Darren, Val, and Phillip. After that silent greeting, I glanced at Guerra.

The old wolf nodded at the group. "Coast is clear—no sign of dead for miles around. You can talk, but keep it low."

Instantly, the boys began chattering, each speaking over the others even as they made room for Guerra to unlock the heavy-duty padlock on the gate to let us inside. We could've easily vaulted the wall, but the boys didn't know our origins, and I saw no reason to reveal that information. As I slipped through the gate, the kids surrounded me, tugging on my arms and sleeves to get my attention as they shared every bit of news I'd missed while I was away.

"I hit a rabbit on the run with an arrow—right through the eye!"

"Mr. Guerra is teaching us rapier and dagger..."

"We're growing tomatoes and strawberries in the garden..."

And on, and on. It was easy to get caught up in their enthusiasm, and to forget about my problems for a time. This was why I came back to the Hellpocalypse, and it was why I was going to risk it all to save a world gone to shit. I was doing it for millions of survivors the world over. People deserved a life free from hiding from vampires and revenants at night, and running from hordes of the dead during the day.

But these little chatterboxes remained at the heart of why I was stuck on this mission. Back when Gwydion had stranded me in this timeline, I'd connected with them on a level that defied description, and while I was busy saving them, the boys gave me something in return.

Hope.

Losing Brian had broken my heart. Yet I didn't get to grieve, because it wasn't my place to do so. I didn't have the right, not really. But the hell if I was going to lose another one of these kids to the Hellpocalypse. Uh-uh, not on my watch.

Now that I had command of the Oak and Grove in this timeline, I had the magic to ensure that never happened. The question was, would my paltry knowledge of druidry be enough to rescue these kids? Would I be able to save this world's survivors from being trampled by the never-ending march of a few billion rotting feet?

I set that thought aside, choosing to enjoy the moment by giving the boys my undivided attention. After passing out sticks of gum and other small treats I'd stored in my pockets, I nodded toward the house.

"Mr. Guerra tells me that Mr. Mickey has lunch waiting. Why don't you savages go get cleaned up, and after we eat, I might just have another surprise for each of you."

Their reaction was muffled by the noise discipline they'd learned, but no less joyful for it. As fifteen boys went running for the well and trough, Guerra chuckled softly.

"What?" I asked.

He shook his head. "When you first came to the Pack, I couldn't understand how someone who was so softhearted was going to make it through the trials. I'd seen Samson break candidates before—and you know what happens to shifters who can't handle the beast."

"Yeah. And?"

He met my gaze squarely, his piercing green eyes turning hazel around the edges. "What I didn't realize at the time was, it wasn't weakness I was seeing, but heart. What makes you good is also what makes you strong. Samson knew it all along."

I chewed my lip, nodding almost imperceptibly. He wasn't wrong.

"Look, you ain't fooling me. I know you got some plan to try to turn things around and save what's left of humanity." Guerra cradled his crossbow in the crook of his severed arm, so he could poke me in the chest with a single, calloused finger. "You care about people, druid—that's what makes you special. You want to save this world? Then hang onto that, and remember who the fuck you're fighting for."

CHAPTER
NINE

WE ATE outside on picnic tables and rough-cut benches Guerra, Anna, and Mickey had set up among the trees in the yard. Eating outdoors like this was risky, since food smells could travel quite a distance. Yet I didn't think any humans were dumb enough to venture this far into Austin, and Guerra said he'd killed all the revs and vamps in a five-mile radius of the castle house. Despite that, when no one was looking, I cast a cantrip to disperse and mask the scents.

Better safe than sorry.

As for the food, it was excellent. Guerra hadn't been kidding when he said Mickey could cook. Before we set up camp here, we'd always been on the run. That meant eating cold food from cans, and barely cooked fish and game when it was available. Thus, I never really got the chance to appreciate the guy's culinary talents.

After polishing off my third *picadillo* taco, I nodded my approval at the wiry, studious-looking middle-aged man across the table. "Damn, Mickey. If I had known you could cook like that, I might never have left."

He offered a wan smile in response, and that was all. It had been years for me since I'd left, but mere weeks for them. Brian's death was still fresh in everyone's' minds, and speaking of leaving was like pouring salt on new wounds.

I decided to change the subject. "By the way, where's Anna?"

Guerra winced, although he tried to hide it. Mickey merely stared at his hands. One of the boys, Thomas, sat nearby, and on hearing my question he spoke up.

"Dame Sweetlove? She's probably up in her room. That's where she stays, most days."

Raising an eyebrow, I looked at the two men seated across from me in turn. "Dame Sweetlove?"

Thomas was busy stuffing his face with the last of his taco, but he somehow managed to respond. "S'what she wants us to call her. Like, when we used to play knights and castles. You know, before."

"Ah," I said, nodding, although I wasn't entirely certain of the full implications.

"It looks like you're done," Mickey said to Thomas. "Why don't you go on and play with the other boys?"

Knowing what being dismissed by an adult meant, the kid lifted his plate to his mouth and bulldozed the remaining scraps of food into his pie hole. Then, he wiped his hands on his shirt and took off.

I glanced at Guerra. "You might teach them not to do that. The smell—"

Guerra waved his hands back and forth, interrupting me. "I know, but you gotta let them be kids sometimes."

Mickey still stared at his plate in silence. Based on how much he'd eaten—not much—and how he was avoiding eye contact, I figured he was pissed at me.

Can't say I blame him. Better rip this scab off now, before the wound festers.

"So," I said as I addressed him. "What's with this 'Dame Sweetlove' nonsense?"

The older man pushed a few scraps of food around on his plate as he replied. "It's what they used to call her, back when they held LARPing sessions." He shifted his gaze to the 'thrope who sat next to him, then back to his plate. "You want to show him, or should I?"

"Show me what?" I asked.

Guerra sighed, rubbing a hand over his face. Then, he stood. "C'mon, it's just inside the house."

Guerra had been busy in my absence. Most of the ground floor doors and all the windows had been bricked over. The werewolf had done the same with the windows on the second floor, but he'd left arrow slits in each of the upper story openings. Everything was buttoned up tight with masonry, except for the front entrance, which I'd personally shored up and warded using druid magic. I followed him to a ladder that leaned against the first-floor wall, leading up to a second-story balcony.

We entered the house through a bedroom which had been converted into a kill zone, featuring plywood-reinforced walls complete with even more arrow slots, and a sturdy metal door, of the kind you'd find in an industrial building.

"Love what you've done with the place," I remarked.

"You ain't seen nothing yet," he replied.

We walked through the metal door and into a hallway,

up some stairs into what used to be the grand entrance. There, ensconced in a glass display case that used to hold part of the previous owner's collection of medieval weaponry, was a pile of scraped, bleached human bones. They were neatly arranged on a kite shield, just behind a small wooden plaque.

-HERE LIES SIR BRIAN, WHO GAVE HIS LIFE VALIANTLY IN THE PROTECTION OF THE KINGDOM.-

It was then I realized the bones were child-sized. "Holy shit," I gasped.

"You said it," Guerra replied.

After I'd shed a few silent tears, we headed back outside to the picnic table. I sat in stunned silence, staring at my hands for several minutes. Meanwhile, Mickey and Guerra respected the mood by returning the favor. Finally, I glanced up, meeting Guerra's gaze.

"Did she—?"

"Yep," Mickey said, staring off into the distance. "I told her we could build a funeral pyre, but Anna insisted on taking care of it."

"Holy hell," I muttered. "That's—I mean, whoa."

"At least she did it away from the house," Guerra said.

"When I offered to help, Anna said she'd worked as a mortician's assistant for a time, and that she knew what she was about." Mickey spoke in hushed tones, obviously not wanting the children to hear. "When she said she wanted to give Brian a hero's burial, we simply assumed she wanted to put him in a coffin and mark the grave somehow. I had no idea she might do something so grisly."

I considered the situation for several moments, then I shook my head. "You know what? I don't think it's all that big a deal."

"Oh?" Mickey said, meeting my gaze for the first time, eyes narrowed and voice dripping with indignation. "How so?"

"For starters, that's how the church used to preserve the dead. Visit the catacombs under any cathedral in Europe, and you'll find hundreds, and in some cases, thousands of skeletons stored similarly. Just because we didn't do it here before the shit hit the fan, I don't think we should think poorly of how other cultures chose to honor their dead."

Guerra humphed. "Yeah, but boiling and scraping your little bro's bones…" He shivered. "That's cold, *hermano*."

"Better than taking the risk of having him come back as one of the undead," I said. I allowed my gaze to drift over to where the boys played a mostly silent game of tag in the grass. "How'd they take it?"

"They're kids," Mickey said. "Their minds are malleable, and easily adaptable to changing circumstances."

"They visit sometimes," Guerra added. "Some just stand there, others talk, a few cry. But I think it's helped them with the grieving process, you know?"

"And the whole 'Dame Sweetlove' thing?"

The two men shared a look, but Guerra spoke first. "It's a little kooky, honestly. She has them all using their make-believe names when she's around. 'Sir' this, and 'Squire' that."

"They even have a code they recite." Mickey chuckled softly. "And I'll be damned if they all don't honor it, every last one."

"So what you're saying is, this has been Anna's way of grieving Brian's loss." They nodded. "Or, maybe it's her way of preventing the loss of another child."

Mickey perked up at that. "Eh? How so?"

"Think about it. Kids might be adaptable, but tragedy and trauma still fuck them up."

"Don't I know it," Guerra muttered. "But that's what family is for, to help you through it."

"Exactly. Trauma affects people differently, depending on their support systems and how they frame it. For some, it screws them up for life—usually in situations where they don't have someone close to help them through it, to help give them perspective on the experience."

"Hang on," Mickey said. "You're saying it's a good thing that Anna ensconced her little brother's skeleton in a glass case for everyone to see, including all his school-aged childhood friends who survived him?"

"Look around you," I replied, gesturing expansively. "We're living in a zombie apocalypse. The bombs fell, the dead walk, and vampires stalk the night. I think we have to throw the old rules out, and find ways to deal with this new reality, the best way we know how."

Guerra sniffed and scratched his nose. "Can't say I disagree."

"Mickey?"

"I suppose. But do we really want these kids living in a fantasy world? Shouldn't they be taught to deal with the realities as they are?"

I pursed my lips, glancing at the boys and back again. "That sounds cruel to me. Maybe Anna is onto something here. What better way to teach a bunch of kids to survive in this hellhole, than to make it a game?"

"Sort of like the Jews did in the concentration camps during World War II," Mickey said. "Makes sense."

"It does," I replied. "At least this way, we can teach them the skills they need without making it too heavy for them. Instead, we frame things in a bit of make-believe to soften the roughest parts, keeping it just stark enough so they take it seriously." I glanced at Guerra. "What do you think?"

"It's not much different than how I was raised," he said.

"Oh?" Mickey cracked a slight grin as he continued. "Did you grow up in Western Europe during the Dark Ages?"

"During the Renaissance, actually," Guerra said, straight-faced. "And if you wanna be exact, it was central Iberia."

———

That night, we had unwelcome visitors.

I'd volunteered to take watch, to allow Guerra to get some much-needed rest. Sure, he was a 'thrope, which meant he could get by on very little sleep for weeks on end. But, even a werewolf has limits, and I could tell he'd been nearing his.

No way was I going to let him continue to take night-time guard duty while I was here. Despite that, Guerra had insisted on sleeping outside, saying something about me being a shit magnet, and muttering something else about all hell breaking loose now that I was back. As he slept on a cot nearby, I sat in the lotus position on the rooftop terrace, keeping watch over the surrounding woods using my druid senses.

As it turned out, the old wolf hadn't been wrong.

There were a couple of ways to monitor a large area using druid magic. The first was with the use of alarm wards and tripwire spells. That method was very effective, but unsubtle. Any supernatural creature with the ability to see magic might spot the enchantments, and find some way to circumvent them.

A more elegant solution was to drop into a druid trance, extending your awareness outward by connecting your mind to that of the surrounding wildlife. It took skill and practice to do it properly, as it was easy to lose yourself inside an animal's mind and impulses. You could also spook an animal by making your presence known to them, causing them to flee—which obviously defeated the purpose.

I had plenty of experience using the latter method, and I could cover a fairly large area easily by "skimming" the minds of multiple animals. Initially, it took a bit of time to find all the suitable species in the area—in this case, night-jars, owls, opossums, raccoons, bats, coyotes, and the like. After that, I had to acquaint myself with each animal's consciousness, one at a time.

But once I had a network set up, it was simply a matter of flitting from mind to mind. I observed what they observed and paid attention to anything they thought out of the ordinary. A mama opossum noticed the disturbance first, the odor alerting her and causing her to scurry up the nearest tall tree with a full clutch of babies on her back. Ordinarily, the smell of carrion would be irresistible to the nocturnal marsupial, but she was a survivor, and knew that this scent wasn't a sign of a meal, but of marching death.

Shit.

At first, I hoped it was merely a lone straggler, one that would be turned away by my wards. But as my consciousness drifted from the mama opossum to a bat swooping high overhead, I knew there'd be no such luck. Bats had shitty vision but great hearing. Based on the noise, the smell came from a sizable horde, one that was headed this way.

Must be a thousand deaders, maybe more. Shit, shit, shit.

There were many different kinds of wards. Some would cause a sentient being's attention to slip and skitter off whatever was protected, essentially making that thing invisible. Others would drive creatures away, often by instilling a gradually increasing sense of fear in trespassers, mounting into terror the closer they came. Still others might alert the caster to an interloper's presence, silently or otherwise.

Then there were ward barriers. That was what I'd cast all over the perimeter fence that stood around my junkyard —spells to keep out all manner of supes. Such enchantments were incredibly effective, yet they were only as good as the physical objects they were cast on. If the targeted physical barrier was solid, then the more you reinforced a ward over time, the stronger it became.

Unfortunately, I'd barely had time to enchant the perimeter wall that surrounded the castle house. Sure, the wall itself was a sturdy structure made from stone, brick, concrete, and wrought iron, so it took the ward spells well. But I'd not had the opportunity to reinforce it since my return, and I doubted it'd hold up to the concerted efforts of hundreds or perhaps thousands of undead trying to breach it.

Maybe they'll turn away. It's not like this neighborhood is easy to reach.

That was one reason why I'd chosen this location. The house sat atop a tall hill with steep sides, and it was tough to access on foot except by the street that led here. I'd blocked the lane off with vegetation and an earthen berm, so there was little chance a lone zombie would find its way here. Never mind the look away, go away wards I'd cast at key geographical points around the property, places where humans and undead alike would be most likely to wander.

Yet as I continued to monitor the situation, it became clear that this was no ordinary horde. Rather than moving with the typically random, chaotic advance I'd seen from other large groups of zeds in the past, this mob was marching with a clear purpose.

They're headed in a straight line—one that intersects with this property. Well, fuck.

That could only mean one thing—someone or something was driving the undead in our direction. Someone who knew our location, who also had the ability to control the undead. Either a higher vampire, or a necromancer. Whichever it was, it was bad.

I latched onto the mind of a screech owl and sent it soaring high above the trees, catching an updraft that allowed it to cruise above the desolate neighborhoods between us and the horde. As the owl flew closer to the mob, I began counting their numbers, and it was worse than I thought.

There were easily three thousand undead marching our way, enough to push right past my spells and tear down the walls protecting our home by sheer numbers alone. At my subtle mental suggestion, the owl swooped lower, following the leading edge of the horde and then banking around the backside.

It wasn't long before I spotted the cause of the undead stampede. Trailing the center of the mass of ghouls and zombies walked one of the largest deaders I'd ever seen, standing easily a full head taller than my buddy Hemi.

With his broad shoulders and long arms, I imagined the tall, pale zed had been an athlete in his former life.

The giant deader lumbered along with slow, unhurried strides, moving with the sort of balance and poise that only a ghoul under the direct control of a higher intelligence could manage. As for who or what controlled him, that was no mystery. On his shoulders perched a child-sized, ashen-skinned humanoid, one who looked almost tiny in comparison while being no less frightening because of it.

Fucking Richard.

———

When I'd first met the kid, he was just a malnourished, school-aged child with close-cropped, curly hair, ashy skin, soulful eyes, and a hollow, haunted expression. The poor child had reminded me of a lost kitten, just a little scrawny thing who begged to be rescued. And rescue him I did, much to my current regret.

Little did I know it at the time, but Richard was a fully enthralled servant of the undead—more commonly known as a Renfield.

It was rumored that master vamps could keep their human servants in thrall by allowing them to feed on their vyrus-tainted blood. In turn, the vyrus supposedly gave humans limited superhuman powers. Of course, once a Renfield got a taste of that good-good, they were hooked, forever enslaved to their wicked vampire master. Or so the stories went.

Whether that was true was anyone's guess, but it would account for some of the weird shit I'd seen a few Renfields do. Crawling up walls backward, tossing manhole covers like Frisbees, walking off gunshot wounds—shit like that. Either they were getting juiced on vampire blood, or they were possessed. If you asked me, it could go either way.

As for Richard, he was obviously fully undead now, beyond a shadow of a doubt. Yet, it was also clear that something had gone very wrong during his transition from human to vampire. Either his maker had botched it, or they'd altered the process somehow. I was just spitballing, but if I had to guess, I'd say they either accelerated it, or maybe they added something to it, possibly to provide him with powers no baby vampire should possess.

Like controlling thousands of undead, for instance. But sheesh —whatever they did, the kid looks like shit.

For starters, his face, chin, and chest were covered in fresh, bloody gore; apparently, Richard was not a neat and tidy diner. In addition, his skin had lost all trace of warmth and human color. Even worse, the kid's eyes were pitch black from eyelid to eyelid, and he moved with the sort of unnervingly twitchy mannerisms that only newly turned vamps and revenants displayed.

Watching him was like observing a tweaker who was really far gone—if you turned them up to 10x speed. Richard's head and arms would pop and jerk, almost blurring as he gesticulated in an odd, inhuman manner. Then his head would snap fully back, and his jaw would open unnaturally wide, displaying a mouthful of needle-like teeth as he screeched like a banshee at the midnight sky.

Jiminy fucking Christmas, what the hell did they do to him?

Whatever it was, one thing was certain: I didn't want that spooky little fucker anywhere near my people.

Snapping out of my trance, I tossed a pebble at Guerra's barely moving form. "Wake up, wolf. We got trouble."

Guerra's eye snapped open immediately, his green pupils turning a hazel, almost yellowish color that gathered and reflected the wan moonlight. The werewolf sat up, sniffing the air as he did so, and he grimaced in response.

"How many?"

"A few thousand, heading at us from the southeast," I said. "A lot more than my wards can turn."

Guerra strapped on his prosthetics as he spoke. "Coming at us from downwind. I take it that's not a coincidence?"

"Nope. From what I can tell, Richard is driving them."

Instead of grabbing his crossbow, he threw a baldric over his shoulder, from which he hung a cutlass and scabbard. "So, Dauphine did turn him. I guess that was his reward for infiltrating our camp?"

I considered his question for a moment before shaking my head. "Nah, she wouldn't have had time. Besides, there's no way some run-of-the-mill baby vamp could control that many undead. Naw, something else is at play here."

"We can figure that out after he's dead," Guerra hissed. "What's the plan?"

The house had a wine cellar—a fancy-ass basement, really—that I could easily seal with druid magic to keep the kids safe. But if something happened to me, it would end up being their tomb. I could always have the Oak portal them out if it came to that, but I really didn't want them to know I could perform magic.

Why? For starters, I was worried it would freak them out. From a psychological perspective, humans had a hard enough time dealing with the undead apocalypse, and the kids were no exception. The last thing they needed was to learn that magic existed, and that they were being protected by some sorcerous demi-immortal.

Besides that, I didn't want them to know. This was one of the few places I could just be Colin, instead of having to play the role of a druid master. Yeah, it was selfish, but I didn't want to lose that. Thus, I'd only portal them out of harm's way if there was no other choice.

I shifted my awareness back to the bats to get a read on the horde's position, then I locked eyes with Guerra. "Get everyone into the cellar, and have them lock it from the inside. Stay out here and listen for my signal. If I tell you to run, take them on foot away from the horde. I'll slow the fuckers down and catch up."

Guerra winced. "I don't think it's a good idea to abandon this place. What you've built here—it'll be hard to find somewhere else."

"Believe me, it'll be a last resort. Now, please, go and keep them safe."

"You got it, *ese*," Guerra said, then he was gone.

Fuck, he moves fast for a dude with one leg.

Three thousand undead were way more than I could quickly handle on my own. Given a few days, I could slay that many with Orna while in my full Fomorian form. Yet, based on my best guesstimate, I had maybe thirty minutes before they reached the edge of the neighborhood.

Not nearly enough time. Magic it is, then.

Taking off at a run, I leapt from the terrace, landing lightly in the courtyard as I sprinted toward the horde. Vaulting the wall at a run, I was soon moving at near vampire speed through the woods, roughly fifty miles per hour, even as I telepathically reached out to the Oak.

Guard the castle, was the message I sent. Specifically, I

instructed my Oak to remain hidden outside the perimeter wall, and to take out any undead that came near without revealing his presence.

Sure, it'd be easier to face a zombie horde with a pissed off minor nature deity at my side. Yet this whole thing had my spidey-sense tingling, and the last thing I wanted to do was to expose my druid oak at a time like this. That meant I'd be going it alone.

No problem, I assured myself as I raced through the oak and cedar trees toward thousands of undead creatures. *Easy-peasy.*

The good news was that the mob would have to cross the river to reach us, and that meant crossing the Penny-backer Bridge. I briefly considered taking the bridge out, but that would mean cutting the group off from the only nearby vehicle escape route to the south. Again, that was something I would only do as a last resort.

That said, the bridge was a hell of a place to make my stand, so I altered course slightly and headed for the north end of the structure. As for the bridge itself, it was a minor engineering marvel. The Pennybacker consisted of two rust-colored metal arches suspending a series of cables that supported a span of concrete and metal across Lake Austin, also known as the Colorado River, some 1,150 feet. Of course, it was jammed up with vehicles in both directions, a situation I'd contributed to not long after I brought the group to the castle house.

Picking my way through cars, trucks, and semis that sat overturned and askew across the length of the bridge, I traversed the length as quickly as possible. By the time I reached the far side, the cacophony of moans and groans made by the horde was clearly audible. They were no more than fifteen minutes from reaching me, which gave me little time to prepare.

Time to get to work.

Stripping out of all but a pair of lycra skivvies, I shifted into my full Fomorian form. Once I'd become a ten-foot-tall cross between the Hulk and Quasimodo, I drew Orna from my Craneskin Bag, laying it on the ground close by as I quickly devised a game plan for the task ahead.

Predictably, the sword immediately started chattering at me. "Oh, master—it is good to see you again in your full Fomorian glory."

For once, I was glad for the sword's company. Hearing it natter on would distract me while I worked. "Greetings, Orna."

The sword paused a beat before answering. "Is that a stampede of the undead I hear rumbling in the distance?"

"It is," I said as I stroked my chin with a thickly calloused, almost claw-like left hand. "We'll both earn our keep this night, I think."

"Oh, joy!" the sword exclaimed. "It has been ages since we took on overwhelming odds and slayed a horde together."

"Have we ever slain a horde?" I asked absently, nodding to myself as I decided on a course of action.

"Hmm, yes. I'm not certain. Perhaps it was with Tethra that I undertook such a task. I say, did I ever tell you about the time…?"

The sword was only marginally intelligent, and hard-wired by its enchantment to recount the deeds of its masters, both present and past, regardless of appropriateness of circumstance. In other words, it would chatter on and regale all and sundry about all the crazy shit that I and its former owner Tethra had done, at least until I told it to shut up. For once, I resisted the urge, instead choosing to let it talk while I worked.

With the sword rambling on in the background, I started pushing cars and trucks into place, end to end, across all four lanes. Then, I flipped them on their sides, effectively creating a low wall that would impede the leading edge of the mob from crossing.

Not good enough. That many undead will flip these cars in a heartbeat.

My time was precious, and slipping away by the second. Even so, I spent another five minutes pushing more vehicles up against the back side of my makeshift wall, piercing any intact rubber with Orna to make them harder to move. After I had buttressed the wall with cars and trucks three deep, I hastily cast a repulsion ward on the whole thing.

The ward wouldn't last long, but it might stop the leading edge of the advancing mob, giving me enough time to retreat further down the bridge's length. Speaking of which, said leading edge could now be seen trudging north on Loop 360 in my direction. Their passing churned up a righteous cloud of dust as the dead trampled the weeds and brush on both shoulders and the center divide of the highway.

With only a couple of minutes to spare before they were upon me, I sat heavily on the hood of a nearby Honda Accord, the greatsword laid across my knees. While the blade prattled on about how Tethra had once slain a huge pack of *cu sith* sent by Cernunnos to kill him over some slight, real or imagined, I quietly prepared a handful of druid battle spells. Once done, I waited to unleash hell upon Richard and the coming zombie horde.

CHAPTER
TEN

MY PLAN WAS simple and direct, with two objectives. First, to keep the horde from crossing the bridge. And second, to reach Richard and off the little fucker, just as quickly as possible. My rationale being that, once I accomplished the second objective, the horde could easily be led away by yours truly.

At least, I hoped that would be the case. Most of my experience with mobs this big was in avoiding them entirely. I sure as hell hadn't ever planned to take on a group of zombies this large in direct combat.

As for tactics, they'd also be fairly straightforward. Human teeth and nails were unable to pierce my skin in this form, but past experience taught me to avoid getting zed juice in my mouth, nose, or eyes. That's how I'd contracted the vyrus previously. While my Fomorian healing factor fought the modified Z-vyrus off, it had been a highly unpleasant experience.

For that reason, I'd be using spell work to decimate the central column of the horde, which should allow me to get closer to Richard, who rode herd behind them. The highway and shoulders were littered with vehicles, which I intended to use as stepping stones, leaping my way to the rear of the column. Orna would be sufficient to deal with any ghouls or revs that got close. And, if luck was with me, the mob would turn their attention on me, instead of crossing the bridge.

And if not? I'd have to retreat and make my stand. If it looked like I couldn't hold them off, I'd send a signal to Guerra and tell him to get the kids out of Dodge.

Let's hope it doesn't come to that.

The blacktop beneath my bare feet thrummed as they closed the distance, bringing me back to the present—and the oppressive stench of three thousand rotting corpses on the move. Now that they could see me, their moans and groans had gotten louder, sitting as I was out in the open. The horde had picked up speed, at least as much as they were able, with the leading edge now a mere 300 yards or so from the bridge.

I briefly worried that I was giving up my secrets to Ateas. This very moment, he might be looking at me through the eyes of one of the approaching undead. Then, I realized that the vamps already knew about my ability to shape-shift. And if they hadn't?

"No sense crying over spilled milk," I muttered as I stood with Orna in my left hand. "Now, time to make the doughnuts."

I took off at a run toward the leading edge of the horde, even as I let the Fomorian side of my brain take over. If I didn't, I might lose my nerve. Looking across that massive roiling sea of decaying limbs, rotting faces, and missing body parts, it'd be easy to get cold feet.

Thankfully, the Fomorian side of me didn't think about losing. To a Fomorian, losing in battle was never an option to be considered. Oh, we accepted the possibility of death as a hazard of combat, sure—but defeat was never a consideration.

The only thing a Fomorian thought of when approaching battle was how he or she might dismantle the enemy. And that was precisely what I focused on as I closed with the horde at over fifty miles per hour.

"MacCumhaill! MacCumhaill! MacCumhaill!" I shouted, the battle cry of my ancestors springing forth from my lips almost unbidden as I cut loose with the first of the spells I'd readied.

I was no more than one hundred feet from the leading edge of the seething mass when I loosed a fireball the size of a bowling ball at them. As it flew forth at twice my current speed, it grew, doubling and tripling its girth and then some, until the projectile was eight feet in diameter. I was fifty feet from the horde when it struck, exploding in a conflagration of burning gas and heat that incinerated the undead in a twenty-foot radius.

Beyond that, it cooked those that remained intact for another fifteen feet from the blast, knocking their charred and desiccated corpses to the ground. That left me a seventy-foot hole that brought me that much closer to my goal. Switching Orna to my right hand, I sped into the gap before other undead could flood into the void.

"Oh, how glorious, Master!" the sword cried. "Surely, this battle will rival the feats of Tethra. Master, did I ever tell you about the time…?"

Ignoring both the sword's droning and the crunch of blackened bones beneath my feet, I looked for an island in the sea of walking dead. *There.* Roughly fifty feet beyond the outer edge of the blast zone, a tractor-trailer laid on its side. Could I make it?

Only one way to find out.

I poured on speed, heading straight toward the jack-knifed trailer, even as the undead howled and lunged at me, filling in the space left by my spell much more quickly than I had expected. By the time I reached the approaching mass of deaders in front of me, the trailer was a good seventy feet away.

No way I'll make that. Gotta get closer.

Focusing my will and intent, I released the second spell I'd prepared—Mogh's Scythe. Instantly, a column of air several hundred meters high compressed itself in front of me, then it shot forward in a sheet roughly fifteen feet wide and as thin as a razor's edge. When it hit the horde, it bisected several dozen zombies and ghouls horizontally, cutting them off at the knees.

A swathe of undead fell to the ground before me, fifteen feet wide and twice as long, writhing and groaning where they lay. I'd briefly considered hitting them at neck level. However, that would leave too many unaffected, potentially forcing me to fight my way through a dozen or more in the spell's wake.

This was messier, but more efficient, and as I crushed them underfoot with my size twenty-fours, I gauged how far I needed to advance before I could reach the trailer.

Just a bit more...

I took a last, bounding stride, choosing the spot where my foot landed carefully, so as not to slip on zombie goo. As the pad of my forefoot hit a small patch of dry pavement, I bent my knee and pushed off hard, propelling my massive body in the air, even as a pair of ghouls leapt at me from the crowd.

One of the ghoul's hands barely brushed my toes as I sailed over their heads, heading in a high arc toward the overturned trailer. Now some twenty feet above the horde, I realized for the first time how daunting this task looked from this perspective.

In the distance, I spied Richard on the back of Stretch Goonstrong, with a good quarter mile of milling bodies between me and my goal. Vehicles dotted the landscape, but those that were tall enough to keep the undead off them were few and far between.

Completing my arc of travel, I landed on the tractor trailer's side as lightly as possible, causing it to crumple and nearly cave in due to my weight. That was another thing I hadn't considered, the physics of an 800-pound behemoth hurtling through the air and landing on vehicles that had been rusting and decaying in the hot Texas sun for a year. What if I crushed one completely, ending up in the center of the horde?

Shit! I'll never make it. Need a new plan.

Whether that was me or my Fomorian brain talking, I wasn't certain. What I did know was that leaping into that mass of bodies would be certain death. It'd be Bryan-College Station all over again, except this time I'd be stuck underneath a mountain of bodies a hundred times what I'd faced back there.

I caught my balance, moving to an uncompromised section of the trailer as I cut down a ghoul who'd managed to climb atop my temporary platform. Turning slowly in a complete circle, I took in the surrounding landscape, making note of every feature, as well as the enemy's position and general trajectory. When I'd almost completed my circuit, something above the river caught my eye.

There.

———

Why I hadn't thought of it before was clear, and that was because I hadn't been thinking like a Fomorian at the time. My human brain had devised this plan on the fly, deciding to engage an overwhelming force on unfamiliar terrain from a disadvantaged position. It had been foolish, brash, and typical of my former ways.

Now that my other side was crunching the numbers, it was easy to see what a mistake that had been. Yet, there was still time to correct it—I just needed to get free from the horde to do it.

Unfortunately, the undead already filled in the gap my spells had made, making the distance to freedom a good eighty feet. With the mob advancing, that span increased by the second. Jumping into their midst was flirting with death, even in this form, but it was either that, or allow them to cross the bridge and overrun the castle house.

Normally, that might be an option. Even if the house collapsed, which was doubtful, the children were safe downstairs in the cellar. After all, I could always dig them out—or if push came to shove, portal them out—after the mob passed.

Yet, there was also Richard to contend with, and I had no idea how powerful he'd become after being turned. Like most who existed outside the closed doors of the Vampire Nations, I knew little regarding how the process of birthing vampires worked. The Vampyri held such secrets close, and what little I'd gleaned came from my lessons with Finnegas, as well as bits and pieces I'd picked up from Luther over the years.

Based on what I'd gathered, the older the maker vampire was, the stronger the offspring. Any reasonably powerful vamp could repel undead from their territory. But generally speaking, only a master vampire—one that was several centuries old and born of a powerful bloodline—could control other undead. For a newly made leech like Richard to have the power to herd this many undead, he must've been turned by either Alalngar or Ateas.

Meaning, he was an unknown quantity, and one I couldn't risk leaving to chance. For all I knew, he might be able to rip through the wards I'd placed on the cellar doors, or perhaps even smash through the poured concrete floor above. That was obviously what he wanted, revenge for me slaying Dauphine. Just the thought of leaving those kids to their fates at the hands of that little sociopath... ugh, it was too much to even consider.

Obviously, leaving them there is too great a gamble. Gonna have to go for it.

Just as I was about to take a running leap, hoping I could fight my way through the last thirty feet of the mob, a cloud of dark mist began to coalesce in front of me.

Who the hell...? Is that Crowley?

But the way the darkness formed looked quite different from how the wizard's magic worked. This cloud was less substantial and tar-like than the stuff my shadow wizard frenemy created. I panicked for a second, thinking it was Dauphine come back to life—or worse, Alalngar.

Oh, I'd definitely welcome a rematch, especially in this form, but not in the midst of thousands of undead. Not wanting to take any chances, I crouched in a fighting stance with Orna held in a cross-body guard, ready to cut whatever appeared before me in two.

In the time I took to process the decision and prepare to strike, the shadowy mist took form. The black smoke coalesced into a tall, athletically slender black man, dressed in black combat fatigue pants, a lavender silk shirt, and shiny red, patent leather combat boots. The individual was familiar, yet different, with a nasty scar that ran vertically down his forehead, across one of his pale gray eyes, and onto his left cheekbone, marring his otherwise flawless chocolate skin. His eyes were haunted in a way they'd never been on the person I knew from my timeline, but I'd recognize the Austin coven leader anywhere.

"Luther?"

He pursed his lips in a slightly amused, but mostly distasteful, moue. "I take it you've decided this approach wasn't the wisest choice," he said in his usual effeminate, upper-crust Louisiana drawl. "Just so you know—that child-sized abomination is receiving outside help to control the horde."

"Ateas, I presume?"

"I see you've been acquainted. The best I can do is to clear a path out of here for you, but the rest will be up to you."

"Um—" I said, pausing momentarily. There were a million things I wanted to ask, but now wasn't the time. "Yeah, do it."

His brow creased, and his eyes narrowed, even as his skin turned slightly ashen. The vampire swayed a bit, as if he might swoon. Moments later, he righted himself, brushing his shirt off and glancing away as if nothing had happened.

"Done. If you survive this, I'll find you before morning."

Before I could say anything else, he disappeared in a swirling cloud of black mist that rapidly dissipated after him. As it did, my gaze was drawn beyond the fading mist toward the bridge, where the horde had parted like the Red Sea between the trailer I stood upon and open ground.

No need to tell me twice.

Without a second's hesitation, I headed for daylight and the space I needed to execute my Plan B. Needless to say, I hoped like hell it would work. If it didn't, that bridge might just end up being my Little Bighorn and Waterloo, all rolled into one.

I leapt off the trailer at a dead run, headed for the bridge. Thanks to Luther's intervention, clearing the mob was a cinch, although I noted that the zombie horde was quick to pour into the gap not long after I passed. Ignoring them for now, I slung my Craneskin Bag off my neck, clutching it in my left hand as I vaulted the makeshift wall of vehicles I'd made earlier.

My goal was not to reach the opposite side, but the spot at which the support arches intersected with the bridge's surface. There, I leapt over the side, barely breaking stride as I sprinted up the right side arch, only stopping when I'd reached the apex of the structure.

Time to roll the dice.

Even as I questioned my sanity, I laid down on the cold, hard, metal surface of the bridge arch, and I began to shift back to my half-Fomorian form. This first required me to change into my fully human form, which was risky considering that a rev or nos might be lurking close by. If they were on the horde side of the bridge, my wards would slow them down. If not, well—I'd be fucked if they caught me mid-shift.

My transition from Fomorian to human took roughly ten seconds, which may as well have been a lifetime considering the situation and what was at stake. When I finished, I started to sit up, just as something large, gray, and altogether inhuman swooped past, moving on a trajectory that told me it must've been lurking beneath the bridge.

Motherfucking nosferatu—an old one. Well, piss.

I laid flat again as it banked above me, gliding on chiropteran wings easily fifteen feet from tip to tip. There I was, nearly naked and clutching a sword I could barely lift in this form, atop a three-foot wide steel girder some 250 feet above the water, and 130 feet or so above the concrete span below.

Ten yards above me, the primitive vampire hovered by flapping those massive wings, *whoosh… whoosh… whoosh*, moving enough air to bathe me in a malodorous wash that smelled of graveyard dirt, desiccated flesh, and congealed human blood.

Whelp, nobody said saving the world would be easy—not even my little corner of it.

Meeting the vamp's red-eyed gaze turned out to be a mistake, as it shrieked and beat its wings harder, gaining altitude in apparent preparation to dive and attack. Whether it had seen my actions as a challenge, or as a sign of fear, I couldn't say. All I knew was that I'd triggered its prey drive, and now it was time to shit or get off the pot; or the bridge, as it were.

There was no way I was jumping 250 feet into the river below, not in this form, no sir, no how, no thank you. At a minimum, I'd break my legs on impact, possibly my pelvis, most certainly my spine, and chances were good I'd start to drown before I could shift back into my full Fomorian form and heal myself. That was if the nos didn't catch up with me on the way down, piercing my torso with its clawed, almost raptor-like feet, at which point I'd be caught in an airborne battle with no wings.

No fucking bueno.

Thus, I took the alternate course, dropping Orna on the bridge and reaching into my Bag for the first thing my hand touched. I came up with my Glock, which was loaded with a full mag of silver-tipped rounds, holstered as always with one in the chamber. As the nosferatu reached the apex of its climb, swooping down at me with supernatural speed, I recalled the words of the immortal Wyatt Earp.

The veteran gunfighter once famously said, "Fast is fine, but accuracy is final. You must learn to be slow in a hurry." Meaning, shot placement is everything in a gunfight, and those who rush the shot often hurry to the morgue.

I'd been in the habit of carrying a nine-millimeter pistol since my early days as a hunter. Yes, I understood that a slow, heavy bullet would do more damage than a lighter, slightly faster-moving one. Yet, I preferred more rounds over more damaging rounds. I also trusted modern loads and the specialty rounds I carried to do the heavy lifting in taking down my targets.

Nine mike-mike would do the trick, but Earp's advice was critical when you were dealing with a creature whose ancient skin might turn normal bullets. When it came to gunfighting advice, trusting a dude with epic facial hair was almost a mandate, so I took my time, drawing a bead on the nosferatu's mouth full of needle-sharp teeth as it descended toward me.

The first round I squeezed off took it in the cheek, where it expanded to form a perfect mushroom that remained embedded and smoking in the old vamp's gray, leathery skin. Round number two missed completely as the nos reacted to the first round, shaking its head and screaming bloody murder. Round three, however, found the mark, slipping right between that shitstain's chompers, hitting it in the soft palate at the back of the throat and punching a neat hole through its brainstem.

I don't care how old and powerful a leech you are, taking a round to the medulla oblongata is going to fuck up your night. Black blood and gray matter shot out the back of the thing's neck as the lights went out in its eyes mid-flight. The nos went limp, going into an awkward, counter-clockwise spin that took it slightly to my right.

As it passed, I was forced to roll to my left to avoid being clipped by its mostly hollow-boned but still formidably tough wing, which struck the bridge's arch with a resounding, solid *tong!* Much to my detriment, that evasive move took me over the other side of the span. I only barely managed to hang onto the edge as I tumbled over, still clutching the gun in my right hand and the Bag in my left.

To my amazement, rather than causing my fingers to slip off the edge of the metal girder, the Craneskin Bag snagged on a rivet. That provided me just enough friction to hang on for dear life. Realizing when luck was throwing me a bone, I discarded the pistol, allowing it to clatter to the pavement below.

With a groan that would've made any zombie or middle-aged dad proud, I reached up with my other hand and pulled my pale, skinny ass back to relative safety. Arms shaking and chest heaving, I collapsed on the hard, cold surface of the arch.

Man, being human sucks.

CHAPTER
ELEVEN

I RESTED ON THE COOL, rough surface of the bridge's support structure, breathing heavily as I gazed at the stars above. Far below, the undead were already straining against the wall and wards I'd hastily erected earlier. While I'd rather have remained there until my human body fully recovered, the sounds of breaking glass and metal screeching across pavement reminded me my task was not yet done.

Wards must've failed. Whelp, no rest for the weary when there's a job to do.

I shifted into my half-Fomorian form as quickly as I'd ever managed the process, then I reached back into my Bag for the object of my current passion. That passion being, to do to Richard what I'd just done to the nosferatu, only on a much more impressive scale.

Yes, I felt bad about having to off a child, undead abomination or no. But only in the way I felt every time I crushed the skull or severed the spine of a child-sized zombie. Such acts always made me regret that another kid had been turned and robbed of their childhood, of all the years and opportunities and potential that had once lain before them.

But killing them was necessary. Better that than to risk the chance that some small part of those victims remained trapped inside whatever was left of their minds. I couldn't begin to imagine the suffering that might cause, wandering the Earth for decades without any hope of release or escape.

No, killing them was a mercy—albeit one I didn't relish.

Besides that, I'd had it with this zombie horde and the reason it was here, threatening my territory and loved ones. I didn't know what had broken Richard inside, to cause a child to want to serve a murdering, bloodthirsty vampire, sacrificing and betraying good people who'd saved him and taken him into their safe haven.

And honestly, I was beyond caring at this point. Because fuck that little sociopathic bastard. He wasn't human anymore, and he had it coming.

There was no telling how many humans a single, deranged vampire could kill over the course of its lifetime. Call it thousands of lives, just to be safe, and weigh that against the morality of killing an undead creature that used to be a child. The math left no room for questioning my decision; there was only the matter of handling it, as quickly and efficiently as possible.

One of the first things I'd done when Gwydion stranded me in this timeline was to acquire as much ordinance as possible. Honestly, it was pretty easy to do in the early days of the Hellpocalypse, what with police and military outposts being overrun right and left. For the most part, the undead have no use for weaponry of any kind, leaving such items behind after feeding or being turned.

It only took a few side quests to decimated checkpoints

for me to amass a considerable arsenal of firearms, ammunition, and other ordinance. Sure, I rolled snake eyes a couple of times, getting to locations and finding them stripped clean. But in the first days of the undead apocalypse, things were moving fast, and zombies were rolling over our defense forces like a tsunami. By the third week here, I'd filled my Craneskin Bag with everything I might need to fight a small war.

Not that firearms were the best solution, mind you. They were noisy, a pain in the ass to keep clean in suboptimal environments, and they tended to fail at the worst possible times. Yet, with the right accessories and a little druid magic, I could take out zeds at a distance with relatively little exposure, making it easier to secure food and shelter as I scrambled to keep almost twenty people alive.

Among the firearms I'd liberated from the battlefield, the most useful were small arms that could fire subsonic ammunition and be fitted with suppressors. There was the .45 submachine gun I'd snatched off a dead homeowner who bugged in when he should've bugged out—fantastic at close quarters—and an M4 rifle chambered in .300 Blackout, an excellent rifle for engaging targets at midrange distances.

Yet when I really needed to reach out and touch someone, or rather, some*thing*, I went for the granddaddy of all anti-materiel rifles, the big Barrett .50 caliber sniper rifle. Chambered to fire .50 BMG, which contrary to popular opinion stood for "Browning Machine Gun" and not "big motherfucking gun," it fired a half-inch diameter, 750-ish grain round at roughly 3,000 feet per second.

In short, the Barrett would straight up tear a nosferatu or revenant in two at ranges of up to two miles. Granted, I was not some spec ops trained elite sniper who was capable of pushing the platform to such limits. But out to 1,000 yards, it was my preferred way to do business.

I'd since lost the original rifle I acquired on my first trip here, but I made it a point to replace it with an upgraded version before coming back. The rifle I pulled from my Bag was the latest model I could get my hands on, the M107A1. Back home, I'd hired an extreme long-range sniper rifle competitor to help me set it up with a Schmidt & Bender 5-45x scope, a non-scope killing muzzle brake, and custom match-grade loads that would "cut a full-grown wild boar in two."

My request, not his words, mind you. It'd cost a pretty penny, and hopefully, it'd prove to be a wise investment tonight. As I set it up on the integrated tripod, I reminded myself that by taking one undead life, I'd be saving countless others.

Obviously, there was no room for error, so I'd be using magic to help me seal the deal. As I scanned the field of battle, I cast a cantrip to enhance my already superhumanly sharp Fomorian eyesight to tengu-like levels. Soon I spotted the odd little leech, still riding on the back of the giant zombie at the rear of the horde.

There you are, you little shit. Boy-fucking-howdy, let's get this show on the road.

While sighting him through the scope, I cast another cantrip, one I'd created specifically for engaging targets at long range. The spell used physics and druid magic to determine distance, heat, humidity, barometric pressure, wind speed, and direction, calculating against bullet weight, velocity, drop, and dope to tell me how to set the elevation and windage on the scope.

It was easier than using modern electronics, and more

reliable by far. Plus, the spell displayed the results inside the scope, overlaid directly on the sight picture, so I didn't have to take my eyes off the target to make adjustments. Or, for that matter, give away my position at night.

In truth, between the magic and my Fomorian sight, I could've used open sights, even from this distance. But the scope combined with the spell made it dead simple to hit targets at long ranges, and in situations like this I did not want to risk a miss. If I spooked him, he might disappear into the night, leaving the horde with instructions to continue on to the target.

No way am I risking that.

Seconds later, all adjustments had been made, and it was time to take the shot. I clicked the safety selector to "fire," settling into my final shooting position as I centered the reticle on Richard's chest. A headshot wouldn't be necessary, as the round would likely cut him in two, destroying his heart and killing him instantly.

As I prepared to squeeze the trigger, I couldn't help but observe the monster I was about to put down. Out of respect, I took a moment to look at him, to really see him, and to commit to memory what those fuckers had done to that poor kid. I took it all in; his sallow skin, ashy complexion, lamprey-like dentition, anthracite eyes, and bizarre, twitchy mannerisms.

I reminded myself that he'd once been a child, a human being. And, I recalled how I'd felt when I rescued him from that church over on Bee Caves Road, not far from here. Call it self-flagellation, but I forced myself to remember how sad and helpless he'd looked, and how he'd briefly seemed genuinely relieved, even happy to have been saved from Dauphine's cult and back among his own kind.

Then I tried to imagine what his life must've been like before the Hellpocalypse. What were his parents like? Did he have siblings? Had he enjoyed attending school, had hobbies, played sports or video games?

Was there a time before the leeches had taken him when he'd been just a normal, innocent, carefree ten-year-old, one with his whole life still ahead of him? Of course there was, and of course, he'd been that child, once. But that was before the Vampyri conspired with the Fae to destroy this world and plunge it into this present chaos of death, un-death, and destruction.

My eyes welled up with tears, but I forced myself to keep them open, to maintain the sight picture as I processed the true weight and burden of what I was about to do. This thing I was about to kill wasn't just a monster, it wasn't only an undead abomination created by Ateas or Alalngar or Dauphine to destroy that which I held dear. It had once been a child, a being as close to pure and innocent as anything left on this accursed Earth since the two supernatural races chose to plunge it into darkness.

Richard snapped his head back, arching his neck at an unnaturally acute angle. He screeched at the night sky, releasing a cry that was both frightening and horrible. I realized then he wasn't screaming in anger, or hunger, or frustration, but in horror.

At that moment, I was fairly certain some small part of the kid remained, enough to recognize what had been done to him, enough to feel terror at being turned into a twisted servant of the Vampyri Council. It was all I could do to say a silent prayer while keeping the reticle centered on his chest.

Lord have mercy.

I squeezed the trigger, not even registering the recoil or the report of the round as it left the muzzle of the barrel. The bullet hit low, taking the top of the giant's head off as it tore through Richard's chest, obliterating the boy's torso through massive and instantaneous hydraulic displacement. His head, shoulders, and arms fell in one direction, while his lower half remained atop the giant zombie as it toppled to the pavement.

It might've been my imagination, but in the instant after the round ripped through him, I could've sworn that his tortured facial features relaxed into an expression of relief.

Maybe I was fooling myself, my mind playing tricks on me for the sake of alleviating some of the guilt I felt. Deep down, I knew I'd just granted Richard the eternal rest he so richly and humanly deserved. Yet, it damned sure didn't feel like I'd done the right thing.

Rest in peace, kid. And if you're watching or listening from the other side, please try to find it within yourself to forgive me.

———

Slowly, almost reverently, I drew my gaze away from the eyepiece of the scope, and I laid the rifle to rest on the bridge. Down below, the dead seemed to have lost the singular sense of purpose they'd had just moments before. However, they were still moving in a general northerly direction, and by sheer weight of numbers they threatened to smash through the barrier I'd placed earlier to prevent them from crossing the river.

To be honest, I wanted to lay my head on the cold, rusted surface of the bridge and cry my eyes out for a few hours. Not for me, but for what had just been truly and finally lost, forever. Richard deserved that much, at least.

But someone had to disperse the horde and lead them away from the castle house. Obviously, that someone was me. It'd be safer to do it in my full Fomorian form, but I didn't have the energy or mental willpower at the moment to shift again.

I decided to stay in my current form, which was risky but more likely to attract the attention of the mob below. After putting the rifle away in my Bag, I quickly got dressed, which was harder than one might think while standing on a metal beam hundreds of feet above a river.

Once done, I set about the task of leading the horde away. There was just one thing I needed to do first.

I sat and dropped into a druid trance again, extending my awareness outward until I located the screech owl I'd commune with earlier. Making the connection a second time was easier than the first, and soon we were circling above the spot where Richard's remains were located.

Honestly, I'd never done druidry at a distance by proxy before, at least, not on this level. Yet, Richard deserved better than having his remains trampled into the ground by a few thousand undead. For that reason, I figured it was worth a shot.

If Ateas can do it, why can't I?

At first, I tried channeling my magic through the owl, which proved to be impossible. Animals weren't meant to perform magic, and the bird's body and nervous system lacked the ability to direct my energy and intent. Once that effort failed, I did the next best thing, which was casting magic from the bridge while guiding my spells through the eyes of the owl.

That approach worked surprisingly well, although I found my powers diminished due to working at a distance. It took all of thirty seconds to use druidry to part the cracked concrete and bury Richard's body several feet beneath the soil. Once he'd been safely ensconced under the highway, I replaced the pieces of roadway, taking care to mark the spot for future reference.

When I'd finished that task, I released the owl again, then I took my time in raising a tall dirt berm in front of the bridge. That had the dual effect of displacing the front of the zombie horde, and also making it that much harder for them to break down my ward wall. Once that was done, I cast a chameleon spell on myself. With my Craneskin Bag slung over my shoulder, I sprinted down the archway toward the zombie horde.

Standing on the berm to avoid the nearest undead, I extended the righthand side of the earthen structure a few hundred feet along the edge of the cliff that overlooked the river. That allowed me to run past the outside edge of the horde, escaping all but the odd straggler, which I could easily avoid as I worked my way around the mob.

After I'd made it to the southernmost side of them, it was merely a matter of dropping the chameleon spell, making enough noise to get their attention, and then leading them in the opposite direction from my people. A few flash-bang cantrips later, and I had three thousand deaders following me at a slow jog down the Capital of Texas Highway toward south Austin.

It was only after I was certain I had the entire mob moving south that I began to pull away. Zombie hordes tended to operate as if in accordance with Newton's First Law. Once you had them moving in a direction, they'd keep moving that way until the terrain prevented it, or something warm and living caught their attention. It was my hope they'd head south and keep going, and that I wasn't putting any survivors out there at risk.

We'd need to monitor them until they either dispersed or moved out of the area, but for now, the compound and my people were safe. Once I'd drawn the horde off a few miles, I lost them by sprinting over a rise. As soon as I was out of sight, I connected with my Oak, calling off the general alarm and asking it to portal me within a few blocks of the castle house.

As I walked the final distance home, I reflected on what had just transpired. Knowing I'd done the right thing gave me little comfort. It wouldn't bring Richard back, and it wouldn't stop the Vampyri from doing the same thing to some other kid, either.

As I walked, a growing sense of unease swept over me. Druid magic was an odd thing, as the longer I practiced it, the more in tune I became with nature. It was as if my surroundings served as a sort of sixth sense, even when I wasn't paying attention—and right now, they were screaming at me to take notice.

Sensing I wasn't alone, I stopped in the middle of the street, reaching into my Bag for Dyrnwyn's hilt.

"We had rules against such atrocities, once," Luther softly said in his oddly feminine yet baritone voice.

I followed the sound to the speaker, locating him just as he emerged from behind a tree trunk some twenty-five feet ahead. "Turning children into vampires, you mean? Or plunging the world into an undead apocalypse?"

"Touché. Although I can assure you, I did everything in

my power to prevent the latter. And, I had nothing to do with the former, either."

I'd responded with a bit more venom in my voice than intended, so I modulated my tone appropriately as I continued. "You don't have to tell me that. I'm just upset, for obvious reasons. For the record, it is good to see you, despite the circumstances."

"The same, obviously." He paused to make a show of surveying the area. "Are you headed somewhere in particular?"

As he was looking around, I noticed that his nose twitched, ever so slightly. Whether it was an involuntary human affectation that was the result of centuries of feigning life, or a reaction to something he detected on the breeze, I couldn't say.

What I did know was that humans were food to vampires, and they'd become scarcer than mice at a cat convention since the bombs fell. I might've once been friends with the former Austin Coven master, but I honestly didn't want him within ten miles of the children who currently cowered in the basement of a house just a half-mile up the street.

The realization fairly stunned me, as Luther had been the only vampire I trusted, back in my primary timeline. Yet this version of him was an unknown quantity. I had no idea what his maker had done to him in that dungeon in Dallas, or what had happened to him since I released him from his prison. Until I did, I thought it unwise to bring him to my base of operations.

Forcing a smile I didn't necessarily feel, I glanced at the eastern sky and back to Luther again. "The sun'll be coming up soon. What say we find someplace where you can hole up for the day, then we can catch up on what each of us has been up to since Dallas?"

———

Roughly an hour before sun-up, we ended up at some millionaire's bachelor pad, a modern five-bedroom home cantilevered off a cliff overlooking the Colorado River. It was one of those concrete, glass, and steel monstrosities, located on a property that had nothing going for it but the view and the zip code.

The whole thing was built on round metal pillars that had been bolted to the cliff. The house had once been connected to the driveway and promenade by a catwalk, but someone had detached the footbridge, allowing it to crash to the rocks below. This meant it was safe from zombies, but also impossible to leave without climbing gear —unless you were making it a one-way trip.

I was looking over the deck's banister at what I presumed to be the former owner. He was little more than bones in board shorts and a Hawaiian shirt, dashed against a boulder more than a hundred feet down. A makeshift rope made from bedsheets was tied to the railing, the other end swinging in the breeze roughly half the distance to firma terra below.

"Poor bastard," I said, shaking my head.

"Thankfully, he did it before he managed to drink all his good liquor. Here." Luther handed me a beverage in a fancy, oversized martini glass. The contents were red, white, and blue, and it was garnished with something white and crystalline around the rim. "I apologize for the lack of ice, but at least he had a properly stocked bar."

"What is it?"

"Very likely the last bit of civilization you'll experience for a while. Enjoy."

With a noncommittal shrug, I took a sip. It was cloyingly sweet, slightly tart, and at least 100 proof. "That's… surprisingly good." I glanced over the side again. "What do you think happened?"

"My guess is that he climbed down and couldn't make it back up. It's likely he waited until he'd run out of food, and was too weak to escape."

"Yeah, but why would you climb down when you knew the rope only reached halfway?"

Luther chuffed. "Delusion? Desperation? Stupidity?"

"Hmph. Probably all of the above. It's astonishing how ill-prepared the majority of the population was for an event like this."

"Indeed, something the Vampyri didn't prepare for, either. They assumed a far greater portion of the human population would survive the fall of modern civilization."

"And now?"

He flashed a rueful smile. "Now, there is dissension among the rank and file. Younger vampires have been left to fend for themselves. Only those privileged by age and power are allowed to live within the Vampyri Enclaves in cities like Dallas, Chicago, Los Angeles, and New York."

"Where humans are treated like cattle, and vampires live like royalty." I gave a nod to his boots. "Speaking of which, love the outfit, king."

He scowled. "You try being a gay black man in an apocalypse, and we'll see how well you dress."

I chuckled softly, sipping my drink and enjoying the view. For a moment, I pretended to be back home, hanging out on Luther's rooftop deck while attending one of his exclusive vampire soirées. The effect only lasted until the screech of a revenant in the valley below shattered the illusion. Survivor's tension began to creep back into my body, a reaction ingrained by months spent running from the dead and keeping sixteen kids alive in the early days of the Hellpocalypse.

Fifteen kids, now.

"Why'd you track me down, Luther?"

"For one, I owe you. Had you not rescued me in that mad assault on the Dallas Vampyri headquarters, I might've rotted in that cell for centuries."

"It was ill-advised, but worth it. And had Crowley not rescued me, I might've taken your place."

The master vampire nodded slowly. "That was the other reason I decided to locate you, to apologize. I am sorry for leaving you to fight Alalngar alone."

Tossing my drink back, I set the glass lightly on the banister. "What's done is done. And while I nearly died springing you from Garr's dungeons, it's not like it was the first time I risked life and limb to rescue a friend."

"Again, th—"

I held up a hand. "You can thank me by answering a few questions. First off, what've you been doing since Dallas?"

The corner of his mouth twitched, ever so slightly. "Rebuilding my coven, for one. Not by making new vampires, mind you, but gathering those whose attitudes... er, *differ*, from that of the current ruling class. And, planning my revenge."

"Well, what do you know? It looks like our goals align."

"Oh? How so?"

"If you haven't figured it out, I intend to take your people down. If I have my way, the Vampyri will be back to sleeping in graveyards and hanging upside down in caverns, hiding out in fear of a visit from the local village mob."

"You understand that I cannot assist you in this, yes? Despite my hatred for Garr, the moment I come within the reach of his influence, I'd be his puppet once more. Beyond answering your questions, the best thing I can do for you is to stay far away from my maker."

"He might be dead."

Luther shook his head. "He isn't. I'd know it if he was, believe me."

"Well, shit. I'm still going after them. The Council, I mean."

"That would be pure suicide," Luther spat. He glanced down at his beverage, which he'd hardly touched. "And thus we come to the third reason I found you, to talk you out of this madness."

"Oh?" I said, crossing my arms over my chest. "Do fucking tell."

"Can't you see what's right before your eyes? Your kind lost, Colin. They are short-lived, ephemeral sheep who couldn't even plan a decade into the future, and that proved to be their downfall. While your people were posting selfies and watching streaming videos, we were putting a plan into motion that had been centuries in the making."

"We?"

"Pfah, you know what I mean. It's not like I had anything to do with it. I wasn't on the Council, and I fell out of my maker's favor a long time ago."

"Yet you had to have known something was going on," I said, scratching my nose with a knuckle. "To put so many important people in thrall, and to modify the vyrus, then unleash it on humanity—I can't imagine the Council could do such a thing without the complicity of coven leaders in every major city."

"Colin…" Luther said in an admonishing tone.

"Tell me I'm wrong."

He averted his gaze, staring off into the distance. "You're not wrong. But someone had to be on the inside, trying to get them to see reason."

I slammed my fist on the metal banister, denting it deeply. "You could've warned someone, Luther! Maeve, Samson, the Circle. Hell, you could've warned me!"

His voice was a whisper as he replied. "Indeed, I could not. You forget, druid, not all of us are born free. My second birth came with certain conditions, not the least of which was inviolable fealty to my master."

"You were under a compulsion not to speak?"

"Of course, we all were. The bond between maker and get is stronger than a geas, more powerful than a glamour, and crueler by far than slavery. No matter how much I wanted to tell you, to warn you of what was coming, I simply could not."

"Then how did you—?" I had to stop myself before I gave away the fact that I was not, in fact, the Colin that this Luther knew.

In my timeline, Luther had helped me stop part of the plot to cause the undead apocalypse. There, things had gone much, much differently. Yet, it would be difficult to say which of a trillion different events were altered in my timeline to allow Luther the freedom to act on my behalf.

Perhaps Alalngar had been killed in my timeline, or Luther had found a way to free himself from his maker's grasp. Or, had he been under orders to help me? Truly, it was impossible to know. What I did know was that, once I returned home, I'd be hunting down elements of the Vampyri Council and convincing them it was a terrible idea to cross me.

First things first, though.

Luther cleared his throat softly. "You were saying?"

I waved his question off. "Doesn't matter. What does matter is that I'm going after Ateas, and I need to know how to stop him."

Luther hissed. "Like I said, that's suicide. As one of the oldest of our kind, he's practically a god—more than a god, really. And then there's the fact that he's spent millennia studying the dark arts."

"Man, where's Snape when you need him?" I muttered.

"Huh?"

"What? Nothing." I hesitated to ask the next question, wondering if I'd get a straight answer. "Is Ateas really Patient Zero for the new vyrus?"

"Yes, as far as anyone knows. He's had his hands in biotech since the inception of the industry, and before that, necromancy." Luther's cheek twitched slightly with just the smallest facial tic, an aberration that was there and gone instantly. "I can tell you no more than that."

"Can't, or won't? Anyway, you were telling me how I was committing suicide, blah, blah, blah."

The vampire stamped a red, patent leather boot on the deck. "You are as pigheaded and infuriatingly stubborn as ever."

"Now you're just being redundant."

Luther snarled, his face transforming for an instant into something feral, a side I'd only seen once before—back when he was incarcerated in Garr's dungeon. "Do not try my patience, you foolish boy. I am trying to save you."

I rubbed a hand down my face and sighed. "Alright, Gandalf, I'm listening. Tell me why I shouldn't go after Ateas."

"Didn't I just tell you?" He counted off on his fingers as he continued. "Ancient. God-like. Dark magic."

"Hmm, yes." I sucked air as I frowned lopsidedly. "But he has to have a weakness."

"Colin, Ateas possesses powers that set him apart, even from our own kind. He doesn't even feed like a normal vampire anymore."

I arched an eyebrow. "Oh, really? And just how does ol' Ateas the vampire god sate his cravings, hmm?"

"He feeds on other vampires. It's something to do with the necromancy that sustains him. Now, he can only survive on the blood of our own kind."

"That's my in," I replied, snapping my fingers. "All I have to do is find a way to exploit it."

"By the blood of Sekhmet, you are mad."

"Yep, and the supernatural world made me this way," I replied with a sardonic smile. "You say you owe me, and that you're trying to save my life? Then tell me everything you know about Ateas—every last detail."

CHAPTER
TWELVE

HOURS LATER, I left Luther in the mansion's wine cellar, reflecting that it was a sure bet plenty of vampires were sleeping in wine cellars these days… and closets, and attics, and basements. If I had my way, a mass eviction was coming soon.

The primary obstacle was Ateas. Luther and I had a long talk in which I'd gleaned everything that he knew about the vampire behind the Hellpocalypse. The picture Luther painted was not a rosy one, that was for damned sure.

One would think that "The Deadlands" would consist of a gloomy expanse of forest, complete with gnarled, twisted trees, dank caverns, and death-loop trails that all inevitably led to Ateas' lair. But according to the former Austin vampire coven master, one would be dead wrong in thinking that, no pun intended.

In fact, Ateas's home turf was in an area formerly known as The Woodlands, on the outskirts of northern Houston. In my timeline, Houston was a virtual no-creature's-land in the World Beneath, a place where no 'thrope pack, coven, fae court, or any other group of supes could set up shop.

And why was that? Because something had claimed Houston as its territory, something old, powerful, and ruthless. Whatever or whoever tried to encroach on that thing's territory got wrecked. Sometimes they disappeared, other times a mangled corpse would show up on the nearest responsible faction's doorstep.

Fallyn once told me that every so often a lone wolf's remains would mysteriously appear on the Clubhouse steps. Nobody ever questioned it. The presumption was that they'd ventured too far into Houston city limits, and paid the price. The Pack incinerated the bodies, spread the ashes at their hunting grounds, and no one spoke of it after.

It's no secret that werewolves heal pretty damned quickly. I'd personally seen them come back from injuries that would easily end the average vamp or fae. Wrecking a 'thrope so bad they didn't heal was no mean feat. Whatever was doing it must be something far worse than a master vampire, werewolf alpha, or fae queen.

Yet there Ateas was, living right on the border of that thing's territory. That told me the lich was at least its equal in power, which had to be saying something. And I had to go up against him.

Based on what I'd seen of ancient vampires, combined with what Luther had told me, fighting Ateas head on would be my very last mistake. Imagine a creature that was as strong as your average god or goddess, craftier than a fae, faster than any vampire, and as resilient as a werewolf alpha, with skin like granite to boot. Now, make that thing a master necromancer with legions of undead at his disposal, and you had Ateas.

Moreover, he guarded his territory carefully, even meticulously, and for good reason. That was where the vamps conducted their most sinister work, among which was the task of solving their food shortage... or so Luther had suggested. When I'd asked for clarification on that detail, he'd merely shaken his head and changed the subject.

After I pressed him on the matter for the third time, only to have him ignore me and turn the conversation elsewhere, I realized he couldn't speak of it. Like the plan to plunge the world into an undead apocalypse, Luther was under a compulsion to stay close-lipped about what Ateas was currently working on in the Deadlands. Thus, it had to be something abominable that had horrible implications for the future of mankind.

Unquestionably, I had to penetrate the ancient vampire's territory. Not just to acquire a sample of the lich's blood for our anti-vyrus. I needed to find out what the hell was going on in the Deadlands.

Challenge number one would be sneaking in. Challenge number two was dealing with Ateas.

If it came down to it, how would I even fight something like that?

The answer was somewhere between praying and portalling away. I had Alalngar's number now, sure, but I'd only defeated him with Crowley's death magic on my side. Without that edge, Garr would likely have beaten me bloody a second time, without breaking a sweat.

Yet Crowley readily admitted that his magic paled in comparison to that of the ancient vampire. Absent a necromancer's ability to lock the lich down, it was hard to imagine my chances against Ateas, mostly because those chances were non-existent.

Thing was, I didn't need to kill Ateas. Hell, I didn't even need to beat him. All I really needed was a sample of his blood.

As I headed back to check on the kids before returning to Crowley's hideout, I decided to stay focused on that singular goal. Needing time to think, I'd intended to have a nice, leisurely stroll back to the compound. By the time I hit the Pennybacker Bridge, that plan was interrupted when my sensitive hearing picked up the distant sound of a child sobbing.

Ah, shit.

I reached out to the Oak for teleportation, just as near as it could get me to the perimeter without being seen. It sent back a string of images, including one of a robin's nest full of baby chicks, screeching to be fed but safe and sound.

You're telling me they're safe?

It sent back the same image, the closest thing to a "yes" I'd get from it.

Wait a minute—are you still there?

The Oak responded by showing me a current image of the compound. Contrary to my instructions, apparently it had stuck around after I called it off. That wasn't too surprising, as the Oak and Grove were not my slaves, despite my position and function as druid master over each of them.

Yet, something had to have caused it to stay last night. I asked it why it decided to hang around, and the Oak sent back an image of a patch of darkness in the forest. That nonspecific answer told me it had acted on a hunch; it had sensed something was amiss, but it didn't know exactly what.

Bring me there. Now.

Instantly I stood on the far side of the Oak, near the compound yet hidden by its bulk. For a moment, I wondered if anyone might notice the comings and goings of a sixty-foot-tall oak, then I recalled how the tree used to conceal itself in plain sight at the junkyard. If it didn't want to be seen, it wouldn't.

As for the noise I'd heard, it was one of the younger boys—Pip if I wasn't mistaken. The abrupt separation from family, friends, and home had been hardest on the youngest among the group. Since we left Plantersville, we'd spent many a night comforting kids who were crying for their parents and siblings.

After I'd gotten my powers back, I'd searched for every one of their families, starting with their home addresses. It was a futile gesture, since a nuke had leveled their neighborhood. If any of their family members were still alive, they'd long since been scattered to the four winds.

Eventually, the kids had come to accept that they were never going home, and the nightly crying ceased. Honestly, I didn't know what had been worse, hearing them sob each night, or seeing the look of resignation in their eyes when the crying stopped.

Putting those memories aside, I patted the Oak's trunk, taking comfort in the warm, rough surface of its bark. Then, I jogged to the wall and pulled myself up, stepping gingerly over the sharpened iron spikes and embedded broken bottles that lined the top. No one stood outside except for Guerra, who maintained his post atop the building.

I gave him a single quizzical look, which he returned with a shrug. "Kids say they heard Richard last night, begging to be let in. And no, I never saw nuthin. Been up here all night. Besides all that racket down by the river, it's been quiet as fish farts."

After I'd joined him on the rooftop, I asked him to repeat what the kids had told him. According to Guerra, they'd heard Richard whispering as if he was outside the cellar door, all night long. As for Anna and Mickey, they hadn't heard a thing.

"That's impossible, man," I said with incredulity in my voice. "I granted Richard his final release last night."

Guerra shifted his crossbow to the crook of his injured arm, using the prosthetic to keep it carefully pointed away from me. "What time?"

"I dunno, around two in the morning, maybe?"

The werewolf's eyes narrowed. "Like I said, the boys heard it all night."

"Man, I buried him myself. Believe me when I say that he's six feet under and then some."

"Maybe," the old wolf said as he spat off the terrace. "But we're dealing with *brujería* here."

"Yeah, no shit. Everyone else inside?" He nodded. "Give me a sec."

I had the Oak portal me to Richard's grave, and I verified that his corpse was still there before teleporting back.

Guerra didn't miss a beat when I reappeared. "And?"

"Still there, still twice dead. I'm going to go talk to the kids."

He stopped me with a firm hand on my biceps. "Fair warning, Anna is in a mood," the old wolf warned.

I winced, and not because of Guerra's grip. "So, what else is new?" I muttered as I headed for the entrance to the house.

Anna had been friendly with me before Dauphine killed her little brother. Now, she blamed his death on me. So did I, but that didn't mean it didn't sting to be the focus of all her anger and grief.

I entered the house from the terrace, following the sobbing sounds to the kitchen. There I found Anna, Thomas, and Pip sitting at the breakfast bar, Anna with her arm around the young boy, and Thomas sitting catercorner to them. Pip was obviously at the end of his crying jag, suffering from the occasional involuntary sob spasm as he whimpered softly.

Thomas kept his head down, keeping his steely gray eyes fixed on his interlocked hands. The lanky red-haired boy twiddled his thumbs, not out of impatience, it seemed, but frustration. When I entered, I caught his gaze momentarily, but he simply shook his head and continued glaring at his hands. I took up a position across from them, leaning my backside against the stove.

"Is everything okay?" I asked in a flat, calm voice.

At the sound of my voice, Anna drew her mouth into a hard line. "It's under control. Page Pip here seems to think he heard something last night, something that frightened him. Yet, Chancellor Merlin and I heard no such thing, so I've been explaining to Pip that it was just his imagination."

"Chancellor Merlin?" I asked.

When Anna ignored me, I glanced at Thomas. The boy looked up, mouthing "Mickey" silently. So, all the adults had nicknames. It seemed Anna was playing the medieval knights thing to the hilt.

"Pip, tell me what you heard, please," I said.

The pale, mouse-faced boy wiped his nose on his sleeve before speaking. "We were all in the cellar, where Mr. Guerra—"

"Master at Arms Guerra," Anna corrected as she tucked a strand of his stringy brown hair behind his ear to keep it out of his eyes.

Hmph. At least he got to keep his name.

"Master at Arms Guerra," Pip said, continuing. "Anyway, we were down there hiding with the doors locked, and I started hearing whispering at the door."

"What sort of whispering?" I asked.

"I dunno, kinda soft at first." Pip's shoulders shook as he inhaled, as if his lungs were threatening to send him into another crying fit. Then he exhaled, only shuddering slightly before continuing. "Then it got louder, but not like I could hear it in my ears."

"What do you mean?"

Thomas answered my question before Pip could do so. "It was inside our heads. The voice, I mean. Richard was talking to us with his mind."

"Like a mind flayer!" Pip blurted out. "Matthew ran a campaign once where we went into the Deeps, and that's how they start. I don't want to get my brains eaten by no mind flayer, Dame Sweetlove."

Obviously, this was about to go south, and rather quickly, if someone didn't redirect the conversation. If my hearing served me, the rest of the boys were down the hall in the dining room, eating breakfast quietly under Mickey's supervision.

Chances were, the other kids could hear everything, and the last thing I needed was to get the kids worked up over imaginary monsters. We had enough problems keeping them safe from the real ones as it was.

"Phillip, there are no such things as mind flayers," I said in the most reassuring tone I could muster. "That's just a creature someone made up for a game."

Pip's voice was that much more strained as he responded. "Yeah, but there wasn't no such thing as zombies or vampires, either. They turned out to be real, so why can't mind flayers be real, too?"

"Colin, just let it go," Anna admonished. "You're just getting him upset again."

"It was Richard," Thomas said, keeping his gaze lowered. "We all heard him."

To be honest, I had no idea what to think about the matter. Clearly, the boys had experienced something, but whether it was some sort of auditory illusory spell, telepathy, a curse, or some other enchantment, I couldn't say. That the adults hadn't been affected clearly indicated the children were the targets.

Someone was trying to scare the kids, possibly to cause pandemonium within the compound, making it harder for us to function. Or worse, they were trying to harm the children by driving them insane. It was nefarious, without a doubt, but then again, we were dealing with vampires. To them, a child was nothing more than a midnight snack.

That said, I wondered if this were an isolated incident. "Has anything like this happened before?"

In response, the boys both turned suspiciously silent. Thomas became even more interested in his thumbs, and Pip buried his head in Anna's shoulder. I turned my gaze on the older boy, clearing my throat to get his attention.

"Thomas, if there's something you're not telling us…"

He frowned, glancing at Pip before responding. "We've been seeing Richard outside the compound."

"You're not supposed to tell!" Pip blurted, his eyes filled with tears. "We all pinky swore!"

I crossed my arms over my chest, then I realized how intimidating that must look, so I relaxed and leaned forward with my elbows on the counter. "Why aren't you supposed to say anything?"

"Because Richard said bad things would happen to Miss Anna, Mr. Mickey, and Mr. Guerra if we did," Thomas replied.

"Wait a minute—you've been talking to Richard?" I glared at Anna, softening my expression and tone before the boys picked up on it.

"This is news to me," Anna said, clearly picking up on the vibe I was putting off, despite that she'd not seen the look I gave her.

Thomas gave a quick nod. "At first it freaked us out. He looked the same, but different. He looks sick now, and his eyes are black and shiny." The kid shuddered. "It's really creepy, but he never hurt us or nothing. After a while, we just got used to seeing him."

"How long has this been going on?" Anna asked.

"I dunno," Thomas shrugged. "Since Brian died."

Well, shit.

"What sort of things did you talk about? With Richard, I mean?"

"He'd do things that helped us. Like bringing us candy, and letting us know when zombies were near."

I shared a look with Anna. For once, since her brother's death, there was only concern in her eyes, and not accusation.

I tried keeping tension out of my voice as I spoke. "Thomas, did he ever ask anything of you?"

"Oh yeah, all the time," the boy said. "He wanted to get inside. None of us let him, though. After what happened to Brian, we didn't trust him."

"Good man," I said. "All of you. But I still don't understand why you didn't tell anyone."

Thomas averted his gaze once more. "He said he'd kill the adults, without even lifting a finger."

"How?"

"Well, with necromancy, Mr. Colin. How else?"

———

I spent all day altering and strengthening the wards on the perimeter wall, tweaking them to keep out curses, illusory magic, and necromancy. The job was a slog, since I had to make it look like I was physically working on the wall. Chink a few bricks, do some magic on the sly. Add some barbed wire, do a little more druidry when no one was paying attention. It was a total pain in the ass.

In addition, I painted some druidic glyphs on the inside surface of the wall. The glyphs were pure nature magic, the antithesis of necromancy. Not only would they make Mickey's garden grow like crazy, they'd also weaken any undead creature who managed to breach the wards.

Of course, I couldn't hide the fact that I was painting glyphs on the garden wall, so instead I gave the kids a lesson in Ogham script. The Ogham alphabet druids used was way older than the standard script, and modified, but it was basically the same thing. Kids being kids, they asked countless questions.

"Why are you doing that, Mr. Colin?" Pip asked.

"Oh, I'm just livening up the place."

Someone who'd lived in the castle house had been an artist, and they left a buttload of art supplies behind. I took advantage of that by using a visual panoply of acrylic paint colors to do my work. Nothing said magic had to be dull and ugly, after all.

"What's it mean?" D'Wayne asked.

"Well, that circular design says, 'Let all living things thrive.' The sort of diamond-shaped one is hard to translate, but it roughly means, 'Diminish the power of the evil dead.' And the one that looks like a curly cue pyramid..."

It wasn't long before they got bored and left me alone.

The sun was low in the sky by the time I finished the job. I'd tried to have a rational discussion with Anna about what the kids heard, but she insisted that they were imagining things. I realized she wasn't being bitchy by blowing me off, she was just going through the grieving process. If using me as her emotional punching bag made her feel better, so be it.

Besides, I'd rather not encourage any talk of magic among the human members of the group. It wasn't so much a tactical decision as a mental health issue, one that was based on my years of experience in observing how people dealt with discovering that magic, mythology, and folk tales were real.

There was a reason why the supernatural races had been able to keep The World Beneath concealed from humanity for much of modern human history. Human psychology made it easy to keep the masquerade going, as most human minds simply could not deal with the supernatural. Then, with the advent of the age of reason, humankind stopped believing in it, and the human psyche adapted accordingly.

Now, when a human witnessed creatures and events that challenged their worldview, it could shatter their sanity. For that reason, the subconscious mind had a tendency to suggest alternate narratives, essentially rewriting memories to fit known facts.

That huge demon-shaped shadow flying overhead last night? That was just a very large owl. The gnome you saw ducking behind a tree in the woods? Just a kid playing hide and seek with her friends. The ghostly playmate you used to hang out with in your childhood home? Why, that was your imaginary friend—all kids had them, right?

Meanwhile, the conscious mind tended to block out what was going on around humans all the time. I'd seen people straight up ignore vampires feeding on their victims in public bathrooms, werewolves in full shift running alongside cars, and fae doing magic in plain sight.

When sensory input doesn't compute, the conscious mind filters it out. The same brain that relies on logic, math, and the laws of physics to make sense of the world will tell itself that the vampire feeding was two people making out, the werewolf was a dog, and the fae doing magic was a street busker performing cheap tricks for cash. This information is then classified as irrelevant, and summarily cast aside as extraneous and therefore not worthy of notice.

Or, as Finnegas always said, "People hear what they want to hear, see what they want to see, and believe what they want to believe." The old man was right. All you had to do was spend a few minutes on social media to prove that theory.

But when events transpire that are so blatantly obvious

they can't be ignored, that's when supes call in the local fae court to perform a cover-up. Or they used to, in this timeline. That's how it still worked back home, at least.

The same went for when a witness just wouldn't shut up; they usually got mind-wiped in the middle of the night by a fae mind magician. So they lost a few brain cells and possibly some core memories—big whoop. Better than getting offed by the local vampire coven for blathering on and on about the immortal blood drinking Illuminati cultists who just moved in next door.

Yet, the Hellpocalypse was a special case, an event that was unprecedented in modern human history. Needless to say, when the dead started to rise and feed on the living, a lot of people quite literally lost their ever-loving minds.

I'd say that as many people died from suicide on that first day as died from the bombs or having their faces eaten off by zombies. Reports were widespread about people leaping from rooftops and upper story windows on day one. You couldn't go scavenging without coming across a corpse with a pistol in its hand and a hole in its skull to match the caliber. Hell, when Gwydion dropped me in this timeline on Day Zero, I witnessed more than a handful of people who just stood and waited to be eaten.

The mind could only take so much warping of reality, and dealing with zombies and vampires was enough for the members of this group to deal with. The last thing I needed was to have a group member go off the deep end after learning one fact too many about The World Beneath. That was why I didn't want them to know about magic, or the fae, or werewolves, or that I could change into a ten-foot-tall finalist in the world's ugliest giant contest.

So, for now, I'd continue to hide my magic and keep all

that other stuff to myself as well. Hopefully, it wouldn't get anyone killed.

Before I left, I gave Mickey and Guerra explicit instructions to keep the kids inside the compound for a few weeks. With Richard gone and the wards refreshed, I didn't think there was any immediate threat to them, but it didn't hurt to be careful.

Once I was certain that things were under control, I gave the perimeter wards a last once over. Finally, I had the Oak portal me back to Crowley's underground lair.

Time to head to the Deadlands.

CHAPTER
THIRTEEN

WHEN I RETURNED to Crowley's lair, the shadow wizard and Saint Germain were playing chess, of all things. I wasn't exactly an aficionado of the game, but it didn't take an expert to see that Crowley was winning, having gathered more of Saint Germain's pieces on his side of the board. As I walked into the break room, neither of them turned to address me, so intent were they on the game.

"The druid returns," Saint Germain said. "Has he come to a decision?"

"He has," I said.

That got Crowley's attention. He turned his swirling black gaze on me, swiveling in his seat to face me fully. When he did so, Saint Germain moved one of his pieces behind Crowley's back, his hand flickering so quickly I almost didn't catch it.

"What did you decide?" the necromancer asked.

"For starters, we're not bringing Finnegas back," I said as I sat on the edge of a nearby table. "But I do have a plan."

"Oh? Do tell," Saint Germain said.

"We're going to infiltrate The Deadlands—from the south."

Saint Germain laughed aloud. "How does that human saying go? 'Have you lost your ever-loving mind?'"

"Personally, I prefer 'motherfucking' over 'ever-loving.' And no, I have not."

Crowley kept his creepy gaze on me, his expression indecipherable as he searched me for signs of insanity or premature dementia. Presumably finding none, he absently reached to the side, moving Saint Germain's piece back to its original position while keeping his attention on me.

This elicited a soft hiss from the vampire. "How do you keep doing that?"

I shifted my attention to Saint Germain. "Don't waste your breath—not that you really need it. Crowley is one to keep his secrets."

"It is uncanny," Jacques replied. "There is absolutely no way he could've seen my hand move."

I chuckled softly. "He grew up around the fae, and nobody cheats like them. You'll never pull one over on Crowley."

"What is your plan?" the shadow wizard asked, turning the conversation back to the topic at hand.

"We all know something lives in Houston, and that it doesn't suffer any encroachment on its territory. We also know that Ateas had the balls to establish a territory that directly borders the no-trespass zone in Houston. Whoever or whatever rules that place has to be pissed off about it."

"He did it so he wouldn't have to guard his southern border," Saint Germain interjected as he studied the chessboard intently. "Quite a brilliant move, when you think about it, if a bit bold. I doubt that any other vampire could get away with it."

"You intend to recruit it as an ally." Crowley frowned before turning his attention back to his game. "You are insane."

"Understatement of the century," the vampire agreed. "The minute you enter Houston city limits, you'll be a dead man walking."

"Only if it kills me."

Saint Germain scoffed. "Entering that territory while hoping for leniency is like jumping off a cliff while hoping for gravity's mercy. You will not survive."

I raised an index finger in the air. "Ah, but you two are forgetting something. Before the bombs fell, Houston was full of humans." I turned that finger on myself. "Human."

"Pfah!" Saint Germain spat. "Being fae-touched, you're about as human as I am."

"My magic's not fae at all. I'm a demigod. That means I'm half-human."

"I find it doubtful that the Terror will be interested in such technicalities," Crowley said.

"Be that as it may, to my knowledge, no demigods have been killed while trespassing in the Houston demesne."

"Wrong," Jacques replied. "One of Coyote's kids got obliterated there not long before Day Zero. Rumor has it he risked it for a meal at the original Ninfa's on Navigation. He wanted fajitas and ended up being the main course."

"Well, that's disappointing," I said with a tsk. "But unlike Coyote's kid, I have the advantage of a fully human form. Maybe it won't notice my Fomorian DNA if I stay completely mortal."

"I doubt it," Crowley observed. "You have the stink of

god-blood and magic all over you. The more time you spend in your other form, and the more you learn about druidry, the more apparent it is to the initiated that you are not entirely human."

"Speaking of druidry," Saint Germain said, scowling as Crowley moved a piece, taking one of his. "Need I remind you that wizards were killed by the Houston Terror just as prejudicially as supernatural beings? And witches, and voudon priests and priestesses, and sorcerers, and shamans —shall I go on?"

"It's a risk I'm willing to take."

"Your funeral," Jacques replied. "Perhaps there will be enough left of you for the wizard to reanimate. I'm sure you'll make a passing house servant after all is said and done."

"Despite the risks, I'm going. Obviously, you two will stay here and wait for me."

"Obviously," Saint Germain said, rolling his eyes as he moved a chess piece on the board.

"If I'm not back in twenty-four hours, assume I'm dead and carry on the plan without me."

"If you die, there is no plan," Crowley replied. He moved a piece into position with an air of finality. "Checkmate."

"Damn it to Hades," Saint Germain muttered. "I'll set the board up again."

"You have all the lab notes and research," I replied. "You'll figure something out."

"Colin, if you meet your end while attempting to broker some sort of alliance with the unknown entity that presides over Houston, this entire undertaking is finished. Should that happen, I intend to march an undead army through

Dallas, killing as many of the Vampyri as I can before they lay me low."

I glanced at Saint Germain, who shrugged. "I'll probably be right there with him. If fate favors me, one of those weaklings will get in a lucky swing and behead me."

"Don't go writing your suicide notes just yet. I still think I can get in and reason with this being, based on the fact that I'm sort-of human."

Crowley closed his eyes and shook his head slowly. "Druid, I've practiced necromancy since I was a child. I can tell you for a certainty—one cannot reason with death."

———

When examined on a map, The Woodlands—now the Deadlands—was situated far north of Houston city limits proper. On paper at least, Spring and a slew of other bedroom communities sat between Ateas' territory and the city's edge. However, the Terror's territory extended well beyond Houston's cartographical borders.

The borders of the entity's actual defended demesne roughly followed 99 to the East, North, and West-Southwest. Then it was delineated by 69 North for a few miles until 69 hit 6 in the Southwest corner of the city. From there, the territory was demarcated by 6 South all the way out to Galveston Island and the West Bay.

It was a huge territory, which caused many in the World Beneath to speculate that it was not held by a single entity alone. Yet Maeve had once slipped and referred to the Terror as "it" and not "they," which told me it was a singular entity—"singular" having more than one meaning, in this instance.

How did I know that Maeve knew the thing? She had to be on negotiating terms with it, as its territory had directly bordered her own, and still did in my timeline. Maeve was no "mere" fae queen, but a goddess in her own right. If I knew the crafty old broad, she'd have worked out a treaty with the damned thing centuries ago.

If only I had Maeve here now. Where's your fairy grand-mother some seventy generations removed when you needed her?

I fully intended to pull the same trick that Maeve had, but first I needed to find the entity so I could parley with it. Based on the story Saint Germain had just told me about Coyote's kid, I figured that wouldn't be too hard. My guess was that the Terror headquartered out of downtown Houston. The OG Ninfa's was located on the Eastern edge of downtown. If that was where the kid got ganked, it gave even more credence to my hunch.

Rather than trying to hide and be sneaky, I wanted to be seen. That's why I had the Oak plop me down in Discovery Green, one of the parks downtown. For maximum visibility, I chose to appear at the end of the big dock jutting out into Kinder Lake. That way, I figured I'd be easy to spot, and I'd see whatever "it" was coming from a mile away.

Moreover, it'd be hard for the dead to sneak up on me here. If I got swarmed before the Terror showed, I'd just blink out and try again later.

Speaking of the dead… where are they?

I stood almost at the end of the dock, which tilted precariously to one side, threatening to sink into the lake. As for the lake itself, it had become choked with weeds around the shoreline in those areas that were not covered in concrete. The jogging trail was still barely visible within the brush, but nothing moved within the park—nothing human, at least, living or undead.

Weird. You'd think there'd be some Zeds stumbling around or something.

Yet, the place was empty, save for healthy populations of squirrels, rabbits, foxes, coyotes, dogs, and cats. But no deer. I knew this because I'd checked the area using my druid senses.

Maybe the coyotes chased them off?

It was also odd there were no humans around. What with the Terror running off all the 'thropes, vamps, revs, and so on, it seemed like Houston would be humanity central. If outsiders weren't settling Houston, at least the surviving native population should've ended up thriving here.

But nope. Besides the chittering of an angry squirrel, the occasional trill of birdsong, and the *ploop* of a frog jumping into the lake, it was dead silent. I had only the wind and the sounds of the local wildlife to keep me company.

Man, this is creepy. Never thought I'd miss the moans of the undead.

For the first few minutes, I was pretty tense, jumping at every sound. After thirty minutes or so, I began to relax, considering that nothing was happening except for a minor dust-up between two squirrels over a territorial dispute. With plenty of wildlife around to use for surveillance and nothing better to do, I sat down cross-legged on the dock. Once I'd gotten comfortable, I dropped into a druid trance and lost myself in monitoring the area using my druid senses.

If it hadn't been for its shadow, I'd never have seen it coming. In fact, that shadow never fell across the dock, at least not until the very last second. I just happened to be looking through the eyes of a squirrel when a swathe of darkness passed at speed over the open space behind me— headed right for the dock.

I barely had time to move, much less connect with the Oak to ask it to teleport me out of there. One second I was deep in my druid trance, enjoying the quiet of the park in the afternoon sun. The next moment, I was diving into the lake and swimming for dear life.

To be honest, I hadn't actually seen what "it" was; I only knew it was large, airborne, and moving fast. When I dove into the lake, I was moving on instinct, and my gut told me to swim for the bottom. It was a good thing I did—if I'd stayed just below the surface, I'd have been snatched by the massive taloned feet that raked through the water above me.

The pond was full of muck and scum, murky and not at all suitable for a swim, so all I caught was a flash of green, iridescent scales and a foot-long black claw slashing through the sudden roil and turbidity. As I backstroked, kicking and paddling myself as far into the vegetation and murk at the bottom of the lake as possible, my mind did the math regarding what I'd seen.

Scales. Foot-long claw. Flying predator.

My mind went straight back to the vault in Vegas, and the massive titan that once guarded it. That was, before I'd cut a deal with the ancient beast to set it free in exchange for not being eaten or burned to a crisp. Having had plenty of recent experience with the species, it didn't take a genius to figure out what was hunting me. Hell, I even had one for a guest at home—in this timeline, at least.

Dragon.

And if the size of that claw was any indication, a big one, too. Not quite as big as Typhon, but possibly large enough to give the big guy a run for his money. Suddenly, it was all starting to make sense.

Dragons were the ultimate predators. Creatures of fire, scale, and magic, they were big, fast, highly intelligent, and relentlessly territorial. If a dragon this large and old had claimed Houston as its dominion, there wasn't a vamp, 'thrope, or fae who could challenge it or depose it.

Everything I knew about dragons had come from what I'd learned from Smokedancer since I invited her and her brood to stay in this timeline's Grove. Smokedancer was roughly the size of a two-story residential home, yet she could move absolutely silently when she chose. She could also slag solid rock with her breath, and she was immune to most forms of magic, something I'd discovered when I tried to cast a tracking spell on her offspring.

I hadn't meant any insult or harm by it. I simply wanted to know where the dragonlings were and how they were doing, as the Grove had flat-out refused to keep tabs on them for me. Rather than being angered by my attempts, the elder dragon had found my efforts and resulting failures to be quite amusing. She'd then explained how dragon scales radiated a natural anti-magic field, repelling almost all forms of basic magic.

Not only that, but Smokedancer's scales were also nigh on impregnable, despite being light and somewhat flexible. If you could take boiled leather and make it tougher than diamonds, you'd have dragon scales. For that reason, their scales were highly valued for use in armor and other protective items.

The bottom line? To say that dragons were dangerous

opponents was a major understatement. Imagine fighting a creature that was the size of a small apartment building, yet it could strike as quick as a serpent. Then, give that creature a breath weapon, claws and teeth like spears, an impenetrable hide, and make it nearly impervious to magic.

That's what I was facing here, and from the worst position possible. Sure, I was sitting pretty at the bottom of a lake. That said, I was far from safe, as the dragon's breath could heat the water up and boil me like a crayfish.

Yet I doubted that was the thing's ploy. If my experiences in observing Smokedancer hunting inside the Grove were any indication, my opponent was currently climbing for another dive. Despite the silt the initial attack stirred up, I'd easily be spotted from above.

Ah, shit. Time to move.

———

In hindsight, staying in my fully human form had been a huge mistake. In my half-Fomorian form, I could've already leapt out of the water and ran for dear life. That wouldn't necessarily mean I'd have gotten very far, but at least I wouldn't be a sitting duck.

Of course, I could have the Oak portal me someplace safe. But that wouldn't get me what I wanted, which was a chance at negotiating some sort of treaty with the dragon. If I cut and run, I'd simply be back to square one.

So, I did the least likely thing that I could do.

In my human form, I had an even greater affinity for plant and animal life, and druid magic came that much easier to me because of it. Maybe it was because druidry had been uniquely intended for humans to wield, or perhaps it was because my Fomorian blood was resistant to certain kinds of magic. I wasn't certain, but what I did know was that I could much more easily connect with the natural energies all around me in this form—so I did exactly that.

There was a ton of vegetation growing in and on the bottom of the pond—hornwort and pondweed were growing in abundance all around me. I reached out, physically and mentally, connecting with the plant life so I could pour my druid magic into it. As the life magic flowed into the vegetation, it grew at a tremendous rate, lifting me up and out of the water as it wrapped around my legs to hold me up.

I managed this just in time to see a speck high in the sky that was growing larger by the moment. If I hadn't been looking for it, I'd not have seen it, as I had to stare into the sun to find it. Obviously no stranger to hunting ground prey, the dragon was attacking from the direction in which it would least likely be seen.

Just as it did before, when I was on the dock.

For a moment, I marveled at the skill required to gauge elevation, position, and vector, all in relation to the sun's position and that of your target on the ground. The dragon had come at me in such a way that I would not have seen its shadow cross in front of or over me, not until the last second. It made me think of fighter pilot aces and how they mastered four-dimensional combat, using the sun and their opponent's blind spots against them.

Magnificent.

Then I remembered that this dragon was trying to eat me, or at the very least trying to end me. Gaping wide-eyed at the majesty of the natural and supernatural worlds is well and good, but it's best done at a distance from each world's apex predators. I'd be damned if I was going to become a cautionary tale of what not to do when you're being hunted by a dragon, so I got to work.

First, I connected with my Oak, making that priority one on my "not becoming human barbecue" list. Then I caused the hornwort and pondweed to lift me as high as possible above the surface of the lake. Finally, I formed the remaining vegetation into five letters that spanned nearly the entire length of the lake:

DRUID

This all happened in the span of a few seconds, and admittedly, my penmanship was not the greatest. Meanwhile, the speck in the sky rapidly became a dot, and then a dark blur, and finally, a building-sized mass of shiny green scales, talons, and teeth that was hurtling right at me. It took all the nerve I had not to tell the Oak to portal me the hell out of there.

However, my plan required me to stay put, and that's what I did. I needed to show this dragon that I wasn't a threat, and that I wasn't afraid of it, either. In truth, only half of that statement was correct.

Standing on my dais of pond vegetation, I had a front-row seat for the dragon's speedy descent. By rights, something that large diving that fast should've made some sort of sound, like that of a plane in a nosedive, or a bomb whistling to the ground. On the contrary, the creature was absolutely silent, just a glistening green mass of furious death come to collect the debt of my life at one hundred twenty miles per hour.

I knew it had to have seen my message. How could it not from that perspective? For a moment I wondered if I'd blundered, thinking it might not be able to read. I immediately recognized this fear as preposterous, then I wondered if maybe it just couldn't read English. The creature wasn't slowing at all, and if anything, it had gained speed—so either it had never attended first grade, or it liked the taste of roasted druid.

I had just seconds to react, but if I moved too soon, it might show fear on my part. Too late, and I'd be nothing more than human burnt ends, a people-kabab. So, I held my ground—or pondweed, as it were.

Steady now…

The shadow now loomed over me, allowing me to make out every detail of the massive draconid's form and features. The iridescent green scales, dark along its back and fading to lighter green, then yellow on its stomach. The eyes, a deep lustrous red at the outer edges, shifting a fleck at a time into orange hues that lightened nearer to its vertically slitted pupils. Teeth like spears, half as long as I was tall, in a mouth spread wide to reveal the light of her fire glands being stoked deep within her gullet.

Her body was muscular and elongated, more like an Asian dragon than the stumpy, squat creatures sometimes depicted in early medieval European artwork. And yes, I could determine her sex now, as she lacked a beard. According to Smokedancer, females of the species had none.

Much like lizards, dragons possessed no external sex organs between their hind legs. Speaking of which, her rear legs and feet were extended toward me, talons wide and pointing forward, ready to skewer me when she struck.

Her wingspan must've been a football field wide, although her wings were pinned back against her flanks so as not to impede her dive. Finally, I noted her tail, which had vertical fins top and bottom, surely designed to help guide her in flight.

She was superbly impressive, frighteningly exquisite, and most terrifying of all, definitely not slowing down.

Even still, just seconds from death, I held my position, at the same time briefly meeting the dragon's gaze. Hers was the stare of the apex predator, and as I met it, I felt small and insignificant. I wanted to portal away, but I remained, waiting until the last millisecond to escape.

This is going to be close.

Just when the dragon was near enough for me to feel the heat of her breath, I had the Oak portal me atop a nearby parking garage. Yet, the scaled huntress didn't crash into the water like I might've expected. Instead, she snapped her wings wide, swooping out of her dive as she banked right for me.

How did she know where I'd be?

There was little time to figure that mystery out, as the dragon barely slowed in changing directions. Almost before I knew what was happening, she was coming after me at near terminal velocity. This time, rather than relying on her taloned feet to do the job, she looked to be resorting to her ranged weapons.

Most dragons—and I say "most" reservedly because I've only met a handful—have their fire glands in their throats, not in their stomachs as is often depicted in popular media. Yes, they have to take a deep breath before they breathe fire, but they're not stoking flames in their tummies or chest when they do. The heat and combustion came from the glands in their gullets, where chemical secretions and magic melded together to create a blaze hot enough to slag stone.

Without a doubt, dragon fire is one of the deadliest weapons in all the magical animal kingdom. With it, wars have been won, civilizations vanquished, and dynasties toppled. When you see the glands on either side of a drake's throat start to glow, it's not time to take cover—it's time to pray.

The typical range for a dragon's breath weapon was a multiple of their length. Based on some very rough math, I'd say this behemoth could spew that liquid and gas inferno over 1,000 feet, placing me well within her kill zone. She was already exhaling and spitting flames at me before I had a chance to tell the Oak to teleport me elsewhere.

There I was, standing on the top level of the parking garage in my human form with no cover in sight as several hundred cubic meters of burning liquid and gas were about to envelop me. There was no time to think, barely even time to flinch, so I reacted instinctively—not with prayer, but magic.

Dropping into a semi-crouch with one foot in front and one behind, I spread my arms wide and brought them together in front of me, fingers together in a clapping motion. The movement was something I did without thinking about it, the result of years of practice, directing magic with gestures and sound. Just as my hands met, I connected with the air molecules all around me, directing them to form a miniature jet stream that came up from behind the building, pulling the cooler air from within as it passed.

Using nothing more than instinct and my affinity for nature's energies, I directed the air into a tight, sharp, powerful gust of wind that wrapped around my body, shooting out ahead of me in a narrow, focused flow. As the airflow passed, it picked up speed, turning into a cyclone that met the dragon's breath head on, splitting it so it passed up, over, and around me.

This effectively created a bubble of cold air that reached roughly five yards in every direction. The heat inside my air shield was still tremendous, but not so hot as to cause me any harm. Tongues of flame licked all around the flow of air, scorching the cement surface of the parking garage and leaving small eddies of molten glass in its wake. Yet, within my bubble, I was safe.

As a side effect of the spell, the airflow forced the dragon to pull up and gain altitude, swooping over me as she made her pass. Knowing that it'd be mere seconds before she came at me again, I had the Oak teleport me once more, to the roof of the convention center. There I had a clear view of the lake, so I quickly directed the vegetation to reform into five different letters:

TRUCE

It didn't take but the span of a few breaths before the dragon was once again diving at me from the direction of the sun. I looked at my billboard of pondweed and mud, and back up at the dragoness, making certain the word was visible and legible. It was, and from her vantage point, there was no way she could have missed it.

"Son of a bitch, this isn't working," I muttered aloud.

Oak, take me to the Grove.

CHAPTER
FOURTEEN

AS I BLINKED out of the park, the first licks of the dragon's breath had just reached the convention center rooftop. When I appeared in the Grove a moment later, my nostrils were assaulted by the odor of burned hair. Almost instantly, I was soaked by a deluge of rain that dropped from the sky in a virtual waterfall of dime-sized raindrops.

"What the hell, lady?" I cursed as I spat and wiped water from my face.

The Grove responded by sending me an image of myself with my hair on fire. I reached up to feel my scalp, and yep, there was a bald spot, right in the middle of my noggin.

Great—I'm a cuckold, and I'm experiencing male pattern baldness. All I need is an exotic sports car and my midlife crisis will be complete.

"Um, thank you," I said in the most apologetic tone I could muster. The Grove responded by sending me another image, one of me with a cap of bright-green moss on my scalp. "No, that's quite alright, I don't need a poultice, or a hairpiece for that matter. I intend to shift shortly, so it should heal on its own."

Just as I was about to ask the Grove if she knew where Smokedancer was, the dragoness came swooping out of the sky, landing thirty feet in front of me. Her dorsal spines were raised, and the fire glands in her throat were all aglow as she snaked her head this way and that.

I smell dragon fire, druid. Is all well with you?

I could speak to Smokedancer telepathically, but telepathy had always felt weird to me, especially when I was under duress. As stressed as I was from my recent brush with death, it was easier to converse with her aloud.

"Yes, yes, but everything is fine." I pointed at my scalp, flashing a sheepish grin. "Well, except for my hairline, and my pride, but both will recover shortly."

Smokedancer's hackles settled slightly. She arched a scaly brow at me as she lowered her head to my level.

Why do you smell of dragon fire?

"Yeah, about that. I was just about to come find you, so I could ask for your advice. See, I just came from Houston—"

YOU WENT TO HUGH'S TOWN?

I'd never heard Smokedancer "shout" before. As it turned out, hearing her voice echo telepathically inside my mind was a headache inducing experience. Placing my fingertips on my temples, I lowered my head while meeting her gaze from beneath a hooded brow.

"Yee-ouch! A little softer next time, maybe?" Something about the way she was looking at me told me I'd better start explaining, so I did. "Yes, I went there to meet with the entity that rules the place, to broker a treaty with it for safe passage."

Why did you not consult me before embarking on this jour-

ney? I could've warned you of the dangers of undertaking such a foolhardy endeavor.

A dragon's facial expressions were sometimes difficult to read, but in this case, Smokedancer was clearly glowering at me. The tilt of her head, the flare of her nostrils, and the way in which she narrowed her eyes—yep, that was definitely contempt. The dragon thought I was stupid.

Not stupid, druid, but foolhardy. What made you think you could simply walk into a great wyrm's demesne and escape unscathed?

"Well, it's not exactly common knowledge among my kind that the 'Houston Terror' is a Godzilla-sized dragoness. Had I known, I might have come to you first for advice."

I do not know this 'Godzilla.' Is she mighty?

"'He.' And yeah, very mighty."

Perhaps not as mighty as The Pyre of Nations, hmm?

"I'm sorry—did you say they call this dragon 'The Pyre of Nations'?"

Among other titles, yes. She is the Flame of the Western Skies, the Wing that Blots the Sun, Frostender, Hellbender, Scalepiercer, Kingscorcher—shall I go on?

"That's an impressive list of titles. I take it she's a big deal among your people?" Smokedancer made a sound in the back of her throat that was similar to a cat coughing up a hairball. It took a moment before I realized she was scoffing at my remark. "Okay, so she's a big deal. One question, then… what's she doing in Houston?"

The dragon continued to glare at me, but after several moments, her expression softened as her eyes searched mine. She snapped her wings before laying them against her flanks, then she settled into a more comfortable position that brought her lower to the ground and closer to my level. When she was finished, her chin rested on her forelegs, with her back-end laying slightly on her right haunch. She had her tail wrapped around her left side so that the tip was raised and twitching nearly in front of her.

All in all, it was a very cat-like thing to do. I was reminded not for the first time how similar dragons were to house cats in their mannerisms and personalities.

Druid, there is a secret that has been closely guarded for generations among dragonkind. Few outside our kind know this —only certain gods and leaders of the other mystic races. As the last master druid, you are a keeper of arcane knowledge and influential among humankind. That alone makes you worthy to learn this secret. But it is only because I have named you dragon-friend that I choose to divulge this information. However, you must swear never to tell a soul what I am about to share with you.

"Of course." She stared at me as if waiting for something, so I hastily added, "I swear."

A promise made to a dragon is not a thing to be taken lightly, and I will hold you to it. Let your vow be a lasting pact between us, now and forevermore.

A tingling feeling passed over me, one I recognized immediately. It was the ineffable sensation of powerful magic passing through my very being, locking itself into the molecular bonds in my tissues as it settled into spirit and bone. The experience triggered a flashback to years past when I was forced to serve Maeve, and I shuddered reflexively.

"Did you just cast a geas over me?" I said, trying my best to avoid frowning.

Only regarding your promise to maintain confidence. As I said, this is a closely guarded secret.

"I suppose that's okay, but next time, warn me first."

Of course.

Silence followed, so I waited to see if there was some other formality to observe. From what I'd seen of Smokedancer's behavior, dragon culture was full of quirks and rituals. I supposed certain polite observances were necessary when you lived in a society full of fire-breathing kaiju, if only to prevent minor Armageddons from happening every other week. But that didn't mean I didn't find it to be annoying at times.

Like the fae, dragons were odd creatures, being long-lived and magical in nature. That meant Smokedancer did things on her time, often seemingly oblivious to the schedules and preferences of her much more ephemeral human companion. Again, it was easy to see why they acted as they did, but the eccentricities of dragonkind could be quite unnerving.

I tapped my foot, wondering when I was going to hear this closely guarded secret. Meanwhile, the dragoness stared at me intently. I didn't want to be rude, but I had things to do and liches to kill. Sure, dragons lived for thousands of years, and my lifetime was just a speck floating on the wind to her, but my patience was wearing thin.

"Ahem—you were saying?"

I was waiting for you to recover.

"Consider me recovered."

Are you certain? You still look a bit piqued.

"I'm fine," I said, doing my best to keep the irritation out of my voice. "Please, go on."

As I was saying, we dragons hold our secrets closely. This is because we have been enslaved by other races in times past—shackled, bridled, and chained like mere beasts of burden.

"You've been used as weapons of war."

To win wars, yes. You've seen what a single dragon can do; now imagine what a flight of dragons might accomplish.

It wasn't hard to envision. I had no idea how many dragons were in a "flight," but even a dozen flying over a city or fortress, raining hell down from above, would quickly bring the strongest adversary to their knees.

"Which is why you've taken sanctuary in my Grove. Certain of the Celtic gods would like to enslave your brood."

Indeed. This is why my people left your earth centuries ago. Much as the fae created Underhill as a refuge to escape the advance of humankind, we found a home on another plane of existence.

"Except in your case, you were escaping the influence of the supernatural races and the gods."

Precisely.

"I see. So, what does this have to do with the dragon in Houston? And more importantly, if your home is on another plane of existence, why is that dragon there?"

That dragon guards the portal that leads to our realm. Every magical dimension requires an anchor on a natural sphere of permanence. You'll note that Underhill maintains several connections to the physical realm, linking to your world in multiple locations.

"So I've noticed."

When planning our exit, we thought this to be a liability and a major tactical error. For that reason, we created only one anchor to this world, a portal that we hid in the middle of nowhere, in a land populated by a primitive tribe of humans who possessed no knowledge of interdimensional magic.

"But little did you know, that location would later become a major population center for my people."

At first, we rationalized away the threat. The entrance was hidden, so what danger did humankind pose to us? But when they brought with them their gods and myths, along came the real threats.

"Meaning, the pantheons and the fae. But what about the gods of the Native Americans? Weren't they a threat to you?"

They wanted nothing to do with us. They saw us as just another sacred animal, and they left us alone.

"Interesting. From what I heard, Coyote's kid couldn't leave well enough alone."

And he paid for it, dearly. Eventually, we realized that the anchor to our realm might be in jeopardy, and that some in the supernatural world might try to sneak through to steal our young. That's when we appointed one of our kind to guard the entrance.

"Obviously, you chose the biggest, toughest, deadliest dragon you could."

Obviously.

"She sees me as a threat because I'm not just a human, but also a creature of magic." I thought about it a bit longer, making an obvious connection—one that only made sense in light of the story Smokedancer had just shared with me. "And the fact that I can portal makes me twice the menace."

Correct. If you can create portals and teleport from place to place, then it stands to reason that you might be able to travel between realms like the fae and the gods.

"Well, shoot. I need to convince her to allow me safe passage through her territory. Trust me, my reasons for it will benefit both her and your kind. I intend to remove a threat that sits on the border of her demesne."

And?

I took a moment to choose my words carefully. We both knew what was coming, but I felt the need to speak delicately regarding this matter. Smokedancer obviously wanted to help me, but I also got the impression that her agency was limited due to her current responsibilities.

"Do you happen to be acquainted with this 'Pyre of Nations'? Because it might help to have another dragon to speak on my behalf."

Smokedancer drew herself up to her full height. *Of course I know her. She's my mother.*

———

It took a few hours for Smokedancer to explain the whole story behind her family tree and why she was on the lam, despite having the most badass mom ever. It wasn't that the story was all that complicated; it was just that Smokedancer felt compelled to explain the most minute details of dragon society, stuff that really had no bearing on her immediate background. Thankfully, we were in the Grove, so only minutes passed on Earth while I got the entire history of her clan.

What it boiled down to was pretty simple to understand. While "The Pyre of Nations"—known to her family as Emberlance—was busy guarding the portal to the alternate dimension where dragons fled, Smokedancer had met someone. This male dragon, Hearthclaw, happened to be the eldest son of the king of dragons or some-such. I didn't quite understand the politics, as it sounded like there was more than one regent. Regardless, having Hearthclaw and Smokedancer as bond-mates was a pretty big deal.

Unfortunately, the political machinations of dragons are as underhanded and convoluted as fae and vampire politics. Which is to say, spying, secret alliances, and assassinations are a matter of course. There was a considerable to-do over their "engagement," because other royal families felt that the union would make Hearthclaw's clan much too powerful if they were allowed to align with Emberlance's clan through marriage.

Wouldn't you know it, Smokedancer and Hearthclaw eloped. They got "married" on Earth, although I have no idea how that worked, ceremony-wise. Being a couple of dumb kids, they decided it would be cool to "honeymoon" in Underhill. I guess that's the dragonkind equivalent of a human couple deciding it would be cool to backpack through narcoterrorist country in Mexico or something, and it turned out roughly as you might expect.

When all was said and done, Smokedancer was pregnant. As for Hearthclaw, he'd been either assassinated or killed trying to protect his new mate from one of the Morrígna—a detail I wasn't quite clear on, to be honest. However, it had happened, the prince's family blamed her for his death, and they wanted to take her children, ostensibly to raise them in safety.

It sort of sounded like a power grab to me, but I didn't press Smokedancer on the matter. As one might imagine, back home, all of dragon society was in turmoil over the scandal. To make things worse, Smokedancer couldn't get home because yours truly had fucked all the portals between Underhill and Earth, in an effort to screw over Maeve and her people.

But Smokedancer was no dummy. Rather than having her kids get nabbed by her enemies or the Celtic gods whilst trying to sneak through one of the few remaining portals back to Earth, she hid—right under their noses, in fact. That's how I happened to find her, smack in the middle of Fuamnach's territory, lying low and doing her best to keep her brood hidden from the gods and fae.

Little did I know, the gods had been closing in on her location before I got her and her kids the hell out of there. Even though it was my fault she got stuck in Underhill, Smokedancer still felt like she owed me for rescuing her, and she was pretty sure her mom would feel the same way. All I had to do was convince Mom I was friends with her daughter before I got flambéed and served as a mid-afternoon snack.

"Okay, so I get why you were hiding out in Underhill," I said as I lounged on the grass in front of Smokedancer, sipping coconut water through a reed straw. "But what I don't understand is why you haven't fled to Houston yet. Seems to me like your mom would want to know you're okay, and that her demesne would be the safest place to raise your brood."

Doing so would put both my mother and my brood at risk. Guarding the gateway to our world is her first priority. Placing my family under her protection would only distract her from her duties.

"'The hunter who chases two rabbits catches neither.'"
What?

"Oh, nothing—it's just something my fencing instructor says."

In this instance, I'd say that maxim applies—and there are many rabbits to chase. Besides the royal family, there are likely other factions among dragonkind hunting us. Given the opportunity, oppositional clans would gladly capture me and my offspring, holding us hostage in order to control the royal bloodline.

"Control? Or kill off?"

That is another possibility. I've had no contact with my home-world since my mate's death. I therefore have no idea what the political climate is like, nor do I know whether it's safe for our return. I can only make guesses from afar, basing my decisions on conjecture and past experience.

"I see. If you went to your mother for protection, she'd give it to you, splitting her attention between her duties and protecting her family."

Correct. Leaving the realm potentially exposed to incursions by the pantheons and the fae.

"Am I right in thinking that, if your mom allowed an enemy to sneak past her, it would reflect poorly on her, negatively affecting her standing in dragon society?"

Absolutely. I suspect there are those who envy and fear her, who might use such an opportunity to portray her as a traitor to the realm.

"Which means you'd rather stay here, and keep yourself and your kids out of dragon politics entirely."

Until my offspring are old enough to fend for themselves.

Something told me that Smokedancer's plans involved more than mere self-preservation. I wondered whether she intended to avenge her mate's death at some point, and it occurred to me that the time differential between the Grove, Earth, and other realms offered her and her brood a distinct advantage in that regard. Her enemies were searching for a teenaged dragon mother and three young dragonlings. What a shock it would be instead for them to find four fully grown dragons, every one of them a power in their own right.

If Smokedancer stayed here long enough, she and her kids wouldn't need to worry about a damned thing. Hell, they could go to Houston and help grandma take control of the portal to the dragons' home world. Wouldn't that throw a wrench in the opposition's gears?

The more I thought about it, the more it made sense, but I kept my speculation to myself. The politics of dragons were none of my business, after all. I merely inclined my head as I assured her of my continued support and protection.

"Thank you for sharing your story with me. I want you to know, this changes nothing between us. You're welcome to stay here as long as you like, and your secret is safe with me."

As always, you have my gratitude, druid. Finally, it seems I have the opportunity to repay your hospitality. Let us devise a plan so that you might return to Hugh's Town and convince my mother that you are no threat to her or our people.

Although hours had passed in the Grove, when I returned to Houston on the alt-timeline Earth, only minutes had transpired. As expected, Emberlance was waiting for my return, high up in the clouds. After I appeared in the park on the concrete jogging path, it was only a matter of moments before she dove out of the sky at me.

Getting a dragon to stop and have a rational conversation with their prey was hard enough; doing it while they were dive-bombing you was that much more difficult. Since my earlier pleas for clemency and parley had been ignored, Smokedancer had suggested a different approach. Following her instructions, I appeared in the park just long enough to flash a plate-sized item, then I laid that item on the sidewalk and teleported the hell out of there.

As expected, the dragoness landed lightly beside the "gift" I'd left for her, settling to the ground with gentle beats of her wings so as not to blow it into the bushes. Once Emberlance had enough time to recognize the object for what it was, and to analyze it accordingly, I portalled back into the area.

This time, rather than appearing out in the open, I instructed the Oak to drop me off inside a nearby building, hidden in the shadows and concealed by my chameleon spell. From where I stood, I still had a direct view of the location where I'd appeared moments before. But more importantly, I was within telepathic range of Smokedancer's mother.

Where did you get this?

The elder dragon's voice echoed inside my head. Rather than overwhelming my thoughts with sheer amplitude as her daughter had, Emberlance's tone was even and calm, if authoritative and stern as well.

"I got it from the owner," I replied as I walked to the window.

"Obviously," the dragoness said, turning her head slightly, so she could see me out of the corner of her eye.

Emberlance's voice sounded quite human, albeit louder, deeper, and more resonant than the typical human female. Yet, it was still very feminine in quality, and husky as well. In fact, it reminded me of a certain alpha werewolf with which I was acquainted. To my surprise, I experienced a momentary pang of longing and regret as I adjusted my expectations for how this conversation would go.

That she'd spoken aloud was quite a surprise, as Smokedancer hadn't mentioned her mother might do so. I'd never heard the daughter's voice, except when she released a shriek of triumph after a successful hunt. Or, when she was chirping at her children. I thought I'd heard her purring once, but she was bedding down for the evening with her brood, and I considered it to be too personal a moment to eavesdrop further.

"Well, this is a pleasant surprise," I said, recovering as I dropped my chameleon spell. "Smokedancer always communicates via telepathy."

Emberlance crouched with her left flank to me as she examined the object I'd brought for her, holding it by the edges between her thumb and foreclaw. In handling the item, the dragon displayed a delicate precision that I previously thought to be impossible for a creature of her size. Although her full attention seemed to be on the object in her talons, I had the feeling she was watching me all the while.

"The ability to use human speech fluently is a rare trait among our kind," the great dragoness replied. She paused for several long seconds, turning her daughter's dragon-scale over to look at it this way and that. "Is she well?"

"Quite. She's been under my protection for some time, and both she and her children are thriving."

A low rumble emanated from the huge green dragon's throat. At first, I thought I'd upset her, then I realized she was purring. Emberlance turned to face me, slowly enough to show she intended no threat, but fast enough to remind me how dangerously quick she was, despite her bulk.

"We dragons can convey a great deal of information by scent, which is likely why Smokedancer gave you this scale. It's a great privilege to be entrusted with such a gift."

"She was clear that it wasn't meant for me, but for you."

"Even so, I hope you understand what an honor she has bestowed upon you."

I bowed my head while keeping Emberlance in sight. "I do now."

"My daughter names you dragon-friend, and master druid. Is Finnegas no more?"

"He…" That question caught me off guard, and my voice caught in my throat as I answered. "My master has passed into the Land of Youth."

Truthfully, I had no idea what had happened to Finnegas in this timeline. Yet, Smokedancer had said her mother would know if I dissembled even the slightest bit. I didn't want to divulge too much, so I answered as honestly as possible.

"I am sorry to hear that. He was a great druid, and a friend to our kind." She tucked her daughter's scale somewhere up under one of her own on her breast. "I asked you earlier *where* you got this scale."

"I'm sorry, but that I will not say. Smokedancer chooses to remain in hiding, and I have offered her my protection. I'm sure you understand why I will not break that trust."

Emberlance sat back on her haunches while lifting her upper body on her forelegs. Her head snaked forward on her long, serpentine neck, until her Mack truck-sized head hung level with the window where I stood on the third floor of the building. She snorted puffs of smoke as she fixed me with her hubcap eyes. It was intimidating, but I stood my ground.

"It is good for my clan to have such a loyal friend among the druids," she finally said, breaking the silence. "Perhaps someday circumstances will change, and my daughter will be able to visit me with my grand-drag-onlings."

I thought it best to avoid telling her that her grand-drag-onlings were quickly growing into dragons themselves, so I kept my mouth shut on the matter. "She saved my life, at great risk to her own. I've vowed to do everything I can to ensure their safety until that time, and after."

"Then you have my gratitude. Tell me, druid, why did you trespass into my territory? Was your mission merely to bring me news of my daughter, or do you have other business?"

"I came to ask a favor. You see, I'm about to attack your neighbor to the north, and I'd like permission to cross through your lands. That way, I can take Ateas by surprise."

A loud rumble came from the great dragoness' chest, which soon turned into a sort of coughing wheeze as it escaped her throat. It quickly became clear that she was laughing, and I felt my face flush.

"I'm sorry—did I say something funny?"

"I am not laughing at you, druid. I'm simply wondering where you keep that sizable pair of gonads."

I lifted the Craneskin Bag at my side as I flashed a smile. "I keep them in here, actually. It's the only place big enough to store them."

Emberlance's eyes widened, then she laughed even louder and more enthusiastically than before. As she did, she filled the air with smoke, which I casually blew away by conjuring up a soft breeze. Her wheezing laughter died away after a few moments, and she wiped her eye with a scaly knuckle.

"Ah, but you are your master's apprentice," she chuckled. "Knowing that The Seer is gone, I'd hate to see his successor killed in a vain attempt to rid the world of Ateas. Not that I wouldn't want to see that crusty old leech put in his place. He's been a thorn in my side since your civilization fell to the Vampyri-Fae alliance and their machinations. Always sending the dead into my territory, forcing me to patrol more often than I'd like." She spat flaming spittle on the ground contemptuously, scraping the fire out with her tail immediately after. "May he someday rot in Hades, where he belongs."

I inclined my head slightly. "Then I'd be correct if I said you'd like to have him removed from your doorstep?"

"You would. I'd have done it myself, but I haven't been able to draw him from his seat of power. Destroying him would require that I abandon my post. However, the moment I did so, the fae would take advantage of my absence by sneaking across our borders. Or even worse, their gods."

I crossed my arms over my chest, sucking air through my teeth as I shifted my gaze to the north. "I see. What if I had a way to hobble him considerably—perhaps even to force him to retreat entirely?"

"I'd be most interested in hearing about it."

"I couldn't divulge too much, since he seems to have eyes everywhere." I leaned forward, lowering my voice conspiratorially for effect. "However, what I can say is that I think I have a way to weaken him, effectively reducing his ability to control the undead. But I need a way to get close enough to him to unleash it, without tipping him off that I'm coming."

Emberlance blinked twice, then her forked tongue snaked out across her scaly upper lip. "Tell me more, druid. We dragons love a good plot, especially when it's designed to undermine our enemies."

CHAPTER
FIFTEEN

"YOU CAN'T BE SERIOUS." Crowley's eyes might have made his expression difficult to read, but there was no mistaking the derision in his tone. "Going in alone is suicide—surely you realize that."

Smiling broadly, I snapped with both hands and shot Crowley the ol' finger guns. "That's why you two will be attacking from the north while I'm sneaking in from the south."

"A distraction," Saint Germain said. "How droll."

Crowley glanced at the vampire before turning his attention to me again. "And not at all obvious. Do you not think that Ateas will notice your absence during our attack?"

"Got it covered. The Oak will create a simulacrum that'll be right there beside you. Anyway, it's not like you'll be making a full-on frontal assault. All you need to do is harass his border patrols and make him think we're probing his defenses."

Saint Germain leaned back in his chair with his fingers

interlaced over his stomach, which was decidedly paunchier than it had been when we captured him weeks earlier. He'd been eating well since he arrived at Crowley's hideout. The central Texas area was rife with humans who preyed on other humans to survive, and we'd given Jacques carte blanche to cull their numbers.

I didn't even want to think about what I was going to do with him when he ran out of evil people to kill—never mind what would happen when Crowley's spell wore off and Le Boucher came back. There were only so many cannibals and slavers in the area, after all. I needed to get this mission finished so I could end him for good, just as I'd promised.

The vampire steepled his hands as he tapped his index fingers together. "His plan might work, at least until Ateas probes the decoy. It's a better plan than anything we've come up with yet."

The shadow wizard sneered as he side-eyed the vampire. "Fine, but he still hasn't explained how he intends to overpower Ateas by himself."

"'He' has it covered." I spread my arms wide. "C'mon, guys—it's me. Don't you trust me?"

"No," the two of them said simultaneously.

"Sheesh. Sure is good to be loved." I grabbed a package of peanut butter crackers from a basket on the break room table, tearing it open as I spoke.

"I am a genetically altered, spiritually possessed, supernatural hyper-predator," Saint Germain quipped. "And therefore incapable of love."

"Figure of speech," I replied, rolling my eyes.

Crowley sighed heavily. "It's not that I don't admire your pluck, druid. It's that I don't wish to see you killed before we even have a chance to put our plan in motion. As we've previously established, no druid, no plan. Forgive me if I fail to see the wisdom in allowing you to enter an ancient master vampire's seat of power alone."

"Ancient master vampire *and* necromancer," Saint Germain added.

Crowley inclined his head at the vampire. "I stand corrected."

"Look," I said, pointing at our necromancer with a bright orange, cracker-and-peanut-butter sandwich, "we've already established that neither of you can face Ateas directly. He'd have Saint Germain hanging from puppet strings in no time, and you already admitted that your magic can't hold a candle to his."

"Yes, but—"

"But nothing," I continued. "I can deal with Ateas by himself, but I can't deal with him *and* Alalngar at the same time. Based on the intel I gathered while I was gone, Garr is still alive. If he's with Ateas, that indicates that he's healed and at full strength. That means I need you two to deal with him."

I tossed the cracker in my mouth, chewing it and savoring the flavor. Crowley's lair was stockpiled with crap like peanut butter, snack crackers, jelly, and coffee—stuff that had long ago become difficult to find in the Hellpocalypse. Since neither the wizard nor Saint Germain ate regular food, I'd been pigging out on it every chance I got.

"Disgusting," Saint Germain said, turning his nose up at me. "Those things smell like dirty feet and unnatural chemistry."

"You have no idea what you're missing," I replied as I shoved the rest of the pack in my mouth.

Crowley scowled. "Please avoid leaving crumbs on the floor. It's difficult enough keeping rodents out of this place as it is."

"Don' uh deh' ee 'em?" I asked, spitting crumbs out as I spoke. Crowley arched an eyebrow, so I used a little druid magic to turn the crumbs to ash. It still left a mess, but at least it wouldn't attract mice.

"My minions eat rodents when they're able, but for the most part, their reflexes are too slow to catch them." The wizard made an offhanded gesture. "I'd get a cat, but—"

"Not many of those left."

"Precisely." He glanced at Saint Germain. "Getting back to the issue at hand—could Garr have healed in such a short period of time?"

"He could with the necromancer's help." Saint Germain made a flippant gesture with his hand. "The *other* necromancer, I mean."

"Right," I said. "The one thing we do know is that Ateas never leaves his HQ. For whatever reason, he sticks close to home at all times.

"Why would he roam?" Crowley said. "He can project his consciousness through his minions. Thus, he has no need for travel."

I tapped a finger on my chin, staring off into the distance. "Yeah, I'm not so sure if that's the only reason he's a homebody."

The vampire arched an eyebrow at me. "Oh? Is there something you know that we don't?"

I didn't want to share my suspicions in front of Saint Germain, so I simply shrugged. "Call it a hunch. But it's pretty much a given that the old fart will send out his best boy if he thinks he has a chance to take me out. And

I'll bet dimes to donuts that Alalngar is raring for a rematch."

"Thus, we're to deal with Garr whilst you sneak into the Deadlands and do what needs to be done." Crowley crossed his arms over his chest, stroking his chin. "I don't like this, not one bit."

"Give me a better plan, and we'll do that instead."

"As you well know, I have none." He side-eyed the vampire again. "Germain?"

"Don't look at me. I'm simply here to destroy your lesser enemies and commit suicide. I'm perfectly content to leave the planning to you two human geniuses."

"Your enthusiastic endorsement leaves me absolutely giddy," Crowley deadpanned. He turned his attention back to me, frowning slightly. "I suppose that means we'll do it. Be advised, should you get caught, there'll be no 'nick of time' rescues on this mission."

"I'm well aware." I said, crossing my arms as I glanced back and forth at the two of them. "Nothing further? Then get your collective shit together. We'll execute this plan at sundown."

———

Leaving Crowley and Saint Germain to their own devices, I spent the remainder of the day getting ready. That meant spending a few days inside the Grove preparing spells—the equivalent of minutes in Earth time. Then, I used the rest of my time to meditate and pig out on graham crackers and peanut butter, of course. I couldn't go into battle on an empty stomach, after all.

Once night fell, it was time to gather the troops and

transport them into position. Crowley had a considerable retinue of the undead under his control. Interestingly, his horde consisted completely of ghouls and revenants outfitted in black leather armor that had been painted with runes and glyphs.

When I asked him about it, he gave me a look that could peel paint. "How else will you and Saint Germain know which undead to attack and which to leave alone?"

I wasn't about to admit that I hadn't thought about it before he mentioned it, nor was I going to ask him about his new obsession with dressing corpses in black leather. He was entitled to his hobbies, after all.

Crowley went on to explain that he had to reinforce his necromantic spells to avoid losing troops to the enemy. Without the glyphs on the armor, Ateas would wrest them from his control in short order.

"Makes sense to me," I replied. "Whenever you're ready, open a portal, and we'll move out."

I'd have preferred to attack at dawn, as we'd have a greater chance of catching Ateas' forces off guard at that time. There would also be fewer of the more powerful undead for Crowley and Jacques to deal with—nos-types, revenants, and the like. But, for my plan to work, my timing would be essential.

As for the big guy himself, I doubted I could catch him with his pants down, no matter what time of day or night I showed up. I also had no idea how long it would take to reach the heart of his territory, so timing wouldn't be a factor. I only hoped that Saint Germain, Crowley, and his undead troops could keep up their attack until I was able to reach my goal.

Jacques stood by, looking bored, as Crowley fussed and frittered over the few dozen undead he'd managed to prepare for the mission. Unlike the feral, undisciplined hordes I'd seen throughout the Hellpocalypse, these deaders stood as still as soldiers in four even rows. Each row comprised a "squad" consisting of two revs and a dozen ghouls, all armored and equipped with weaponry—just like living humans.

The revenants carried light swords, which suited them well, considering their greater speed and agility. Apparently, the kind of blade didn't matter as much as the weight. Some had katanas, others machetes, and still others carried the odd gladius or Bowie knife.

As for the ghouls, they wielded blunt weapons—maces, clubs, and hammers. Again, the exact type didn't seem to matter. Crowley's ghouls had everything from medieval reproductions to heavy metal pipes to baseball bats with nails sticking out of them.

I'd never seen the undead use tools before, but they held their weapons as if they knew how to handle them. I could only assume that Crowley had amped up their intelligence somehow via necromancy, which was a scary fucking thought. The last thing the world needed was smarter ghouls and revs running amuck with weapons in their hands.

Crowley must've noticed the look of concern on my face. "Never fear, the spell that enhances their cognition only lasts a short while. By the time the sun rises again, they'll have reverted to their former savage selves."

"Those that haven't been torn to pieces," Saint Germain muttered.

"The bottom line is, the clock is ticking." I checked my

watch, noting that we were thirty minutes past sundown. "Let's get this show on the road."

Crowley nodded, opening a portal inside the underground tunnel large enough for his troops to walk through four abreast. As we'd previously agreed, the other side of that portal opened just south of College Park, on the north side of Ateas' lands. That was where we'd stage the first attack.

Before the undead apocalypse, The Woodlands had been the brainchild of a Texas oil magnate, his idea of the perfect urban utopia. It consisted of ten master-planned "villages," each set up like small towns, with residential areas, retail zones, grocery stores, and so on. Everything surrounded a central commercial hub, with manmade lakes, walkways, a shopping mall, restaurants, a medical center, and a few sky-rise buildings, which was where Ateas was said to have set up shop.

The whole thing had been this kind of weird, upscale metro-suburban hell, and I found it odd that it was where the lich had decided to make his home. But who was I to tell an ancient master vampire-slash-necromancer where he could set up shop? Maybe the guy liked having a Nordstrom's and a P.F. Chang's close by—hell, I didn't know. All I did know was that it'd make him that much easier to find, and that's all I cared about.

As for the lich's defenses, they were extensive. Interestingly, besides the anti-portal wards, they were primarily based on numbers alone. Emberlance had informed me that Ateas had countless small hordes of a few thousand undead that marched in circles around the perimeter of his territory. The route they followed had been set by their master, and the hordes did not deviate from it.

All told, roughly 1,000,000 undead patrolled the border of the lich's territory, split into groups of 1,000 to 2,000 deaders. That, combined with the stragglers, made it virtually impossible for anyone who didn't belong to penetrate the outer perimeter without getting swarmed by zombies. Whenever scavengers or a group of survivors entered the area, they'd soon be spotted by one of the mindless sentries. That zed would sound the alarm, and all the rest of the undead within earshot would answer the dinner bell.

But that wasn't close to the extent of Ateas' perimeter defenses. He also had nosferatu and revenants camped out in abandoned homes and retail stores all around the outskirts of his lands, just beyond the loop where the undead patrolled. Despite the natural territoriality of revs and nos-types, their assigned areas overlapped enough to create a second net that kept the living out of the area.

In short, sneaking into The Deadlands was suicide. If the revs and nosferatu didn't catch you, then the zombie hordes would. Having never seen the place, I couldn't figure out why any living person would want to get in there at all. Moreover, it didn't make sense that the ancient lich would want to keep everyone out, humans included.

What was inside The Deadlands that would make it worth trying to sneak past more than a million undead? And what was Ateas hiding in there that made it so vital to keep humans and the other supernatural races out of his home?

Guess I'll find out once I get inside.

———

When we exited the portal, the first thing that hit me was the stench. Despite that the wind was blowing from a northeasterly direction, the smell of rot and death hung on the air like a fog. With every breath, that miasma of decay clogged my airways, triggering my gag reflex and making it difficult to breathe.

Knowing that the odor was literally microscopic pieces of decayed human flesh, it gave me an idea. On instinct, I crafted a living, breathing mask made from wood, moss, grass, and druid magic. After clamping it over my mouth, I grew straps to hold it in place. The mask fed on the particles of dead flesh floating on the breeze, filtering them out and releasing fresh, oxygenated air each time I inhaled.

Geez, why didn't I ever think of this before?

On reflection, I realized my bark skin armor spell worked much the same way in allowing me to breathe; I'd just never made the connection. Necessity was always the mother of invention, and having missed out on much of what comprised a proper druidic education, I was forced to make stuff up on the fly. Briefly, my thoughts turned to Finnegas, and I wondered if I had made the right call in refusing to recruit him from the time streams.

The crunch of bones under my feet forced me to refocus on the current situation. I hadn't noticed the landscape while I was conjuring the mask, so focused was I on trying to get clean air in my lungs. Glancing down, I saw I was standing on a carpet of skeletal remains that stretched out all around me.

Turning a slow circle, I took in our surroundings. We had landed in the parking lot of a Walmart, adjacent to the intersection of the I-45 freeway and Texas State Highway 242. According to Emberlance, this was the northernmost border of Ateas' claimed territory, and 242 made up much of the route where his undead hordes patrolled.

Everywhere I looked, bones and skulls covered the ground. Most were human, but some were fae. I even saw signs of other species, including a giant's skull that sat on the hood of a rusted Ford F-350 pick-up, like the devil's own hood ornament. On closer inspection, I noticed that all the bones had teeth marks.

Good heavens—it's even worse than Tethra's killing fields.

"Look alive, druid." Crowley's voice came from my left, drawing my attention to where he stood next to his four squads of undead. "It won't be long until—"

A loud screech cut him off. It came from the roof of the Walmart, and it sounded like a cross between fingers scraping across a chalkboard and metal grating on metal, amplified by a factor of ten. Silence followed, but only for a moment. Then, the call was answered by the moans of thousands of undead, coming from the roadway to the south.

I snapped my head around, spotting the revenant that had alerted the horde to our arrival. My goal in coming with Crowley and Saint Germain had not necessarily been to support them in their attack, but to be seen in battle. I needed Ateas to think I was here, and that meant sticking around long enough to know he'd spotted me participating in these harrying attacks.

Being identified required me to keep my skin exposed, for a while at least. I had to get the lich's attention before I covered myself with my bark skin spell. Only then could I switch places with the Oak's simulacrum and portal the hell out of here.

My best bet was to engage with one of the more capable

sentries, as they were most likely to be monitored by their master. The revenant was the closest candidate, so I marked its position before getting Crowley's attention.

"I'm going after that thing on the roof of the store. Follow the plan, alright? Hit-and-run—*run* being the operative word. Capiche?"

Crowley tsked. "Why you insist on using obscure slang terms at times like these is beyond my comprehension. Doesn't it make more sense to limit your vocabulary to standard language, so you might communicate your intentions clearly?"

I hid my face with my hand for a second before meeting his gaze. "Do. You. Understand?"

"Yes, I 'capiche' your meaning, although only by inference. We will stick to the plan. Good luck, druid."

"Luck is for losers," I replied.

"Good hunting, then," Saint Germain called as he turned to face the coming rush of undead.

"That's more like it," I yelled. "Right back at ya', Jacques."

The last thing I wanted was to be surrounded by a flood of undead while unprotected in my half-Fomorian form. Once I covered myself in a thick layer of magic bark, being in the thick of things would be less problematic. Even so, I still didn't want to be stuck here fighting zombies and ghouls.

I allowed myself one last glance at Crowley and Saint Germain, watching for a moment as the vampire leapt into the center of the horde with reckless abandon. Soon after, a zombie's head came flying out of the crowd where the vampire had landed. Meanwhile, Crowley's troops created a cordon around him, with the ghouls on the outside and the revenants creating a smaller, inner circle of protection.

For a moment, I was concerned about his well-being. Then, a sickly yellow mist floated above Crowley's troops, gliding across the parking lot to settle over the giant's skull. The skull began to glow brightly with that same pale-yellow light, then it and hundreds of other giant bones floated up out of the skeletal garden.

The giant's skeleton assembled itself, even as it was knit together with Crowley's shadow magic. Black, tarry mists settled in between every joint, giving the thing ligaments that enhanced the necromantic magic that animated it. The giant skeleton stepped inside Crowley's cordon, scooping the wizard up and setting him on its shoulders. From there, Crowley began laying about with death magic and shadow tentacles, tearing into the undead that already surrounded his minions.

Yeah, he'll be fine.

I chuckled softly to myself as I marveled at the shadow wizard's resourcefulness, then I sped off toward the roof of the superstore.

CHAPTER
SIXTEEN

ZIPPING across the parking lot at full speed was impossible due to all the skulls, femurs, and other large bones littering the ground. Instead, I skipped and hopped between bare spots, finding my footing as I landed, then pushing off immediately, gaining momentum as I went. As I traversed the lot, I examined the storefront, marveling at the fact that most of the glass was uncovered and intact.

Never seen that before.

Seeing a post-apocalyptic Walmart that hadn't been looted and trashed was a miracle, as most such stores had been picked clean in the weeks following Z-Day. Despite worldwide societal collapse, radioactive fallout, and mobs of undead walking the streets, people still had to eat. That was how the second wave of humans died—by venturing out in an effort to avoid starvation.

The third wave of deaths included those who were smart enough to remain hidden. Most of them either committed suicide, or they starved to death. I guess it was better than being eaten alive, but to each their own.

Clearly, this area had been under inhuman control soon after the bombs fell and the dead rose. That made me even more suspicious about what had been going on here. Was this where the enhanced vyrus had been created—in the middle of upscale suburbia?

Hell, this might even have been one of the locations where it was released.

I could figure that mystery out later. Presently, I needed to confront this revenant, kill it, and then slip away to the northern edge of Emberlance's territory. Then, I'd sneak into the heart of Ateas' territory, beat the fuck out of him, get my blood sample, and boogie.

Yep, no pressure.

By the time I neared the store, I was leaping twenty to thirty feet in a bound—more than enough to propel me onto the building on my final jump. I landed on the edge of the roof, balancing on the raised lip, pistol in hand. Thirty feet in front of me, the revenant crouched atop an HVAC unit like a caveman, ass to heels with her arms between her legs.

Like most revenants, this one had been young in life, a teenage girl from the looks of it. She was slender, almost waif-like, perhaps fourteen or fifteen at the time of her death, and built like a ballet dancer or a distance runner. Why the infection tended to turn young adults and children into revs, I'd never know.

Yet another young life, taken by the vyrus.

Revs were an oddity among the undead. They had thick, dark blood like vamps, but their flesh was somewhere between a vampire and a zombie. It was denser than healthy human tissue, and they usually didn't rot like zeds.

Yet they stank like zombies, and when injured they didn't heal right after feeding like vamps did.

They were also smarter than the average deader, but nowhere near as bright as a higher vamp, or even a nos. A revenant's intelligence was more feral and predatory in nature, focused on finding prey and luring it into places where they could make an easy kill. Yet, there was nothing easy about killing a revenant.

And honestly? I was not looking forward to killing this one.

The girl had long, dark, stringy hair that hung over her face, hiding her facial features. She wore gore-stained yoga pants that were torn at the knees, and a loose Misfits t-shirt that revealed thin, pale arms. Where her skin wasn't obscured by ink, gangrenous veins popped out just beneath the surface. The venous distention was caused by the infection rushing through her system, transforming blood and tissue alike as it went.

Her black fingernail polish was chipped where it clung to nails that had been thickened and elongated by the vyrus. I knew from experience that those nails carried the infection, as did her saliva and all other bodily fluids that remained in her system. One scratch and my Fomorian immune system would be fighting the vyrus for days, even weeks.

Like I said, revs were quick, wily creatures. As far as the danger they posed, they were only surpassed by nosferatu and higher vampires.

The trick in dealing with them was to always do it from a distance. Unfortunately, I needed to make sure that this one's master knew I was here. That meant getting up close and personal.

But maybe I can make it safer for me.

I began to raise the pistol, slowly, so as not to startle her. Just as I was about to shoot her kneecaps out, the revenant arched her neck and screeched at the overcast sky. Then, she leapt backward, disappearing behind the HVAC unit.

"Shit. Why can't things ever be easy?"

I hopped off the roof's edge and ran after her, careful to watch for areas that looked soft beneath the roof's membrane. It wasn't that I thought the roof was rotten; I was looking for traps. Some revs were known to weaken roofs and flooring, hoping that the odd stray human would fall through. A sprained ankle or broken leg made for easy prey, after all.

Thankfully, I made it to the spot where the rev had perched without incident. Once there, I slowed my pace, tiptoeing around the HVAC unit in a crouch with the pistol at the ready. As I rounded the large, rusting metal box, I cursed under my breath.

Fucking skylight. Great.

The rev had jumped through a broken window into the darkness below. That was likely where it lived during the day, where it waited for unwary humans to invade its domain. The thing likely knew every inch of the interior of the store, and it probably had dozens of places from which it could hide and pounce.

Jumping into that hole would be like pissing on an old, rusty electric fence. Sure, you might not get shocked, but why take the risk? Yet, I still hadn't seen any sign that Ateas was monitoring what the rev saw, so my options were to go back and join the battle or drop into the darkness below.

I looked over my shoulder at the parking lot, which was now swarming with undead. Saint Germain was going through them like a ripsaw, but it was like shooting the ocean with a laser beam. No sooner would he cut down a dozen zombies, than a dozen more would pour in to take their place.

As for Crowley, he appeared to be safe enough sitting atop the giant skeleton. The bone golem now had shadow tentacles growing out of its ribcage, and whenever a ghoul tried to climb its legs, a shadowy limb would pluck them off and hurl them into the distance. His troops were holding their own, but they looked to be missing a few of their original number.

My companions might've been doing okay for the moment, but I'd be torn to shreds in a heartbeat out there. I needed to make sure Ateas saw my face before I armored up, and no way was I facing that horde without protection. Getting infected again was a big "nope" for me, thank you very much.

I peered into the darkness below one more time, hoping to catch a glimpse of the revenant. The rev was nowhere to be found, but I did spy a familiar sight in a beam of pale moonlight that had pierced the clouds above. There, some twenty feet below, sat a box of snack cakes in the middle of a grocery aisle.

Fuck it, Ima kill this thing, then Ima grab me some raspberry Zingers and a Sunny D.

Two items that were guaranteed not to spoil in the apocalypse were cellophane-wrapped snack cakes and anything with high-fructose corn syrup in it. With a prospective reward of orange-flavored drink, cream-filled sponge cake, and a massive sugar high to goad me on, I cussed silently and dropped into the dark interior below.

———

Rather than leap all the way to the floor, I stealthily landed on the topmost level of a line of shelving ten feet beneath the skylight. As I touched down, my feet kicked up a cloud of dust, making me thankful for the moss mask I wore. Yet, through the mask, I still detected the faint but unmistakable scent of decomposition and death.

Somebody's done a lot of killing in here.

In a spot of faint moonlight that shone through the skylight above, I saw signs of the revenant's predation. There sat an open and discarded backpack, spilling its contents across the floor. A bag of potato chips, a few cans of corn, and two water bottles marked a haphazard trail that ended where another, bloodier one began.

A wide, thick smear of blood started at the water bottles, leading off into the deeper recesses of the store. Something —or rather, someone—had been dragged away from their haul. Ambushed while they were celebrating their unbelievable good luck, no doubt.

Coulda told them there's no such thing as good luck in the Hellpocalypse. Only the careful, and the dead.

Swiveling my gaze left and right as far as possible, I performed a rapid assessment of my position. The shelves on which I stood separated the bread aisle from the canned goods in the grocery section of the store. I waited for my eyes to adjust to the gloom, crouching stock still as I listened for any movement in the surrounding darkness.

Nothing. All clear, for now.

No matter how still and quiet I remained, being silhouetted by the moonlight was no way to hide from a nocturnal predator. As soon as I was certain I wasn't about to be attacked, I glanced at the bread aisle below, seeking a safe place to leap. There, something of interest caught my eye. Every bag of bread was full of mold, but next to a clear spot in the aisle, I spotted an entire section of snack cakes that was virtually untouched.

Jackpot.

I wasn't about to go traipsing off into the pitch-black interior of the store, enhanced Fomorian vision or no. Sure, I could see in minimal light, but my night vision was nowhere near that of a vamp or a werewolf. And yeah, I could cast a cantrip to enhance my vision, but some sanguivores could also see in the magical spectrum. Casting that spell would light me up like a Christmas tree.

Besides, I needed to appear helpless. Otherwise, I'd be chasing that damned rev all night. I wanted it to come to me—when I was damned good and ready for it, of course.

Vampires had excellent night vision, like that of a cat, and many could also see in the infrared spectrum. Of course, revenants also shared that advantage. I was certain this rev was counting on having the superior vision of the two of us, and she was likely waiting to ambush me from the deepest shadows of the store. So, I used my druid powers to tap into the abilities of one of the store's other inhabitants.

Texas is home to dozens of bat species, one of the most common being the Mexican free-tailed bat. There was a massive colony under the Waugh Bridge near downtown Houston, and as expected, this area was full of them as well. It took only a moment before I was able to psychically connect with one that was flitting around the interior of the building. As soon as I did, I tapped into its sonar to scan the room.

There.

The bat's superior senses revealed that the revenant hid atop an overhead ventilation duct, deep within the recesses of the gloom-filled store. She was in the back, near the spot where the majority of Walmarts stocked water. That was the first place most people would go when scavenging a new location.

Looks like she's not going to come to me after all. Figures.

The rev was smart, I'd give her that. But if she was acting on instinct, did that mean Ateas wasn't tuned in? This was getting tedious, and I needed to be spotted, so I could end this creature and roll.

"Fuck it," I muttered. "Fortune favors the bold."

So did Death, but I wasn't about to split hairs. With a shrug, I jumped off the shelf and onto the floor, making as much noise as possible in hopes the rev would take the bait.

After landing, I snagged a box of Swiss Rolls, some Oatmeal Creme Pies, and a package of raspberry Zingers as I marched down the aisle toward the back of the store. Everything but the Zingers went into my Bag, then I tore that box open, grabbing one before stowing the rest.

Cellophane is so very loud when handled. It's something you don't realize until you're opening a bag of chips in a quiet theater—or in a spooky, abandoned Walmart in the Deadlands after dark. But it was noise I wanted now, as I figured it would make me an irresistible target for the revenant.

I hit the end of the aisle, munching on a Zinger as I rounded the corner. After pausing to get my bearings, I turned right and headed down a central walkway toward the rear of the store. As I went, I kept an eye on the almost invisible shadow that still sat atop the vent, right where the bat's sonar had pegged it.

Damn, this one is hellaciously stubborn. Or lazy. Take your pick.

For a moment, I considered taking a pot shot from where I was, but I didn't want to risk accidentally killing it. Knowing my luck, I'd get a headshot and have to go hunting for another one before I could portal away. Yet, I didn't want to get too close, either, due to the risk of infection.

Finally, I settled on stopping a few rows from the vent, where I could brace the pistol against a support post and get a nice, clear shot. There I stopped, popping the last sticky bit of raspberry-covered, creme-filled pound cake into my mouth. Resisting the urge to lick my fingers, I wiped my hand on my pants. Then I lifted the pistol, rotating it slightly to brace the magazine against the top of a self-service pricing station as I lined up the shot.

The pistol had Tritium sights, so it was easy to get a decent sight picture and alignment. Aiming for the creature's leg, I squeezed the trigger with a slow, steady rearward pressure.

"*Screeeeeiiiiiiitttcccchhhhh!*"

Something howled in the darkness to my right, a split second before a small, dark figure tackled me from the side. The thing was moving fast enough to bowl me over on my side, slamming me to the ground. The gun fired, and the muzzle flash momentarily lit up the gloom, even as the creature attacking me shredded the side of my face with its nails, tearing away my mask in the process.

Acting on instinct, I backhanded the creature with my gun hand, pistol-whipping it across the jaw. I was strong in this form, if not thick-skinned, and the crack of the gun smacking my attacker's flesh echoed in the confines of the store. Hot blood ran down my cheek as I rolled to my back, popping off two more rounds while aiming for center mass.

Like a freeze-frame photo, the muzzle flash illuminated my attacker with daylight brilliance in the darkness. Each shot revealed what had tackled me, unveiling the surprise second predator that had been waiting for me in the darkness. Although I saw the thing's face clearly, I couldn't believe my eyes.

———

This cannot be happening.

Despite the absolute unlikelihood of his return, Richard crouched not six feet from me with blood dripping from his hands. It was the same motherfucking kid I'd rescued from that church—the very one I'd split in half with a fifty-caliber rifle round and buried beneath the Mopac Expressway.

I couldn't understand it—I'd put the kid six feet under myself, and then checked his remains the day after to be certain he was dead. How the hell could he be lurking there, with no sign of injury to the bare, ashen skin of his abdomen and chest?

Granted, he looked like the thing that had led that horde to our doorstep in Austin, and not like the kid I'd saved. No, this version of Richard was the one that had been changed into something *other*, down to the mouthful of needle-like teeth and his creepy black eyes.

"What the actual fuck?"

Richard flashed a wide smile, transforming his expression from one of feral rage to intelligent maleficence. "Hello again, druid. Did you miss me?"

Richard's voice was the same, but different—ragged, raspy, and deeper, with that calliope resonance I'd heard before from people possessed by multiple spirits. Yet I had a feeling that just one mind was riding Richard's.

"Ateas."

Blood dripped down my jaw and onto my jacket, and the wounds on my face burned like salt had been poured into them. The flesh around the cuts throbbed with every heartbeat, even as they were starting to close. Healing wouldn't make much difference, as the damage had already been done.

Shit. I'm infected.

"I can see from your expression that you've just now realized your predicament." Richard raised a hand to his lips, sucking the blood off his fingers, one by one. "Oh, now that is interesting. Not quite human, are you?"

At that moment, I wanted to panic. I could feel the disease spreading through my system, much more rapidly than it had before. I resisted the urge, getting a grip on my nerves as I let my focus expand and soften. That way, I could pull in as much information as possible, allowing me to pick that data apart later when I had time to think.

To my left, I made note as the revenant I'd been stalking earlier dropped from the vent to the floor, disappearing behind a row of shelving. As for Richard, I noticed he wore only a pair of hospital scrub trousers, and nothing else. He also had no scars or marks on his torso, save for those made by the rounds I'd just put in him.

Outside, Crowley called urgently to Saint Germain. I couldn't make out specifics, but his voice sounded strained and insistent. At the front of the store, deaders began to beat violently on the glass. In the entrance, where a glass door had been shattered, I heard the crunch of shards on the concrete floor as the dead forced their way through the opening.

Meanwhile, Ateas babbled on using Richard's vocal cords, spouting empty nonsense about how he was going to enjoy using my DNA in his experiments. Something about the new Vampyri, a better vyrus, and a new dawn for his species.

Villains—always with the monologues.

Now the moans of the undead came from within the store, and they were getting closer. Somewhere off in the darkness, a predator flitted through the shadows. The other revenant was positioning herself to attack me from behind.

Time to go.

I triggered my bark skin armor spell, letting it cover everything but my eyes, nose, and mouth. The bark hissed and sizzled on contacting the blood that dripped off my cheek—that was my druidic magic protesting as it clashed with Ateas' necromancy and the vyrus. Yet, as the soft inner membrane covered the wounds, it offered some relief from the pain.

Richard clapped softly, almost silently. "Oh, bravo druid, bravo. A shame you didn't think to spell yourself before you were infected. I doubt even druid healing magic has a cure for—"

I shot Richard between the eyes, watching his brains blow out the back of his skull with casual indifference. As he fell, I leapt forward to stand over him, looking for any signs of un-life. He twitched, so I shot him twice more, then I willed the bark to cover me completely.

Once fully disguised, I ran for the entrance to the stock-room at the rear of the store, with the other revenant and a few dozen zombies in full pursuit. Bursting through the swinging double doors, I skidded to a stop some ten feet ahead. There I turned and raised my Glock to eye level, and I waited.

When the rev came through the doors after me, I planted a round in her left eye, dropping her instantly. As the other, slower undead entered, I took my time giving them the same treatment until my magazine was empty. Backpedaling at an unhurried pace, I maintained my distance as I reloaded, then I dispatched the remaining undead that pursued me.

Knowing more were on the way, I cast a chameleon spell on myself as I told the Oak to portal the simulacrum into the store. When it appeared, I gave it a quick once over, instructing the Oak to change a couple of details, so it was as convincing as possible. Once I was satisfied that my double would pass muster, I handed it my pistol, then I ran into the employee bathroom, locking the door behind me.

CHAPTER
SEVENTEEN

AFTER CHECKING each stall to make sure I was alone, I had the Oak teleport me inside an abandoned home on the northern edge of Emberlance's demesne. Already, I felt a fever coming on, one of the first signs of a vyral infection. Soon my Fomorian immune system would be in an all-out fight with the vyrus coursing through my veins.

Well, this isn't fucked up at all.

The skin around my wounds throbbed beneath the bark, but I ignored the pain, focusing instead on what I'd just learned. Regarding Richard's reappearance, it jibed with what Guerra had told me. Maybe the kids had actually seen Richard, and not just some illusion or mental projection.

But how? There were three possible explanations, none of them good. One was that Ateas could teleport extended distances, and he'd portalled himself to Austin to recover Richard's body. In that scenario, Ateas would then have used necromancy to repair Richard's injuries and raise him from the dead… again.

The second possibility was that Ateas had done the

same thing, but from a distance. Meaning, his ability to use necromancy at a distance was much more potent and formidable than we'd seen. In many ways, that was even scarier than having an ancient vampire that could be anywhere at once. Somehow, though, I doubted it.

I had a theory regarding why Ateas guarded his territory so fiercely, and why no one ever saw him in person. If I was right, I might be able to find an advantage when I faced him in his lair. But for now, it was only a theory.

Then there was the third possibility, a scenario that was so far-fetched as to be ridiculous. Just thinking about it made me want to laugh out loud, but I couldn't completely dismiss the possibility. That possibility was, Ateas could somehow be cloning humans through an unholy marriage of science and dark magic.

Yeah, that explanation was way out in left field. Yet, it would explain a lot. In light of the vampires' food shortages, I could see how they might want to investigate the possibility.

I'd never heard of magic being used to clone a person's DNA. Sure, the fae had glamours and illusions, but that magic was only good enough to fool the mind. Illusory magic couldn't change reality.

Then there were doppelgängers, who could copy someone convincingly enough to fool their own loved ones. Yet, that was an innate magical skill. To my knowledge, it wasn't something a spell could replicate.

That still didn't mean it couldn't be done.

However, there was one major problem with my third theory. Science and magic just didn't mix—not well, anyway. It was powerful, but way too unreliable and unpredictable. That was why almost no one used techno-magic. Besides the government, that is, but those fuckers at CERBERUS were clueless as all hell.

That said, this was the Vampyri we were talking about. Like the fae, they were very long-lived, and they planned in centuries, not days, months, and years. Given enough time and resources, there was no telling what Ateas might have come up with.

Now I really want to see what he's hiding in the Deadlands.

From my current position, I had a seven-mile hike to get to the high-rise that I suspected to be Ateas' seat of power. There was one universal truth about higher vamps, and it was twice as true for the oldest of their kind: every single one of them was a pathological narcissist.

The Occidental Petroleum Corporation building jutted up from the shores of Robbins Lake as the last remaining evidence of some random oil billionaire's microphallic compensation. Being the tallest building in the area, it was the logical place for Ateas to set up shop. That's where I was headed. Whether I could get there unseen, before the vyrus laid me low, and get what I needed from Ateas was another story entirely.

One crisis at a time, Colin.

A large shadow passed overhead outside, momentarily blotting out the moonlight that shone through the broken windows of the home. Stepping over shattered glass, discarded picture frames, and a strangely intact Lego sculpture of a fire truck—all covered in blood, no less—I exited the front door, where Emberlance awaited me.

So close was she now, the dragoness appeared even more massive this time around. Emberlance had landed in the center of the residential street, her bulk reaching from one side of the lane to the other, with her tail trailing off somewhere around the corner. She must've had surprising control in flight; despite the tight quarters, she hadn't disturbed a single car or mailbox when she touched down.

When I allowed the bark armor to recede from my face and head, the dragon leaned over and sniffed me. After getting a good whiff, she snarled and snorted a cloud of smoke. I did my best not to cough, thinking it might be rude.

"You smell of The Walking Death." She was whispering, but a whisper for a dragon was like my outdoor voice at best.

"Shouldn't we be communicating via telepathy?" I asked. "I wouldn't want Ateas to find out that I gave his guards the slip."

"Don't worry, none of the vampire's minions are near. I can smell them from a mile away."

"Good to know." I pointed to the scab on my cheek, touching the surrounding flesh gingerly. The skin around the wound was puffy and hot to the touch. Moreover, I could smell the infection, even though the wound hadn't started draining. "I got scratched. It happens."

"Will you die?"

"What? No, not even. I've been infected before. My immune system is pretty strong. I'll fight it off in a few weeks, maybe a month at the outset."

"Perhaps you should wait to pursue this mission, then."

It wasn't like I hadn't already thought of it. I could go to the Grove, heal up, and come out in a few hours of Earth time, completely healed. Yet Crowley and Saint Germain were risking their asses for me right now, and I had no easy way of calling them off. Besides that, a delay of even a few hours might give Ateas time to figure out our plan.

I waved her suggestion off. "Ateas already knows I'm close, and he probably suspects that I'm coming for him. The longer I delay, the greater the chance he'll be ready for me."

The dragon snorted again. "This is a stupid plan, druid."

"I know. But I can't portal in, and a frontal assault is suicide. Stealth and subterfuge are my only hope."

She blinked, snapping her wings against her flanks. "I wish you good fortune in your mission. You will need it."

"Thanks, Emberlance. If I don't make it, a creepy shadow wizard with empty pits for eyes might come looking for me. Do me a favor, don't kill him. He's a friend."

"I wouldn't dream of it. Shadow wizards tend to be stringy, and they taste like tar pits."

"Hah! Somehow, I don't doubt that." I glanced around awkwardly, wondering if she'd actually been serious. "Look, I gotta be going. If you see a few hundred-thousand undead headed this way, you'll know I made it out alive."

My exit strategy after getting the blood sample was to haul ass south, where the dragon could cover my retreat from the air. I didn't care how many undead Ateas had at his command, they wouldn't do shit against a sustained assault from a kaiju-sized, fire-breathing dragon.

If I make it out, that is.

Emberlance bowed her head slightly. "I look forward to your return, druid."

———

Sneaking past the undead wasn't all that difficult, if you had the right spells at your fingertips. I used a combination of a chameleon spell to help me blend into the shadows, some druid magic to cover my scent, and a silence spell to prevent them from hearing me. Zombies couldn't see for shit, but they were attracted to sound, so the silence spell was a must-have for being stealthy in the Hellpocalypse.

I briefly considered using Gunnarson's cloak, but that thing was way too unpredictable. When it worked, it worked flawlessly, but it still held a grudge against me for killing Siegfried's last remaining heir. The last thing I needed was for the cloak to purposely crap out on me at the exact moment I was sneaking up on Ateas.

So, my dime store invisibility it was, and it worked well enough as I jogged into the Deadlands. As I crossed State Highway 99, heading for the greenbelt that ran along Spring Creek south of Grogan's Mill, I thought I had the whole "Deadlands" name figured out. Like the Walmart parking lot earlier, the ground here was littered with bones and corpses—most of them charred and blackened by dragon's breath.

The undead were everywhere along 99, thousands upon thousands of them. They dutifully trudged along the highway, mindlessly patrolling Ateas' southern border, following the route their master dictated—walking widdershins around the territory, of course. They were so numerous that I had a difficult time finding a gap through which to cross. I ended up following the highway west, finally crossing at an underpass that was clogged with wrecked cars somewhere near Willow.

Understandably, I assumed the place had been named for the presence of the dead—moving and not. It wasn't until I exited the greenbelt heading into The Village of Grogan's Mill proper that I realized I'd been wrong. On entering that formerly quaint, middle-to-upper-middle-class bedroom community, it wasn't the presence of the dead that struck me, but the complete lack of them.

I found zero signs of life in those neighborhoods. No zombies or ghouls shambling about, no revenants or nosferatu lurking in the shadows, and no corpses of those who'd fallen prey to said undead. Everything was oddly silent, deathly still, and picture postcard perfect as well.

There wasn't a single car wreck to be found. I saw no luggage carelessly strewn across lawns, no bicycles left in driveways, and no strollers on sidewalks. No matter where I looked, I saw none of the typical signs left by residents making a hasty exit from their homes on Z-Day.

Despite that I was short on time, and even though I could feel my temperature rising, I had to stop and look around. Out of sheer curiosity, I picked a house at random, a nice little ranch-style home with a two-car garage and a minivan parked in the drive. I crept around the side of the house through the tall grass, jumping the fence into the backyard.

Besides the fact that the pool desperately needed a cleaning, there was nothing out of order back there. Sure, the landscaping was a mess, and fallen leaves and debris covered everything, but all was in place, just as the owners had left it. Feeling perplexed, I snuck onto the back deck, staying close to the wall as I took a peek through the sliding patio doors.

Again, nothing was out of place. The table was clear, the dishes were put away, the sink empty. There were no schoolbooks laid haphazardly across the coffee table, no toys left on the floor, no bags of pet food ripped open for the family dog in hopes that they'd survive in their owner's absence. Unlike every other house in every other community I'd seen in this hellscape of a world gone mad, this home revealed no sign that the vyrus had ever struck here.

There had to be an explanation, right? Like, maybe the person who owned this house had OCD, and they'd cleaned up before blowing their brains out in a back bedroom. But after looking in every window, I saw no bodies there. It was almost as if the house had never been occupied in the first place.

Thinking that the house had to be an anomaly, I checked four other houses on the same street. In every single case, the homes had been left in an orderly condition, barren of any sign that the owners had left in a panic. Nothing out of order, everything in place, no signs of violence anywhere.

It was like the people of this community had been abducted by aliens or something. If I didn't know any better, I'd say that the former occupants had marched right out of here of their own volition. The question was, where did they go?

I desperately wanted to poke around inside the house in an effort to unravel the mystery. Yet, I needed to be on my way, and something told me I'd find more answers where I was headed than here, where only ghosts and memories stirred. With a last look through a darkened window and a shake of my head, I took off at a jog to the north, where Ateas and the fate of the world awaited.

———

The map I'd referenced before heading here said I could follow Grogan's Mill Road north to Woodlands Parkway, then cut east and head north again to the high-rise. Despite this place being as empty as a Chik-fil-A on Sunday, I still didn't want to risk following a main artery to my destination. After leaving the greenbelt, I'd followed a more direct route, cutting through neighborhoods and taking side roads to reach Ateas.

Initially, I'd intended to use my druid senses to navigate, but there were no animals anywhere in the Deadlands, not even a single insect. Thankfully, the trees and vegetation were still alive; otherwise, I'd have gone nuts from being cut off from nature so completely.

As it turned out, I didn't need any help to navigate. By the time I reached the center of Grogan's Mill, the Occidental Petroleum Building jutted up in the distance like the world's biggest hard-on. You could see the damned thing from virtually any point in the township, regardless of where you were. If I didn't find Ateas there, I'd eat my socks.

Yeah, right. Throat's so raw I can barely swallow.

The last time I got the vyrus, it was a lot like having the world's worst case of the flu, and this time was no different. I wasn't quite as sick as I'd been the last time, but I still felt feverish, and I ached all over. Besides that, my throat was sore, my skin clammy, and my mouth dry, so I decided to take a break.

The place wasn't called "The Woodlands" for nothing. With trees and vegetation everywhere, there were no shortage of places to hide. I took cover in a small copse that had a nice, thick layer of undergrowth at ground level. There I grabbed some water from my Bag and sat silently, sipping slowly as I savored the reprieve it provided my sore, scratchy throat.

Just as I was putting the cap back on the bottle, I heard a familiar noise in the distance.

"*Skrrrrrrreeeeeeeee-iiitttcccchhhh!*"

It was the same screeching cry that Richard had made after he'd been turned into a revenant. For a moment, I worried that Ateas had resurrected him a third time, and somehow tracked me here. Yet, even in my feverish state I could work out the improbability of that happening, so I remained still and listened for a time.

When I heard it again, I was able to get a lock on the direction. It seemed to be coming from the same direction I was headed, a realization that did little to bolster my confidence. My gut told me this was important, and since I was going that way anyway, I decided to investigate.

I headed north to within a few miles of my destination, until the screeching sounds led me west toward Interstate 45. The loop that the lich's legions of undead followed went far east of here, so when I came upon the freeway, it was devoid of sentries. I continued hearing the occasional shriek, so I followed my ears in an effort to unravel the mystery.

Like any highway in the Houston area, the North Freeway was lined with retail strip malls, restaurants, and big box stores. I soon came across an area with a large grocery store, a Wally World, a giant hobby store, and a massive liquor store, all within a stone's throw from each other. This wouldn't have been anything of note, except for the loud, shuffling footsteps I heard as I approached from the rear of the Walmart.

By this time, I'd been fighting the infection for a couple

of hours, and the vyrus was in full swing inside my body. I was nauseous, and my head was throbbing, especially around the wound. My chameleon spell was good, but it wasn't foolproof, so I needed a place where I could see what was going on without attracting attention.

I finally decided I needed to get on the roof of the building. Rather than attempting a twenty-foot leap in my current, weakened condition, I opted to climb a drainpipe instead. Even that relatively minor effort was taxing, and I collapsed at the top, breathless and weakened from the exertion.

While I was recovering, I heard the shriek again, this time coming from within the building. I pushed myself off the roof and onto my feet, doing my best to avoid disturbing any rocks or debris as I snuck to a skylight nearby. Making sure to approach so I wouldn't cast a shadow into the area below, I peered into the store's interior.

The building had been cleared of all its former contents, including the shelving, counters, clothes racks, and check out stations. In their place were rows upon rows of metal cages, of the kind that might be used to transport large prey animals like lions or bears. I could make out humanoid figures inside the cages, but it wasn't until one of them shrieked that I determined they weren't human.

At least, not completely. Not anymore.

There were no lights on inside the building, making it difficult to see exactly what Ateas had caged up. Finding out would require getting a closer look, and the quickest route was through the skylight. I tried prying the window, which was designed to open to allow ventilation, but it was lodged tight with rust and debris.

Risking external magic was still a no-go, as it might draw the wrong kind of attention, so I opted for strength. The silence spell should block any noise from escaping, and it was a risk I was willing to take. After producing a small pry bar from my Bag, I wedged it between the window and the frame and levered away.

CRACK!

As I pried at the frame, the window glass cracked, right down the middle. Of course, I could hear it inside my silence spell, just as I could hear external noises coming in, but no sound could escape the spell. I waited to make sure I'd not alerted anything to my presence, then I went at it again, moving the window just a tad bit more.

Almost there...

Then, the crack split and spread, spiderwebbing the entire windowpane. Again I watched and waited, and nothing seemed to be coming to investigate, so I tried a third time. This time, a small piece of glass dislodged from the window, just a dime-sized sliver, falling to the concrete floor below.

The noise it made wasn't enough to be heard outside the building, but it was enough to set a few of those things in the cages shrieking. As I vacillated over trying the window again and risking a complete collapse, the loud footsteps I'd heard earlier began to get closer. I glanced up and saw what looked like a giant egg, floating in the air roughly level with the edge of the building and moving in my direction.

Nope, not an egg—that's a skull.

I ducked down as low as I could behind the skylight, accidentally kicking a rock across the roof in the process. In the still silence of the Deadlands, I might as well have been Pippin knocking a bucket down a well in Moria. The small stone clattered across the roof and well beyond the radius of my silence spell, making noise enough to echo between the buildings.

The footsteps stopped, and the skull turned toward the building. A skeletal hand large enough to palm a truck tire reached up and over the building's topmost edge, hanging on as a huge, eyeless skull searched the roof for the source of the noise. It seemed Ateas had taken a page from Crowley's manual, animating a giant's corpse with necromancy and using it as his night watchman.

Hunkering down as best I could, I watched through dirty and cracked windowpanes as the bone golem proceeded to investigate. Its head swept back and forth, the only indication regarding where the skeletal giant's empty eye sockets searched. Finding nothing out of order, it released its grip, returning to its patrol of the shared parking lots between the buildings.

That bone golem was obviously here to guard whatever Ateas had stored inside these buildings. That meant it was of some importance, and I wanted to see what it was. Since the window was no longer an option, I decided to climb back down the drainpipe and break in through the back door.

CHAPTER
EIGHTEEN

THE VYRUS HAD MADE me so sick, I almost lost my footing climbing back down the drain. I ended up half-sliding, half-slipping down the last ten feet, but thankfully I managed to land without alerting the whole neighborhood. Between that little misadventure and my poor judgment in attempting to pry the window open, I realized just how badly the vyrus was impeding my ability to reason.

Not good.

The best thing I could do was to go lay my trap for Ateas, get my sample, and leave. Yet, I was already here and my curiosity had been piqued, so I decided to trudge ahead. It took me a while to find my lock-picking kit, as I'd not had to use it in ages, and then there was the matter of picking a lock after not having done it in months. After five minutes of fumbling, I had a door next to the loading docks unlocked.

Moving ever so slowly, I cracked open the door, pausing and bracing in case something waited for me on the other side. When nothing happened, I opened it halfway and slipped inside, shutting it carefully behind me. On surveying the space, I found myself inside the unloading area adjacent to the stockroom, where goods would be offloaded from trucks for storage and restocking.

Surprisingly, this was the one part of the store that seemingly hadn't been cleared out. Pallets, boxes, and crates were stacked everywhere, which set my mind at ease since they provided plenty of places to hide. Not that I should have needed to hide, but I was sick and feeling spooked as all hell, and I'd take any small comfort I could find.

Knowing now that whatever was in those cages could easily be set on edge, I moved through the stockroom as carefully as possible, only stopping to snag a dozen bottles of water, which I tossed in my Bag. After slaking my ever-growing thirst, I poured some water on the swinging door hinges, then I cracked them just enough to slip through into the main area of the store.

The cages were lined up in neat rows in a grid pattern that covered the entire floor, a space that was easily 100,000 square feet. Each cage was just tall enough for a grown man to stand in, but the occupants all appeared to be squatting or sitting. Not every cage looked to be occupied, either, although it was too dark for me to make out details at a distance.

Time to find out how well my dollar store invisibility performs in a roomful of revenants.

I tiptoed over to the nearest occupied cage, being careful to stay out of any incoming light so as not to cast a shadow. When I got to the cage, the occupant had its back turned to me, preventing me from seeing its face. It wore nothing but a pair of stained and torn hospital scrub trousers, just as Richard had worn when last I saw him.

It was male, or it had been in life, that much was apparent based on its musculature, skeletal structure, and the broad expanse of pale white skin that made up its back. Its dirty brown hair was shoulder-length and matted, and it stank of offal, feces, and blood. On rounding the cage, I got a good look at its face, which bore the same empty black eyes and lamprey-toothed mouth Richard had after he'd been turned.

Yet, this unfortunate soul was no one I knew. As I turned to go to the next cage, I noticed something on its shoulder—a number, tattooed into its flesh.

97-651

It took a moment for the realization to sink into my fever-addled brain, but I realized it had to be some sort of lot and subject number. I checked the cage and found a matching tag, which also had some other info such as the revenant's race, age, sex, and most interestingly, his blood type, O+.

Huh. The thick plottens.

I moved to the next cage, first checking the tag. This one was numbered "97-649"—almost the next number in sequence, but not quite. The next cage was "648", and so on. It wasn't until I got to "642" that I noticed something creepy.

Each of the revenants in cages marked "97" were identical in race, sex, and build. Could it be? I went back and got a good look at their faces. While some were disfigured from decomposition and what appeared to be self-imposed injury, they all essentially looked to have been the same man in life.

Ho-lee shee-it. This is fucked up.

Moving through the shadows as quickly and quietly as possible, I began checking other rows. Due to the size of the place, I was only able to search a quarter of it in the time I allotted myself. Twenty minutes later, I'd marked six more series numbers, all with multiple, identical subjects.

Either Ateas had gathered every set of septuplets and octuplets he could find, and then turned them into revenants, or he was cloning humans. It looked as though my nutty, far-fetched theory wasn't so crazy after all. Even with the evidence sitting right in front of me, I could hardly believe what I'd discovered.

Whelp, even a broken clock can be right twice a day.

The question was, why? Why clone a bunch of people, turn them into revenants, and keep them locked up in cages? Unless…

Maybe he hadn't intended to turn them into the undead at all.

That would make the most sense; it wasn't like there weren't enough undead in the world already. If he was building an army, all he'd have to do is swing a dead cat, and he'd have his pick of zombies, ghouls, and revenants galore. The only logical reason for Ateas to experiment with cloning would be to solve the Vampyri's food shortage—which was what I'd suspected in the first place.

Could it be that necromancy is unable to create another living human?

Considering what Luther had told me, it made sense. Not only were the Vampyri facing a serious crisis due to their "food" shortage, but vampires were notoriously conniving and power-hungry. If Ateas solved the problem, he might be able to leverage that knowledge into a complete coup over the Vampyri Council.

The lich had obviously failed to achieve the desired result, but he was keeping the rejects around for some reason. Cannon fodder, maybe?

That he'd missed the mark thus far was somewhat comforting, although I hated to think what might happen if he unleashed this many revenants on humanity. I wondered if that was actually part of his plan, after he perfected a working human cloning process.

Speaking of humanity—where are all the original test subjects?

A revenant in a nearby cage arched its head to the sky as it released a random shriek, startling me back into the present. It was too much of a risk to stay here any longer. Besides, I had places to go and ancient vampires to bleed.

Time to find that motherfucking lich.

———

By my best guesstimation, I was less than two miles from the Occidental Petroleum Building. The easiest way to get there would be to follow I-45 north, but I'd be too exposed. Instead, it made more sense to go overland through the neighborhoods south of the lakefront and plaza area.

If I could use druid magic without the risk of being noticed, it would be no problem to cut through the woods and underbrush. That would've allowed me to remain concealed virtually the entire way. Slogging it through the brush without using my powers wasn't an option, not the way I felt, so I took to the streets and sidewalks instead.

At first, it was business as usual—a virtual ghost town, with no people and no undead. After a quarter mile or so, I noticed that some yards were being maintained. Soon, a pattern emerged. It was only the upscale homes that had maintenance going on, and never the run-of-the-mill houses.

When I started seeing lights on inside some of the homes I passed, I knew something was up. It wasn't until I spotted movement inside one of those larger homes that I realized what was going on. If Ateas was doing research, then he'd need personnel to help him carry it out.

Of course—vampires are always going to live in the most upscale, luxurious places they can.

The closer I got to my destination, the more homes appeared to be occupied. No doubt, the vamps wanted to live as close to their place of work as possible. I found that amusing, considering how they liked to think of themselves as superior to humans. In many ways, they weren't so different after all.

I wondered who the poor slobs were who got stuck doing all the grunt work around here. Ateas couldn't simply use the undead to do that sort of work, as they were too dumb. Did they have humans working for them, or low-level vampires?

Call me petty, but I hoped it was vampires. Heavens knew, there was no way a vamp would be caught dead driving a garbage truck or running a power plant before Z-Day—no pun intended.

Surprise, motherfuckers—running a functioning civilization is a lot harder than it looks. Wouldn't you know it, you always need people who are willing to do the manual labor.

I was deep into thinking about how that division of labor would work in vampire society, when the distraction almost got me run over. There I was, jogging down the middle of the street, when an electric vehicle came up behind me, lights off, doing about twice the speed limit. I barely had time to leap out of the way.

Of course, the vamps had also discovered that gas and diesel got scarce awful quick after the bombs fell and society collapsed. EVs were about the only vehicles you could keep running these days, if you had a power source to charge the batteries. A vamp wouldn't need headlights to drive at night, so they probably cut the wires to save on juice.

And only a vamp would drive sixty miles an hour through a residential district at night. Fucking jackasses.

Even at that speed, I caught a good look at the female vamp behind the wheel. She was studious and mousy looking, with a pinched face and light-brown hair pulled up in a bun. The lab coat she wore told me I should follow her, since she might be my way into the building.

No way would I catch up to her at that speed, so I'd have to cut her off. After I watched her turn the corner, I gambled and took off at a run between two houses, hoping she'd have to cut back this way on the next block. Just as I reached the street on the other side, I heard the soft whine of electric motors getting closer to my position.

I would only have one chance at making her stop. The options were endless, but almost all of them involved magic. Too risky. In the end, I drew my hunting knife, flipping it so I held it by the blade's tip. As the car neared, I drew back, throwing the knife with all the force and speed I could muster.

The blade spun through the air, end over end, as the hundreds of hours of practice I'd had with weaponry of all kinds paid off once again. The knife pierced the right rear tire, blowing it out and causing the car to swerve dangerously close to the curb. The driver, being a vampire, had the reflexes to pump the brakes and counter-steer, skidding to a stop in the middle of the street.

As I approached the car from the blind spot, I drew a silver-plated stiletto from my Bag. Crouching on the passenger side of the car, I heard the *clunk* of a car door opening and shutting, then the *tap, tap, tap* of pumps on pavement. Before the female vamp knew what hit her, I'd grabbed her from behind and had the knife at her throat.

"Don't even think of shouting for help," I said. "No one will hear anyway."

"If you're working for the fae, you should leave while you can. Take this any further, and you'll be just another body walking the border by morning."

"I assure you, lady, I'm no fae." I dropped the chameleon spell, but not the silence spell. "Turn around."

As she did, I kept the knife at her throat before pinning her against the car with my free hand. I could tell by the resigned look in her eyes, she wasn't a fighter. Chances were good she'd been recruited for her technical or scientific expertise before the bombs fell, then turned as a reward soon after.

I'd just so happened to carjack a new vamp, one who'd probably never had to use her powers for anything more urgent than getting to work on time. Just to be safe, I patted her down for weapons, finding none. As I did, I noticed she had a name badge that said "Karen Walters" clipped to her lab coat.

Of course, I'd mug a Karen.

"Where do you work?" I asked.

Karen Walters sneered. "Like I said, you won't last the—"

Quicker than the eye could see, I stabbed her on the right side of the chest. The sliver-plated blade slid in below her breast and under her lab coat, where a little blood wouldn't be noticed. Her expression turned from defiance to surprise to agony, all in the span of two seconds. As she gasped and staggered, I caught her with my free hand, twisting the knife as I did so.

"Been a while since you felt pain, eh, Karen? That could've easily been your heart—game over for a vamp. I know you're fairly new to this, so let me speak plainly. I'm no normal human, and I've killed more vamps than you have years left in your miserable, tainted lifespan. I'll carve your heart out without thinking twice, unless you tell me what I want to know. Understand?"

Karen nodded, lowering her gaze and grimacing in pain as she did so. I withdrew the knife, whipping the blood off it quickly before laying the edge against her neck again.

"Once more, with feeling. Where do you work?"

The vampire's gaze briefly flicked up as she answered. "I work in the main building, in genomics."

"Well, shit—it's your lucky day, Karen. Know why?" She shook her head, eyes lowered again. "Because it's take a druid to work day, and I'm your guest of honor."

———

The clock was ticking. I didn't have time to change her tire, and I honestly didn't feel like it in my condition. The street was empty and the night still, save for the occasional shriek of a caged revenant in the distance. With no alternative, I risked the tiniest bit of druid magic, re-inflating her tire and causing the hole to seal and self-vulcanize, so the sidewall wouldn't blow out again.

I did all this while holding Karen at knifepoint, which was no mean feat in my condition. Once the tire was fixed, I shoved her into the passenger seat of the car as I followed after her.

"Get in the driver's seat, and don't you dare try to bolt."

She did as I asked, stealing a furtive glance at me as I settled into my seat. "You're a mage. I thought they killed all the mages during the purge."

"Weren't you listening? I'm a druid, not a mage. Now start driving, and shut the fuck up unless I ask you a question."

"They'll never let you through the gates."

"Didn't I tell you to shut the fuck up? Let me worry about that."

She drove on, remaining silent for the mere span of half a minute. "You're infected, I can smell it. How have you not turned?"

"I'm special, I told you that."

"No one is immune to the vyrus," she replied with certainty. "Our virologists have proven that beyond a shadow of a doubt."

"Whatever." She was right, however. I was sick as hell, but I couldn't let her know that. I resisted the urge to close my eyes and rest as I changed the subject. "Tell me about the revenants you have in those cages. The ones with the tattoos."

Karen glanced toward the knife I held at her neck, brow furrowed. "I guess it can't hurt to tell you. One of us will be dead by morning anyway."

It seemed this vamp wasn't as clueless as I'd first thought. "Talk."

"How much do you know about the work we're doing here?"

"Nothing. Speak to me like I'm a new hire." I frowned when the vampire snickered at my remark. "Something funny?"

"It's just that it reminds me of when they recruited me. That's what the suit called me, a new hire."

I sneered. "Out of curiosity, what makes a human side with a race of supernatural predators in an effort to collapse society and take over the planet?"

The vampire inclined her head slightly as she frowned. "Anyone with half a brain could see where humanity was headed. If World War III didn't end us, it'd be a pandemic, or climate change. They promised me immortality, and survival through the coming Armageddon. Once they showed me what they really were, I took the bait. Little did I know I'd be slogging away in a lab for yet another nameless corporation, even after the world ended."

"If you saw what the world is like now beyond The Deadlands, you wouldn't complain. Anyway, you were saying?"

"I know a little of it. The subjects they bring in talk, you know, when they think we aren't listening. That's as good a place as any to start with the test subjects. They bring them in every few weeks, a new batch for us to work with."

"Who brings them in?"

She shrugged, her hands blanching from pale to stark white as she gripped the wheel tighter. "Sometimes they come from Dallas, other times our security teams gather them from the Wasteland. The Master requires us to work through each batch as soon as they arrive. A few are earmarked for feeding and breeding, half for him, and the rest for research."

"You're trying to clone humans for food."

"You're smarter than you look."

I pressed the flat of the blade against her neck. "Don't push it."

The vampire shrunk into her seat as she continued. "I didn't mean—never mind. As I was saying, no one anticipated how quickly the new vyral strains would spread through the populace. The Master is trying to find a way to grow them more quickly, without breeding. Breeding is too messy, too time-consuming, and far too unreliable."

"What's the event horizon on a crisis situation for The Vampyri? How long until the point of no return?"

"Ten years at the outset. Possibly sooner, if the humans continue to die off at the current pace."

"Oh, the irony. Not that I don't want to see your kind starve. But at the cost of humanity's future? Not worth it." I laughed humorlessly. "How close are you to a solution?"

"A few decades, at least. We keep telling The Master to let us work without magical integration, but he insists on it. His goal is to clone mindless cattle." She tsked. "It's a pointless and foolish endeavor."

"I'm sure he wants to eliminate free will and control the clones, and he thinks magic is the ticket. You're right, it is pointless and foolish. Not even the gods can create life from nothing."

"There are no gods. Only monsters."

I chuckled again. "You're half right. Now, tell me about the humans who are earmarked for Ateas."

"The Master? Nobody calls him by his name—he doesn't allow it."

"Like I give a shit. Just tell me what he does with them."

"They're turned into vampires, and he—" her voice broke a little as she paused. "He eats them."

My voice dripped with sarcasm as I responded. "Aw, what's wrong, Karen? You drink human blood, but balk at a little cannibalism? Please."

"No, you don't understand. It's *forbidden*. Only a few of us know he does it, and that knowledge guarantees we'll never leave this place. Not that I have anywhere to go at the moment, but still."

That made me wonder how Luther had found out. Did he work here, was he held captive, or was he a double agent? I kept having to remind myself that this wasn't the Luther I knew, so anything was possible.

"Yeah, yeah, cry me a river. You made your bed—or coffin, in this case."

"It doesn't mean I have to serve him forever."

Something in the way she said that caught my attention. I watched her out of the corner of my eye for a moment as I tried to put my finger on it.

Ah, there it is—hope.

"You think you're going to escape or go free at some point, maybe once you solve 'The Master's' great cloning dilemma." I gave a rueful shake of my head. "Lady, for a scientific genius, you sure are stupid."

"You don't understand what it's like to know you'll live forever," she said softly, with just a hint of venom in her voice.

"Nothing lives forever, not even a god. How often does he feed?"

She pursed her lips and narrowed her eyes before answering. "Every morning, I think, based on when security comes to replace them."

"Well, this just gets better and better. Do you have access to the area where your master's cattle are kept?"

"Like I said, only a few of us know. So, yes, I can get you in there. But why?"

"None of your beeswax, Karen. You just keep driving, try not to bleed too much, and get me in that building. I'll take it from there."

CHAPTER
NINETEEN

BY THE TIME we'd driven within a few blocks of our destination, I had a suppressed .22 sitting in my lap that I'd pulled from my Bag. Just before we reached the gate to the parking garage at the main building, I ducked into the back seat, knife in one hand, pistol in the other. Once I got comfortable, I stabbed the stiletto far enough through the driver's seat to make Karen mewl.

"Oh, quit your whining. One feeding, and you'll be good as new."

Her tone was much more venomous this time—and more than a little strained. "If I look like I'm in agony when I pull up to the security checkpoint, they'll suspect something's wrong. What happens to your ingenious plan then?"

"Fine," I replied as I backed the blade out half an inch. "Satisfied?"

"That's better. I hope you can turn invisible. We're almost there."

I triggered my chameleon spell again, adding some

extra druid magic to neutralize my scent. If Karen could smell the deader vyrus on me, chances were good the guards could, too. Hopefully, they wouldn't look in the back seat. Up close, I doubted the spell would fool a suspicious vamp.

"Roll down all the windows. If I have to shoot these flunkies, I don't want the sound of shattering glass to bring others to investigate."

As I felt the car slow to a halt, I tensed in anticipation of the likelihood that I might have to take the guards out. The pistol was loaded with subsonic silver-tipped ammo, and while it wasn't completely silent, I could fart louder than the gun's report. My main concern was accuracy, as it might be difficult to line up two headshots from where I crouched.

Footsteps approached the vehicle, so soft as to be nearly silent. It seemed that Ateas' security guards were no rookie vamps. I peeked over the door sill just as a trim, young, Anglo guard with a blond crew cut stopped next to the car, his gaze trained on my driver. About ten feet behind him, a second vampire sat inside a metal and glass guard shack, reading an old copy of *Ricochet* magazine.

Each guard wore a black LEO uniform, neatly pressed, with a silver badge over the left breast pocket, a small name placard over the right pocket, and a generic "security" patch on the shoulder. The one next to the car wore a police officer's duty belt that held hinged handcuffs, a collapsible baton, and a holstered Ruger 9mm.

The guards here looked to be organized and disciplined. I'd need to be careful once we got inside the building. It was one thing to take out a few rent-a-cops, but another to fight a bunch of armed vampires with military and police backgrounds who were trained to operate as a unit.

The guard leaned in, placing his left hand on the door. "Dr. Walters. Running late again?"

"Ugh, don't remind me," she replied convincingly as she held her badge out for the guard to see. "If Dr. Patel catches me one more time, he's going to dock my vacation time."

"Supervisors, amirite?" The guard swept her badge with a handheld barcode scanner. "They don't realize how much those trips to Vegas and Bermuda mean to us grunts. A few nights at the tables with some nice-looking cattle at your side—it almost makes this job bearable."

"I know what you mean, Harris. Sometimes I just want to run away, then I think about the consequences."

The security goon's cheerful demeanor slipped momentarily, his eyes narrowing. "Everything alright, Doc?"

I slid the blade forward a hair, just to remind Karen what was at stake.

"What? No—I mean, yes, of course." She giggled and brushed a stray strand of hair behind her ear. "Sorry, I haven't fed yet. And here I am rambling on while a shift's worth of work awaits."

"Big night ahead?" the guard asked, a bit too pointedly.

"Isn't it always? I need to get on those blood samples from last night. We had a promising batch come in last week, and I have to make certain I record the results before Patel checks in." I held my breath as she paused. "Are we good here?"

The guard's smile slowly returned. "Sure, we're good." He patted Karen's arm before stepping away from the vehicle. "Don't work too hard, Doc. Gotta' save some for that vacation."

"I won't, Sergeant. Have a good night."

"You too, Dr. Walters."

The barrier gate arm lifted, and the car crept forward, rounding a short curve down a decline that led to the parking garage entrance. We waited for a metal garage door to open, then Karen pulled through into a well-lit underground garage. After the door had closed behind us, I chuckled softly.

"What?"

"I think Harris back there wants you to be his lucky charm in Vegas."

The vampire hissed softly. "As if. Like I'd date a sergeant. They live in those condominiums on Woodlands Parkway. Can you imagine, living in an apartment? Ugh."

"Perish the thought. Now, tell me there's a freight elevator or a private stairwell that'll take us to the holding area for your test subjects."

Karen frowned at me in the rearview mirror. "Every elevator and stairwell is covered by FLIR security cameras. They'll spot you as soon as you enter. If you want to get to the 10th floor, you'll have to go another way."

"Park in your normal spot while I think this over."

"They're all assigned. If I parked anywhere else, security would be on us in no time, flat."

"You're being awful cooperative. Any reason for that?"

"Besides not wanting to get killed?"

"Fair enough," I said, withdrawing the blade from the seat. "Check yourself over to make sure no blood is showing through your lab coat."

"And if it is?"

"I'll handle it."

While she gave herself a once over, I considered my options. Option A was that I kill Karen, spell her body to cover the scent of blood, and stuff her in the trunk. Then I'd have to make my way through the building on my lonesome—not the most attractive prospect.

Option B involved using druidry to mask my body temperature, hopefully making myself invisible to the cameras. Yet I knew how FLIR cameras worked. They'd see an outline regardless of whether I was able to match room temperature or not, and in my condition, it'd be tough to get it just right. Scratch that one as well.

My third option? Scaling the outside of the building. I might be able to do it using druid magic to cling to the walls, but this building was all glass and steel. One slip, and I'd be a stain on the sidewalk—and I wasn't sure my Fomorian healing factor had enough juice to save me, considering the strain the vyrus had me under.

Karen shifted in her seat as her eyes searched the rearview mirror. "Have you figured something out yet? Because I need to get to my station before someone comes looking for me."

Finding myself out of options, I decided to take a chance on Option D—Karen power. "Tell me something, Karen. Do you really want to get out of here?"

"Well, yes. I don't know where I'd go, though."

I thought about Luther, and whether he might be able to find her a place in his new coven. He'd certainly do it for me, or at least, I thought he might. Besides, I only needed to convince Karen that there was a *chance* for her outside The Deadlands. After that, it was on her.

"Look, I know someone—a coven leader from one of the major cities. If I vouched for you, he'd take you in."

"Are you offering a trade? I help you, and you take me with you when you go?"

"If I get out of here, yes."

"That's a thin promise to rest my future upon."

I laughed. "You really think they're going to let this go? Once they find out you helped me, you're dead meat anyway."

"Pish posh. They can't afford to lose me. It's not like geneticists are growing on trees these days."

"My point is, Ateas will make you pay for this slip, eventually. If not now, at some point in the future after your usefulness has expired. Are you willing to risk that, just to stick around and work at a job you hate?" I paused, letting her stew for a few moments. "It's me or 'Patel,' Dr. Walters. Make your choice."

She sighed heavily, which must've been an unintentional reflex, considering that she didn't need to breathe. "You know what? Fuck Patel. He's a moron anyway, and he's been taking credit for my work from the start."

"That's the spirit. Now, tell me—how are you going to get me to the 10th floor?"

———

Fifteen minutes later, I was climbing inside an insulated metal cart that had biohazard symbols on the side. The thing normally held lab transport coolers, but Karen had cleared them out to make room for me. I also had to remove a shelf by melting the welds that held it in, yet I still had a hard time fitting inside the thing.

To make it work, I had to toss all my gear and weapons inside my Craneskin Bag. If things went south, I'd be fighting barehanded, after blasting my way out of a metal box with magic.

The whole thing was pretty fucked, but it was either the cart, or crawling up a ladder for twelve stories inside the elevator shaft. I chose the cart.

"You sure no one will look inside here?" I asked while I was half in and half out of the cart.

Karen stood next to the thing, casting furtive glances up and down the storage hall as she answered. "Not unless they hear you. Trust me, no one in this building is interested in anyone else's work. Everyone has enough of their own workload to keep them busy."

"Earning those vacation days, working for the promise of sucking some slave dry in Vegas, eh?"

She turned her gaze on me, pursing her lips as she shook her head. "Believe it or not, few of us asked for this. What they promised us was a far cry from what we got. If I'd known?" A lopsided frown flashed across her face. "I'd have taken my chances with the apocalypse."

Was the scientist's professed regret all an act? I didn't know. I'd only ever trusted one vampire—Luther—and even he deceived me. Finnegas had taught me that the only trustworthy supe was a dead one, and that had kept me alive this far.

"Hindsight's twenty-twenty," I said as I shoehorned myself the rest of the way into the cart. "Go ahead and lock me in. And just remember, if you cross me, we're both dead."

"Don't I know it," she muttered as she closed the door.

I heard the latch click, and soon we were rolling off down the hallway. The thing had a squeaky wheel, which was deafening inside the cabinet. The noise vibrated through the chassis, causing it to reverberate with a sort of *ree-reeeee, ree-reeeee, ree-reeeee* sound.

I was almost ready to silence it with magic when I felt the cart hit a couple of bumps. Then there was a *ding*, followed by the unmistakable hum and momentary sensation of heaviness caused by an ascending elevator.

"When we exit, don't make a sound," Karen whispered. "This level is full of researchers and support staff."

"Why didn't you mention that before?"

"Sshh, we're almost there."

I heard another *ding*, then the whoosh of the elevator doors opening. The bustle and clamor of an occupied office building followed immediately after. Straining my ears to isolate every sound, I picked up multiple sets of footsteps, the whir of computers and lab equipment, several low conversations, and the rattle of a loose ventilation cover further down the hall.

Karen pushed the cart out of the elevator and down the corridor. Based on the frequency of the squeaking wheel and the sensation of momentum I felt, she seemed to be moving at a rapid pace. We continued for what felt like an eternity as lab noises, footfalls, and chatter came and went, with each new sound setting me on edge.

After a time, the cart slowed. I felt our inertia shift as we rounded a corner, causing the research lab sounds to fade behind us as we continued on. By this time, I was quite ready to get out of the cart. My fever had me sweating like a pig, not to mention that it was getting stuffy in there.

"Almost home free," the vampire whispered.

Somewhere nearby, I heard a toilet flush, followed by the swish of a heavy door opening. Karen released a kind of *meep* as we abruptly stopped.

"Ms. Walters," a male voice with a slight Bengali accent said. "So nice of you to finally arrive at work."

"Dr. Patel, good evening," Karen replied, obviously flustered. "How's Jaya doing? I haven't seen her in ages."

"Do not change the subject," Patel said in a clipped tone. "You've been late six times this quarter, making you dangerously close to yet another red mark in your personnel file." He paused, and I could almost picture him noticing her payload for the first time. "What *are* you doing with that transport cart?"

"Huh? Oh, you mean this? I was just taking it to Sanitation for disinfection. Clumsy me, I spilled a lab sample, contaminated the whole thing. I just wanted to get it taken care of before someone else suffered from my mistake."

Inside the cart, I began to queue up a spell, keeping the energy within my body but ready to release at a moment's notice.

Patel tsked. "Can't you get a lab assistant to take care of that? There's an environmental chamber full of unprocessed samples waiting for you in Lab Two. Or have you forgotten?"

"Of course not." Karen's voice became more and more strained with every syllable she spoke. "Let me just run this over to Sanitation, and then I'll get right on those samples."

I heard someone's foot tapping, and it wasn't Karen's. "Ms. Walters, what do you have inside that cart? Are you sneaking work home again?"

"What? No, I—"

Patel's voice got louder as he carried on, speaking over Karen's verbal protestations all the while. "Just because you can't keep up with your workload, it doesn't give you the right to remove company property from—"

Suddenly, the cart door opened, leaving me face to face with a stunned-looking, middle-aged Indian man with salt and pepper hair, wire-rimmed glasses, and an RDJ goatee. His eyes widened, and he stammered something incomprehensible. My palm began to glow as I prepared to release my sunbeam spell, straight through the guy's right eye.

Just as I was about to release the incantation, blood filled the eye I'd been aiming for, turning it dark red. Patel's facial muscles spasmed as he slumped forward, sort of half on me and half on the floor, with a metal ballpoint pen sticking out of the base of his skull. I reabsorbed the magic I'd been about to release, even as I fumbled to push Karen's supervisor off me.

When I looked up, Karen was standing over the guy, fists balled up and practically vibrating with barely bridled tension. Her eyes were wild, her jaw taut, her teeth gritted. As she stared down at her now deceased supervisor, she snarled, showing more than a little fang.

"It's *Doctor* Walters, you dimwitted misogynist prick!" Karen spat. "Submit that to HR, why don't you?"

Karen started kicking Patel's semi-prone body, first timidly, then harder, gaining momentum as she went. Within seconds, she was punting his corpse with abandon, snarling and muttering crazed insults all the while. Clearly, this Patel had been a shit, putting mousy little Karen on the verge of going postal, where she must've remained for some time.

I couldn't very well calm her from within the cart, but I didn't want to get caught, either. After toying with the idea of shutting the door and leaving Karen to her own designs, I realized it was a crappy thing to do, and a poor plan as well. Cursing under my breath, I began to squeeze and lever myself out of my temporary means of conveyance.

A rapid survey outside the cart revealed that we were in

some kind of side hallway, hopefully with no cameras. Someone would be by eventually, though. If I didn't get Karen under control soon, that might happen sooner than we'd both like.

"Karen. Karen… Karen!" I whispered with more and more urgency, finally nearly shouting her name as I finished prying myself out of the cart. "Get a grip, before you bring the whole building down on us."

"And get your own fucking coffee!" she said, punctuating each word with a kick.

I was out of the cart now, and dangerously close to being on the receiving end of Karen's size seven flats myself. Risking self-harm, I grabbed her by the upper arms, squeezing and shaking her to get her attention.

"Karen, stop," I hissed urgently, pushing her away from Patel even as she threw one last kick at his inert figure.

All at once, she seemed to deflate. Karen stood there, chest heaving with her shoulders slumped, strands of hair in her face, her blouse half untucked under her lab coat. She blinked several times, shaking her head like a boxer trying to shake off a hard right to the jaw.

The vampire looked down at her former supervisor's misshapen corpse. Her face became drawn and her skin even more pale as she covered her mouth. "Oh, I think I'm going to be sick."

"Steady there, Roy Kent." I released her arms, brushing her shoulders off and patting them before stepping back. "You can do that later. Right now, I need you to help me stuff Patel's body in that cart."

"What? Why?"

I knelt over the body, thanking my lucky stars that she broke bones without breaking any skin. Working quickly, I pulled his lab coat off, making certain I retrieved his badge as well. Then I pushed the cart against the wall, locking the wheels. Finally, I grabbed Patel under the armpits, flipping him over as I inclined my head at his feet.

"Grab his ankles. C'mon, we don't have all day."

Karen complied, revealing her vampire strength in the ease with which she helped me heave the supervisor's body into the cart. He was of smaller stature than me, but he still didn't fit all in one go.

I stood and pointed at the body. "Shove him the rest of the way in there. I don't care how you do it."

"Do I really—"

"Do you want to get caught? Just do it."

Glancing around quickly, I searched for a door marked "storage" or "maintenance." There was an unmarked door down the hall with a ventilation grate on its lower half. I quickly checked inside—it'd do.

After pulling several large boxes of paper towels and cleaning supplies out of the closet, I motioned for Karen to bring the cart. "Hurry, roll it inside. No, flip it around so the biohazard thingy faces the back."

"Someone will find it here," Karen said, her face contorting with horror.

"Naw," I said as I stacked boxes on top of it. "It's like you said, overworked people tend to be incredibly self-involved. No one will even bother moving the thing until his corpse starts to decompose. And considering that he's a vamp, that could be a while."

Karen stared at the cart, then she turned away, hugging herself. "What now?"

I grabbed a blue PPE suit, a surgical cap, and a surgical

mask off the shelves. It wasn't exactly the ideal disguise, but it'd have to do.

"How far to the section where they keep the humans?" I asked as I stepped into the jumpsuit.

"There's a service corridor at the end of this hall. We can take that to the other side of the floor. It exits around the corner from the security checkpoint that leads to the holding area."

"Cool beans. How long until feeding time?"

She glanced at the old-school digital watch on her wrist. "About an hour. But how are you going to get past the security checkpoint?"

I rummaged around in my Bag, grabbing the suppressed .22 and shoving it in my waistband inside the suit.

"By any means necessary."

CHAPTER
TWENTY

WHEN WE GOT to the end of the service corridor, I stopped in front of the exit and faced Karen. "Tell me about the security checkpoint."

The vampire's brow furrowed as she replied. "The checkpoint is just two goons standing outside the entry, along with a keypad and a badge reader. The room itself is secure. I think the guards were placed there strictly to prevent employees from stopping in and snacking on our subjects."

"Cameras?"

"Nope. Patel had them removed."

"Why?"

She smirked. "It was rumored that he sometimes promised leniency to subjects in exchange for sexual favors. Of course, every human who comes into this building dies eventually, so..."

"Hmm. Most vamps simply rape their victims. There's not much a human can do to prevent it. Why engage in all that deceit?"

"I think he got off on seeing their hope fade after they arrived in the lab. A couple of times I caught him watching a subject being bled out, and he was, um, aroused."

"That's just sick."

She frowned. "Now you know why I hated him."

"Anything else you can tell me?"

"Let me see," she said, tapping her chin. "From what I'm told, The Master doesn't like subjects who've been previously fed upon. When they pick humans to be turned for his purposes, they have to be free from fang marks or other major scars and deformities."

"Has he ever let one of them live?"

She shook her head vigorously in the negative. "Never."

"Are the vamps he feeds on already turned? Or do they turn them right before he takes them?" Karen gave me an odd look, so I held my hands up in response. "I don't know much about how the whole process of turning someone works. You'll have to help me out here."

"Well, it can take a while to turn someone, and it depends on the subject. Some change overnight, while others take multiple—"

All at once, Karen's eyes glazed over. For a moment, I thought she was falling under her master's influence. Fortunately, it was merely a compulsion implanted in her subconscious taking effect.

She shook her head and rubbed her temples. "Gah, how I hate that. Sorry, there are certain secrets the Vampyri keep a lid on, and the process of making vampires is one of them. That's all I can tell you."

I waved her apology off. "It's fine, I get the picture. Just curious, though—aren't new vampires obsessed with the thirst? How do you control them?"

Karen averted her gaze. "We feed them."

"Right." I had a feeling there was something more there, but she wasn't offering, and I didn't have time to pressure her about it. "You say they'll be coming to retrieve his meal soon?"

"Within the next half hour."

"Then we need to hurry." I glanced back the way we came. "Find someplace to hide until I call for you, and be ready to move when I do."

Karen licked her lips nervously, then she scurried off to do as I asked. I watched her leave, wondering if I was placing too much trust in her.

She's a vampire. Of course I am.

It was too late to worry about that now. I checked my pistol's magazine and chamber, making sure I was carrying in condition one. Lastly, I donned the cap and mask, then I stepped into the hall with the gun shoved into my waistband behind my back.

As an afterthought, I ducked my head back into the service corridor. After I found what I was looking for, I reached in and snatched a clipboard from where it hung on a hook next to the door. I sauntered around the corner, out of the service hall entrance and into the main hallway, staring at the clipboard and flipping through random pages as I walked.

"Should've told him he could get the damned subjects himself," I muttered as I continued to approach the door. "Always bossing me around. 'Get this, Colton. Clean that, Colton.' We'll see how they like it when I get promoted to lab tech two. Then someone else can fetch their crap."

The guards shared a glance. I sized them up beneath a hooded brow, keeping my gaze on the clipboard all the while. Two males, one Hispanic, the other Anglo, the latter more or less my size.

This will do.

The Latin guard held a hand up as I neared their checkpoint. "Stop there. You're not the regular transport tech. Where's Smitty?"

"Who's Smitty? All I know is that Dr. Patel told me to come down here and get a suitable subject ready for The Master." I flipped through the forms again, which were actually cleaning checklists for the sanitation staff. "I take it one of them is fully turned?"

The guards looked at each other again, and the Anglo shrugged. The Latino dropped his hands as he relaxed, hooking his thumbs in his duty belt.

"Yeah, but you're going to need a form eighteen-dash-oscar-lima for retrieval."

"An Oscar who?"

They shared a knowing look, and the Anglo hid a chuckle behind his hand. "It's the form that looks like half a sheet of paper. Printed in triplicate, like everything else around here. You know, white paper on top, pink and yellow on bottom?"

"Oh yeah, I got that one right here."

I reached behind my back, grabbing the pistol and drawing it in one smooth motion. The Anglo guard's jaw dropped, just as I put a round through his upper incisors—perfect placement to plug him right in the brain stem. His eyes rolled back, and he started to drop, even as I was pivoting toward his partner.

Needless to say, I was moving fast and feeling pretty good about my chances of ending this quietly, when I realized the other guard wasn't there anymore.

"What the actual fuck?" I said as I swiveled my head, scanning the entirety of the hall's terminal end in a single sweep and finding nothing.

I heard the *shickt* sound of an expandable baton opening, then I felt something hard and cold impact the back of my hand. The pistol went flying, and my hand went numb, stung by an ASP baton moving with vampire speed. Acting on instinct, I shelled up boxer style, covering my face and temples just as a barrage of strikes landed on my forearms and shoulders.

Holy shit—he's invisible.

Many older vamps possessed unique magical talents, and apparently this guy's was invisibility. It was just my luck that I hadn't shot the guard who could turn into Casper the Unfriendly Ghost first. A sunlight spell might've evened the odds, but it would've been a mistake to cast it, for multiple reasons.

First, it might alert Ateas to my presence. Second, I couldn't yet tell if the guard was in front of me or behind me. And third, I needed to conserve that particular bit of magic for what would come next.

Acting on instinct, I did what I'd been trained to do, long before I had the highest levels of druid magic at my disposal. I waited until the next strike landed, then I snapped my hand out, catching the baton and yanking on it in one quick motion. As I did, I used the pulling motion for counter-rotation, popping out a palm-heel strike where I thought the guard's chest would be.

Thankfully, I hit something with that strike. Based on touch alone, I realized I'd caught him in the shoulder. No matter—it allowed me to snag the strap on his plate carrier, which was what I actually wanted.

Holding on to the baton and the strap, I pulled the vamp toward me hard as I delivered a Muay Thai thrusting knee at waist level. That connected with something soft, causing the guard to let out an *oof* that was atypical for a mature vamp.

Immediately, I felt his grip on the ASP loosen. I yanked it out of his grip, tossing it away, then I started hockey punching at speed, over and under my other hand, sometimes connecting, sometimes not.

It only took three or four blows before the guard began to shimmer back into view. His image stuttered and faltered as it reappeared, revealing his body position as he attempted to fend off my strikes. I faked another punch to his head, drawing his arms up high, then I delivered an oblique kick low, stomping his knee sideways with a short series of pops.

As he staggered, favoring his now injured knee, he blinked fully into view. Upon finally realizing what kind of trouble he was in, the guard began fumbling for the sidearm at his hip. The last thing I needed was a round to the chest, so I stuffed his draw by grabbing his right wrist with my left hand.

He was strong, and I knew it was only a matter of seconds before he managed to draw that weapon and even the odds. Stepping in, I popped a quick palm jab under his chin that snapped his head back. Stepping to his right side, I kept my hand there for control as I performed an outer reaping throw, sweeping his legs as I drove his head into the floor.

There are few judo throws that hit as hard as a proper *osoto gari*, and man did I ever put some smoke on it. I kicked my inside leg back hard, tossing his legs and lower body up in the air even as I slammed his head into the ground. The end result was that he came down on the back of his skull with force, snapping his neck with a sickening crunch as his cervical spine took the brunt of the impact.

When all was said and done, the vampire lay on the floor in a heap, his head and neck twisted at an unnatural angle. Cruelly enough, the guy was still alive—or as alive as a vamp could be—but quite paralyzed from the neck down. Since his head was twisted away from me, he was looking at me sideways, working his jaw as if trying to get a few last words out.

I didn't have time for tender mercies, nor did I possess the empathy to deliver them. Fumbling around in my Bag, I grabbed the silver-plated stiletto I'd used on Karen earlier. Without hesitation or remorse, I plunged it into his heart through the gap in the side of his plate carrier. The vampire expired instantly, leaving me with two dead bodies and a quickly approaching deadline for the subject transport team's arrival.

———

I heard the service corridor door open behind me, and snapped my head around to see who was coming. Luckily, it was Karen and not a staff member.

"Yikes!" she said as she saw the bodies.

"Seriously? After what you did to Patel?"

"That was out of character."

"I'll say." I pointed at the Latino's body. "Hide that one while I deal with the other."

This time, Karen did as she was told without question or complaint. As she carried the guard off, I began to strip the other guard of his uniform, then I dumped him in the service hall.

"Him too," I said when Karen returned from dumping the first body.

The vampire grimaced distastefully. "Gross, he's in his tighty-whities. And aren't you going to help?"

"I need to get changed. Do you want to pull this thing off or not?"

"Fine."

While Karen dealt with the second body. I stripped out of the PPE suit, my boots, pants, shirt, and jacket, replacing them with the guard's uniform. Once done, I looked myself over, using my phone as a mirror. I needed a shave, so I donned the surgical mask again.

"None of the guards wear masks. Really, none of us do, unless we're in a clean room. I'm surprised that mask didn't tip them off."

"Let's hope whoever comes for tonight's snack is too busy to pay much attention." I pointed at the keypad and badge reader. "Tell me about this thing. Do I need a code to get in?"

"No, just a badge swipe."

"There's no biometrics, nothing to prevent someone from accessing all parts of the building with a stolen badge?"

"Biometrics don't work with all vampires. Badges are the most reliable method of controlling access. Since no human or fae has ever successfully trespassed into or out of The Deadlands, we've stuck with them."

That was interesting. Most all higher fae possessed magic that kept them from being discovered by humans. Their innate abilities blurred their image in surveillance camera photos and footage, muddled their fingerprints, and prevented them from being identified by facial scan technology. Very handy.

Karen was inferring that some vamps possessed similar talents, which wasn't surprising. Yet I knew that wasn't a universal thing, as Luther had called in Maeve's fixers to clean up a crime scene on more than one occasion. Still, it was info that was worth tucking away.

I cocked my head as I stared at the badge reader. "Whelp, let's see if anyone has found Dr. Patel yet."

One swipe was all it took to get a green light on the reader and a *bzzt-click* from the door lock. I yanked on the heavy, brown metal door, swinging it wide as I gestured for Karen to enter first. "After you. Just in case."

"Still don't trust me?" she asked, rolling her eyes.

"Well, I did stab you."

"Twice. I haven't forgotten. It's not the stabbing that pissed me off, it's that you ruined a nice blouse."

The blouse was hideous, but I wasn't about to tell her that. She entered the room and I followed, whistling softly as I took the whole thing in at a glance. "Now this *is* fucked up."

The space consisted of a large open area, surrounded on three sides by cells with plexiglass forward enclosures. The cells were very *Silence of the Lambs* looking, except that they were more favorably appointed. Each had a nice single bed, a side table, lamps, a desk, a chair, a rug, a sink and mirror, a shower, and a toilet.

I counted twelve cells in all, but only six were occupied. There were two males, one a teen, one middle-aged, and four females, all in their early- to late twenties. The first five of those occupants hardly registered our arrival, so cowed was their behavior in the presence of what appeared to be facility staff.

Unlike the others, the captive in the last cell popped off her bed like a gymnast when we walked in the room. She snatched her chair and held it over her shoulder, bouncing on her toes in an offensive crouch as she snarled and spat at us. The girl was barely out of her teens; thin, but not unhealthy, with brown hair just past shoulder-length and eyes to match.

"We keep them drugged—the humans, I mean."

"I figured," I snarked venomously, even as I wondered how I was going to rescue these people on my way out. I pointed at the last cell. "I take it that's your master's designated meal?"

"You motherfuckers will never take me alive!" the woman shouted in a natural East Texas accent. "Just come in here and see what I do to you shit lickers."

"Relax, I'm human, and I'm not going to hurt you," I lied as I pulled down my mask and approached the cell. "That's because I need your help."

"She's not," the girl said, nodding at Karen. "Human, I mean."

I glanced at Karen and back to the subject again. "I know, but she's decided to help me. What's your name?"

"Dottie. And don't make fun of it, it was my gramma's name, and I'm proud of it."

"Hi, Dottie. I'm Colin, nice to meet you."

"Nice to meet you too," she snarled. "Now get me the fuck out of here."

I shook my head, keeping my voice level as I replied. "I can't do that. You've been turned, Dottie. For all I know, if I let you out, you'd break into one of the other cells and rip another captive apart."

"I wouldn't do that," she countered.

Even as she said it, her eyes darted over to a cell that sat cater-corner from hers. Inside that cell, the teenage boy sat on the floor in the corner, hugging his knees as he rocked back and forth. The boy's eyes were distant, haunted, and devoid of any evidence that he'd even registered our presence.

Dottie's tongue flicked out, lightning quick, as she watched the boy. Having just been turned, it was doubtful she had any control at all over her blood-hunger. Given the opportunity, she'd pounce on any one of the poor souls in the other cells, ripping their throats out with her fangs as she lapped up every last bit of blood in their bodies.

Fixing her with my gaze, I clucked my tongue at her. "You know that's not true. Even now, the hunger is gnawing at you, telling you to feed. I bet you can smell my blood inside there, and hear my heart beating, too."

Dottie lowered the chair a bit as she sniffed the air. "Yeah, but you smell bad." She inclined her head at Karen. "Wrong, like them."

"Like you as well. You're just like them now, Dottie, whether you like it or not. Because of that, I can't offer you freedom, but I can offer you revenge."

The captive vampire's shoulders slumped, and she set the chair down on the floor facing backward in front of her. The girl sat in the chair, straddling it as she rested her forehead on the chair. After a moment, she looked up at me, combing her fingers through her hair before crossing her arms over the chair back.

"How do I know you're not lying to me?" Dottie asked.

"Look at the name tag on my uniform." I glanced down at it, noticing for the first time it said Stephenson. "You've come to know the guards here. Do I look like Stephenson?"

"Nope. What happened to him?"

"I killed him."

Dottie shook her head. "Uh-uh. Humans cain't kill them things. Ain't possible."

"Oh, it's possible," I countered. "Just not easy. But I've been doing it for a long time."

"Then get me the fuck out of here!" she demanded, glowering at me.

"Again, I can't do that. You're driven by bloodlust now, Dottie. By the hunger for human blood. If I release you, you'll kill, guaranteed. I've seen it happen a hundred times. As I said, the best I can offer you is a chance at revenge."

She closed her eyes, lowering her head. "You're right —'bout the killin', I mean. They put Tommy in here with me, mister. My own little brother! An' I—" Dottie choked up a bit, although she sounded more feral than human. "I killed him. Couldn't help myself. Didn't even realize it 'til it was over, when they was in here cleanin' up the blood. An' you know what's fucked up, mister?"

I shot Karen a hate-filled glance before softening my gaze as I turned it back on Dottie. "That you keep thinking about it, even now. The salty, mineral taste of the blood. The way it warmed your gut, chasing away the cold for a short period of time. The way it made you feel invincible. That you'd do it again, if they could somehow bring Tommy back. That you still couldn't stop yourself, no matter how much you loved your little brother."

Dottie nodded, almost imperceptibly, as she answered in a whisper. "Yes."

"They did this to you, kid, these pricks in lab coats, the guards, and their boss. Because of that, you're going to die, and there's nothing I can do about that," I lied, for the second time. "But if you help me, you can get back at them, for you and for Tommy. This I promise."

Her voice was frail and weak as she replied. "What do you want me to do?"

"You're going to help me kill the guy who's in charge of this place."

Dottie glanced up at me without lifting her head, her piercing gaze meeting mine through strands of greasy brown hair. "I seen that thing, an' he ain't no guy. Don't know what he is, but he ain't human."

"I'm aware. That's why I need your help." I turned to Karen. "They drug them before they take them, right?"

Karen gave a single nod. "Yes. We gas them with a mixture of ketamine, fentanyl, and a few other drugs. None of the subjects feel a thing when they are taken to The Master."

I shifted my gaze to Dottie. "They'll be in here to take you within minutes, so we don't have much time. I know this is hard, and I can't offer much in the way of comfort for the shitty hand you've been dealt. But at least I can help you get back at the monster who's responsible for your current condition."

Dottie ran her fingers through her hair again, grasping it close to her scalp and tugging on it so hard I thought she'd rip it out. She growled in frustration for several long seconds, then all the tension went out of her at once. She looked up, and when her eyes met mine again, they were wet with pink tears.

"Fact is, I hate what I've become—what they made me. Couldn't live like this, no how. Tell me what I got to do."

CHAPTER
TWENTY-ONE

IT TOOK only minutes to prepare Dottie for Ateas. The kid didn't scream once, the whole time—she really took it like a champ. I said Tommy would've been proud, which was the third lie I told her that night.

Karen wouldn't let me gas Dottie before I did it, claiming it would raise suspicions with the transport team. Little did she know that wouldn't be an issue. I saved that little tidbit as a surprise, partially because I'd originally intended to include her in the festivities.

But then I decided I still needed her.

If she gave me any trouble, I could always kill her later. After finding out what she and her team had done to Dottie and her kid brother, I couldn't care less.

When I was finished, Dottie lay wrung out on the floor of her cell. Meanwhile, Karen seemed transfixed by what I'd done to the other vamp, clearly horrified that I possessed such power. I snapped several times in front of her face to get her attention.

"Look alive, Captain Theranos. The party's not over yet. We still have work to do."

"How?" she asked as she pushed her glasses up on her nose. "It makes no sense, from a scientific standpoint."

"And vampires, zombies, and shit do make sense?"

"Well, yes. I can look under a microscope and see how the vyrus alters human cells—"

I cut her off with a chop of my hand. "It's still magic, dumbass, no matter what you've seen under a microscope. Eons ago, something came across the Veil from another dimension, something dark and twisted. It possessed a human body, altering that person's DNA. Then it fed, and created others like itself." I made an explosive gesture with my hands. "Ka-boom! Magic."

"Sure, but certainly that event could be quantified, perhaps explained even, by quantum mechanics or another branch of science."

"Oh yeah? Then riddle me this, Batman," I said as I cast various cantrips on myself to mask my scent and heartbeat, and to make my skin even paler than it was. "Can you quantify what your master does with necromancy? Explain that with science."

"Well, I can't," she stammered. "It's not my field—"

"Karen, just stop. No amount of science is ever going to justify what you did to these people, and it'll never make you human again."

Her expression was stricken as she responded. "That's not what I was getting at."

"Yeah, but it's what you hope. I've fought your kind and others like you since I was just a kid, and I've heard and seen it all. Every evil fucker who becomes tainted by the dark side tries to rationalize it away. You're wasting your breath on me, believe me. I just don't fucking care."

She hugged herself and faced away from me. "You're cruel. In many ways, crueler than the people I worked for here."

Despite how weak I felt, both from the vyral infection running through my veins, and the magic I'd spent, I was on her instantly. I snatched her by the lapels, picking her up off the ground as I snarled at Mentos range.

"Don't ever compare me to them. Ever."

Something in my voice must've caused her to think twice about pushing her luck. Karen closed her eyes tight and cringed, shrinking into herself. Disgusted by her cowardice—both in the moment and for going along with this whole operation—I tossed her away like so much refuse.

"How many people do they send when they retrieve his meals?" I asked.

"A team of two. One tech, and one guard," she said as she picked herself off the floor. I chuckled, and her eyes widened as she realized my intent. "You can't be serious."

Just then, the badge reader at the entrance beeped. "I guess there's no time for debate now," I whispered, so softly only she could hear. "It's go time, Bunsen britches. Brace yourself—this could get messy."

The hall door opened. A guard entered with his sidearm drawn, followed by another vampire in a lab coat. Before they could react, and while I still had them stacked in the doorway, I shot a tight, laser-like beam of sunlight, right through their chests.

The guard instantly shriveled as he died, aging

hundreds of years instantaneously. That happened to the old ones, sometimes, the moment you beheaded them or burned their heart from their chests. As for his buddy in the lab coat, that guy simply collapsed with a smoking hole in his rib cage.

I walked over to them, kicking the lab tech to make sure he was dead. "See? Magic."

Karen made a gagging noise. "I think I'm going to be sick again."

"Pfft. Some doctor you are. Now help me hide these bodies while I bring in the gurney they brought."

We shoved the corpses in a closet, then we gassed Dottie before getting her ready to move. Karen insisted that we had to undress and bathe the girl for her master, so I made her do it, averting my gaze until the job was done. After Dottie was loaded and strapped in tight, I nodded at the not-so-good doctor.

"Lead the way, Madame Curie. We have an appointment to keep."

My vampire accomplice's hands were visibly shaking as she replied. "I don't know if I can do this."

"Hey, you agreed to this, remember? In for a penny, in for a pound and all that."

She turned on me, grasping the end of the gurney for support. "How can you be so calm, when we're about to face the most frightening creature I have ever known? He's practically a living god."

"From what I understand, he's hardly living. And, I have a plan."

Karen shook her head. "The Master will see right through your ruse, the moment you walk into that room."

"That's why I'm not walking in there. You're going to deliver poor Dottie here, while I wait outside."

"Oh no, not me. First, that's not how it's done."

"It is now."

"And second, I'm not made for this sort of thing. I'll screw it up, and then this whole crazy plot will be revealed."

I crossed my arms over my chest and sighed. "Look, either you do this, or you end up like them." I jerked a thumb at the broom closet where we stashed the guard and tech just moments before. "Choose."

Karen closed her eyes and gritted her teeth, screeching softly as she dug her nails into her palms at her sides. After her hissy fit was over, she visibly relaxed, regaining her composure. For several moments, she busied herself with adjusting her blouse and skirt, tucking her hair behind her ears, and tugging her lab coat straight.

When she was done, she squared her shoulders before looking me straight in the eye. "Fine. But when this is over, I never want to see you again."

"Trust me, the feeling is mutual. Now, let's go before we're late and someone gets suspicious."

"God, I hate you," she muttered as she headed out the door, pulling the gurney behind her.

"God has nothing to do with it, lady. Not a damned thing at all."

———

We entered the main elevator, and once we were inside, Karen swiped her badge before punching the button for the top floor.

"Of course he's in the penthouse," I observed. "The blackout curtains must've cost a fortune."

"You're lucky there's no security up there," Karen hissed. "He likes to be by himself, doing who knows what rituals with all the things and pets he keeps up there."

"What kind of pets?"

She glanced at the ceiling of the elevator and shuddered. "You have no idea. *Things*. Hideous things. Unholy things. Creatures that would make Frankenstein cower in fear."

"The monster, or the scientist?"

"The scientist, of course. I know my Shelley."

"You would," I snarked. "Are these pets mobile? How many does he have? And do they serve as his guardians?"

"Yes, many, and definitely. You'll see when we get up there." She raised a trembling hand to her forehead. "I honestly can't believe I agreed to this."

"Steady now. It's almost over."

"Liar."

"That makes two of us."

"Quiet, we're nearing the top floor. He'll hear us."

I clammed up, hunching over and lowering my gaze to look suitably cowed when we exited. When the elevator stopped, there was a *ding*, then the doors opened. I glanced up, and what greeted me was a world of madness.

At first, everything looked normal. Or rather, normal-ish, if you thought baroque interior design was the standard for high-rise penthouse office suites. The elevator opened directly into a hallway foyer, which looked to have been decorated by a fifteenth century torturer.

A Persian rug ran the length of the floor, which was appointed with dark, rich wooden planks, likely from some exotic species that didn't grow in this hemisphere. Gothic, wrought-iron chandeliers hung from the ceiling, each very authentic looking except for the LED bulbs in the sconces. A few torture devices sat here and there, including an iron maiden and a rack that looked to have been recently used.

But that wasn't the extent of it, not by a mile. Lining the walls were stone archways that had clearly been removed from some European castle; carved, high backed ebony and ivory armchairs upholstered in red leather so dark it was nearly black; and suits of armor from every era, each standing on a separate dais, lined up like soldiers every ten feet or so on either side of the hall.

Although I kept waiting for Taika Waititi and Jemaine Clement to walk in wearing pirate shirts and speaking with horrible Romanian accents, nothing seemed out of place. On closer inspection, things took a decidedly eerier turn than even I might've suspected.

First, I noticed the chairs—or rather, the upholstery on the seat nearest to me. What I first took for an embossed design turned out to be a face, a feature they all had, I noticed. I soon realized those faces looked human; then it occurred to me that they might actually *be* human skin. It was only when one of those faces opened its mouth and yawned, revealing crooked and yellow, but very human teeth with pronounced canines, that I realized what I was seeing.

He'd taken the skin from his victims, tanned it some-how, and reanimated it with necromancy. On reaching that conclusion, I examined the chairs more closely, noticing that they weren't made from carved ivory and wood, but of bone. Some of it had been stained to appear like ebony, and some left natural, then polished to a high sheen, but it was definitely osseous tissue.

Then I noticed that each one of those chairs moved slightly at intervals, revealing their true nature by way of small twitches and tics, or the occasional yawn or sneeze. It was all I could do not to shiver, but that wasn't the worst of it. Not yet.

Karen pulled the gurney into the hall and I followed. As we proceeded down the corridor, the first two sets of armor stepped off their platforms, taking up positions alongside to accompany us in lockstep. I observed them in my peripheral vision, noting that one set of armor was 14th century European, the other, samurai armor circa the early 18th century.

The European armor might've been French, consisting of a full salet, cuirass, pauldrons, vambraces, greaves, sabatons, and the like. It was nigh on impossible to see what was under that armor, but the way it moved was all too smooth and animated for my liking. As for the Japanese armor, there were plenty of gaps between each piece that let me view what made it move.

Honestly, I wished I hadn't looked.

When the two sets of armor began to stir, I immediately suspected they each contained an undead creature within. However, once I got a good look at the samurai armor, it became clear that the armor *was* the undead creature. Like the chairs, dead flesh was integral to their creation and design, with skin and sinew holding each piece of armor to the others without a notion of seam or stitch.

The sick son of a bitch had fused tissue to those suits of armor, turning them into golems of metal, lacquered wood, and flesh. I glanced down at the samurai's feet, which were shiny and discolored, like the tanned skin covering the furniture. Then I stole a look at the face behind the *mengu,* and my gaze was immediately drawn to the creature's eyes —dead, clouded, and lifeless. Never had I seen the like.

It occurred to me then that each armor set was fully armed with period-accurate weaponry. I wondered if the poor souls who'd been necromantically integrated were the original owners of each set, and whether they were renowned warriors of their time. Golems could be incredibly difficult to kill, and considering how effortlessly these things moved, it might be a tough fight.

By the time I'd finished discovering, examining, and assessing Ateas' handiwork, we'd reached a pair of ornate, double wooden doors at the end of the hall. A Greek Hoplite and a Roman Centurion had stepped down from their podiums, moving to take up positions in front of the doors. The pair had plenty of source material showing in places their armor didn't cover, revealing leathery skin pulled taut over desiccated flesh and presumably reinforced bone.

I reflected that it must've taken an insane amount of magic to reconstitute even that much tissue from a corpse so old. Either that, or Ateas had done this to them shortly after their deaths, perhaps even causing said expirations to occur for that precise purpose. Or, he'd pieced them together from multiple individuals.

We stopped in front of the ancient duo, and our escort did the same. The Hoplite and Centurion opened the doors, revealing absolute darkness beyond. Each stepped aside to allow the gurney to pass, and I allowed Karen to pull it along without me, intending to wait in the hall with "The Master's" menagerie.

However, I never got the chance. Just when I expected the doors to shut ahead of me, I received a powerful shove from behind that sent me stumbling through the doorway into the lightless space beyond.

———

I was weak, sick, creeped out, and pissed off about my plan being foiled by an armor golem. Since I couldn't think of a better name for them, that's what I called them—armor golems. It fit, no pun intended. At least I could say I solved one conundrum over the course of the evening.

Still, there was the odd chance that Ateas wouldn't recognize me, so I played it cool. I'd bumped into the back of the stretcher on my way through the doors, so I grabbed the back and tried to avoid looking freaked out.

Unfortunately, it was too dark to see without using magic. Moreover, I was exposed and weakened, and a lich was bouncing around somewhere in the immediate vicinity. No bueno.

Not long after I'd gathered my composure, someone spoke out of the darkness. "I see you've brought my meal. Excellent."

The voice was like sandpaper sifting broken glass. Yet I recognized the timbre and cadence from my long-distance brush with Ateas in Bryan-College Station. It was him, alright.

"If she's—" That was Karen speaking. Her voice had gone up a couple of octaves on that second syllable, so she coughed and gave it another go. "Ahem, to your liking, with your permission Master, we'll take our leave."

"I can smell your fear, grandchild," Ateas said. "Don't be afraid. I might kill those who displease me, and perhaps even make a lampshade out of the most irksome, but I never feed on my offspring."

Karen let out a small *meep* at that. Based on the odor of ammonia I detected, I was pretty sure she pissed herself, too. I had no idea vampires needed to eliminate, but I guess with all the fluids they drank, it made sense.

It was also fucking gross because the smell was even worse than asparagus piss. If I had to describe it, I'd call it a cross between moldy bread, dirty pennies, and day-old mop water. My strategy was to pretend I was used to it while shutting the fuck up. I was doing a pretty good job of that when Ateas addressed me directly.

"And you, druid? Would you take your leave as well?"

Well, fuck a duck.

Knowing the plan was completely blown, I pulled the sheet over Dottie's face, then I shot my hand high overhead. In one extended burst, I released the remainder of the sunlight I'd stored up inside my body. It was going to suck for Karen, but screw her, she was complicit in running this whole biotech loony bin anyway.

The room lit up with the bright, warm glow that can only come from one hundred percent pure, unfiltered daylight. Immediately, three things happened. First, Karen screamed as her hair lit on fire, and she fell to the floor trying to put herself out. Second, I spotted a mottled gray and maroon blur zipping across the room to a shadowed spot behind what might've been the original version of *Laocoön and His Sons*.

And third, I reached into my Bag to grab a handful of silver buckshot and silver-plated ball bearings that I'd left sitting in a bowl next to the opening. I tossed the balls into the air, resisting the urge to yell, *"No one can resist my Schweddy balls!"* Then I cast Cathbad's Planetary Maelstrom.

The powerful spell snatched the metal spheres I'd thrown, as well as a few dozen random objects that littered the room. Almost instantly, the space became a cyclone of silver pellets, ball bearings, marble busts, compact discs, an ashtray, a couple of lamps, an end table, some pens and stationary, a couple of skulls, and various other assorted items. I kept the pattern tight due to the confines of the area, which turned out to be the lich's living room.

However, to call it that was an understatement. The space was easily the size of our shop back at the junkyard, which was three full garage bays by three car lengths deep. The room had been decorated in a style that was just as gothic and eclectic as the entry hall. The place was adorned with creepy antique couches, chairs, and settees, expensive-looking, period oil paintings and sculptures, and a clawfoot tub and vanity, located on the far side of the room.

I imagine the tub was where he fed, to avoid getting blood all over the weird-ass furniture. There were also windows along the far wall, curtained, of course, and a few carved wooden doors that presumably led to his sleeping quarters, apothecary, laboratory, and torture chamber. Honestly, I was spitballing on what was behind those doors, as I was basing it on what Crowley would have in his house if he was a five-thousand-year-old lich.

Of course, I should've kept my focus on the situation at hand. Unfortunately, my mind was muzzy due to the effects of the vyrus, and I wasn't thinking clearly. By the time I realized I'd become distracted, Ateas had started zipping around the room—or rather, he was zipping across the room in my direction.

How he could manage to do that while I had all those objects spinning around me at several hundred miles an hour was anyone's guess. So quickly did he move, my eyes could barely track his progress. But progress he did, in spurts and starts that sometimes made it seem like he was in two places at once.

Initially, I couldn't figure out his game. Did he want to get perforated and pulverized by all that flying silver and marble? Or was he impervious to it? Then, I realized what Ateas was actually doing.

Holy shit. He's dodging the fucking debris.

It was such an unbelievable feat of speed, timing, and precision, I would not have thought it possible if I hadn't witnessed it myself. Yet, it was happening. And if I didn't do something about it, that lich would be on me within seconds.

With an effort of will, I sped up the rotation of my maelstrom, pushing the spell to its limits. There were limitations on how quickly objects could orbit the caster, of course. It mostly had to do with overcoming centrifugal force to prevent the missiles from flying off in all directions, and the faster the circuit, the greater the willpower needed to keep the spell going.

I must've had the cyclone pushing five hundred miles per hour—way faster than I'd ever had the spell cycling before. At that speed, it was taking everything I had to keep it going, and in my current condition, I didn't have much. But the quicker the objects flew, the blurrier that Ateas became, until eventually, I lost track of him completely.

The next thing I knew, the lich was in my face. One moment I was safe inside the eye of the storm, and the next I had an ancient vampire lord standing nose to nose with me. Before I could even react, he grabbed me by the legs and slammed me, Loki-style, overhead and against the floor about a half-dozen times.

Despite my enhanced durability in my half-Fomorian form, I'm far from invulnerable, as it's a far cry from fully shifting. Moreover, I was greatly diminished and weakened by the vyrus. By the time I counted the sixth impact, I blessedly, thankfully blacked out.

CHAPTER
TWENTY-TWO

ONLY ONE THOUGHT went through my mind when I regained consciousness:

I have to stop getting knocked out like this.

I was broken, that much was clear. I couldn't feel my legs, one of my arms was twisted at an odd angle behind me, and I had fluid coming out of my nose and ears. Not only that, but my pulse was throbbing at my temples and I wanted to puke.

That meant I likely had a skull fracture—not the ideal condition to be in when facing an ancient, god-like vampire. Yet, he seemed to have diverted his attention from me for the moment, as the beating had stopped.

Despite the pounding in my skull, I heard the lich speaking to someone in soothing tones. Strangely, it sounded as if he were far, far away. Either I had also suffered hearing damage, or we'd moved locations.

I doubted the latter because I couldn't have been out for that long. Thus, it was probably due to a busted eardrum.

Look on the bright side. At least he didn't snap your neck.

That thought provided small comfort, considering my present condition. Still, I was alive, and that was more than I could say for most humans who entered this place. Figuring I needed to keep my living streak going, I cracked an eyelid to get a handle on the current situation.

The lights were on, something that Ateas had to have done for my benefit. He must've tossed me against the wall when he was through beating me, as I was slumped against it in the corner of the room. Dottie was still strapped to the gurney with the sheet over her head, and hopefully still unconscious as well. As for Karen, she lay in her master's lap in the center of the room, suckling at his wrist like a babe at her mother's teat.

The lich spoke to her like a parent consoling a child, cooing as he stroked her remaining strands of hair while she fed. I wondered what it might do to her, feeding from a vampire who was so clearly tainted by necromancy. As for Karen, the terror I saw in her eyes was genuine, that much was clear.

Paralyzed as I was, there wasn't much I could do to save her—not yet. Rather than draw attention to myself, I sat still and willed myself to heal, which was the only thing I could do at the moment. While I did, I took a good long look at Ateas, cataloging every last bit of his bizarre appearance.

At first glance, he appeared as any normal little old man farting around his house in a silk smoking jacket, matching lounge pants, and leather house shoes. He was a wizened, frail-looking, hunched thing with paper-thin skin and a few wisps of white hair adorning his scalp. Yet, on closer inspection, if became clear that he was anything but normal. In fact, the longer I looked, the more horrific his visage turned out to be.

First, there was his skin, which was devoid of any warmth or color, and hairless save for those few strands on his head. Having gone long past the typical pale tones most vampires developed, his hide had taken on a gray, waxy sheen, almost like polished granite, but lighter by several shades. I recalled how powerful his grip had been, how it had felt like iron bands wrapping around my ankles, and I intuited that no mortal weapon would pierce that flesh.

Then, there were his hands. Again, at first blush they appeared normal, until you examined his fingertips. Each ended in a thick, clubbed, black fingernail that curved into a short, sharpened tip. The vyrus did weird things to human flesh, often causing keratin to harden into an almost stone-like substance. If I had to guess, those nails could rip through the skin of a car door just as easily as human skin and muscle.

Surprisingly enough, his teeth seemed like normal vampire teeth—human except for a set of long, pronounced canines. That said, the guy could certainly benefit from the attentions of a dental hygienist. His enamel had yellowed like aged ivory, and his gums were clogged with thick black tartar that looked like it might harbor a variety of deadly infectious diseases.

But worst of all were his eyes. Unlike most vampires, who possessed normal enough eyes save for a pronounced red eye shine at night, Ateas' orbs were pitch black. On seeing them, I immediately thought of Richard and the rest of the cloned revenants I found in that Walmart earlier.

I wondered, was it due to the influence of necromancy? Or was there something else going on—something having to do with those eyes being a window into an empty, soulless vessel? On instinct, I began sweeping the room with my gaze, hoping to find a detail that might give me an advantage.

"Ah, you're awake."

My attention snapped back to the lich in a heartbeat. I pointed at my ear with my one functioning arm. "Can you speak up? I seem to have something in my ears."

Surprisingly, he did just that. "I was simply remarking that you'd awoken. How do you feel?"

"Barely conscious, but alive," I croaked. "And wondering why."

Ateas pulled his wrist away from Karen's mouth. He licked the wound with his gray, slimy tongue, after which it healed almost instantly. The lich moved his "grandchild," as he'd called her, off his lap, setting her head gently and almost tenderly on the floor. The younger vampire curled up into a fetal ball, eyes closed, her lips moving soundlessly as she rocked in place.

The vampire lord stood in a manner that could only be described as abrupt—one moment he was sitting cross-legged on the floor, and then he was on his feet. It happened so quickly, he might have been teleporting, except I caught the movement as a blur when he did it. Of all the vampires I'd met, he had to be the fastest of them all, and that scared the hell out of me.

"If I said it was because you intrigue me, I'd be lying," he said in his raspy, drought-stricken voice. "You are a threat to my plans, and I had to evaluate that threat. Now that I have, I'll eliminate you shortly."

"You're not going to feed on me?"

"I'd intended to, but I can see you've been tainted by the lesser vyrus." He closed his eyes and gently shook his head. "How I regret creating that strain."

"Yeah, you kind of fucked yourself, didn't you? Killing off your food supply will do that, you know."

"Such a crude youth you are, and so bitter for one so young." He tsked. "You'd have made a good vampire. Such a shame that I won't be able to add you to my get."

"What, so I can end up being a midnight snack for you?" I chuckled, hoping it didn't sound too much like false bravado. The last thing I wanted was for him to realize I was playing for time. "Or a seat cushion?"

Ateas perked up at that. "Then you noticed my handiwork in the entry. Tell me, what did you think?"

He sounded almost proud that he'd turned vampires into living furniture, like he expected me to compliment him on his craftsmanship. Instead, I made a sour face.

"It sucks. The stitching was coming loose on the Queen Anne, and you failed to match the leather on the Louis the XIV."

He ran a single, clawed index finger down the side of his jaw, pointing it at me as he spoke. "You, young man, are a sore loser."

I sighed. "Yeah, you'd think I'd be used to it by now."

The lich's eyes widened, then he cackled at the ceiling— it was a barking, hollow sound. When he was done, he fixed me with a sinister look.

"Perhaps I won't kill you after all. I'm sure I can find a way to force the vyrus to overpower your druid magic. After you've turned, with new legs, you might prove to be a useful servant." He shifted his gaze to the stretcher. "But first, I shall dine."

My heart thumped in my chest from a sudden jolt of hope-induced adrenaline. Clearly, the lich thought that Dottie had merely been a ruse to get me in here, and not the actual trap. I maintained a poker face as I checked to ensure that the silence spell I'd cast on myself was still intact.

It was. So long the lich didn't see my chest moving in time with my pulse—or, for that matter, the pulse in my neck—I might just have a shot at getting out of here alive.

Thankfully, his attention was fully on Dottie now, having discarded me with as much ceremony as a redneck loosing a fart in public. Ateas drifted over to the gurney in an almost balletic manner as he drew close to the poor girl. Once there, he leaned over her and took a long, creepy whiff, from her crotch to her face.

"Intoxicating," the lich declared.

"Gross," I countered. "She's like, one thousandth your age."

"One more word," he said, raising an index finger while keeping his attention on Dottie, "and I will crush your skull."

I wisely shut my fool mouth, observing in silence as Ateas removed Dottie's sheet. He then released the gurney's straps before carrying her to the clawfoot tub. After lowering her into the basin, he laid atop her like a lover, then he began tearing into the baby vampire's neck.

———

The act was bloody, brutal, and obviously final for poor Dottie, but she'd already been doomed when I met her. At least now, she'd have a shot at revenge. Sadly, she'd get it posthumously, but I would keep my promise. The downside to this stroke of luck was that I had no idea how long it'd take the lich to feed, and I needed all the time I could get to heal. I couldn't very well get my sample in this condition, after all.

As for why I wanted Ateas to feed, it had everything to do with Dottie's blood and what I'd done to it. Once the ancient bastard had his fill, that was when I'd spring my trap.

Ironically, the lich's own maker had made this plan possible. Working out the spell to weaken Alalngar had cost me plenty of time and effort, but casting it hadn't been so difficult after I figured it out. The only question was how to keep Garr still long enough to do it.

That it might work on Ateas had always been a foregone conclusion, but I faced a similar challenge in his case. How do you manage to hit an undead speedster with a spell that takes half a minute or more to cast?

It was only when I learned about his feeding habits that I realized I didn't have to cast it *on* him; I just needed to get him to feed on blood tainted by sunlight. At the moment, the guy was filling his gut with it, guzzling it by the quart. He was quick, too. I supposed several millennia spent in practice made you a fast eater, if not a tidy one.

When his hunger was finally sated, he raised himself from his victim, grabbing a towel from a nearby vanity drawer. Slowly and methodically, the lich wiped off the bulk of the blood that now covered his hands, face, and neck. As he completed the task, he dabbed the towel at the corners of his mouth, like some effete foodie finishing a meal at a Michelin-starred restaurant.

That he intended to kill me, I had no doubt. All the talk about letting me live was bullshit. He had to have witnessed how easily I dealt with his offspring and staff, either through their eyes or via hidden cameras that I failed to spot on the way in. I was a threat, and vampires always eliminated threats to their person and brood.

The only problem was that I was far from healed. My spine must've been crushed when he slammed me against the hardwood floor. I had almost no sensation below my waist, which was a blessing from a pain perspective, but a curse considering the present situation.

After that, the vampire lord calmly washed himself in a basin that had been outside the range of, and thus spared from, my maelstrom spell. While he went about that task he ignored me completely, back turned, until he shook the water off his hands and toweled off.

Contrary to various folk tales and legends, most vampires cast reflections, except when they chose not to do so. After Ateas was done examining himself, he locked eyes with me through the mirror.

"Now, what am I going to do with you, druid? Hmm?"

"Saying 'hmm' after you ask a question, in reference to said question, is a bit redundant, don't you think?"

"So is asking a rhetorical question after a declarative statement," he replied as he picked a bit of bloody skin out of his teeth. "But let's not split hairs. You've disrupted my research, killed members of my brood, and destroyed my living room. That calls for retribution, I think."

"What are you going to do, cancel me?"

He smiled broadly, but there was no humor in it. "In a manner of speaking, yes."

That's when I knew I couldn't wait any longer. Without hesitation, I spoke the trigger word for the spell.

"*Solas.*"

While he was feeding, his smoking jacket had fallen open, revealing his upper torso and stomach. When I spoke the trigger word, light flared through the weird, gray, semi-translucent skin that covered his stomach. Almost immediately, the flesh there ignited, burning and spitting like a road flare.

I expected him to go up like a torch, but he didn't. Oh, that shit burned a hole right through his torso, and it kept on burning, but somehow the fucker kept standing with half his abdomen missing. He gripped the sides of the basin to hold himself up, staring at me in the mirror with sheer, unadulterated hatred in his eyes.

"What. Did. You. Do?" he roared in an animalistic voice, emphasizing each syllable fully.

"Just fucking die already!" I shouted as I used druidry to seal and bind the doors.

The thing is, it is damned fucking hard to avoid folding right in half when your abdominal and back muscles have been burned down to the spinal cord. I could see the mirror and vanity at which Ateas stood *through* the huge gaps in his torso that my spell had caused. Not only was that fucked up, it meant that the second he let go of that basin, he'd collapse in a heap.

Normally, a freshly fed vampire will heal at a rate close to that of your standard werewolf. I'd seen vampires lose plate-sized chunks of flesh then heal in under a minute, just from feeding alone. Ateas should've been healing, except for the fact that all the blood he just drank had been incinerated inside his stomach when I unleashed my sunlight spell.

Unfortunately, he wasn't dying, and that was a problem. The upside was that he wasn't going anywhere in his current state, and he wouldn't be able to heal without feeding.

Ateas realized that as well. Simultaneously, we both looked at Karen, who was still lying on the floor having a complete fucking meltdown.

Ah, shit.

Ateas smiled, even though he still had some embers burning around the edges of the wound in his midsection. The smug son of a bitch pushed himself off the sink all at once, landing flat on what was left of his back on the floor. He then began using his arms to push himself across the floor toward the scientist, inch by inch.

"Karen," I shouted at the top of my lungs. "Run!"

It was no use. Being in such close proximity to a vampire as old and powerful as Ateas had scrambled her brain. Heck, for all I knew he was using necromancy to control her mind. Clearly, she wasn't going anywhere, and I needed a plan B, fast.

I doubted that small caliber firearms would harm the lich. Even injured as he was, there was a good chance that bullets would bounce off or barely wound him, silver or not.

Then there were elemental spells, and I had plenty. Yet, casting a fireball in an enclosed space was a no-no. And if losing half his gut didn't kill Ateas, I doubted a lightning bolt would, either.

Finally, there was time magic, but it took focus, energy, and willpower to cast. Damaged as I was, I was short on all three at the moment.

Damn it, I need time to shift.

Ateas wasn't moving quickly, but he was making steady progress. At the rate he was going, he'd reach Karen long before I made the change. I needed to stop him, fast.

With little alternative but to act from where I was, I

quickly formulated a plan. First, I dug around in my Bag until I found *Gae Dearg*, The Red Spear, which I laid on the floor beside me. Now, I just needed room to throw the damned thing.

Next, I covered my legs, pelvis, abdomen, and chest in my bark skin spell, leaving my arms free to move. Then I hardened the bark enough to give my body support, while still allowing a bit of give. That would help me stay upright for what came next.

Grasping the spear in my right hand, I used it for support while I scooted away from the wall. As I did, I used druidry to anchor my left hand to the wooden floor, releasing it again with each small bit of forward progress.

Anchor, scoot, reset.

It was precarious, but it helped prevent me from falling over as I worked. Soon I found I had enough room behind me to wind up for a throw. I anchored my left hand one last time, then I sighted in on Ateas, who'd nearly reached his goal by this point.

Only one chance to get this right.

I reared back, took aim, and threw the spear with everything I had. Thankfully, I didn't have to throw it far, no more than twenty feet at most. The Red Spear flew true, piercing the lich's left shoulder then exiting just above the charred edge of his anterior ribcage, left of his exposed spine. As it did, the spearhead bit deeply into the wooden floor, anchoring Ateas in place.

Thick black blood spilled out over the leaf-shaped spearhead, pouring out onto the floor. Ateas wailed silently like a trapped honey badger, mouthing curses and gnashing his teeth as he stared daggers at me from where he lay.

"That's right," I screamed. "Liches get stitches, bitch!"

To be honest, it was a lucky hit. I'd been aiming for his left side, hoping to pierce his heart, but I wasn't certain I could make the shot. Thankfully, my aim had been true.

Gae Dearg was the sort of weapon that you didn't use except in dire circumstances, due to the effect it had on mortal flesh. A wound from the spear would never heal, and having once felt its bite, I could attest to its effectiveness. In short, Ateas was a goner.

Now that I had bought some time, I could finally shift into my full Fomorian form. Doing so would be painful, but by rearranging my anatomy down to the cellular level, I'd heal completely. Then I'd stomp that smoking pile of parchment and bones to dust.

Closing my eyes and focusing inward, I triggered the change. My clothing shredded as my bones lengthened and thickened, becoming dense to the point of nearly being unbreakable as they did so. In the process, ligaments and tendons tore from their anchor points. Likewise, most of my muscles ripped completely in two, only to reform and reconnect in new and larger configurations that suited my now massive, ten-foot-tall frame.

My human skin split and shed to allow for this growth, even as new dermal layers formed that were as thick and tough as rhinoceros hide. My right hand grew into a large, club-like appendage, the fingers like small tree limbs and knuckles covered in thick callouses. Simultaneously, my left hand morphed into a thinner, more claw-like limb, still humanoid but clearly designed for ripping and tearing flesh and viscera.

All this happened in a matter of seconds, but as always, it felt like an eternity, such was the agony I experienced during the shifting process. Less than thirty seconds later, it was done, and I was fully healed in my most powerful form. Now, it was time to deal with Ateas.

I opened my eyes, searching the spot where I'd left him. The Red Spear was there, the tip still driven deeply into the floor, along with a small pool of black, viscous blood. But as for Ateas, he'd somehow vanished without a trace—and Karen as well.

Hunching slightly as I stood, I stomped over to examine the evidence. Within two strides, I was there, kneeling at the scene of the crime to see how he'd escaped. By rights, he should've been dead, but a thin, black, bloody trail across the floor told me he'd pulled himself off the spear and dragged himself to safety.

The fact that there was no other blood told me he hadn't fed on Karen. Either he'd ordered her to help him escape, or she'd fled. My guess was that he'd used her to escape, determining that he was in no state to fight me after having nearly been destroyed by the magic and magical weaponry of the Celts.

I stood, retrieving the spear as I did so. Following the trail across the room, it stopped in front of a picture that had been torn from the far wall. In its place, a wall safe lay wide open, emptied of whatever had once been hidden inside. Based on the size of the safe, it had to have been something small and easily carried.

A teleportation amulet? Or a phylactery of some sort? I'd never encountered a lich before, but often art echoed legend, which often reflected reality. If that was the case, then my hunch had been right.

I'd never know for sure, not until our next meeting. That I would face Ateas again, I was certain. Like I said, a vampire always eliminated threats to their person and brood.

As for this entire escapade, it seemed I would get my blood sample. But to collect it, I'd need more delicate hands. I shifted back into my half-Fomorian form, shivering both from my near nakedness and the return of my vyral infection symptoms.

I searched the apartment for a vial of some sort, finding several in an adjacent laboratory. Then I used druidry to gather every last drop of the lich's blood I could find, storing the vials in my Craneskin Bag when I was done. Finally, I dressed and armed myself, then I prepared myself mentally for my impending escape from The Deadlands.

CHAPTER
TWENTY-THREE

ONE OF THE benefits to shifting into my full Fomorian form and back again was that it reduced the vyral load in my bloodstream. That was how I survived the vyrus the first time, by shifting back and forth to cleanse my system. Eventually, the demigod side of my immune system kicked it for good, but I was sick for weeks on end during that first bout with the vyrus.

This time I seemed to be handling it well, but I was nowhere near fully immune. Still, I felt much better than I had before I shifted. For the first time since I entered The Deadlands, I was ready and raring for some action.

All the messed up shit I'd seen had me riled, and I wanted retribution. No—I wanted to make sure it didn't continue, and I wanted to make it as difficult as possible for Ateas to start over again. In short, I intended to take this place down on my way out.

But first, I needed to rescue the humans I'd come across on the way in. Step one would be fighting my way through the lich's armor golems. Standing in front of the sealed double doors that led to the entry hall, I covered myself in bark skin, then I drew Dyrnwyn from my Bag.

The sword flared bright along its length with white-hot flames, the way it always did when evil was present. I unsealed the doors and kicked them open, then I waited for the armor golems to come through.

Not one of them budged. They all stood on their podiums, statuesque and creepy as all get out. Slowly, I moved forward, and it was only when I crossed the threshold that the first armor golem stepped off its dais.

The Greek Hoplite was the first to come at me, clanging the medium-length spear in its hand against the round, painted shield it held in the other. The ancient, undead warrior took a shield-forward stance, holding the shield high to cover as much of its torso, neck, and head as possible. It shuffle-stepped forward, keeping the spear pointed at me with its arm protected behind the shield, waiting until I was in range before it thrust the weapon at my abdomen.

In the background, the other warriors had turned their heads. Each still stood on their own dais, apparently patiently waiting their turn. I had no idea how skilled each one of these soldiers had been in life, but for all I knew they were the champions of their time.

Which meant there'd be no fucking around with these things. Before the Greek golem could get close enough to skewer me with its spear, I blasted its legs out from under it with a small fireball. Before it even had a chance to tumble to the ground on the charred stumps that were left, I burst forward and lopped its head off with Dyrnwyn.

On witnessing how I'd dealt with their fellow undead warrior, foul play and all, the remaining eleven golems stepped off their podiums in unison. Each readied their respective weapons as they turned to face me. Suddenly, the long hallway rang with the sounds of steel being drawn, metal ringing on metal, and leathery palms slapping wood and leather.

I parried a thrust from the Roman centurion, lunging and thrusting Dyrnwyn through its skull and helmet on the riposte. Twisting the blade as I withdrew, I was forced to kick the golem off the sword to free it. That gave a Mycenaean warrior in a full bronze cuirass the opportunity to slash at my flank with a long bronze sword.

Kicking the centurion away had left me with my weight on my forward leg. Rather than try to turn, face, and parry the Mycenaean all in one movement—a losing proposition when fighting a second opponent who had the jump on you —I pushed off my back foot and stepped forward. I still took a shallow gash to my ribs on my right flank, but the bark absorbed the brunt of it, and it was better than getting split in two, Rob Roy style.

Still, it was a reminder that I wasn't exactly in tip-top condition to face down a roomful of undead champions. I spun on the Mycenaean, stepping in and slicing through sword, armor, and cuirass in one long, committed angular downward forehand stroke. Then I turned to face the rest of the warriors, and I cast Mogh's Scythe.

A barely molecule-thin sheet of compressed air shot down the hall at mach-three, slicing through the golems at chest level. It took a moment for the result to reveal itself, but two heartbeats later they each fell into assorted pieces, having been bisected and then some by the spell.

Depending on their body position at the time I cast it, some of their arms were cut into multiple segments, but at least half remained standing from the torso down. Those armless, head-and-shoulder-less torsos soon began walking around aimlessly, bumping into each other and the walls. When they happened to bump into one another, they continued to do so in an increasingly aggressive manner, like so many headless Don Quixotes tilting at windmills.

I stifled a laugh. It didn't seem right to mock these warriors, considering what they might've been in life. I reminded myself that they'd once had wives, children, and careers as soldiers, before they met their current fate at the lich's hands. Instead of amusing myself at their expense, I made my way down the hall, cutting each of them down and fully dispatching them with chops and thrusts through their skulls.

When the last dismembered golem stopped twitching, I called the elevator and stepped inside. When the doors were closing, I cast a small fireball through the gap, lighting the entire hallway on fire. As smoke began filtering through the door gap, I punched the button for level ten, thinking carefully about my next moves.

———

Next stop, lingerie, evening wear, and human captives, I thought as the elevator came to a stop at the tenth floor. I stood aside as the door opened, only to be met by a hail of gunfire that likely would've ruined my day. The rounds struck the back wall of the elevator, mostly harmlessly, although I did get grazed on the arm by a ricochet.

At the first lull in the gunfire, I peered around the corner and blasted a guard in the chest with my chain lightning spell. The spell arced to the next guard, and the next, until a half-dozen vampires were writhing and spasming on the floor. From there it was a simple matter of chopping their heads off with Dyrnwyn.

Killing vampires was a task the sword seemed all too happy to complete, if I were to gauge its pleasure by how it flared even brighter, each time I beheaded a guard. When I finished, the hallway was still, and I had a clear path to the captives' quarters. On reaching the entrance, I swiped Patel's badge, only to find it had been deactivated since the last time I used it.

Fine, we'll do this the hard way, then.

Dyrnwyn worked well when I was fighting evil beings, as that was its entire purpose for existence. However, it was unwise to use it for more mundane tasks, like cutting through deadbolts and locks. The blade was only metal, after all, albeit the best that a god could forge with the technology of that era.

It was the laser-like heat Dyrnwyn emitted that allowed it to cut so well, and not its edge. The last thing I wanted to do was to chip it while doing a simple B&E, so druidry would have to do. I sheathed the sword in the scabbard I wore over my shoulder—awkward, but convenient when I had to cast magic with both hands—then I set about opening the door.

Most electronic locks rely on magnetism to keep the door shut. A powerful electromagnet held the door closed until the security badge reader or keypad shut off the circuit. I could've short-circuited the lock with a lightning spell, but instead I simply used druidry to shut the current off.

Since I was out of contact with my Oak, I decided to save the last of my magical reserves until I really needed it.

I pulled an M84 stun grenade and an M4A1 rifle from my Bag, setting the grenade aside.

I dropped the rifle's magazine to check the action before reseating it, making certain it was in good working order and ready to rock and roll. After that, I chambered a round and flipped the selector switch to *pew-pew*, then I grabbed the flashbang.

Standing aside as I opened the door, I pulled the pin on the grenade and tossed it through the door. When it went off, I shouldered the rifle, sighting with the red dot as I entered the room at near-vampire speed. Two guards had been waiting inside in the dark, but thanks to the grenade I caught them off guard, plugging each with a round to the cranium.

I put another round in each of the guard's skulls as I passed. Before I flipped the lights on, I dropped all trace of my bark skin spell. Once I had the lights back on, I started unlocking cell doors with one of the guard's keycards.

Despite the open doors, the captives stayed put. At least two of them cowered in the rear corner of their cells, backs turned, shaking like dice in Vegas.

"I'm human, I swear it. Come with me if you want to live."

"Who are you, John Connor?" the older man asked.

"You're thinking of Kyle Reese," I said. "You saw me cap those guards. Think of me more like The Ex-Terminator, only I kill the undead instead of bugs."

"Same thing if you ask me," a young, college-aged brunette said as she walked out of her cell. "Can you get us out of here?"

"That's the plan. We have to get to the parking garage, and unfortunately, we can't use the elevators because they'll be able to track us. That means going down ten flights of stairs, possibly fighting all the way. Can you do it?"

"Does a goldfish drink its own piss?" The brunette grabbed a sidearm off one of the dead guards, checking the chamber and racking a round with practiced skill. "Lead the way."

I looked around, counting only four prisoners. The fifth was the teen boy, who was still rocking back and forth in the corner of his cell. "What about him?"

"He's been like that since they took his mother," a redhead said. She was short, stout, and looked to be in her late twenties to early thirties. "Let's just go, mister. He'll only slow us down."

"How about I leave you behind, instead?" I hissed. "You want out of here? Look after the kid. If he falls behind, you fall behind. If you fall behind, you get eaten by them. Understand?"

The redhead gulped and nodded. "Uh-huh."

She stood there, like a dope. "Then go fucking get him," I said, pointing in the general direction of the young man's cell with the barrel of the rifle. While she complied, I turned to the other woman and the old man. "Can you two shoot?"

"My dad taught me when I was a little girl. I think I can manage," the other young woman said. The old man merely nodded.

"Then grab a firearm and be ready to use it. You're going to cover our rear. Do not fucking shoot over my shoulder—you'll likely end up shooting me in the back of the head. Just watch our backs during the descent, and shoot at anything that comes up behind us. Is that clear?"

"As daylight, which I pray to see again," the old dude replied.

I looked at the brunette. "You, you're with me. Stick to my back like glue, you got it? If I have to reload, you unload." I reached down and grabbed two spare mags from a guard's duty belt. "Stick these where you can get to them, alright?"

"I know how to fucking do a combat reload," she griped.

"Military experience?" I asked.

She nodded. "Plus two years as a beat cop in Corpus before all this shit happened."

I flashed her a friendly grin. "You can tell me all about how you survived—after we get out of here."

"Deal."

———

By that time, the redhead had returned with the boy. He looked emaciated, frightened, and not at all ready to make it down ten flights of stairs under gunfire. The thing was, I really needed him to make it, because I was not leaving any of them behind. I turned around and reached into my Bag, digging around until I found a Pepsi and a Snickers bar.

Holding the soda and the candy bar out in front of me, I approached the kid. The sight of the soda and candy elicited a few gasps from the others, but a sharp look from me hushed them right up. When I was close to the boy, I set the can and the Snickers on a table nearby, then I got a wet washcloth from a nearby cell.

By the time I came back with the washcloth, he was

eyeing the candy. "It's alright, you can have it. I know you're hungry."

The boy tentatively reached for the candy. I pushed it toward him, and he snatched it, tearing off the wrapper and devouring it in a couple of bites. I watched him eat, then I popped the tab on the soda and handed it to him. He drank that, chugging half until he let out an involuntary belch.

I chuckled, then I reached toward his face with the rag. "May I?"

He nodded, so I began wiping the accumulated filth off his face and neck, then I cleaned his hands as well. Once most of the dirt was gone, he appeared to be a boy of about fifteen years of age, with olive skin, curly dark brown hair, and green eyes. Remembering what it was like to lose my dad at a young age, I really felt for him.

"I'm Colin. What's your name?"

"Mateo," he said.

"That's a good name. Mateo, I'm going to get you out of here, and then I'll take you someplace safe. But before we leave this room, I need to know that you can keep up. If you can't, I understand—"

"Give me a gun," he said, cutting me off.

"Wait, what?" the redhead asked.

I looked in the kid's eyes, and I saw he was dead serious. "I take it you want to kill some vamps. Can you shoot?"

"I'm from South Texas, mister Colin. Down there, everybody knows how to shoot."

"Fine." I handed him my sidearm, a Glock 17. "Aim for the head. It's loaded with silver-tipped rounds, but only headshots are really reliable on those fuckers. And pick your shots."

"What the hell?" It was the redhead again. "Everybody else gets a gun, and I don't?"

I sighed. "Have you ever, in your life, used a firearm before?"

She frowned. "No, because I don't believe in them."

"Then you don't get a gun. Now shut the fuck up and get ready to move." The redhead's jaw dropped to the floor at that, but she was smart enough to stay quiet. I glanced around at the rest of the group, meeting everyone's gaze in turn. "Alright, let's move out."

We made it down seven flights of stairs before we ran into trouble. Somewhere around the third floor, the vamps got wise, and they came at us from above and below. Rather than get caught in a pincer maneuver, I led the group out of the stairwell and onto the third floor, which was full of cubicles and offices.

I grabbed the cop's arm as she passed, pulling her aside. "Take them around the corner a ways, and tell them to cover their ears when I yell."

"You're the boss, Reese," she said. "Just don't leave us here, alright?"

I watched the group disappear around the corner, then I laid my ambush. Hiding inside a cubicle just thirty feet from the stairwell exit, I cast my chameleon spell and I waited for the vamps to come flowing through the door. A team of six entered in full battle rattle, including M4 rifles like the one I currently carried.

Once they were all taking up positions in the hall, I pulled the pin on a Willy Pete grenade and I rolled it out across the floor at them. While their attention was on that grenade, I pulled the pin on a second one, counting off before I tossed it at the ceiling above the vamps.

Then I hit the deck.

The grenades went off around the same time, showering the area with burning chemicals and lighting everything in a thirty-foot radius on fire. Thankfully, the sprinkler system wasn't working. Not that it would have put the phosphorous out, but it would prevent the building from going up in flames.

Two of the vamps were stupid enough to get caught, while the other four had taken cover. I ignored the flaming leeches as they rolled around on the ground, opting instead to stalk the others while they were in disarray.

I caught one of the remaining vamps when he popped his head above a cubicle wall, giving him a fatal case of lead and silver poisoning. Sadly, the vamps were onto me, and they triangulated my position via the sound of the gunshot when I took out their buddy. Within seconds, I found myself pinned down in a crossfire, caught cowering inside a cubicle in the middle of the room.

Let me tell you, cubicles make good concealment but shitty cover. Rounds were piercing the cubicle walls all around me, and it was only a matter of time before I got hit. Just when I thought I was going to have to use my last bit of magic to escape, one of the vamps went down under a hail of bullets.

Now, gunfire was coming from two directions—from the area nearest the stairwell exit, and from deeper within the building. Wondering what the hell was going on, I heard the cop yelling over the clamor of the firefight.

"Colin, are you still with us?"

"Fuck yeah!" I replied.

"Then get your ass moving. We can't keep laying down covering fire forever."

"Moving!" I shouted, recalling an afternoon long ago spent training small unit tactics under Maureen's watchful eye.

I leapfrogged from position to position, sprinting just slow enough so I didn't look like a vampire to my human companions. When I made it around the corner to their position, I found the cop, Mateo, and the old man waiting for me. I popped another Willy Pete and tossed it in the center of the room behind me.

"Thanks, now, let's get the fuck out of here," I said, motioning for the three of them to precede me toward the exit sign down the hall.

———

After gathering the other two captives, I led them down the other stairwell to the parking garage, finding it all clear the rest of the way there. I didn't know if they'd run out of guards, or maybe the rest of them just decided it wasn't worth it, now that their boss had beat feet. At least, I hoped he had.

It seemed like Ateas had some taboo against eating his offspring, and I didn't know if it was for practical reasons, or just personal preference. Either way, with Dottie gone, Ateas didn't have another source of blood here that could heal his burned, permanently wounded, necromancy-tainted corpse. For those reasons, I was betting that he'd split town to heal and regroup.

It was too bad about Karen, though. She was just starting to grow on me. Like a fungus, sure, but still.

Once we exited into the garage, I surreptitiously sealed the doors, then I pulled the cop aside. "Yo, Lady Jaye—

thanks again for the save."

"It's Aredhel, but everyone calls me Del," she said.

"Wow—did your parents read Tolkien much?"

"Just a wee bit," she said, squeezing her thumb and forefinger together. "Considering all the shit I took for that name as a kid, Lady Jaye is almost an improvement."

"She was a total badass, too, so it fits. Anyway, we need transportation. Can you and the others find something suitable? Additionally, it'd be helpful if you chose someone to drive who knows the area. I'd rather be riding shotgun than behind the wheel on the way out of here—just in case."

Del sort of half-frowned, half-smirked. "Normally, I don't take orders from random guys. Not unless they outrank me, and even then, it's iffy."

"It's not an order, just a request."

"Meh, you've gotten us this far. I'll let it slide."

"Gee, thanks."

"Just don't make it a habit."

As Del headed off to organize the troops, I went to the elevator entrance. Once there, I pried open the doors, then I pulled out the ball of muck I'd taken out of Crowley's clothes back at his lair. After the addition of some seeds I'd brought from the Grove and a tiny whisper of druid magic, I dropped it down the shaft.

Then, I closed and sealed the doors, and I hauled ass back to the group. They were waiting in a mid-size electric SUV, a Japanese model. Three of them were in the back seat, Del was in the hatch area, and Mateo was driving.

I walked around to the hatch and opened it. "Um, what're you doing back here?"

"In case I have to shoot something."

"Cool, cool." I glanced around. "But the kid?"

She shrugged. "He says he's from around here. And he has his license."

"What, for like a week?"

"You said you wanted someone who knew the area. If you wanted an EVOC graduate, you should've said so."

She pulled down the hatch, then she shattered the glass with her pistol. I stroked my chin, then I handed her my rifle and spare mags before heading around the vehicle to the front seat. After I got in, I looked at Mateo.

"Hey, good job back there. With all the shooting and stuff, I mean."

"Thanks," he said, brushing his hair out of his eyes. "Where to?"

"Not to doubt you or anything, but you can drive, right?"

"Oh yeah, sure. I mean, I have my learner's permit. And I've played a lot of Gran Turismo."

Yep, we're gonna die.

I smiled. "Okay, great. Head south, avoiding the 45, and stop as soon as you see State Highway 99 in the distance. There's a ton of undead there, and we don't want to draw their attention."

"Got it."

The kid put it in gear and floored it, and I swear he drifted that fucking car the whole way out of the parking garage. Before I knew it, we were heading west on Woodlands Parkway at speed, with clear roads and not a vampire in sight. I could almost imagine we were home free.

Just when I was starting to relax, Del spoke up from the back. "You might want to cover your ears."

"Shit." I rolled down my window, trying to get a bead on what was following us in the sideview mirror. Meanwhile, Del started dropping brass in controlled three round bursts. "Talk to me, Del—did you hit it?"

"I don't even know what 'it' is," she yelled back. "The thing keeps disappearing and reappearing. It's like it can read my mind. Every time I squeeze the trigger, it vanishes!"

"Ah, hell." I leaned out the window, craning my neck to get a good look behind us.

Finally, I spotted what was following us. It was Alalngar, *bamfing* along behind us, fast enough that he'd catch up soon. And once he teleported inside this car, it was all over.

"Motherfucker... I do not have time for this. Mateo, stomp on it. Del, keep firing on him, and let me know when he's within fifty feet."

"What are you going to do?" she hollered back.

"I'm about to fuck some shit up." I closed my eyes, leaned back in the seat, and tried to relax.

"By meditating?" Mateo asked, his voice dripping with incredulity.

I cracked an eye open. "Just drive, kid."

Then I closed my eyes and focused inward, using druid breathing techniques to harness every last bit of magic and willpower I had left within me. I'd need all of it for what I was about to attempt, and my timing would have to be perfect. Otherwise, we'd all be dead.

"He's getting closer," Del said. "And he looks pissed!"

"Fifty feet, Del."

"On it."

Just then, Mateo took a sharp left, nearly getting the car up on two wheels as he did so. "Mateo, what are you doing?"

"Sorry, but we have to hit Gosling, and I took Panther Creek because it's faster. Once we hit Gosling Road, it's more or less a straight shot."

"So you can punch it?"

"Yeah."

I cracked an eyelid again. "You do realize that getting us all killed defeats the purpose of this exercise, yes?"

"Hey, man, do you want to drive? Because I'd be perfectly happy meditating right now." Mateo bit his lower lip as he gripped the wheel tighter. "Hang on!"

He cut another sharp left, slowing enough to avoid taking us over the curb. Then he punched it, and all I heard was the low whine of the electric motors, which quickly rose in pitch. I glanced at the speedometer.

"Keep it above sixty, if you can. But don't go so fast you lose it." Mateo gave me the side-eye. "Right, I'll go back to meditating now."

"He's still on our ass," Del said. "One hundred feet."

"I think I just peed my pants," the redhead squeaked from the back seat.

I shouted over my shoulder at Del, ignoring the whiner. "Let me know—"

"Yeah, yeah," she said, punctuating her words with another three-round burst. "Fifty feet."

Garr's voice echoed like thunder over the whine of the engine. "McCool, I know you're in there. You had help to best me the last time, but now you're all alone. There's no place to run, and no escape. Give up, and I might even spare those humans you worked so hard to save."

The old man spoke up after remaining silent for the entire ride. "Who is this person, anyway?"

"He's danger personified," I answered. "Now, be quiet and let me focus."

Everyone did as they were told, and the only sound we heard for the next minute was the vehicle's whine, the occasional tire squeal, and Garr screaming at me between ports. Finally, Del shouted again.

"Hang on, it looks like he's fading out... now!"

As soon as she said the word, I triggered an area of effect stasis spell. The spell was designed to cover a large area—basically the car and a one hundred fifty-foot diameter around us. Covering that much area was a stretch, even when I was at my best, and I definitely was not at the moment.

So, I compromised on the spell effects by only slowing things down without completely freezing them. This had the result of making everything around me look like it was going through molasses. It was like the prototypical movie slow motion scene, but throttled down by a factor of ten.

Of course, I wasn't affected by my own spell, so I climbed out the window and onto the top of the car. Once there, I dug around in my Bag, and I waited.

Garr's teleporting ability wasn't quite instantaneous. He went somewhere when he was traveling from point A to point B. Where, I didn't know—maybe through a wormhole, or something.

It didn't matter, but what did matter was the hunch I had about it. And that hunch was, when Garr was in transit, he couldn't see what was going on around him. Meaning, he couldn't change his trajectory mid-teleport.

It only took a matter of seconds in real time, less than half a minute, but soon a dark cloud began to appear just ten feet behind the vehicle. I counted off the seconds, basing my calculations on how long it had taken him to disappear and reappear while affected by the stasis spell.

If I got this wrong, I'd be fucked. I was not going to get this wrong.

Three... two... one... now!

I leapt from the roof of the vehicle, with Dyrnwyn held high overhead in a two-handed grip. While I was airborne, the sword burst into flames, shining so bright it lit up the immediate area as if it were noon. I reached the peak of my leap, and I began descending toward the spot where Garr would hopefully appear.

Then, Alalngar coalesced in the center of that dark cloud of mist, suddenly becoming corporeal. He wore an expression of supreme triumph on his face, his mouth curled in a smug smile, his eyes widened with all the zeal of a man possessed. Then, something shifted in his expression, something that was reflected in his gaze.

It was the realization of his own impending death.

This was a creature who could move at tremendous speeds, whose brain had adapted over the centuries to process information at a rate to match. His reflexes were more than uncanny—they were superhuman, almost godlike. That's why I had to time my attack just so.

Garr was just that fast. I'd witnessed it myself. If he realized what I was doing, he'd just teleport somewhere else before I could reach him, and that would be it. Sure, I could freeze him in place completely, but to do that I'd have to cast the spell when he couldn't see it coming.

The only way to do that was to cast it while he was mid-teleport.

Garr materialized, just as Dyrnwyn's white-hot length intersected with his forehead. I swung downward as I descended, cutting with all my strength, following through as my feet hit the ground. The blade passed clean through, cutting the vampire from stem to sternum, so to speak.

The vampire's eyes conveyed a single emotion as I completed my cut—that of disbelief. I sheathed Dyrnwyn over my shoulder, then I braced myself for the momentum that was about to hit me. I had been traveling at sixty miles an hour when I jumped off the SUV, after all.

Finally, I released the spell. Time sped back up to normal all at once. I slid along the road for roughly twenty-five feet, ruining a perfectly good pair of boots. The SUV screeched to a halt some two hundred feet down the road. And Garr's now truly lifeless body fell in two perfect halves on either side of the center stripe.

I heard Mateo shift the car into reverse. Not wanting to get run over, I turned to watch as he backed it up, the whole two hundred feet. When he screeched to a stop, Del was the first to jump out of the car.

"What in the hell just happened?"

"If I told you, you wouldn't believe it," I said.

"Try me," she answered back, eyes narrowed so much she was nearly squinting.

"Maybe someday."

Mateo ran out of the car next, but he kept his distance from me as he approached. The kid looked at Garr's corpse, then he looked at the SUV, then at me.

"You're like one of them," he said, hugging himself.

"Not quite, Mateo. I'm still human."

"*Nombre*, I saw it," he said, his tone and mannerisms becoming ever more hysterical as he went on. "One second you were there, and the next, *poof! Eres un brujo, un vampiro, cabrón.*"

And that's when Mateo went into full hysterics. It took over an hour to calm the kid down. By that time, the sun was up, and the worst of the danger was over. It was time to call Emberlance in to have her burn us a path through the dead, so we could cross the border back into safety.

Unfortunately, I had no idea how I was going to explain away a dragon to these people. Del was going to love it, but poor Mateo? He'd be traumatized for life.

CHAPTER
TWENTY-FOUR

I SOLVED the dragon problem by taking the captives to raid a completely untouched convenience store. While they did that, Emberlance torched us a way through the undead gauntlet. In fact, they were so busy stuffing their faces with candy, soda, and chips, they didn't even notice when I slipped away to destroy the lich's clones.

Once I got within a half-mile of the border, I was able to contact the dragon directly via telepathy. She'd promised to stay close to the northern edge of her territory, keeping an open line in case I needed help getting back across. Emberlance was also all too happy to destroy a couple of Ateas' anti-teleporting wards as well, which allowed me to contact my Oak again.

The first thing I did was deliver one of the vials I'd collected to Crowley. He tried to conceal his relief at seeing me alive and well, but I knew what was up. As for Saint Germain, Crowley said he'd gone to feed, and he was likely sleeping off the battle somewhere. I left the shadow wizard to start the research without me, telling him I'd return in a day or two, three at the most.

Then it was party time. I started by nuking the clone warehouses I'd come across earlier, ripping the roofs off with the Oak's help, and burning anything the sun didn't kill. Then I activated the seed pod I'd dropped in the elevator shaft at the Occidental Petroleum Building. If you've never seen a thirty two-story high-rise building destroyed by a massive, four hundred fifty-foot tall complex of telephone pole-thick vines, you're missing out.

The best part was watching all the vamps jumping out of windows or getting pushed out by vines, only to burn to a crisp in direct sunlight. It was glorious.

The only downside? I couldn't find any trace of Ateas or Karen. Wherever they went, it must've been far, far away from The Deadlands.

By the time I was done searching for the lich and destroying everything he'd built, Emberlance was finished clearing a path through the undead gauntlet and into her territory. She agreed to stay out of sight, resting in her aerie in downtown Houston while we crossed safely through her territory. When the captives asked why there were no undead to be seen, I told them it was because local vampires had chased them out of the area. That made them more than eager to leave Houston, for good.

Before we left the dragon's territory, I found a charging station at a Toyota dealership that was "mysteriously" still powered. "Must be on a generator or solar or something," I explained. From there, I could think of only one place to take the captives, and that was to Samson and The Pack at Bryan-College Station.

When we arrived at their primary outpost in the old

DPS building, the group was stunned at their set-up and security. I left them with Sledge and a few others who offered to help them get settled in, then I went to see Samson. When I found him, he was planning new supply routes with Trina in the station's former squad room.

"Look what the cat dragged in," Trina said with a smirk as I entered the room.

Samson barely looked up from the maps they were poring over. I figured he was still pissed at me for blowing him off days earlier, and failing to return Guerra to him. Instead of engaging in a power play with an alpha on his own territory, I poured myself a cup of coffee from a carafe on a nearby table.

"Sure, help yourself to our scarcest supplies," the grizzled old werewolf said. "You help yourself to everything else around here."

"Not to mention your daughter," Trina whispered.

That last bit stung, but I hid my pain by flashing them both a broad grin as I spread my arms wide. "Hey, I brought you a carload of new recruits, didn't I?"

Samson scowled. "Dead weight until proven otherwise."

"And," I said, pointing an index finger in the air, "I can get you more coffee."

"Now you're talking," Trina replied, rubbing her hands together.

"How?" the alpha asked.

"Came across a huge untouched cache, with plenty of dry foodstuffs. Plenty of coffee, some of it even canned. I'll bring you a few boxes, next time I roll through."

Samson's scowl softened a bit, and he leaned back against the table with his bare arms crossed over his chest.

The guy tended to dress to type, often wearing nothing more than a pair of jeans, boots, his leather vest, and whatever biker accessories he decided to wear that month. This time around, the theme seemed to be bandanas, but he also wore a thick black leather watchband with metal rings on it that looked to have come straight from the 70s.

The old alpha fixed me with a look, then he raised his chin at me. "Tell me about the group you brought in."

I spent the next half hour telling him how I found them, giving them the rundown of what had gone down in The Deadlands. Finally, I ended with my opinion of each of the group members. "The kid, Mateo, and the cop, Del, are solid. Fair warning, though, the boy's still traumatized from losing his mom to the vamps."

"Who isn't these days," Trina remarked.

"I like the old man, but he's old. Might not make it through the change. As for the younger girls, the redhead is a pain in the ass, so let me apologize in advance for that. The other one will work out for sure, though."

Samson sniffed and scratched his nose with a knuckle. "Eh, we need more females. Too many males in a pack leads to trouble eventually. It's good you brought them in, druid."

"I'll say," Trina added.

Samson chuffed. "At least give the guys a shot, playgirl."

Trina winked at me. "All's fair and shit—ain't that right, Colin?"

"I'm staying out of this. Pack politics and drama are just not my thing. Oh, and by the way, as far as they know, 'Druid' is my biker name."

The alpha chuckled, and I detected actual mirth in his

tone. "What, you didn't explain how magic works to them yet?"

"Eh, they got a taste, but I didn't want to blow their minds all at once. I figure after they accept the existence of 'thropes, and decide whether they want to attempt the change…" I let my voice trail off as I tossed my hands up. "Then we'll see."

Samson grunted. "Anything else?"

"I'm going to need Guerra for a few more months."

"You're a sack of shit, you know that, druid?"

"So I've been told, Samson. So I've been told."

My next stop was the Grove. I spent two long weeks there, shifting back and forth to flush the vyrus and regain my strength. During that time, the Grove treated me like a guinea pig, tending to me with a variety of herbal concoctions while I laid around the place.

Some of it was nasty, but she did manage to come up with a tea made from medicinal mushrooms and herbs that perked me up quite a bit. Between that and some good old-fashioned druid healing medicine, I was right as rain in no time. Once I was fully healed, it was time to return to Crowley's lair.

Almost three days had passed since I'd last seen him, and I was eager to find out what he'd deduced. However, when I tried to portal directly back into his digs, the Oak informed me that the way was blocked. Instead, I portalled outside his home, then I banged on the metal door that led from the factory to the massive tunnel below.

The fact that the doorway and surrounding area were

covered in necromantic, anti-vampire wards was not lost on me. It took half an hour of knocking for Crowley to open the door. When he finally did, he swept his gaze around the area, then he ushered me in with due haste.

"Come in, come in, before *he* shows up again."

"Wait a minute," I said. "Just what the hell happened while I was gone?"

"Inside, now!" he ordered.

I complied, and Crowley sealed the door behind us with a combination of necromancy and shadow magic. He bustled past me on his way downstairs, which was when I noticed he was walking with a pronounced limp. He also hadn't shaved in days, his clothes were crumpled, and he had bruises covering his forearms and the left side of his face.

"You don't look so good," I observed as I followed him down the stairwell. Once we reached the bottom, that's when my mind was really blown. "Holy crap—what the fuck happened here?"

Every surface of the massive tunnel was covered in old, dried goo, of the kind that came from killing the undead. Not even the high ceilings at the apex of the shaft had escaped the carnage. I was no blood spatter expert, but it didn't take a genius to see that someone or something had gone through Crowley's undead army like a buzzsaw.

I whistled, long and low. "Was it Ateas?"

Crowley turned around and sat heavily on the stairs that led to the adjoining offices and break room that he used for his living quarters and labs. "Indirectly, yes. After the battle, Germain said he needed to replenish his strength. I brought us back here, then I left him to his own devices. I did not see him again until the evening after you showed up with the sample."

"And then?"

"Then, it wasn't Germain who showed up, but Le Boucher. A tremendous battle ensued. If it had not been for the undead standing between him and me, I might not have made it."

"He took all your troops out? All of them?"

Crowley nodded once. "Went through them like crêpe paper. In the end, I had to fight him off with shadow magic whilst I banished him from the lair using my failsafes." He exhaled heavily, shaking slightly as he did so. "It was a very close thing, indeed."

"Ah, shit. I'm sorry you had to deal with him alone. But we always knew the risks involved with bringing him on."

"Yes, but I didn't expect him to revert so soon. And Colin?"

"Yeah?"

"He bore the marks of necromancy when he returned. I did not think it possible for Ateas to dominate Saint Germain's alter-ego, but somehow, he did. And The Butcher knew exactly what he was looking for when he arrived."

"The sample."

"Precisely. He made it as far as my lab, destroying all the research we'd done." The wizard glanced over his shoulder at the entrance to his quarters. "It's an absolute mess. Ateas must've given the creature the means to set the place on fire. It looked to be alchemical in nature. I am sorry, my friend, but all our work went up in flames."

I clucked my tongue. "Well, not all of it."

Crowley jumped to his feet, grasping me by the shoulders with both hands. "Tell me you had another sample."

A broad smile split my face. "Hey, it's me you're talking to."

The wizard almost looked like he was going to hug me, then he composed himself as he brushed off my upper arms, smoothing my t-shirt out. He averted his gaze as he cleared his throat, gesturing toward the door to the living quarters in an "after you" manner.

"Well then, we should start working on it immediately. I believe I can recreate the work I did earlier from memory." He arched an eyebrow at me. "Do you still have the nanoparticles?"

"Do cow farts keep Al Gore awake at night?"

Crowley's expression went from cautiously hopeful to completely and utterly confused in an instant. "I do not understand that reference."

I chuckled and clapped him on the shoulder. "C'mon, I'll explain it to you while we put your lab back together. I've gotten pretty good at repairing glass receptacles, you know."

EPILOGUE

I LOOKED out over the parapets of Tethra's former citadel in Mag Mell, back in the primary timeline. My gaze swept across the landscape, which had been completely transformed since the last time I'd visited here. Where once only desert and parched earth had been, now stretched mile upon mile of lush grasslands, reaching away to the cliffs, which were topped by dense forests that continued on toward the horizon.

In my absence, the lands had become hostile to intruders. I'd had Oisín's *fian* monitoring the borders, to keep track of who might try to enter the area in an attempt to stake a claim. The lands were mine by rights, and I intended to keep them free of fae and gods alike, by force if necessary.

I needn't have worried.

Those trespassers that the wyverns couldn't chase off were eaten alive by the forests—sometimes, literally. They'd enter the dense woodlands along the border, only to become hopelessly lost, wandering until they fell into a crevasse, got devoured by some carnivorous plant or creature, or died from simply forgetting to eat and drink.

In exploring the region, I'd come across remains belonging to giants, trolls, goblins, dwarves, and other varieties of the lesser fae. I'd also stumbled upon what was left of a small party of higher fae that looked to have been scouts sent by one of the courts. The only magical creatures that could survive in the region were the more feral kinds of fae, such as barghests, cat sith, and the like, but only those who had not pledged fealty to any court or patron.

Of course, all natural flora and fauna thrived in the area, and the land was overflowing with game. You could practically grow anything on the plains, and I'd honestly never seen the like outside of my Groves in either timeline. It was a druid's paradise, and I intended to keep it that way.

I turned and faced my distant relatives, Oisín, Oscar, and Plúr. "Are you certain you're willing to do this? Once you take up residence in this fortress, you'll have to answer to me from this day forward. And after you pledge your fealty, there's no turning back."

Oisín spoke first. "For millennia, our people have struggled ta' survive in Underhill. Ta' land's not made fer humans, as ya' well know, lad. 'Tis a blessin' ta' have a safe harbor, where we can thrive and prosper."

I turned to Plúr. "Cousin?"

"Father speaks true. I have no qualms regarding this arrangement."

Next, I shifted my gaze to her brother. "Oscar?"

He frowned. "I won't lie an' say I like pledgin' to you, druid, but you have proven yourself. From this day forth, I'll give my life to protect you."

I walked past them to the other side of the wall. Leaning on the interior parapet, I pointed to the central courtyard below. "Oh, it's not me you'll be pledged to protect, but that."

Down in the center of the courtyard, inside a raised, walled garden, a single oak sapling grew. Somehow, although I stood hundreds of feet away, it sensed that I was looking at it, and it responded by shaking its leaves a bit. Deep within my mind, I received a mental image of a mighty roe buck, broad-chested and proud, and bearing a huge, multi-tined rack.

Translated, that image could only mean one thing:

Father.

I sent back a message of my own, one of calm reassurance that everything would be just fine. Missive sent, I faced the trio, three demigods out of Irish legend who'd betrayed my confidence at the behest of my mentor, Finnegas. The old man had trusted them with my life, and now I'd entrust them with my own child's life as well.

The three of them shared a glance, and Oscar gave a small shrug. "I don't have a problem with that."

I inclined my head. "Then kneel, and repeat after me. 'We pledge our lives in service to the Oak. Without the Oak, Druidry dies. Druidry exists to serve humankind, and the Oak is the druids' sanctuary…'"

———

This ends *Deadlands Druid*, Book One of The Sylvan Cycle, a Colin McCool Urban Fantasy Tetralogy.

Be sure to visit my website at MDMassey.com to

subscribe to my newsletter. When you do, you'll be the first to hear when a new Druidverse novel is released!

ABOUT THE AUTHOR

M.D. Massey describes himself as the prototypical INTJ. His eclectic background provides him with a rich tapestry of experiences to draw on when crafting fiction, as evidenced by the believable worlds and relatable characters he creates.

Mr. Massey lives in Austin, Texas with his family and a huge American Bulldog that keeps him company while he writes. When he's not in his office or at the local coffee shop writing, you can find him in his garage pummeling inanimate objects, or knife fighting with his friends.

facebook.com/mdmasseyauthor

instagram.com/mdmasseyauthor

amazon.com/author/mdmassey

ALSO BY M.D. MASSEY

The Colin McCool Junkyard Druid Series

Junkyard Druid

Graveyard Druid

Moonlight Druid

Underground Druid

Druid Justice

Druid Enforcer

Druid Vengeance

Druid's Due

Druid Apprentice

Druid Mystic

Druid Arcane

Druid Master

The Trickster Cycle

Druid's Folly

Druid's Curse

Druid's Bane

Druid's Gamble

The Junkyard Druid Novellas

Druid Blood (A Junkyard Druid Origin Story)

Blood Scent (A Junkyard Druid Prequel)

Blood Circus (A Druidverse® Short Story Collection)

Blood Ties (A Druidverse® Short Story Collection)

Blood Bound (A Druidverse® Short Story Collection)

Colin McCool Saves Christmas (A Druidverse® Novella)

Blood Moon (A Druidverse® Novella)

The Shadow Changeling Series

Shade Cursed

Shade Hunted

Shade War

The CERBERUS Paranormal Detective Series

Weaponized Magic (with D. William Landsborough)

Breach of Magic (with D. William Landsborough)

Felony Magic (with D. William Landsborough)

THEM Paranormal Apocalypse Series

Invasion: Zombie Apocalypse

Incursion: Vampire Apocalypse

Counteraction: Werewolf Apocalypse

Gabby's Run: Paranormal Apocalypse

Extinction: Undead Apocalypse